# THE PRISONER OF ROME

# THE PRISONER

## OF ROME

## Tomas W. Schafer

SMB
Sunrise Mountain Books
Boise, Idaho

THE PRISONER OF ROME
Copyright © 2017
Tomas W. Schafer

ISBN 978-1-940728-06-3

**Library of Congress Control Number: 2017933390**

Published by
Sunrise Mountain Books
13347 W. Tapatio Drive
Boise, Idaho 83713
www.sunrisemountainbooks.com

Printed in the United States of America

# PREFACE

*The Prisoner of Rome* is historical fiction set in mid-1st century AD. It was a time of both secular and spiritual significance.

The Roman Empire had experienced a period of expansion and a new Caesar, Nero, was the emperor, assigned the responsibility of maintaining law and order and keeping rebels from overthrowing the government. Rome was tolerant of their conquered peoples, but only within certain strict limitations. Cross that line and the punishment was swift, public, and brutal.

In the mid-1st century, spiritual expansion rivaled the expansion of the Roman Empire. Followers of Christ Jesus were found in virtually every hub of Roman commerce. Paul was one of the main leaders of this new band of people that ignited the curiosity and the wrath first of the Jews, and then of the top Roman ruler, Caesar.

Followers of Christ were initially referred to as "The Way," and they were an anomaly of that particular time. To the Jews, followers of Christ were a threat to their established religious power. To the Romans, the followers' refusal to revere established Roman pagan gods and rituals caused concern over their potential rebellion. In essence, the followers of Christ were caught in the middle between these two ruling bodies. Paul became the focal point of this band of peculiar people. He was scrutinized by both the Jewish leaders and the Roman officials.

This scrutiny came to a head between the years of 60-62 A.D. when Paul was accused of high treason against Rome by Jewish leaders wanting to be rid of him and his teaching. Facing threat of execution by the Jews, and waiting for Felix to judge, Paul finally invoked his Roman citizenship, demanding to be tried before Rome's supreme ruler, Caesar. It became the first of two times he was a prisoner of Rome, and is the centerpiece of this book.

To many, Paul's appeal was risky. Either he would be exonerated or swiftly executed, and there would be no in between. However, Paul's trial before Caesar was delayed for over a year and a half; and no explanation for it has been retained in the annals of history. He was sequestered under house arrest during most of this two-year time period, but no documents survive to suggest what happened other than the Bible's wonderful record in the book of Acts and four of his epistles during that 24-month period—to Philemon, Ephesians, Philippians, and Colossians. Therefore, study had to be made to discover aspects of house arrest for Roman citizens.

It will surprise some readers to learn that uncondemned Roman citizens awaiting trial before Caesar were held without chains or shackles. They were held in closely guarded residences within the Roman garrison or in a well-guarded private house in town.

The biblical record refers twice to Paul having been with a chain when he was in transit with a guard. There, the Greek word *halusis* is used in Acts 28:20 and Ephesians 6:20. The *halusis* was a short length of chain by which a prisoner's wrist was bound to the wrist of a soldier who was guarding him for the prisoner's protection or to prevent escape.

However, in Acts 22:29, the captain of the guard became afraid when he discovered Paul was a Roman citizen and that he had ordered him to be bound. Roman citizens were to be treated more civilly, far better than others. Based on this information, Paul's reference to his bonds and chains at times seem to be a figurative reference to his personal lack of freedom, rather than to iron shackles. Paul refers to himself as "the prisoner of Christ Jesus" which is obviously a figurative inference while he was under house arrest. He could not leave the guarded residence, but he was free to receive visitors, send and receive messages, work and write. His gloriously inspired writings in the Bible are proof of that.

House-arrest Roman prisoners like Paul were expected to pay their expenses from their own resources, and employment was one way to do this. Thus, Paul, like other tentmakers of his time, certainly could have used his tentmaking skills to work as a cobbler, using many of the same materials and tools. This possibility has been incorporated into the narrative.

For many students of biblical history, the questions of who, what, when, where, why, and how pepper one's thoughts concerning details that have no record. This is where historical fiction comes in; it is what this book, *The Prisoner of Rome*, hopes to satisfy. It takes the prominent characters and events of that segment of time and combines it with researched facts to fashion a story of plausibility for curious readers.

To gain plausibility, over 400 hours of research were conducted, delving into both the Roman culture and government of that time. Key elements of Roman citizenship, laws, punishment, commerce, housing, food, clothing, etc., were studied. Most importantly, the Holy Bible's record of Paul's acts and writings were diligently studied and considered while developing the story. A wide variety of sources provided insight and snippets of vital information that were carefully juggled and arranged, similar to assembling puzzle pieces to arrive at a big picture.

Emphasis was placed on the historical facts, as best known, and elimination of some misunderstandings surrounding Paul's house detention as well as his appeal before Caesar Nero. In no way does this narrative attempt to replace truth; but it provides a possible perspective of that particular time in Paul's life, based on historical events and types of persons he would have known. History does record Paul's affability and acceptance by almost all who met him, including Roman guards and officials.

In a sense, all history contains an element of fiction or speculation. Ask several eye witnesses of a single event to describe what happened and there will be variations in the accounts of that event. The eye witnesses will all be adamant that their version is the correct one. All are influenced by their emotions at the time and their reaction to the final result. Enter the historian, and the main question is, "What happened?" All variations are listened to and then sorted out for inconsistencies and blatant misconceptions. The historical fiction writer goes beyond the obvious questions and delves into others such as: "What was it like?" "Why did it happen?" "What influenced the people and events?" "Who would have been directly involved?" and "What might have happened behind the scenes?"

So the role of the writer of historical fiction is not to retell stale lectures that may have been given in school, and were soon forgotten. Historical fiction fuels the imagination and acts as a springboard for further investigation and appreciation of the event, the people, and the results. Historical fiction should be written with great attention to factual details that are consistent with many historians and archeological evidence—to experience that moment, to conjecture, and discover. The exclamation, "So, that's what it was like!" is a satisfying reward to the curious investigator.

Now is the time to turn the page and let yourself go back into a momentous, two-year span on history's timeline.

# CAST OF MAIN CHARACTERS
(in order of their appearance)

- DEMETRIUS—Centurion with FESTUS' contingent upon his arrival home
- FESTUS—honorable new governor (Procurator) over Judaea, married to FABIANA, replacing corrupt FELIX
- CAELIUS and SERVIUS—assistants to FESTUS
- LYSIAS—c ommander of Praetorium guard headquarters
- ANANIAS and TERTULLUS—Jewish high priest and his scribe, out to get Paul executed
- PAUL—the apostle PAUL, formerly Saul of Tarsus
- LUKE and ARISTARCHUS—companions of PAUL, followers of Christ
- AGRIPPA II—local official, similar to a mayor, married to his sister BERNICE
- CAESAR NERO—Roman emperor over the expansive empire, married to OCTAVIA
- JULIUS—Roman centurion assigned to transport prisoner Paul by ship to Rome
- GENERAL CLEATUS—supreme commander of the Praetorium Guard in Rome
- SENECA—Roman senator and consul to Nero; chief investigator into Paul's case
- CATO—Roman philosopher and lawyer; collaborator with Seneca to investigate Paul, spy
- FLAVIUS—Centurion commander, collaborator with Seneca to investigate Paul, receives reports from spies
- TADIUS and LYSIUS—Garrison commanders
- DRABA—Roman soldier guard in Paul's house arrest, spy for FLAVIUS
- LUCILIUS—Roman soldier guard in Paul's house arrest, spy for FLAVIUS
- MARCUS—Roman soldier guard with dogs in Paul's house arrest, spy for FLAVIUS
- JUNUS—Roman soldier front door guard in Paul's rented house
- AELIA—prosperous Roman businesswoman, landlord of Paul's rented quarters

- ANTONIUS—Roman cobbler, business associate of AELIA, employer of PAUL's cobbler skills
- EPAPHRODITUS—follower of Christ, messenger, co-worker with PAUL, former centurion
- ONESIMUS—runaway slave
- PHILEMON—follower of Christ, businessman, owner of runaway slave ONESIMUS
- EPAPHRAS—follower of Christ, friend of PHILEMON and co-worker with PAUL
- TIMOTHY—follower of Christ, messenger and co-worker with PAUL

# Chapter 1

The band of ghost warriors came to a halt within sight of the villa located just outside the city of Caesarea. It marked the end of a two-and-a-half-week journey from Antioch that was long, hot, dusty, and over unpleasant country to view. But now the end was in sight—their target, a villa, lay within easy striking distance. As the dusty horde reined in their mighty steeds, the leader turned to face the column.

His fierce, intense eyes were like small dark pools surrounded by a desert of caked-on dust, sweat, and grime. He surveyed his fellow specters who looked at him with similar sunken eyes and weathered faces. They awaited his signal of attack, were it to come. They welcomed any opportunity to perform their deadly skills.

A soft breeze caused the red plumage atop the leader's helmet to sway back and forth, creating a soft whispering sound. He shifted in his saddle, attempting to restore circulation that would be needed for any unexpected foray. Using hand signals, the leader silently gave the command to proceed toward their unsuspecting target. This force of 81 men continued towards the villa unnoticed, just as the leader wanted to happen.

At the rear of the villa, several servants were picking fresh vegetables from the garden. They were engaged in lively conversation punctuated by occasional laughter. The slaves never heard the approaching stealth pack. One of the slave servants stood up from her stooped position when, out of the corner of her eye, she saw the phantom death horde.

Horrified, she dropped her basket of vegetables with a loud gasp that drew the attention of the other slave servants. The workers looked in her direction and caught their breath at the ominous sight hovering within a stone's throw. Their faces immediately exhibited dread. One slave began to shake and sob as the frightening horde drew nearer.

The red-plumed leader leaned forward in his saddle and stared down at the frightened slaves with his intense dark orbs of doom. He peered deeply into each slave's eyes, one by one, causing some to tremble and cower. Others would not even look, avoiding what they felt certain were the eyes of death.

The leader of the apparition raised up and silently looked over the entire back portion of the villa. Satisfied with what he saw, he calmly spoke, "Have no fear, slaves. We wish you no harm. I am Demetrius, centurion to Governor Quadratus of Antioch. With me is the new Procurator of Judea. You must immediately take Procurator Festus to his office." The leader's voice was not harsh, but his commanding words were spoken in a firm tone that suited his authority.

Sensing no harm was about to befall them, one of the servants stepped forward and in a tentative voice uttered, "Follow me, I will take you inside the villa." One specter dismounted his horse and gave the reins to another of the ghosts. The apparitions then dispersed and seemed to melt in the late afternoon sun. The specter who remained behind motioned for a slave girl to lead him inside his new quarters.

The slave girl escorted the ghost warrior through the kitchen and opened a door, then stood aside for the specter to enter. The strange being cautiously entered the room and stood motionless to take in the surroundings. It was an elaborate indoor courtyard, complete with a vast array of different plants, colorful flowers, and a small pond. The courtyard was bordered in fine marble. Off to his left, he saw a section with comfortable-looking patio furniture. In one of the chairs sat a vision of loveliness.

Sunbeams cascading through the rectangular opening in the partial roof accentuated her beauty. Her dark brown hair was swept upward in the style of Roman upper class women. The ghost warrior saw her gown was made of fine linen, and her posture in the chair created folds in her gown that highlighted her feminine form. The ghost warrior was captivated by the beauty of the woman. So much so, he could not resist exclaiming, "Woman! Your beauty repays me for all the discomfort I've had on my trip!"

The startled beauty abruptly turned in her chair to face the voice that had invaded her solitude. She looked at the apparition, a human form covered in thick dust. Deep blue eyes peered at her from caverns encased in dried sweat and dirt. A broad smile stretched across his face and was bordered by cracked patches like a dried-up riverbed baked in the hot sun.

Slowly, she stood up from the comfort of her chair to face the intruder. Advancing cautiously, she stopped four feet short of the ghost warrior. "Festus! You alarmed me! You should have announced your presence! What is this warrior disguise?"

The ghost warrior feigned a posture of apology and opened his dust-covered arms. As he did so, small clouds of fine dirt tumbled off his armored arms and fell to the marble floor. At the sight of the dirt, the woman stepped back two paces and thrust out her hand to deny the ghost warrior's approach. "No embrace, or anything, until you get out of that wretched uniform and get yourself clean!"

Immediately, he began to undress. Naked, he turned and raced for the nearest door and rushed inside. Quickly he returned, looked at the woman sheepishly, and said, "I forgot, I'm unfamiliar with our new villa. Please show me where the bath is." Without uttering a single word, the woman walked out of the indoor courtyard. The naked body followed. When they were inside the main portion of the villa, the woman pointed to a door. "That's the bath. Now go. Your cleansing water awaits."

The naked ghost waved goodbye, opened the door, and scampered inside. To his delight, he could smell the scent of lavender in the water and feel the rising heat from the spa. In the water were two slave girls, giggling at the sight of the strange warrior who was entering the bath. His dirty hair and encrusted face contrasted with the rest of his exposed body, creating a comical appearance.

The grimy figure ducked under the warm water and remained submerged momentarily. Suddenly, the head broke the surface, shaking off massive amounts of water in all directions. Fabiana entered the bath with a change of clothing. "I've brought you a decent, clean tunic for you once you are adequately cleaned." She looked intently at the slaves and said with exaggerated sternness, "If he isn't sufficiently cleaned, you all will suffer the consequences."

The ghost warrior turned his gaze from the woman to the slave girls, tilted his head, grinned ridiculously, and said with mock horror, "Alas, there is much dirt to eliminate." He then lowered his head so that they could proceed to transform him from an apparition into the man he needed to be for the woman he desired.

While the new procurator was being washed and refreshed, Demetrius, too, was enjoying a much-needed cleansing. The officers' quarters of the garrison had a private bath that was approximately half the size of that in the procurator's villa, but its function was more than adequate, and pleasant for weary travelers.

Demetrius, having been sufficiently washed by slave girls, was relaxing in the adjacent smaller spa of hot therapeutic water when the garrison commander, a man named Tadius, sat down at the side of the spa area. "I'm glad you are enjoying the comfort of the water, Demetrius. When you are ready, I have arranged for a fine meal we can share, at which time I would like to discuss the new procurator with you."

The refreshed centurion wiped water from his face and looked up at Tadius. "I'm about finished here and your proposition of a fine meal is one I cannot refuse."

At the table, Demetrius looked down at the first course of his meal. There was a bowl of Spanish garum, fish sauce, a bowl of fresh hummus, and plenty of flat bread for dipping. "Tadius, you don't know how often I dreamed about eating a fine meal during the long journey down here from Antioch. We ate only dried meat and hard biscuits because Festus did not want any detection. We had no night fires to reveal our position. During the day, we usually traveled 30 miles, the safe limit for our Nisean horses."

Tadius listened to his friend as they savored the appetizers. At his first opportunity, Tadius asked his initial question, "Demetrius, I know very little about our new procurator. What should I know about this man Festus?"

Demetrius wiped his mouth clean, and looked intently at his friend with his dark eyes. "He is not a man to be trifled with in any way." Before continuing, the centurion took a healthy gulp of wine.

"He has been hand-picked by Quadratus to clean up this mess caused by Felix. Because of the severity of the situation throughout Judea resulting from Felix's ineptness, Quadratus is furious because Felix was under his authority and repeatedly lied and hid issues from him. Quadratus is so angry, he nearly executed Felix himself. Only intervention by Egypt's governor saved Felix's life."

Again Demetrius drank from his goblet. As he peered over

the edge of the goblet, he could see that Tadius was gripped by what he was being told. "Quadratus allowed Felix to become the Procurator of Judea and feels deeply betrayed by the man's actions. He is also embarrassed that the situation Felix caused with the Jews has resulted in riots and deaths. To Quadratus, it reflects his failure as a governor. He has chosen Festus to resolve these issues because he truly trusts him based on previously shared duties together."

Tadius interjected his opinion, "It is reasonable to understand Quadratus' thinking. In his place, I would do the same thing. Lysias, commander of the Jerusalem garrison, has spoken to me about the problems caused by Felix. He is quite concerned about the growing hostility there."

Demetrius nodded his head in agreement, "This situation with the Jews and the prisoner named Paul is very volatile." Demetrius tilted his head sideways and gestured toward Tadius, "What was your relationship like, with Felix?"

Tadius closed his eyes and sighed, "Very strained. There was no way he could be trusted and I truly feared he would incite a riot that would imperil my men. Like Quadratus, I sometimes thought about executing the man! Because of this background, I seek knowledge how to proceed with Festus. How should I conduct myself?"

Demetrius' face hardened and his eyes narrowed. "Be forthright with him and do not attempt to deceive him in any way. He can be very severe should he believe anyone lies to him or attempts to hide anything from him."

The centurion let his words resonate with his friend as he continued, "Festus is a man of character and devoted to Rome. He is not corrupt. He always seeks to be fair and impartial in all his dealings. You can trust him because he is consistent."

Tadius relaxed noticeably and took several sips of his wine. "Thank you, Demetrius. This is good to know. Now, what do you think Festus will do here, initially, in Caesarea?"

Demetrius finished a bite of the hummus before he answered. "He will immediately address the situation with the citizen Paul, who has been under house arrest these past two years due to Felix's extortion attempt. In so doing, it will allow him to establish his authority to the Jews and their leaders. Dealing with these despicable dogs is a top priority, not only of Festus but of Quadratus, as well. Rome is wondering about this region and doesn't want things to get out of control."

Tadius nodded and asked, "How do you perceive Festus will deal with this citizen Paul?"

Demetrius was quick to answer, "In three ways. First, he will research the crime he is accused of committing. Second, he will thoroughly interrogate the man. And thirdly, he will render an impartial and fair verdict."

Tadius was relieved. He sighed again, and his facial expression relaxed. "This is good to know. Now, what about the situation with the Jews and their leaders?"

At this question, Demetrius threw back his head and laughed scornfully. "My friend, Festus will descend on them like a severe summer thunder storm. They will quiver in fear! He will leave no doubt who is in charge. I would not want to be in their boots. One additional point—Festus will not dally in dealing with these dogs."

It was evident by Tadius' face that this forecast had a startling impact on the garrison commander. Seizing the moment, Demetrius continued, "You will be given opportunities to establish your capability and your loyalty to Rome in whatever Festus decides must take place. Make the most of them. Do exactly what Festus instructs you, but use your perception to assist him. He welcomes insightful opinion. Do not attempt to display false loyalty to him. He wants you to be loyal to Rome first. In so doing, you will garner the respect of Festus and, believe me, he values and rewards those whom he believes he can trust."

After Festus finished his bath, Fabiana took him on a tour of their new villa. They ambled leisurely from room to room, holding hands during the inspection. The villa was considerably larger than the townhouse they previously had lived in at Antioch. There were more rooms and separate quarters for the slave servants. The walls throughout the villa were adorned with painted landscapes and figures and bordered by fine marble. The floors all were marble and intricately designed.

Beginning at the front door, they entered the vestibule, a spacious entrance hall that led into the atrium. This was the focal point of the villa. It contained a rectangular pool for catching rainwater that fell from the decorated opening in the partial roof. Festus gazed up at this opening and admired the etched border and the plastered high vaulted ceiling supported by marble columns. Highly detailed and carved marble outlined the doorways that led to the variety of rooms. Fabiana stood smiling as she watched her husband inspect the opulent interior. "Isn't it something to behold! We've never had such luxury since we married."

Festus smiled back at her. "It is as we have talked about. Our time has come, and now that it's here, we must not waste a single moment for enjoying its beauty."

The two looked down into the rain pool in the atrium and enjoyed the rippling reflection of the three-foot statue of the Roman goddess Diana. Fabiana led Festus to the various bedrooms located on the side of the atrium. They drifted past the dining room, as they had already shared their first meal together there. In happy anticipation of Festus' reaction and with a broad smile, she opened the door to one of the bigger rooms in the villa, the study.

Festus stood inside, looking around at what would be his central office and meeting room. His official office would be in the palace built by King Herod in the center of Caesarea, but all stategizing would be done here. Pointing at the elaborately carved desk, he turned toward his wife. "Behind that desk, I will make decisions that will propel us to a much higher position in our service to Rome. My first official acts will be to wipe clean the dirt that Felix has wrought."

Fabiana gave her husband's hand a tight squeeze and ushered him out of the room. She led him into the enclosed courtyard in the back of the villa. All traces of the dirt and dust from his initial arrival had been removed. The two sat down in the cushioned chairs of the patio, enjoying their reunion. Servants dutifully brought them wine and fruit snacks.

Festus turned his chair so that he could face his lovely wife of ten years. He grabbed a small fig and popped it into his mouth, moving it around and chewing while he talked. "I'm glad the journey from Antioch was uneventful and that we were able to proceed undetected. I want no one to know I've arrived here in Caesarea until such time as I choose. Since you have been here a month prior to my arrival, tell me, what have you learned from Felix's wife Drusilla, as well as our servants?" Anticipating her report, he took a handful of figs to enjoy while she talked.

Fabiana savored a taste of wine before she answered her husband's questions. "There was much turmoil when I first arrived here. Felix was beside himself over being called back to Rome to face Caesar for his actions here. He was angry, but also greatly fearful of what awaited him in Rome.

"The impact of his dire situation came to a head when commander Tadius had his men restrain Felix from removing anything of value from the villa. They confiscated all his money and possessions, and had to forcefully relocate him to one of the rooms used for house arrest in Agrippa II's palace. Ironically, he was close to where the citizen named Paul is also being held in house arrest."

As Fabiana relayed to Festus what she had learned, his eyes narrowed and his brow creased, reflecting his intense thought concerning his predecessor. Fabiana took another sip from her goblet and continued, "Drusilla was allowed to remain here in the villa, but was constantly under guard by Tadius' soldiers. She was eager and willing to confide to me her feelings about the development. Felix did many things he kept secret from her. Despite this, Drusilla was aware of the extra money that was available to them. She definitely wasn't naïve about some of his dealings."

At that, Festus let out a grunt of distaste. "She certainly revealed her lineage. Her entire family beginning with Herod, her father Agrippa, and now her brother Agrippa II, all are deceivers. But please go on. I could not help myself with this interruption. I apologize."

Fabiana adored her husband. She smiled and continued, "Drusilla realizes she could be executed along with Felix, should Caesar decide to do so. Since Felix is a former slave, but now a freedman due to his brother Pallus paying for their freedom, he can be executed under Roman law. Drusilla isn't a Roman citizen and, as such, she can be executed as an accomplice. She indeed is very scared."

The lovely informer coyly tilted her head to one side and gave Festus a sly smile. "I took advantage of her emotions to secure as much information as possible and she withheld nothing from me. I also verified her statements, just as you would do, my husband." Festus chuckled in delight. Fabiana enjoyed his reaction and carried on, relishing that she had even more to tell.

"Drusilla said Felix would often send for the citizen Paul under pretense of hearing him, but with his actual intent to extort money from him in exchange for his freedom. At the same time, Felix did the same thing to the Jewish leader Ananias and his chief scribe Tertullus who wanted Paul released to the Jews in order that they could kill him. Felix's plan was whoever came across with the money first would be the one to buy his favor. Unfortunately for Felix, neither Ananias nor Paul would pay him anything. He became quite angry over this. He was caught in the middle by his own evil with no escape. He was stymied."

Festus nodded his understanding and agreed with Fabiana's summary regarding Felix's corruption. Without hesitation, Fabiana declared, "Drusilla said Ananias and Tertullus were pressuring Felix to turn Paul over to them; otherwise, they would complain to Quadratus. In response, Felix aligned with a group of zealots and assassins—the Sicarii—to thwart their efforts. It resulted in several riots and many deaths. It quickly got out of hand and Felix lost control over this band of rebels. So much so, he was in fear of his own life!" Fabiana lowered her head as she reacted to the seriousness of the scenario.

"In a certain way, Festus, I feel sorry for Drusilla. Her final words to me were that once she is back in Rome, she will do whatever she can to save herself. She is quite shaken over the fact her brother Agrippa II refuses to intervene on her behalf."

Festus reached out and took his wife's hand. Gently he kissed it, and held it firmly. He attempted to comfort her, "My dear wife, I appreciate your feelings for this woman. Let me tell you the reason why Agrippa II won't assist Drusilla in any way. Agrippa II is responsible for appointing Ananias as high priest of the Jews. He also is fully aware of Felix's involvement with this rebel group of assassins, the Sicarii. Agrippa II is in fear of his own life and position as tetrarch over the Jews. Indeed, this is a mess of a situation; but have no fear. Drusilla will get what she deserves, as will Agrippa II."

Festus released Fabiana's soft hand, and leaned back in his chair. He added, "And so, too, will this citizen named Paul."

Fabiana looked seriously at Festus. Her heart was warmed by his determination and ethical character. With pride, she affirmed, "I am confident, Festus, that you will deal not only with this man Paul, but also with Agrippa II and the Jews, without delay and in a manner Rome will approve."

The morning of his first workday as the new Procurator of Judea, Festus held an early morning meeting with the two assistants who had accompanied Fabiana to Caesarea the month prior to Festus' secret arrival.

Festus was fond of disguises. For their safety in traveling, he had Fabiana and the two assistants disguised as slaves in one of the merchant caravans that frequented Caesarea from Antioch.

Because of the unrest that was rampant throughout Judea, there were numerous spies everywhere, of different interests and groups. The Jewish leaders had spies, as did the Sicarii and other bandits. Foreign merchants paid spies to acquire information that would increase their business. In essence, spies were as plentiful as ants—only more deadly.

In the current political environment, an individual would dare not trust anyone whom they did not know very well. It wasn't uncommon for family members to betray other family members for politics, power, or monetary gain.

Festus knew the extent of the clandestine milieu that permeated Judea as well as other parts of the Roman Empire. As such, he was wary of people, organizations, and things, even though they might appear ordinary. Disguises were a useful protection.

He employed a variety of disguises to combat these ever-present spies whose sinister purpose was to steal vital information or disrupt events pertinent to the daily operations of Roman rule. He also utilized disguises for safety purposes. Fabiana was dear to his heart and he did not want her captured for ransom or killed in retaliation against him as an official of Rome. Neither did he want his two trusted assistants to encounter a similar fate.

"Caelius, how did you fare as a 'slave' to the merchant on your journey to Caesarea?"

Caelius grimmaced and replied, "It was quite the experience, Festus. Both Servius and I performed duties we are not accustomed to doing, and physical soreness is just now leaving my body!"

Servius ruefully added, "I had no idea how obstinate camels can really be."

Festus laughed heartily and said, "Our soldiers stationed here often refer to the Jews as being just as obstinate as the camels." Caelius and Servius joined his laughter, recognizing the fitting comparison.

Festus then addressed Caelius, "What have you learned about Agrippa II and his involvement with Felix and the citizen named Paul?"

Without hesitation, Caelius gave his detailed report, "Agrippa II loathed Felix despite the fact he was married to Drusilla. Part of Agrippa II's hatred was because Felix was a former slave. Another part was because his brother Pallas exercised considerable influence as head of the civil service and had Felix appointed as Procurator here in Judea. Agrippa II felt he had been slighted, not being able to at least influence who was appointed heir to Cumanus." Caelius paused to gather his thoughts. There was much to tell and he did not want to leave anything out.

Festus leaned back in his cushioned chair behind his elegant desk and motioned for Caelius to continue.

Caelius picked up where he left off, "Needless to say, Agrippa II is ecstatic about Felix's removal and what appears will be his execution after he is tried back in Rome."

Caelius glanced down and shifted his paperwork to another document. "Agrippa II has no prior involvement with the man named Paul. However, Agrippa II is knowledgeable about the religious sect Paul purportedly leads. He also was quite aware that Felix has had Paul here under house arrest for two years now, and did nothing to intervene on Paul's behalf. It appears Agrippa II was waiting to find out if Felix would be successful in extorting Paul or the Jewish leaders, to demand his share of the spoils."

At that point, Caelius put down his document, and looked directly at his boss with a crooked smile. "No doubt, Agrippa II is chagrined about losing any monies involved in the extortion of Paul! It is also true that Agrippa II is quite concerned about what might happen to him concerning this messy situation with Paul and also the Jews. He is aware of your reputation, but even that won't stop him from attempting to sway your judgment about him."

Festus did not respond to Caelius' last statement. He thanked him for the report and turned his attention to Servius. "What have you to report concerning the Jewish high priest Ananias and his chief scribe Tertullus and why they are opposed to Paul?"

"I had Tadius, the garrison commander here in Caesarea, send a message to Lysias, the garrison commander in Jerusalem, that I would be arriving there disguised and to have me arrested and brought directly to him. This would avoid any undue suspicion from the plethora of spies that inhabit the city." Servius smiled broadly, "The ruse worked to perfection.

"Lysias informed me that Ananias considers Paul to be a blasphemer against the Jewish religion and its traditions. Paul was a former rising Pharisee within the Jewish religion who suddenly left to become a zealot of a man called Jesus of Nazareth. This Jesus of Nazareth called himself the son of the Jewish god. This Jesus was tried before Pilate, and Pilate turned him over to the Jews to be crucified.

"Legend has it that Paul encountered the ghost of this Jesus while on his way to Damascus to suppress followers of this ghost god. Paul was thrown from his donkey, blinded for three days, and then disappeared into the desert for three years. Upon his return, he began recruiting Jews and so-called Gentiles to be followers of this Jesus."

Servius finally stopped to catch his breath, and to determine if Festus had any questions at that point. He looked directly at Festus who sat expressionless in his chair, waiting for more. The assistant knew he could continue with his report.

"Paul has been going to the major commerce cities where significant numbers of Jews live and work. He goes into their synagogues, advocating this Jesus. Usually he gets thrown out and on several occasions has been imprisoned, beaten and, I believe, twice stoned by the Jews. He is very determined and a true zealot of this Jesus."

Servius paused between each of his next flat statements, "Ananias wants Paul dead. He will stop at nothing to accomplish this. His hatred toward Paul consumes him." He meant to emphasize this significance, "The belief is that Ananias views Paul as a competitor for control over the Jews.

"Ananias also believes Paul is intent on destroying the Jewish religion and its various traditions and rituals. In essence, the situation between Ananias and Paul is a power struggle. It is Ananias' hope you can easily be swayed to favor the Jews and hand Paul over to them. His chief scribe, Tertullus, is a gifted attorney and orator. It is he who will present their argument to you."

This concluded Servius' report. He felt drained and sat down in a nearby chair. Festus casually stood up and walked around his desk. He went over to the lone window in his office and looked out at the activity of birds in the trees. Some were fighting each other while others sat on branches uninvolved. He thought how much they were like humans. He was silent for a brief period of time, before he turned to face his two assistants.

"You both have done excellent work. Tell me, Servius, exactly what did you do to get arrested in Jerusalem?"

Servius beamed as he recalled his adventure, "I dressed as a poor beggar and stole food from a vendor, who in reality is an agent of Rome. We created quite the scene and the soldiers did their part as well." Servius massaged his left shoulder. "In fact, their harshness was real and my shoulder is just now healing from the bruise they inflicted upon me."

Festus laughed, "Servius, you have learned well about disguises and spying. It is unfortunate that part of the ruse can incur pain, but that makes it very believable. Do either of you have anything more to add at this point?"

Servius immediately responded, "When the commander at Jerusalem had three of his cavalry accompany me back to Caesarea—presumably to stand trial for my theft—we noticed several figures monitoring our journey. They stayed with us one third of the way back here. One of the cavalrymen said he believed they were spies for Ananias. Bandits, especially the Sicarii, would not engage in such tactics."

Festus ran his fingers through his dark hair as he verbalized his thoughts, "The garrison commander in Jerusalem and the Jewish leaders know of my expected arrival here in Caesarea. They also are aware of the protocol that requires me to make an official visit to Jerusalem. I must do this now. What they don't know, and I obviously don't want revealed, is that I'm already here. I want to interrogate this citizen named Paul before I engage Ananias and his scribe Tertullus. I also want to speak with Lysias, as well, while in Jerusalem before I meet with these two Jewish leaders."

Festus returned to his chair, sat down, and folded his hands in front of him. "What I can learn prior to this meeting will greatly aid in how I deal with these obstinate people. Make sure no one here lets word out that I'm in my office."

Both Caelius and Servius pledged their support in keeping Festus' arrival secret. Festus finished the meeting with a prophetic declaration to his assistants, "My friends, the game has begun."

After the conference, Festus sought out Fabiana. The couple ordered their mid-day meal and went directly to the flowered courtyard. There Festus relayed to Fabiana what he had learned. "You have always been able to advise me well, dear wife. I have several thoughts concerning this meeting and seek your comments."

Fabiana looked lovingly at Festus. She was grateful for his invitation to share her thoughts on important matters. It was rare for Roman men to honor women this way. She took a deep breath to prepare, and affirmed, "I agree that it would be wise to interrogate Paul before meeting with the Jewish leader and his scribe. This man Paul will give you both information and insight as to the heart of this issue. He probably is the only one involved who will speak the truth."

Later that afternoon, Festus donned his official uniform, a toga made of natural undyed, finely woven, thin wool. At the hem was a purple-bluish band that indicated his social rank as well as government position. The tunic worn underneath the toga also had the same band of color running vertically down his right shoulder. The toga covered his left shoulder and draped over his left arm.

Festus liked the feel of the fine wool. He wore the official toga with pride but did not want to appear arrogant regarding his social class or government position as the new Procurator to Judea. Nevertheless, he relied on Fabiana to make sure his appearance radiated power. She smoothed the fabric and stepped back to admire his appearance. She smiled. Satisfied with his wife's assessment, Festus left the villa and rode in his official carriage to the palace built by King Herod, that was now used intermittently by Agrippa II. His mission was to interrogate Paul.

The garrison soldiers were surprised to see the new procurator arrive at the palace. They resided on the first floor, and were stationed as guards for all that pertained to the palace, offices, and persons housed there. The first floor also held Festus' official headquarters. The second floor was devoted to Agrippa II. The third floor had a series of detention rooms for those accused of various crimes. Festus was escorted by two soldiers to Tadius' office.

After a brief introductory chat, Tadius personally escorted Festus to where Paul was detained. Tadius opened the unlocked door and Festus entered with a flourish of measured authority that indicated his official position.

Paul was sitting at a small desk when Tadius announced Festus' arrival. The detainee turned sideways from his writing and looked up to greet the new procurator who held his fate.

Festus quickly assessed the room and the appearance of the man who had caused such a stir throughout Jerusalem. Paul was not nearly as tall as Festus, who was close to six feet tall. But similarities included their intense piercing eyes, a no-nonsense countenance, and muscular arms and hands that evidenced strength from working a trade. Festus had expected a typical Jewish appearance, but Paul was clean-shaven. He gave credit to Paul's perceptive choice to look the part of a Roman citizen, for the Roman Caesar he would appeal to.

Festus initiated the conversation, "I am Festus Porcius, Procurator to Judea. I have replaced Felix. It is my desire to remedy your case as quickly as possible. To do this, I need information from you that will assist me in my decision-making."

Paul was surprised at the curtness of this new procurator. Actually, he was relieved by his direct, official nature. It was in notable contrast to the vacillating, conniving Felix. Paul sensed this procurator would be impartial.

"As you can see, Procurator, my surroundings are comfortable, but sparse. Please sit in my chair. I will sit on the bed, and I will answer your questions."

Festus immediately fired his first question, "What was your intent in starting the riot in the temple that led to the Jews wanting to kill you?" Paul was glad Festus got right to the point. It confirmed this new procurator was vastly different from Felix. He felt his time in Rome would not be as protracted as the prolonged times he had spent coming and going at the mercy of Felix's whims.

"I took a Gentile to the temple to worship God. Some in attendance were opposed to this because of Jewish traditions. They complained to Ananias that I was blaspheming the temple. The ensuing disturbance resulted in your soldiers taking control of the situation. My intent was simply to worship God."

In a casual voice, Festus challenged Paul, "I have learned you once were a Pharisee, well versed in these religious traditions and rituals. As such, why did you purposely violate them with this so-called Gentile you refer to?"

"We were in a portion of the temple that was open to Jews, women, and Gentiles, and we were not in violation of going into those parts of the temple where Gentiles could not enter."

"Did your accusers know that this section of the temple was permissible to these Gentiles?"

"Absolutely. From early in life, Jews are taught about areas in the temple and any limitations associated with worshiping there." Paul anticipated Festus' next question and gave his answer before it was asked, "I believe these accusers were agents of Ananias, whose purpose was to make a false statement against me, so that I would be taken before the high priest and the Sanhedrin."

"Would this Sanhedrin be a court that would decide your crime and render punishment against you?"

"Yes."

"What would this punishment consist of?"

"I could be beaten or possibly stoned to death if the infraction was serious enough. To the Jew, the crime of blasphemy is very serious and warrants stoning."

"It is my understanding you have also gone throughout Judea and other parts of the Roman Empire espousing conversion to this man-god you call Jesus of Nazareth. Is this true?"

"Most certainly. My divine ordination from Almighty God is to go forth as His vessel, teaching about Christ Jesus, and allowing God's Holy Spirit to move within the hearts of the unsaved, that they may accept Christ's eternal salvation and enjoy a personal relationship with Him."

Festus detected the fervor in Paul's voice, yet there was no ranting or insane emotionalism involved in his words or his accompanying body language. He could tell Paul was intelligent, resolute, and fully committed to this man-god he called Jesus.

"It appears to me that your actions of recruiting Jews to believe in this Jesus are most offensive to the Jewish high priest, who is intent on stopping your efforts. Can't this god of yours, this Jesus, become part of who the Jews worship?"

Paul answered, "They do not recognize Him as their Messiah, because Jesus came in human form, growing from infancy. The Jews believe their Messiah will come down from heaven with a multitude of angels to eliminate the Jews' enemies. Because this did not happen with Jesus, they rejected Him and had Him crucified."

Festus didn't understand. He quickly interjected his next question before Paul could continue. "So, tell me, in your opinion, why didn't this Jesus come as the Jews expected?"

"Jesus came to redeem mankind spiritually, not to set up a kingdom on earth as earthly kings do. He came to show us who God is. He was God with us, walking, talking, healing. The Jewish leaders saw and heard it with their own eyes and ears. He came to be God's own blood sacrifice as atonement for the sin of mankind—sin that separates us from any relationship with God our Father. When Jesus was crucified, it was for no crime. It was the divine plan of God. Jesus the Christ sacrificed His life to offer man forgiveness, freedom, and new relationship with Him for all those who choose to accept it."

Festus looked up and scanned the ceiling in Paul's room, but remained silent while he thought about Paul's words. It was a lot to absorb, and he didn't want to admit that he didn't fully grasp it. With his arms folded and his eyes still on the ceiling, he attempted to verify the essential issue, "In essence, then, the Jews want what they expected their messiah would accomplish for them; and they refuse to accept what Jesus taught—and now what you and others like you teach. I believe I understand their opposition."

Paul confirmed his conclusion with a nod. Satisfied, Festus followed with another question, "So, why did you invoke your

Roman citizenship to the soldiers, who in essence rescued you from death by the Jews? Isn't this solely a religious matter?"

"What I and my brethren teach is not religion. Religion is man trying to reach God through his own efforts. Jesus is God reaching out to man, freely offering forgiveness to all who ask Him." Paul could see that Festus was struggling to understand, so he was more specific, "As you can understand, Festus, a free gift of forgiveness threatens religious rulers' power with their rules and rituals which they claim are needed to earn God's favor. Ananias and the Sanhedrin will resort to anything to stop me. That is why the Jewish high priest Ananias seeks to use Roman law to have me executed, hoping all teaching about freedom in Christ will cease."

"Is this new belief of yours why you have forsaken being a Pharisee?"

"Yes, it is. When I was journeying to Damascus to persecute Christ's followers, Jesus Christ personally intervened. I was blinded for three days. During that time He spoke to my heart, showing me the error of my ways and the falseness of religion no matter how zealous it is. After my conversion, I attempted to speak about him with the Jewish followers of The Way there. But they were afraid. They believed I was attempting to snare them. They feared I intended to beat them or even kill them for their belief in Jesus. They rejected me and set about to execute me.

"But Christ intervened and took me to the desert of Arabia for three years where He imparted His Holy Word to my heart. I received His teaching and had much time to meditate." He smiled at his next thought, "This was the same time period He taught the original eleven who continue to go forth teaching His precepts. I do the same."

Festus sat facing Paul with his arms still crossed. It was just as Fabiana had supposed; Paul would be truthful. He had just verified the information Fabiana had obtained.

Festus unfolded his arms and his facial expression relaxed. He slowly stood up and looked into Paul's earnest face. "I shall cease this interrogation for now. Rest assured, I will evaluate what you have told me. I do not perceive your case will take much longer to resolve." At that, the new Judean procurator left Paul's room and returned to his villa.

Fabiana was waiting anxiously for her husband's return. She knew they would have a discussion concerning Paul's interrogation. It was gratifying to her that Festus valued her input for different aspects of his official duties. His willingness to listen to her comments and suggestions made her more receptive to enjoying his official position in spite of its continual pressures and dangers.

She heard him return to the villa and call her name from the atrium. She hastened from the room that had been set aside and furnished especially for her. Smiling, she opened her arms and embraced her husband.

"Fabiana, there is much to share with you but I also need both Caelius and Servius to attend my debriefing of the interrogation with Paul. I shall summon them and we all will discuss this meeting while we have our evening meal."

Fabiana drew back from their embrace with her sparkling eyes revealing a playful attitude. She had a winsome way about her that always helped dissolve her husband's tensions. "Since this is dreary official business, I say we should offset the starkness of the occasion by having our meal in the courtyard where surroundings are more festive."

Festus acknowledged her playfulness with an expression of feigned remorse, and dramatically placed his hand over his heart. "Alas, my dear wife, Rome would never approve of such a thing, but as Procurator of Judea, I decree we shall do this." The two laughed and embraced a second time, and Fabiana went to the kitchen to instruct the cook while Festus sent a servant to call his assistants.

During the appetizer course, Festus related to Servius and Caelius the conversation he had with Paul, making sure not to leave out any of the details. He did not want to omit anything of importance that would adversely affect the comments and suggestions he sought. When the meal was finished and the dessert course of fresh fruit and honey cakes was served, the discussion of the meeting took place.

Caelius was first to speak. "Your description, Festus, clearly indicates this is a religious issue between Paul and the Jewish high priest. As such, Paul should be turned over to the Jews for whatever decision and punishment they deem is necessary."

Servius concurred with Caelius, adding, "You could also make certain specifications of what you want the Jews to do to reduce or eliminate any future riots and such from these inflexible, stubborn people. This would establish your authority and let them know you are not like Felix."

Festus listened thoughtfully to his assistants, then turned to Fabiana for her cherished input. Fabiana had been listening attentively. She said, "I perceive this matter to be more than mere religion. If that were the case, this man Paul would have allowed his followers to assist him against the Jews. Paul indicated Ananias would utilize Roman law to eliminate this enemy of the Jews. I believe Paul saw that by invoking his Roman citizenship, he would be taken into custody, thereby saving his life, at least for the time being. I think it behooves you, Festus, to find out how Ananias seeks to use Roman law to achieve his purposes. You can be sure he will put his mind to it."

Festus finished eating his honey cake and licked the last bit of sweetness from the ends of his fingers. His counselors showed interest in what Fabiana had suggested. He leaned forward in his chair and cupped his hands under his chin. "Each of you has made compelling statements. Your assessment of this situation is precise. What I intend to do is go to Jerusalem. While I'm there, I shall seek out whatever information I can obtain. I shall also meet with this high priest Ananias and his scribe Tertullus."

Caelius let out a chuckle and conjectured, "No doubt, Festus, you will use one of your disguises to acquire the information you seek?"

Festus returned the chuckle and smiled at his chief assistant. "You know me well, Caelius. I have just the disguise that will allow me access to those that I need to talk with."

Servius enjoyed the parade of possible disguises in his imagination as he asked, "When do you intend on making this trip to Jerusalem?"

Festus responded, "As soon as I secure a position with the merchant caravan that is scheduled to take their wares to Jerusalem. Tadius has informed me this will be within the next two days. I shall become part of their group. I forsee being gone two full weeks. When I return, we all shall meet again.

"In the meantime, Caelius, I need you to make some inquiries for me. Servius, I also want you to talk with some people here in Caesarea. Fabiana, I do wish it possible for you to accompany me to Jerusalem, but this can't be done. I would like you to confer with some of the women here about Agrippa II. There is much to accomplish before I can render the right decision in this case."

 Chapter 2

Festus sent Servius into the working class section of Caesarea to purchase some used clothing that would fit Festus. When Festus showed the clothing to Fabiana, she scowled at the sight of the unsightly garments. "Are you really going to wear such filthy clothes?"

The beaming procurator replied, "Most certainly, my dear. This shall be the disguise that will enable me to secure a job with the merchant caravan! I must avoid detection at all costs until such time that I choose to reveal my presence here in Caesarea."

Fabiana shook her head in amused resignation, shrugged her shoulders, and left Festus' office. Quickly, the procurator donned the soiled, worn garments and adjusted the hat. Satisfied with his working man's disguise, he called for Fabiana. She was startled at his appearance.

With an expression of sadness, Festus informed his wife, "Dearest wife, I go to secure a position with the merchant caravan. As such, I won't be returning to you until my work is completed in Jerusalem. Please inform both Caelius and Servius of my departure." The couple wanted to embrace each other in a loving farewell, but because of the soiled worker clothing, Fabiana leaned forward to gingerly give him her kiss without brushing up against his dirty identity. Festus turned and slipped out the back of the villa to make his way to where the merchant caravan was being prepared. He would be assigned one of the lowest jobs, attending to the camels. Festus relished the opportunity to put his disguise to the test.

Once there, he had no difficulty getting a job. The caravan left the next morning while it was still dark. During the journey, Festus avoided the squad of Roman soldiers that accompanied the caravan. He altered his speech and mannerisms to mimic that of a vagabond. To his delight, no one questioned his identity. Four uneventful days later, they arrived in Jerusalem.

After he received his meager pay from the merchant owner of the caravan, Festus made his way to a small shop. There he attempted to steal a pair of leather working class boots and was caught by the store owner. Roman soldiers were called to the scene. The irate shop owner was indignant and insulting in his report of the theft. He swore and stuck his finger at Festus, and spat in his face.

One of the soldiers restrained the red-faced shop owner while the other hit Festus in his ribs with the blunt end of his short sword, causing the disguised procurator to cry out and bend over in excruciating pain. This placated the smug shop owner who officiously waved for the soldiers to take the thief away.

Festus had difficulty breathing as he was pushed and dragged to the nearby garrison headquarters. There he was taken to the commander, Lysias. After the two soldiers left the commander's office, the prisoner staggered to a nearby chair and fell into it, cringing from the pain. This alarmed Lysias. "You appear to be hurt, Procurator. I shall call for our doctor!"

Within minutes the doctor, Dioscrides, entered the commander's office. "Are you ill, Commander?"

Lysias shook his head negatively and pointed to the doubled-over Festus. "I fear this man is gravely injured. It is he who needs your attention."

Dioscrides peered at the dirty, rumpled clothing of the injured man. He detected the acrid smell of camel emanating from the man's clothing and stiffened. "Commander, my services are intended only for Rome's military and its citizens. This man appears to be a mere gypsy."

Lysias held up his hand to silence Rome's most renowned physician. "Dioscrides, this man is no gypsy. He is Festus, the new Procurator of Judea." Dioscrides became wide-eyed at Lysias' announcement. Breathing through his mouth to avoid the camel smell, Dioscrides had Lysias assist him in getting Festus to lie down on a cot that was in the commander's office.

As the physician examined Festus, it became evident the injury was to his ribs. "I fear you have broken a couple of ribs. How did this injury occur?"

Lysias answered for Festus, "As part of his ruse, Procurator Festus attempted to steal a pair of boots from one of our agents who owns a leather shop. One of my men hit him with the end of his short sword. He did not know who he was actually striking."

Dioscrides raised his eyebrows and looked down at his patient who lay helplessly on the cot. "Procurator Festus, I must have you sit up that I may attend to your injured ribs. This will be somewhat painful, but I assure you it is necessary." Dioscrides called for his assistant who had waited outside Lysias' office and sent him away with instructions.

Grimacing with pain, Festus sat up with the assistance of Lysias. He arched his head back in an attempt to breathe in more air. The painful effort caused him to gasp. Both Dioscrides and Lysias carefully removed the smelly clothing from Festus' body. When they had discarded the last of the garments, Dioscrides' assistant had returned with the items the physician wanted.

Lysias watched intently as Rome's prominent physician made a mixture of herbs that included genugreek as an anti-inflammatory, willow as an antiseptic, garlic for soreness, hyssop leaves for the bruising, and camphor. The herbs were combined in a small bowl and pounded into a powder. Dioscrides then used hyssop oil to make a paste of the concoction. He applied it to Festus' rib area. Finally, the physician took a strip of linen and wrapped it gently around Festus' chest, making sure none of the herb concoction fell to the floor.

The camphor immediately created a cooling sensation to Festus' skin. Dioscrides examined the bandage, then took several of the same herbs, crushed them, and dropped the batch into a goblet of warm water. He mixed them well and gave the goblet to Festus. "Drink this, Procurator. It will help the healing inside your body." Festus first sniffed the brew and detected a hint of mint from the hyssop oil. The aromatic scent of fennel filled his nostrils. He placed the goblet to his lips and obediently drank the entire amount, as Dioscrides looked on.

After the brew was dutifully swallowed, Festus could feel the impact of the various herbs. His pain began to subside and his facial expression displayed his stoic acceptance. "Can you feel the herbs working inside you?" asked Dioscrides. Festus nodded his head. "Good, you should continue to receive its healing power, but I instruct you not to attempt to lift any weight, and avoid any jostling. You are at risk for part of the rib to puncture your lung. This will kill you. Also, breathe deeply as much as you can. This will prevent you from contracting pneumonia."

Before he left, Dioscrides gave Festus a list of the herbs he used and instructions on how and when to make the paste and the liquid potion. "How long will you be here in Jerusalem, Procurator?"

Festus said he must meet with the Jewish high priests. Afterward, he would leave Jerusalem to return to Caesarea.

"I strongly suggest you wait a minimum of two weeks before you travel back to your headquarters. If you cannot ride one of the Nisean horses with their soft gait, ride an old camel. You will still feel some pain and discomfort but you shouldn't do further damage to your ribs or to your lungs."

Dioscrides looked at Lysias. "I will finish my instructions to your garrison doctors at the end of this week, and then make my way back to Rome. If there are any complications, summon me." The physician left the office.

Lysias looked dismayed, knowing the injured procurator could easily have him removed from command for the actions of the soldier. Festus looked up at Lysias. "Don't fret, Lysias. Your soldiers performed their duties as they should have." Festus looked down at the bandage covering his injury, then back up at Lysias. He actually was pleased. "This is proof my disguise worked perfectly. Our Jewish agent who owns the shoe shop did his part very convincingly. My true identity remains hidden, which must be the case while I'm here."

Festus slowly lifted up his chest with a small groan and another grimace. He purposefully took in as deep a breath as he could. "So long as the healing herbs are active, I can manage to breathe as Dioscrides instructed. Now we must discuss the turmoil caused by Paul before I meet with the Jewish high priests."

Lysias easily relayed to Festus the events that led to Paul's detention in Caesarea. As Festus listened, he began to detect what was at the core of the riot caused by Paul. "You say that twice Paul spoke to these Jews? First to the mob, and then to the high priests? Give me your opinion about this meeting with the priests."

"Paul was very eloquent in his speech. He had the high priests listening carefully to his words. Some even appeared to believe him until his last statement where he quoted some god named Jesus. That's when the high priests cried out that Paul wasn't fit to live. As is their odd custom, they tore off their clothes and threw dust into the air. I sensed they would attempt to kill Paul, so I had him brought into the barracks."

Festus' face revealed curiosity in spite of the distracting pain in his body. "What happened back here in the barracks?"

Lysias stood up and nervously paced about his office. He returned and sat on a corner of the desk, where he could watch Festus for his reaction. "One of my centurions was about to scourge and then release Paul because supposedly this is a religious matter. At that point, Paul informed the centurion of his Roman citizenship. The centurion was aghast at their near blunder, and immediately halted the soldiers from laying hands on Paul. The centurion informed me of Paul's statement. I went to Paul and asked him about his Roman citizenship. When I informed him I had purchased my citizenship, he told me he was born a Roman citizen."

Festus suddenly raised his hand to stop Lysias from continuing. "Are you sure Paul said he was *born* a Roman citizen?"

Lysias did not hesitate in his reply. "Absolutely sure, Procurator. My centurion witnessed his statement."

Festus pressed his lips tightly together and his eyes seemed to focus on something deep within him.

Lysias felt compelled to add, "Paul has a sister and nephew living here in Jerusalem. The boy overheard a plot by the Jews. They were to petition me to take Paul to their council the next day to inquire of him. This was a ruse. Their intention was to steal him away from my men and kill him. Instead, I had two centurions prepare a force of two hundred men, seventy cavalry, and two hundred spearmen, and under the cloak of night they brought him to Felix."

Festus sat motionless as he listened to Lysias. When the garrison commander had finished, the procurator gave his thoughts, "Lysias, you have done well in this matter. I perceive it necessary to meet with these Jewish high priests as soon as possible, despite my injury. Please arrange a meeting, preferably here on the day after tomorrow. Also,..." he said with an amused expression, "procure for me some different clothes for me to wear to the meeting."

When he finished making his requests, Festus eased his body back down on the cot with a moan, and placed his left arm over his eyes. Lysias responded, "Procurator Festus, I shall do as you instruct. In addition, you must stay with me where you will be more comfortable. My residence is above this office, so you won't have far to walk."

Festus remained prone and mumbled, "That will be fine." He was exhausted and the herbal medicines were causing some drowsiness. He fell asleep while thinking of his next strategy.

Just as planned, two days later the meeting with the Jewish high priests was ready to take place. Lysias was concerned about the procurator's condition. "Festus, do you feel you want to continue with these people? You looked pained."

Festus smiled reassuringly at Lysias. "The herbs and bandage are sufficient that I can proceed. Where are these high priests?"

Lysias felt relieved about Festus' apparent improvement. "They wait for you in my office. There are two, Ananias the high priest, and his scribe Tertullus."

Festus motioned with his arm and was assisted to his feet. "Let the meeting begin."

Carefully, the two Romans made their way to Lysias' office. They remained outside the closed door a brief moment so that Festus could take as deep a breath as possible without revealing his limitations to his audience. After a few breaths, Festus motioned he was ready to proceed and he walked into the office as ceremoniously as he could muster. Lysias had arranged for a comfortable chair to be placed near the door, so that Festus would not reveal his injury as he walked. Lysias was impressed with how well Festus managed to hide evidence of any weakness.

As soon as he was seated, Festus wasted no time in beginning the meeting. Summoning determined strength, he announced, "I am Festus Porcius, newly assigned Procurator to all of Judea by Governor Quadratus. It appears we have an issue that has been ongoing far too long and must be resolved. It concerns this man named Paul. What is your argument with him?"

Tertullus rose up from his chair. He was smaller in height than Festus, and heavier. He purposely moved his body to draw attention to his attire. He wore a tunic with sleeves that reached to his wrists. It was made of pure natural, cream-colored linen and covered his entire body. He wore a plain white sash of finely twined linen over his left shoulder with several markings Festus did not understand. However, he knew the markings indicated his rank, whatever it was.

On his head was a cone-shaped turban with embroidery of signs or words; again, Festus knew nothing about them, yet he assumed they coincided with his sash, regarding rank. Tertullus made a point of strutting about the room, allowing his tunic and sash to sway with each exaggerated movement. Festus was not impressed. To him it was a garish display of religious nonsense.

Festus' thoughts were interrupted by Tertullus. "We here in Jerusalem have known that a replacement to Felix was on his way to Caesarea; however, your predecessor did not notify us of your arrival. I trust your journey was uneventful."

Lysias noted the tone of Tertullus' voice was condescending, almost mocking, and that he considered it an offense not to have been notified of Festus' arrival. He was curious how Festus would deal with this insolence.

"Before I answer, tell me...," Festus deliberately paused to make his point, "...who are you?"

Tertullus faintly showed irritation at the question, but did not allow it to influence his pompous demeanor. "I am Tertullus. Scribe to high priest Ananias and to the Sanhedrin, the governing body of the Jews wherever they reside." Before Festus could ask another question, Tertullus sought to control the meeting by hastening to add, "Through Felix, our people have enjoyed great peace and prosperity through his foresight. We are most grateful for his involvement with us, which allows our people to continue as servants to Rome and to Caesar."

He swayed with self-importance as he continued, "Felix realized our desire to obey the dictates of Rome. As such, he indicated our case against this creator of dissension and ringleader of sedition was very strong. It is unfortunate this rebel has not been turned over to us render justice. We trust Felix has informed you about this. Is there a date when we can expect Paul's return to us?"

Lysias almost gagged at the arrogance, but controlled his emotions. He looked directly at Festus who sat stoically, not exhibiting any sign of discomfort from his rib injury. A few moments of silence passed, which befuddled both Tertullus and Ananias.

Festus' eyes bore through Tertullus. Festus carefully took as deep a breath as his ribs would allow and slowly exhaled. "Tertullus, it is common knowledge that Felix was a scoundrel whose main intent was his own monetary gain. He was thoroughly corrupt, a thief, and a liar." Festus stopped to give his words their desired impact on this impudent caricature of a man. He was pleased when Tertullus looked startled at his bold honesty. The fool's eyes revealed he didn't know what to do or say.

Festus continued with a second thrust of his imaginary sword. "Felix attempted first to extort money from Paul, and then from you. It made no difference to him. Whoever gave him the desired amount would win the case." Again Festus paused to ready his verbal sword for yet a third strike. Lysias was enjoying the scene. "Felix has been arrested and is on his way to Rome to be tried before Caesar for his crimes. There shall be no special favor shown to you or anyone else in matters involving Roman law and justice. Being a free-born citizen of Rome, Paul shall be tried before me in Caesarea and nowhere else. I remain here in Jerusalem on official business ten more days, at which time I return to Caesarea. Twenty days from now, you must appear at his hearing—with your accusers—concerning Paul's crimes against Rome. I will render my decision at that time. Now go."

Tertullus was stupefied, standing as rigid as if he were stone. He could not speak. Ananias silently stood up, glared at Festus, and grabbed Tertullus by his arm. They speedily left the room with their ceremonious garments flapping awkwardly around them.

Lysias closed the door to his office and turned to the seated Festus. "That was most interesting, Procurator. It certainly did not go as these Jews expected. No doubt they thought you would be like Felix, dispensing favor at a price. Do you believe their case?"

Festus was losing strength. He winced at a sudden sharp pain and let out a sigh, "I'm glad the long-winded fool gave me an opportunity to end his oratory. I've learned much from this brief meeting and will ponder its ramifications. I believe they are lying through their gritted teeth about this matter concerning Paul. It will be interesting what real evidence they present at his trial." Festus took a careful breath. "And it will be most interesting to hear how Paul defends himself against these fools."

The next ten days allowed Festus to heal, and he began to breathe more easily. He still had pain and his face showed it when movement aggravated his ribs, but he knew he was improving. He had several in-depth conversations with Lysias and learned much about the Jewish Sicarii assassins who were creating havoc throughout Judea and especially in Jerusalem. He was appalled to learn that it was Felix who had given these rogues power by entering into an alignment with them. He was determined to ensure they had no influence at Paul's upcoming trial.

On the tenth day, Festus joined a merchant caravan that was returning to Caesarea. Festus had no difficulty securing a spot. This time he did not wear his disguise, only an ordinary Roman tunic. The tunic would not draw any suspicion; it merely suggested that he could be an upper class businessman. Lysias ordered the accompanying cavalry to protect Festus at all costs and made sure Festus had an old camel to ride for the 70-mile trip.

## Chapter 3

Back in Caesarea after a tiring and painful trip, Festus knew he would incur Fabiana's wrath regarding his rib injury. Although the healing was progressing, there were times it was quite painful. As the wounded procurator stood at the front door of his villa, he mentally prepared himself for what was to come.

A servant announced his arrival, and Fabiana came rushing out of her office with a delighted smile and sparkling eyes. "Oh Festus, it is so good to have you back safe and sound! Your lot seems to have improved much since your departure," she quipped, admiring his fresh clothing. She quickly came towards him, arms open for the welcoming embrace they loved to share. This time, it was Festus who held up his hand in a gesture for her to stop. Her face showed confusion and concern, "Festus, what's wrong?"

Realizing he couldn't prolong his confession, Festus reached out for Fabiana's hand and immediately began walking to the courtyard. Surrounded by fragrant flowers and fresh air, he felt it would be the perfect place to recount all the events that had transpired during his stay in Jerusalem.

As he made his way through his narrative, Fabiana's eyes grew wide while hearing about the rib injury. "Festus, you and your disguises! I hope you have learned something from this event." The procurator smiled and lowered his head to offer his heartfelt apology to appease his wife. Inwardly, though, he was quite pleased how effective his disguise had been, and would consider using it again should the need arise.

Fabiana's exasperation with Festus gave way to fascination with what he had learned about Paul and the two Jewish leaders. When the wounded procurator finished relaying the events of his trip, he detected, much to his relief, that Fabiana's earlier testiness had evaporated like the morning dew.

"I must say, Festus, your trip turned out to be quite valuable for you. Many questions were answered during this trip, and despite my annoyance with your infernal passion for disguises, I realize it helped you in your quest. We have talked quite a while, and I'm sure you are hungry after your trip. We shall eat and you shall have a soak."

Festus smiled lovingly at Fabiana. She treasured the tenderness she saw in his eyes and blushed at his gentle love for her. Festus reached over the small table and gently grasped her hand. "Your concern for my wellbeing greatly touches my heart. But before we eat, I must request both Caelius and Servius to meet with me again this evening. We have but a few days until the two Jewish leaders come to make their case against Paul. Every hour is essential to prepare for this trial."

Fabiana called one of the servants and instructed him to summon her husband's chief assistants. Throughout the meal, Fabiana carefully studied Festus for any signs of pain. She was amazed at how normal his vitality appeared. Still, there were times she saw him wince when moving in a way that inflamed his ribs. Caelius and Servius knew his stoicism, and were not surprised at his determination. They were sure neither of the two Jewish leaders, or even the accused Paul, would be able to match Festus in grit, stamina, and mental agility.

After Festus finished his report, Caelius was the first to speak. "With so little time before the trial, what do you propose to do, and what do you want Servius and myself to do?"

"I must limit my activities to give my ribs rest and healing. Reading your reports will suffice to give me plenty of time to prepare a strategy for this trial. I truly believe the Jewish leaders were quite surprised during our brief meeting. Based on my trip, I don't perceive they will have many accusers or will present any new evidence that I haven't already knowledge of." In a lowered voice he added, "I do know the accused Paul will be absolutely prepared."

Festus frowned slightly and twisted his body in an attempt to relieve the quick, sharp pain from his ribs. Sensing the concern of his attentive audience, the procurator raised his hand and slightly hung his head. "Everything is fine. I drew too deep a breath, and my ribs felt the impact. However, I must take a bath and change my bandage as Dioscrides instructed me."

Haltingly, the procurator stood up from his cushioned dining room chair to end the meeting. Slowly straightening, he looked directly at both Caelius and Servius. "I want both of you to attend the trial. I will also request that Tatius be present." Festus turned and smiled at Fabiana. "My dear wife will also attend. Each of your input will be appreciated once the trial is concluded." At that, Festus headed toward the bath. He suddenly realized how tired he was and how much he longed for the soothing water.

Early the next morning, Festus asked Fabiana to accompany him to the garrison barracks to meet the accused rebel Paul. She quickly assented with a smile, "I was hoping you would ask me to do this. We make such a good pair in these matters. I know I can offer insight into this man Paul."

"Fabiana, indeed I value your perspective, and whatever you give me will greatly assist my decision-making in order to close this case."

When Festus and Fabiana arrived at his room, Paul was finishing up a meeting with an earlier visitor. As the visitor left, he greeted the arriving couple. Festus noted the man's cordiality and body language, and committed these details to memory for potential reference later.

After Festus introduced Fabiana to Paul, he informed the detainee that the Jewish leaders would be arriving within the next couple of days for his long-postponed trial. "I'm sure you are relieved this matter is about to be decided," he said.

Paul replied, "I have learned to wait on Almighty God, for in His perfect timing all things come to pass. My needs have been met and I've been able to do God's work while detained here by Felix. I am not anxious or worrisome about this trial."

While Paul was speaking, Fabiana paid particular attention to his mannerisms. In perfect harmony with his statement, he displayed no anxiety or worry. He came across as confident, focused, and ready to meet his accusers. She was impressed.

"Do you require anything that will assist you in preparing for your trial, Paul?" The apostle of Christ smiled and answered that he needed nothing. Festus looked for a moment at Paul, then finished the meeting with a brief acknowledgement, "I wish you well." Festus took his wife's hand and they left the room.

During the carriage ride back to their villa, Fabiana gave Festus her insight, "This man is not the criminal the Jews say he is. Paul is considerate and warm-hearted. He will handle himself well at this trial."

Festus studied her serious eyes as she spoke. He trusted her instincts, as she had been proven correct on many occasions. He said, "I quite agree with you, my dear. This will be most interesting."

The day of the trial, Fabiana and Festus were enjoying their breakfast together. "Festus, I've been thinking how this is your very first trial as Procurator of Judea. Have you given any thought to this? Are you concerned about how it may go?"

Festus appreciated her empathy, and smiled her question. His thoughts had been fixed on that very thing. "The thought has come to my mind about this being my first trial in any capacity as a Roman official. In some ways, it's exciting. But more importantly, I'm acutely aware of my responsibility to render an impartial verdict in this case. Quadratus, as well as Caesar, will review my decision. Their opinions will influence my career, but neither the Jews nor Paul will have any effect. This is about my professionalism and being a servant to Rome, doing what is best for Rome."

Fabiana reached her hand across the dining table and clasped her husband's hand. "Festus, I love and admire your passion for Rome. I know in my heart that this is part of your very being. Your passion carries over into other facets of your life, including your love for me. I'm deeply touched and proud to be your wife."

Festus was moved by Fabiana's comments. They made him melt inside, reflecting the deep, abiding love they shared. He cherished Fabiana's love and would protect it even if the cost were his very life. His eyes closed at her words as he raised her hand and gently kissed it. The two lovers sat contentedly for a while, enjoying the moment, and silently let their hearts sing to each other.

As Procurator of Judea, Festus had a special two-wheeled carriage made available by Rome for official events, as well as for commuting from the villa to the main office located within the palace Herod had built years earlier. The carriage was spacious and comfortable for Festus and Fabiana to ride together.

Inside the palace, Festus and Fabiana were met by Caelius, Servius, and the garrison commander, Tadius. Normally, the accused and his accusers would enter the courtroom before the judge's entrance. But because of his rib injury, Festus decided to be present first.

Carefully, he made his way up the small platform where the judgment seat was placed. It wasn't as embellished as the one

Caesar utilized, but the significance was the same. The fates of humans were decided here; some would live, and others would be executed. As Festus sat for the first time in the judgment seat, he pondered its significance. It was humbling. He peered around the small room. The only seating was for the procurator and his attendants. Both accused and accuser would stand, with the accused on one side of the platform and the accuser on the other.

Caelius noticed how Festus slowly stroked the arms of the judgment seat as he looked down from the platform where the plaintiff and the defendant would be standing. Caelius felt he could read Festus' mind, honing in on the honor and the heavy responsibility of his position. Caelius felt reassured by this thought. He knew in his heart that Festus' first decision would be proper. He was excited to witness and be part of this momentous occasion.

Ananias and Tertullus were next to enter the courtroom. They did so with pomp and swagger. Tertullus led the way. Moving proudly, the hired lawyer wore the traditional garments that denoted his social position. His pure linen tunic covered his entire body from his neck to his feet and included long sleeves that went to each wrist. Over the top of the tunic was a robe-like outer covering that had multi-colored stripes. Fabiana could see it was made of a combination of wool and cotton, certainly expensive. On his head was a stiff brimless cap that appeared to be made of felt. Attached to it was the same material as the multi-striped outer covering.

Tertullus walked with his black-bearded chin held high, his jaw set firm. He projected confidence—tainted with ugly arrogance. As Servius watched the slow procession, he realized his emotions were being swayed against these Jews simply by their charade. He wondered if others seated on the platform of justice felt the same way.

Four feet behind Tertullus came Ananias. His special garments denoted he was the high priest of the Jews. His vestments included a sleeveless blue robe, the lower hem being fringed with small golden bells that alternated with pomegranate-shaped tassels in blue, purple, and scarlet. The tinkling of the bells seemed out of place to Festus in the imposing hall of justice. There was an embroidered apron with two onyx gemstones on his shoulders. Each stone was engraved with the names of the twelve tribes of Israel.

There was an elaborately woven cloth made of the same fine

linen as that of the apron. It was folded back on itself to form a square bag in which were special items only the high priest could wear. This was fastened to the apron. Twelve gems adorned this breastplate, each signifying the twelve tribes of Israel. His head was covered with a taller turban than the one Tertullus wore. It was more broad and flat-topped. On the front of it was a golden plate inscribed with the words, "Holiness unto YHWH." Later, Festus would learn these garments were to be worn only in the place of the temple referred to as the Holy of Holies where only the high priest was allowed; and that *YHWH* referred to the God of the Hebrews, written without vowels because they considered his name to be too sacred to be spoken.

Ananias narrowed his eyes, pressed his lips tightly together, and squared his jaw under his long gray beard. He made sure the members of the judging panel noticed his exalted position as high priest. He walked purposefully and puffed out his chest to enhance the adorned breastplate. His shoulders moved haughtily with each step. Like Tertullus, his head was held high in defiance.

As Caelius watched the two-man parade, he thought how dreadfully hot Ananias must feel beneath his garb, and the back of his neck began to ache as he imagined the weight of Ananias' turban. His overall impression was how foolish these men appeared with their attitudes and regalia. He knew that Festus would not be impressed with the display.

Tertullus stood on the left side of the judgment platform with Ananias slightly behind him and three paces away. No sooner had they assumed their positions, than a Roman soldier opened the door to the courtroom and ushered Paul in to meet his fate. Unlike his Jewish accusers, Paul was dressed in a simple workingman's tunic. The garment was made of wool and hemp, making it both tough and durable. It covered Paul's shoulders with short sleeves. The bottom came to his knees. The color was blackish maroon, a color that reflected he was a freeborn citizen. Underneath the tunic, Paul wore a loincloth adopted by the majority of men and soldiers for a sense of modesty.

Festus and the panel made a mental note of Paul's attire but, more notably, that he had shaved his beard. This was the custom of Roman society. No Roman citizen dared grow a beard because it was thought of as being unclean. This was a point of contention between the Romans and the Jews whose tradition was that men wore long beards.

Both Ananias and Tertullus were startled at Paul's appearance. They had expected him to wear the traditional Jewish garments that were dissimilar to that of Roman clothing. In their minds, this confirmed that Paul was a blasphemer who should be executed. Tertullus smirked at Paul's appearance. He fully expected to use this in stating his case.

Paul walked confidently and smoothly to the judging platform. He took his place to the right of his accusers. Not once did he look at either of them, but turned to the panel and bowed with the traditional Roman show of respect. The panel also made a mental note of this. Fabiana was glad that Paul came attired as the Roman citizen he was. She knew Paul was sending a subtle message to the court. She was anxious to hear his defense.

As soon as Paul finishing bowing to the court, Festus turned to the two Jews and demanded, "Begin your accusation."

Tertullus stepped forward. His exaggerated movements caused the turban to bob and the multi-colored outer garment to make a swishing sound. "We accept this opportunity with all thankfulness and do not wish to be tedious for you. I beg you to hear, by your courtesy, these few words from us."

The gifted orator then launched into the same religious argument he had made two years earlier to Felix. Tertullus emphasized each accusation with a body movement that caused his garments to swirl as if dancing with the air. The Jewish orator was not true to his declaration of being brief. He often rambled and made excessive hand gestures that accented his swirling clothing. Finally, much to the relief of the panel, he finished and arrogantly resumed his position next to Ananias. His conceited smirk made Fabiana want to scream.

Festus breathed a moan of relief that only Fabiana noticed. He turned to Paul and said, "Make your defense."

Unlike his counterpart, Paul was very brief. "Neither against the law of the Jews, nor against the temple have I offended in any manner."

Paul paused before raising his voice for emphasis, "Nor against Caesar have I committed any crime." In a lawyerly manner, the defendant went on, "My accusers have not produced any witnesses to any alleged religious offense. Nor have they presented any proof of sedition that they claim I've initiated or continue to espouse." It was the conclusion of his defense, and Christ's servant bowed and stepped back.

The procurator gripped the arms of his judgment seat and looked down at the accused man. No witnesses? No evidence? His mind was racing as he processed Paul's words of defense. In one brief statement, this defendant had given him the opening he needed to separate the religious and political alleged crimes. A sense of elation coursed through his body.

Festus leaned forward to slowly and deliberately demand from Paul, "Are you willing to go up to Jerusalem and there be judged before me concerning these religious things?" Festus then leaned back in his judgment seat and awaited the answer he hoped would come forth. He hoped Paul would not choose to return to Jerusalem where he would surely be tried unjustly by religious powers who had already proven their malicious intent to kill him.

"I stand at Caesar's judgment seat, where I ought to be judged. To the Jews I have done no wrong, as you very well know." Again Paul paused and looked from one member of the panel to another, then at Festus. The apostle of Christ declared slowly and sincerely, "For if I am an offender, or have committed anything deserving of death, I do not object to dying. But if there is nothing in these things of which these men accuse me, no one can deliver me to them."

Ananias and Tertullus, in tandem, shifted their accusing eyes from the procurator to the faces of the panel. They were chagrined by the quick agreement they saw displayed on each member's face. Anger began to swell inside Ananias. Tertullus felt a sudden cold foreboding he did not like. Their respective emotions boiled and surged like a volcano about to erupt.

Then came Paul's final declaration. Positioning himself directly in front of Festus and standing tall with his shoulders back, the apostle announced in a loud, unwavering voice, "I appeal to Caesar!" To the Jewish leaders, the sound of Paul's words were thunder that shook their bones. To Festus, they were a melodic chirping that delighted his entire body, sore ribs and all.

Paul's thunder echoed throughout the room. Each member of the startled panel visibly reacted. Their eyes were wide at the defendant's appeal. This was most unusual in a case such as this! To appeal to Caesar meant the defendant was putting his life in the hands of Rome's supreme judge. It also meant the defendant must feel very confident about his case and was very learned in Roman law to make such an appeal.

To Festus, there was another more interesting component to Paul's appeal—shrewdness. He saw this defendant was intelligent and knew exactly what his declaration meant to his accusers. Before Caesar, they could not bring forth accusations of a religious nature. Their proof had to be political, overwhelming, and solely focused on their claims of sedition and treason against Rome.

While Festus was inwardly experiencing exhilaration, Tertullus was beside himself. He was fully aware of the ramifications of Paul's appeal. Hearing Paul's words was like the collapse of a dam. All of Tertullus' strategy had crumbled, emptying the wall of water behind it, and leaving a mere puddle destined to dry up.

Paul remained fixed on Festus as he awaited the judge's answer. He noticed the procurator looked ill and ashen-faced. Paul sensed there was something physically wrong with him.

Festus adjusted his position in his judgment seat and stated in a strong voice, "I shall confer with my council and we shall weigh both presentations. You all shall wait outside until we have finished our deliberation."

Ananias and Tertullus sulkily left the room, in noticeable contrast to their earlier prideful strutting. Caelius compared their new posture to a pair of dogs that had just been severely beaten by their master. He wanted to laugh, but managed to contain his emotions. Paul, on the other hand, waited respectfully before calmly following them out of the courtroom.

With the room now emptied, Fabiana went to Festus' side. She looked worried. "You are in pain, aren't you, my husband?"

Festus knew he could not hide the obvious. "I'm very uncomfortable. I must stand so that I can breathe deeper." Both Caelius and Servius assisted their superior to his feet. Once erect, Festus steeled himself and took in a deep breath. He slowly exhaled, repeating the exercise three times. At the end of the third effort, Fabiana could tell her husband was feeling better even before he spoke.

"I'm feeling much better, standing; it's easier to breathe," he admitted. He smiled warmly at Fabiana and lightly touched the side of her anxious face. "I will stand. Let our deliberation begin."

All council members looked to the others, trying to guess what each one was thinking. Tadius opted to be first to speak. "This Tertullus is a known lawyer who has presented cases in both Jerusalem and Caesarea. He knows Roman law and is crafty. I noticed there were no accusers with these two men. Tertullus knows full well that accusers must be present at a Roman trial. He also made no mention of the crime of treason that was made before Lysias and Felix. This tells me Paul did *not* commit any such crime against Rome."

The faces of the other members of the deciding council showed varied emotions. One had wide eyes, another scowled in thought, one had pursed lips. But all nodded their understanding. Servius spoke, "I found it interesting that this high priest did not speak at all. However, his eyes revealed anger, hatred, and malice toward Paul. To me, this is a personal matter with him and I believe he will go to any length to kill Paul."

Again, the council members' heads bobbed with serious consideration. Caelius cleared his throat and spoke next. "I noticed that Paul wore the clothing of a free born Roman citizen. He was also clean-shaven."

Tadius suddenly interrupted, "That's right! Lysias informed me that when he arrested Paul in the Jewish temple, he had a beard in the style of the Jews, and he was dressed as a Jew!"

Caelius resumed his assessment, "I believe Paul was demonstrating to us that he considers himself a Roman citizen, and not a Jew. It also signifies he believes this case should be limited only to any violation of Roman law and not anything religious."

Tadius and Servius emitted an "Aah" sound. The others murmured their agreement with his observation.

Fabiana waited until it was clear the men had spoken all they had to say. She looked at Festus, then at the councilmen. "I believe all these observations are accurate and worthy of consideration in this case. It appears to me that this man Paul wants to go to Rome, for much more reason than to have Caesar hear his case. He is supremely confident he will win before Caesar. So, I wonder—what motivation does he have for appealing to Caesar?"

Festus looked at each of his fellow council members' studious faces. Feeling his strength ebbing, he grabbed the back of the judgment seat to brace himself. Fabiana could tell he was pondering all that the council had stated and that he would not allow hmself to be distracted by his discomfort. No one spoke, respectfully allowing the procurator to deliberate their opinions. After a few minutes, he looked up and announced, "I greatly appreciate your wise council in this complicated case. What each of you has said will be considered for what I have to do."

Festus released his hold on the back of the judgment seat and slowly sat down. "I have reached a decision. Summon the litigants back into the courtroom."

Ananias and Tertullus walked into the courtroom side-by-side. There was no pomp this time, only apparent anxiety and fear. Paul came in behind them, looking serene. All three resumed their positions in front of the judgment seat platform.

Festus avoided looking at the two Jews, but locked eyes with Paul's, allowing his gaze to linger for a few moments. The procurator's demeanor was as relaxed as the defendant's. Without hesitation, he declared the decision that would define Paul's fate. In a controlled, firm, matter-of-fact voice, he declared, "You have appealed to Caesar and to Caesar you shall go."

It was done. Two years of Felix's procrastination and Paul's prayers for progress towards a resolution had finally been adjudicated! The council saw undisguised anger and hatred shooting from Ananias. His teeth were clenched, his lips compressed, and his hands formed tight fists of white knuckles. The high priest was obviously struggling to maintain control of his roiling emotions.

Tertullus, with set lips, merely looked down. His head hung in sullen disbelief. He knew the journey back to Jerusalem with Ananias would not be good. Paul folded his hands together, bowed his head, and appeared to be in prayer.

After announcing his decision, Festus rose from the judgment seat and began a slow descent from the platform. Fabiana followed closely at his side, and the remaining councilmen brought up the rear. The procurator and his council did not linger; they promptly left the courtroom.

Guards quickly stepped forward and ushered out Ananias and Tertullus. Ananias could not contain his anger. He spat at Paul. Immediately, a guard forcefully grabbed his arm and shoved him toward the courtroom door. Tertullus glanced at Paul with a defeated expression before quickly exiting.

Another guard stepped forward and escorted Paul back to his familiar room for the past two years of his life. There he would await Festus' decree for his departure for Rome, the city he longed for. He knew in his heart his wait would not be nearly as long now.

 Chapter 4

Festus felt drained after Paul's preliminary trial. The long-winded Tertullus and the deliberation with his advising council took up more time than what normal trials required. These two factors added to his rib injury to cause him fatigue. Nonetheless, Festus felt pleased with how he had conducted his first trial as Procurator of Judea. "Fabiana, I'm exceedingly tired. Would you care to bathe with me so that we can refresh ourselves and possibly talk about what comes next in Paul's case?"

Fabiana's eyes sparkled like rays of sun bouncing on rippling water. "I was hoping you would suggest a bath together. Had you not done so, I would have insisted on it. You need the therapy for your injury."

With arms around each other, the couple made their way to the awaiting bath.

After the two Jews were roughly escorted out of the courtroom and the palace, they climbed into the waiting carriage and silently began the long trip back to Jerusalem. Tertullus could tell Ananias was seething, so he waited until the high priest was calm enough to discuss what had taken place in the courtroom. The two mules hitched to the two-wheeled enclosed carriage transported them five miles away from Caesarea before Ananias had calmed sufficiently to discuss Paul's trial.

"Tell me, Tertullus, do you believe Festus was bribed prior to the trial?"

Tertullus was enjoying the carriage and hated the interruption of his brief pleasure. He was thinking about Ananias' plunder of the carriage from the appointed high priest, Ishmael, who was known to love luxury and pretty women. Late in his years, Ishmael had been appointed high priest for the second time by Agrippa II just two years before Paul was placed under house arrest by Felix. Ishmael's love of luxury funneled down to the carriage Tertullus now shared with Ananias who had usurped Ishmael's position.

Tertullus reluctantly considered Ananaias' question. Sullenly, he answered, "No, I do not think Festus was bribed. When Festus refused our request to have Paul returned to us for trial in Jerusalem, he sent a clear message he would not be bribed." The lawyer paused before adding, "Nor would he be intimidated by us. This trial proves Festus' intention to be impartial."

Ananias gritted his teeth and snarled, "Is it possible to sidestep Festus in any way to get at Paul?"

Tertullus slightly shook his head in disbelief. He was astonished at the hatred Ananias had towards Paul. "At the present time, no Roman soldier will go against the new Procurator of Judea! They know of Festus' association with Quadratus, who is a very severe governor. Any failed attempt to kidnap Paul and those involved will face crucifixion." Tertullus waited momentarily before expanding on his reply, "Ananias, you must forget about killing Paul. Within a short period of time he will be on his way to Rome. Until such time, Paul will remain under house arrest at the garrison headquarters. It is foolish to think about assassinating him there."

Ananias audibly huffed. "I wasn't contemplating making any attempt on Paul's life while he is under guard at the garrison headquarters," he growled. "He will be transported somehow to Rome. That could very well be the opportune time to assassinate him."

As Tertullus listened to Ananias' madness, he felt relieved that his earlier promise to himself would now come into effect. He turned in his seat to face the high priest of the Jews. "Ananias, I will not be a part of any attempt on executing Paul. It is foolhardy. When we get back to Jerusalem, pay what you owe me; then go about whatever folly you choose."

Ananias didn't look at Tertullus. His eyes remained fixed straight ahead on the backs of the two mules pulling them down the winding dusty road. "You shall have your money in full, Tertullus," he said nastily. The only sound from that point on was that of the carriage bouncing over rocks and ruts in the road and

44

the cadence of the innocent mules' hooves. The hired attorney knew in his heart that Ananias wasn't about to give up killing Paul. He also knew his services pertaining to Paul's case were over.

Festus felt immediate relief when he entered the smaller bath of warm water. In smaller baths, Romans placed heated rocks from a fire into a special porous box. As water flowed over the rocks it became heated. The procurator was glad the Roman architects had the foresight to include such an innovation when the villa was constructed.

Fabiana massaged the back of her husband's neck and shoulders, relaxing him even more than the warm water's therapy. "I'm very proud of how you conducted your first trial as Procurator of Judea. You laid a very strong groundwork as to how you will govern these strong-willed people."

The procurator's head began to hang loosely as the combination of warm water and his wife's massaging took the pain and fatigue out of his body. "Thank you, Fabiana. I did want to send a clear message to the Jews they cannot bribe me or solicit favors from me as they did with Felix."

The now very relaxed Roman official interspersed cooing with his narrative. Fabiana quietly chuckled to herself and listened as he continued, "The hired attorney, Tertullus, fully understood my intent. The high priest's intense hatred towards Paul prevented him from learning this. It is probable I will have more problems with this high priest than what should be."

The couple changed their conversation when they were interrupted by a messenger from the palace garrison. Paul was requesting a meeting with Festus as soon as possible. Festus and Fabiana exchanged startled expressions. Festus looked up at the messenger. "Tell Paul we shall visit him within two hours." The messenger promptly left the bath area.

"I find this odd, Festus. Why do you suppose Paul seeks an audience with you?"

Festus shrugged his shoulders. "I do not have any idea. It will be some time before he can leave Caesarea for Rome. This is baffling."

True to his word, Festus and Fabiana arrived at the palace garrison at the designated time they relayed by the messenger. Paul greeted them warmly, "Procurator, during the trial, I perceived you were in considerable discomfort. Is this true?"

Festus looked warily at Paul, but decided to answer his query, "It is true. I have a rib injury that makes breathing difficult at times. Sitting too long causes the pain to increase."

Christ's apostle nodded his head with compassionate concern. He moved his chair away from his desk and placed it near Festus. He motioned to the chair and invited Festus to sit there. Festus glanced at Fabiana, then back at Paul, but did as the apostle requested.

Paul placed his outstretched hands on the top of the procurator's head. As he did so, he began to pray in Jesus' name, requesting Him to bring forth healing to the Roman's body. Paul's invocation was intense, emotional, and pleading. As he prayed over Festus, the procurator felt a warm sensation coursing through his body and tingling in his chest.

As Paul continued to pray, Festus felt the warmth centering on his ribs and lungs. It was as if someone had reached inside his body and lifted out the pain. With each wave of warm healing, Festus breathed more easily with less pain.

Fabiana was watching and listening intently as Paul administered his faith-filled prayer for healing. She saw the change in her husband's facial expression. Gone was the tightness around his eyes. His lips were no longer clamped tight against unrelenting pain. His whole body seemed more relaxed.

Paul's prayer request did not take long. When he was finished, he sat down on the end of his bed. He looked kindly at his judge and saw his demeanor had softened. Inwardly, he thanked Almighty God for His grace to this lost soul. Fabiana noticed that Festus was breathing easier than she had observed since her husband's injury from the Jerusalem encounter.

Festus slowly rotated his head side to side. He murmured, "I don't know this god called Jesus you prayed to, but he certainly is a powerful deity. My body doesn't ache and the stabbing pain is gone." His tone reflected his surprise. Fabiana turned her attention from her husband to Paul. She could not believe what had just happened.

"Are you a sorcerer, Paul? Ordinary men do not do what you just did. Do you have supernatural powers?" she asked with trembling.

"I am merely a servant to Christ Jesus. It is He who is the Great Healer, not I. I call upon His holy name that He will provide the healing and receive all glory, honor, and praise."

46

A noticeably different man arose from his chair. Festus stood easily without discomfort. Healthy color had returned to his face. He looked at Fabiana with wonder. "I feel very much like I did before getting hit in the ribs by the soldier. Perhaps better."

Fabiana's eyes began to mist over and she took her husband's hand in hers. But she looked directly into Paul's smiling face. "We thank you and this god Jesus for returning Festus to his normal state." Hesitantly, she continued, "Are you seeking some form of payment for this act?"

Paul's head moved backward in surprise. "Absolutely not. I do this only because God chooses to use me. It is His will that you should be healed, Festus, not mine."

Silently, the couple stared at Paul as they considered all that had just happened. "Well, I certainly do feel better, but I must inform you, Paul, this in no way alters my duties as a Roman procurator towards you. I know you agree with me on this."

Paul chuckled slightly and looked at Fabiana, sensing her uncertainty, then turned his attention toward Festus. To reassure him, he said, "Procurator Festus, I would not attempt to sway or otherwise bribe you in the performance of your duties! I stand on God's truth and the facts that have been revealed at my trial. To do otherwise would be a violation of my personal relationship with Christ and my Roman citizenship."

Festus felt the time was right to relay the news to his detainee. "While we are here, let it be known that you shall depart Caesarea within the next couple of weeks. We await a seagoing vessel to transport you, any companions you choose, and other prisoners of Rome. It is too dangerous to transfer you to Rome via land in light of the assassination attempt by the Jews."

Paul's countenance remained serene. "I fully understand, Procurator. It shall be as you say."

With that, Festus and Fabiana left Paul's room and returned to their villa. For the rest of the evening, they exchanged their thoughts on Paul, the healing, and the mystery of this Jesus-god Paul professed his allegiance to serving. Over the course of the next five days, they individually pondered this miraculous event, but never spoke about it together again. Their inner stirrings and wonder were so indescribable they kept their thoughts to themselves.

Word came to Festus that Agrippa II, the appointed tetrarch to Judea, and his sister Bernice were coming from their palace in

Caesarea Philippi for their official visit to welcome the new Procurator to Judea. Festus believed this would also be a convenient time to discuss Paul's trial with Agrippa. As procurator, Festus was required to include the tetrarch in matters of state, although the tetrarch's position was mostly ceremonial. Agrippa and his sister Bernice exhibited a proclivity to pomp and ceremony that rivaled Ananias' and Tertullus' love of attention and adulation. Festus prepared himself.

After several days of dealing with their charade, Fabiana vocalized her feelings to Festus when they were alone in their bedroom. "These people give me the creeps, Festus," Fabiana said in exasperation. "Bernice does not want to spend any time alone with me. She hovers around you and Agrippa and doesn't want to miss any exchange the two of you have."

Festus could see his wife's frustration. She lay on her back with her arms folded tight against her body. Her eyebrows were wrinkled with tension. When she became that emotional, it usually was with good reason.

Festus wrapped his arms around her and soothed her, "I have noticed this about her as well, my love. In addition, both of them have unapproachable demeanors. It is obvious they are searching to find out how I will deal with them during our stay here in Caesarea. I perceive they are fearful because of all that was brought on by Felix's actions."

Fabiana curled up in her husband's arms and leaned her head against his shoulder. "What stands out about them the most to me is how dark and cold their eyes are. Have you noticed this?"

"Indeed I have. I believe it is a sign not to trust them in any way. Tomorrow we shall determine more about them. I've informed Agrippa about Paul and his recently concluded trial before me. He is eager to examine Paul. You and I must be most observant during this examination."

The next day, in addition to Agrippa and Bernice, Festus had invited Tadius and the most prominent businessmen of Caesarea to observe the examination of Paul. This was in accordance with the Roman judicial custom in the outlying provinces of the empire.

The meeting would be in the palace because Festus felt it was a more secure location than having Paul travel even the short distance to Festus' villa. Normal procedure did not allow Roman citizens under house arrest to leave their confined area. In making his decision, the procurator also took very seriously the implied assassination attempt against Paul. Notably absent were Caelius and Servius. Festus had sent them on separate secret assignments. They would not attend as they normally would. Even Fabiana did not know where the two assistants had gone.

Tadius and the businessmen entered the great room of the palace and were greeted by Festus and Fabiana. It was an opportunity for Festus to officially meet the power brokers of Caesarea. His exchanges with the businessmen led Festus to believe they would be allies in his dealings as head of Judea. All their various conversations were very amiable.

Agrippa and Bernice were the last to make their appearance. They strutted into the room like peacocks displaying their plumage, with necks stretched high, chins thrust forward, and steps made in a poor imitation of grace. Their brilliantly colored attire was flamboyantly expensive. Everyone present remained appropriately silent; but all had the same reaction—this brother and sister act was more laughable than laudable.

Unnoticed were the two guards who had brought Paul from his room to the meeting. As Agrippa and Bernice did their peacock dance, Paul silently observed the spectacle. He had knowledge of the incestuous relationship the brother and sister had maintained for some time. Bernice had recently left her third husband after a short marriage of less than one year. Many Jews and Romans felt this was a subterfuge to distract from the rumors circling about her and her older brother. Paul, too, believed they were in an abominable relationship. It was despicable; however, this did not impact his emotions towards either of them. He saw them as lost souls in need of saving grace, like so many others.

The apostle of Christ knew the majority of the people who were present for his examination, and he was not awed by any of them. Instead, his heart was excited for the opportunity to speak to them about his savior, Christ Jesus. He would do this joyfully with a sincere heart.

Festus saw that Paul had arrived for the examination and he motioned for the guards to bring Christ's messenger before the assemblage. When Paul was at his side, Festus announced to the audience, "I have brought this man Paul before you. No doubt, you all are aware of the alleged crimes the Jews have accused him of committing. He has been tried here before me."

Festus took a step closer to Paul and extended his arm in the direction of the apostle. He looked at Paul, then back at the gathering. "I want you to hear his story from his own lips. It seems unreasonable to me to send a prisoner to Caesar without specifying the charges against him." No one disagreed with his statement.

Paul silently surveyed the faces of the group. He saw curiosity, and there were a few doubters. Bernice appeared especially discomforted, while Agrippa seemed bored. Fabiana was eager to hear Paul speak. She hoped to learn more about the man who performed the miraculous healing of her beloved husband.

The apostle of Christ wasted no time after a quick assessment of his observers. Agrippa signaled for Paul to speak. Paul bowed to Agrippa and to the others, "I beg you to hear me patiently." For the next thirty minutes, he spoke with passion about his early life, emphasizing how he had become a zealous Pharisee, especially in the persecution of followers of Christ, "I punished them often in every synagogue and compelled them to blaspheme. I persecuted them even to foreign cities."

The onlookers showed no signs of emotion while hearing Paul's confession, except Fabiana. She heard remorse and sorrow in the humbled man's voice. His tone was genuine and subdued.

Fabiana was moved by the power of Paul's tale of his conversion while on the road to Damascus. As Paul gave his testimony, he moved about the room, energetically gesturing and speaking with a passion Fabiana had not heard from anyone before. She was captivated by his extraordinary narrative.

Now she had a good understanding about this god Paul referred to as Jesus and Paul's relationship with him. This struck her as very odd, considering how the Romans and the Greeks viewed their deities. To them, they were not benevolent, loving, or compassionate. She felt strange inside as she pondered Paul's words.

Fabiana became lost in her thoughts until she heard Agrippa say, "Paul, you almost persuade me to become a Christian." What struck her about Agrippa's statement was the coldness of his voice—the disdain—but also his fury and an element of fear. She could not understand why Agrippa felt the way he did towards Paul.

She was startled by Paul's reply, "I would to God that not only you, but also all who hear me today, might become both almost and altogether such as I am, except for these chains." His voice was earnest, yet vigorous. It appeared to her to also be chastising Agrippa.

When Paul finished, Agrippa and Bernice bolted from their

seats. The rest of the audience suddenly realized the meeting was over and stood up to leave. Festus motioned for the guards to return Paul to his quarters. He then escorted the businessmen out of the palace. When he returned, he motioned for Agrippa and Tadius to go with him into an adjacent room. Festus informed Bernice she could not attend. She was infuriated. Like a pouting child, she followed Fabiana into another part of the palace without speaking.

After Tadius closed the door to their meeting room, Agrippa burst forth in a somewhat high-pitched voice conveying his irritation to Festus, "This man might have been set free if he had not appealed to Caesar!"

Tadius focused on Agrippa's emphasized word "might," and speculated that Agrippa knew of Ananias' plot to kill Paul any way possible. The garrison commander made a mental note to discuss this with his new superior, Festus, when he would have the opportunity to be alone with him.

Hearing Agrippa's angry squeal, Festus quickly shot a look to Tadius that confirmed he also wanted to talk alone with him. Festus turned his steely eyes on the Tetrarch of Judea. In a steady, firm voice, he proclaimed, "You might be correct in what you say, Agrippa, but the accusation against Paul has moved from a mere religious issue to that of treason against Rome! You, as well as the prominent businessmen and leaders of Caesarea, are agreed that Paul is not deserving of death or chains for religious issues!"

Agrippa appeared to be stunned by Festus' statement. Immediately, he realized the focus of Festus and the new direction of the case against Paul. Without any connection to religion, Agrippa II was powerless in this matter. He swallowed hard and became even more fearful for his safety and well-being, a lurking fear that surrounded him constantly. He cringed, recognizing that the new Procurator of Judea was sending him a message of warning.

On the night of Paul's departure to Rome, a lone crippled old man walked the dock where a seagoing vessel awaited Christ's apostle and his entourage, as well as the other Roman prisoners. Amid the hustle and bevy associated with loading the vessel, the man walked with a cane, hunched over, limping slowly but resolutely.

Every so often, the old man stopped to adjust a bag slung over his shoulder. He would turn his head slightly to his left and peer into the shadows of the buildings that lined the dock. He sensed a presence hiding deep in the shadows. Nonchalantly, he adjusted the object on his right side that was hidden by his outer garment. It was important that it not be seen or detected by anyone within sight of his presence. Each time he stopped, he strained to distinguish any human form in the silhouettes of the dark buildings. He saw none. Nevertheless, he took precautions against an attack.

Several observers called out to him, "Old man, are you sure you want to attempt fishing?" Boisterous voices laughed at this unlikely prospect. The old man said nothing, but continued his way to the small sailboat that looked as old and decrepit as its owner. Cautiously, the old man lowered his bent body into the small fishing boat. He began to attend to his fishing nets and seemed to pay no attention to the ongoing final preparations of the seagoing vessel. It was obvious the vessel was about to depart Caesarea's harbor.

His observant eyes, even in the shadowy darkness of the early morning, made out a single male being tightly escorted aboard the ship by ten Roman soldiers. Following the male were several others who appeared to be traveling with him.

On deck of the vessel, a Roman centurion watched the boarding of the secretive group. Once the prisoner was onboard, the centurion ordered the soldiers to take the prisoner to another part of the ship the old man's eyes could not follow. Very intriguing, he thought. This mystery person must be someone of importance; otherwise, there would be no need for so many battle-ready soldiers.

Very soon after the prisoner and his followers were onboard, the vessel unfurled its sails. The ropes securing the ship to the dock were loosed and thrown back to waiting sailors on deck. The huge ship smoothly eased away from the dock and began making its way out of the harbor.

The old man unfurled the sail on his creaking wooden boat and followed the bigger vessel out of the harbor. He carefully adjusted the sail and was able to close the distance between himself and the ship carrying the prisoners of Rome. His eyes remained focused on the stern of the ship. His lips were firmly set. He would not be deterred from his mission.

When both vessels were clear of the harbor, the larger ship adjusted its mainsails. The resulting rush of wind snapped the canvas of the sails and the ship began to turn to the open sea in the direction of Rome.

A sailor suddenly appeared at the stern of the ship and threw over the contents of several buckets that splashed on the water's surface. Doing so, the sailor noticed the small craft in its wake. He bent over the railing and yelled to the shadow directing the boat. "Here you go! Feast on this garbage!" He laughed robustly and returned to his duties.

The old man appeared unbalanced as his boat bobbed with the waves. Yet, he threw his nets in the direction of the ship's garbage. When he could determine the nets had sunk below the surface of the water, he sat back down in the boat and waited. He was content, and keenly watched the seagoing vessel as it became smaller on the horizon.

The gentle undulation of the waves relaxed the old man as he leaned back against the stern of his boat. His right hand repeatedly adjusted the rudder as the boat swelled and dipped with the waves. He allowed his thoughts to dwell on the mystery of the special prisoner who was so guardedly escorted aboard the seagoing ship.

Within a short period of time, he dragged in his nets to find an abundance of fish. Grinning broadly and with a spirited laugh, the old man turned the sail of his boat and made his way back to the harbor.

As soon as his tired old boat was safely secured to the dock, the old man slowly and carefully climbed up onto the dock with his catch. A couple of other fishermen who were in the process of leaving the dock took notice of his bounty. "You did well, old man! Your catch should make you plenty of money at the market!"

The old man merely waved to them and began carrying his catch up the slope to the street where the markets awaited the first catch of the day. He also carried the bag he had brought with him earlier. The concealed object on his right side combined with the bag and his catch made it difficult for him to move.

His cane thumped with the effort it took to carry himself and his bounty. At the first market he came to, he sold all but four mid-sized fish. Putting his reward into a small purse, the old man thanked the merchant and made his way down the street in the opposite direction back to his home. The sound of the thumping cane became lost in the mixed calls of sea gulls and human voices that broadcasted their activities of the new day.

When he was out of sight of the merchant, the old man ducked into a shadowy recess between two buildings. He waited, motionless and silent, listening for any sound of footsteps that might be following him. Satisfied no one was near, he sat down and painfully began pulling at the beard fastened to his face. He flinched at the ripping, but was able to stifle sounds of his efforts and the discomfort they caused.

He looked at the goat hair beard in his hand with disdain and discarded it into the shadows. He rubbed his face and carefully removed the beeswax that had secured the goat hair to his face. The wax had itched and irritated his face. He rubbed his cheeks to remove all vestiges of the adhesive. Next, he removed the pileus, a hat commonly worn by various laborers. He threw the felt hat next to the beard.

He scratched his head and smoothed his hair into place. Now, it was time for his next transformation. From a small bag he had carried with him, he withdrew a fine linen tunic with markings of official Roman status. Quickly, he removed the worker's garments and replaced them with the linen tunic. Next, he threw away his working class boots in favor of the sandals, proper attire for a renowned Roman citizen. He saved only the object that was hidden under the outer garment.

With a sigh of relief, the apparition moved silently to the front of the dark recess and cautiously exposed just enough of his face to the street to determine whether any other presence waited for him. Silently and carefully, he—the new identity—emerged from the shadows. No longer hunched over, the younger man stood tall, confident, and in control. Briskly, he made his way to the better section of Caesarea, carrying no cane, only the four fish he had caught earlier.

Now prominently displayed on his right side was the hidden object. It was both highly respected and feared throughout the Roman Empire. It was the short sword favored by the Roman infantry. The sight of the sword signified the holder was quite adept in its usage. It often served as a deterrent to would-be attackers.

Festus could not keep from laughing as he made his way back to his villa. His disguise had worked perfectly! This time there was no blunt blow to his ribs, only the satisfaction of his deception. He was thankful for the fishing skills he had learned as a youth. It had been quite some time since he had been fishing, and he realized how much he liked feeling the splash of the waves and tasting the salty air.

As he continued to the villa, his thoughts were divided. He could not help but remember his healing brought about by Paul's prayer. It had motivated him to engage in his deception. He personally wanted to observe Paul's departure and determine whose spies were monitoring the event. He was also concerned about a potential attack on Paul by the Jews.

Festus was relieved that his planning and the timing of Paul's departure remained unknown to the Jews. His concern with these obstinate people became another focus. He centered on what lay ahead in dealing with the two deceivers, Ananias and Agrippa. He had no doubt about his ability to handle them effectively. They would create an opportunity for him to demonstrate his authority and to quell future uprisings while he was Procurator of Judea.

As Festus neared his villa, he realized a longing in his heart to be present in Rome and to witness the outcome of Paul's encounter with Caesar. With that wistful thought, he opened the front door of the villa to share his fisherman's catch with Fabiana.

 Chapter 5

Octavia was in her bedroom, arranging her clothes and other personal items for the much anticipated trip she and Caesar Nero were about to take to Athens. Since they would be spending the entire winter there, she wanted to make sure she had sufficient stylish clothing.

Her self-absorbed reverie was harshly interrupted by a piercing scream, one she had heard before. She knew who it was. It was too familiar.

Dropping the items in her hands, she hurried into the next room. There stood beet-faced Nero, clutching a piece of paper so tightly his knuckles were white. Out of the corner of his eye, Nero caught his wife staring at him wide-eyed.

"Oh, Octavia, the most disconcerting news has arrived from the province of Judea." His royal voice was squeaking. Before continuing, Rome's mighty Caesar stumbled to a nearby chair and flopped his portly body down. He looked at his wife with forlorn eyes and lamented, "It appears some Roman citizen named Paul has been accused of treason and petitions me to decide his fate. And you know only Caesar can render a decision on a case of treason."

Caesar lowered his head and placed his hands over his face. After a brief moment, he looked up at the motionless Octavia. "This could not have come at a worse time. It is very close to our departure date to Athens. Should I remain here to hear this man's plea, we won't be able to journey to Athens."

Octavia put on her best face and drifted across the room to his side. She pulled up a chair next to him. She wrapped her hands around his. "Nero, let us reason this out. Is this accused citizen in Rome?"

With tears welling in his eyes, Nero squeaked, "No. He is en route with other prisoners, none of which will appear before me. They recently left Caesarea by ship."

Octavia gently patted the back of her husband's hand. "Ship travel is faster than over land, but it still will be at least six weeks before they arrive here in Rome."

Nero perked up and a hopeful smile formed on his trembling lips. "Aah, I see what you refer to, my dearest wife. By the time this accused man arrives in Rome, we shall be nearly to Athens. Wonderful. This is truly wonderful." The short, portly ruler began to giggle with glee as he contemplated the alternative.

His jubilance was short-lived. Nero abruptly became silent with a troubled expression on his face. He looked away from Octavia in deep thought, and after a few moments turned his body again to look into her eyes. Brightening up, he exclaimed, "I have a solution! I shall summon Seneca and turn this case over to him. There will be many details necessary to understand this case because of its location. It will take time to compile all the pertinent information. Seneca can do this while we are enjoying ourselves in Athens."

Octavia beamed her approval at the quick solution Nero had devised. Now she wouldn't be denied her pleasures in Athens. Nero finished describing his plan to her, "When we return next spring, Seneca should have everything ready so that I can hear this man's appeal. I would delegate these same duties to Seneca even if we remained here throughout the winter."

Mighty Caesar lifted his chin high and commanded with renewed authority, "Continue your packing! We leave per our schedule three days from now! The special caravan will be ready by then and we will proceed as normal." Octavia smiled her approval and giggled. She withdrew her hands from Nero's and happily bounced her way back to resume her packing.

The long, harrowing, four-month journey was finally over. Paul, his entourage, and the other prisoners were now safely in Rome. Their journey had taken much longer than normal, due to the onslaught of the fall season that caused severe storms to develop and wreak havoc throughout the Mediterranean Sea.

Despite his fatigue, a very relieved Centurion Julius and his men delivered their prisoners to Blasius, the captain of the guard.

Julius often was assigned to transport prisoners to Rome via the sea route, but had never before left Caesarea so late in the summer season. Those accused of crimes ranging from theft to murder were taken to holding cells in the prison that was located nearby. Most would be sent to the dreaded mines, which in essence was a death sentence. On occasion, prisoners were allowed to participate in gladiator contests as an alternative to the slow death caused by the toxic air of the mines.

Paul's entourage consisted of Luke the physician, and Aristarchus, a Jewish convert from Thessalonica. They were taken to the Praetorium of Caesar Nero. This section of the palace had numerous rooms that served a dual purpose of housing guests and dignitaries; but some were utilized as holding rooms for Roman citizens accused of crimes.

Luke and Aristarchus were not charged with any crime and were not Roman citizens, and as such posed no problem for Rome. Nonetheless, Julius intervened on their behalf, and Blasius allowed them to stay with Paul in Nero's palace.

After they were secured in their respective rooms with guards posted outside each room's door, Julius and the captain of the guard went downstairs to the main part of the palace. Seeing how tired Julius was, Blasius escorted the centurion to the barracks located in the far outside wing of the palace that housed members of the Praetorian Guard.

Blasius quickly located a room set aside for officers and assisted Julius inside. The fatigued centurion stood dazed, almost falling asleep on his feet. He offered no resistance when Blasius and one of the slave servants assigned to the Guard began to remove his distinctive red cloak, red-plumed helmet, and armor. Once they eased him onto the bed, Julius went into a much needed deep sleep.

After twelve hours, the centurion awoke, feeling refreshed and ravenous. He made his way to the barracks' dining area and sat down. Almost immediately, a slave brought him a bowl of Julian Stew, a staple of the military.

Many times during the arduous trek to Rome, he had dreamt about this quintessential Roman dish that was widely favored by the military. He was carried away by the smell of the pepper, fennel, and cumin mixed with ground pork meat. The stew was enhanced with a wine reduction sauce and spelt served as a binder for the dish.

Julius seemed awestruck at the meal set before him. His favorite fantasy was now reality! He began to devour the savory dish. Served with this delight was a small loaf of whole wheat bread. Normally, soldiers, especially those in the field, ate barley bread. Julius preferred the wheat and was thankful the status of the Praetorian Guard warranted this culinary gem.

Much too soon, the meal was consumed. Julius hesitated and contemplated asking for a second bowl, when a messenger informed him that after his meal he was to report to the office of General Cleatus, the supreme commander of the Praetorian Guard. Julius believed the upcoming meeting would be quite long. It was no contest. He opted for the second bowl of stew.

When a satiated Julius finally stepped into the office of Cleatus, he was surprised to find two other people waiting for his arrival. He recognized one individual; it was his long-time friend and fellow centurion, Flavius. He judged by the striping of his toga that the other person was a high official. Julius assumed this man was associated with either the Senate or possibly Caesar. In any event, the centurion was immediately on his guard.

Cleatus' attire reflected his position as one of two supreme commanders of the Roman military. He was outfitted in black body armor with brass trimmings. On the wall behind him was a solid black helmet with brass trimmings across the forehead portion and on the side face protectors. A red horsehair plumage stood erect atop the middle of the helmet, running from front to back, displaying an impressive colorful statement of his power. The direction of the plumage indicated the highest rank in the hierarchy.

Julius, looking at the barrel-chested General Cleatus, could tell that he was a tall man, even though he was seated. His shoulders and forearms were large and muscular, no doubt from repeated usage of the famous short sword common to all Roman soldiers. His angular face had chiseled cheek bones, a square jaw, thin lips, and a thin, pointed nose. Flecks of gray were scattered throughout his brown hair, especially at his temples.

What most impressed Julius were the commander's eyes. They were brownish, set somewhat wider than the normal Roman male's. Heavy eyebrows accentuated his deep-set eyes. Julius felt those eyes boring through his body as if they were daggers. Despite his forbidding appearance, the commander of the field troops surprised him with a quiet voice when he greeted Julius.

"Centurion, thank you for coming as soon as you did. I'm sure you recognize Flavius." Julius indicated he did. "Good. Now, seated to my right is Seneca, personal consul to Caesar Nero." Cleatus paused for Julius to place both name and face in his memory.

"Julius, this case against the citizen named Paul is quite delicate. There are mysteries surrounding the accusation against him that must be revealed before his appeal to Nero. I must ask you to give us details of your trip from Caesarea to Rome now, while it remains fresh and accurate in your mind."

"Of course, General, I will make every effort to give you as accurate an account as I am able. I assume you will also be questioning my men concerning these same mysteries?"

"That is correct, Centurion, now please proceed."

Julius began his narrative by explaining how he secured a coastal ship for the group consisting of 40 of his men, himself, ten prisoners being sent to their execution, Paul, and his two companions. One companion was named Luke, who was neither a Jew nor a citizen of Rome. The other was a man from Thessalonica named Aristarchus.

He told how the first leg of their voyage was uneventful and they were able to travel the 80 miles from Caesarea to Sidon in a single day. "My men were able to easily control the prisoners. Paul and his companions were very amiable, courteous, and even kind to my men, the prisoners, and me. For this reason, I allowed him to seek things he needed for the trip from friends there in Sidon."

Julius described how, soon after their departure from Sidon, winds from the east intensified, warning of a severe storm. "My concern about the impending storm caused me to seek a different ship at Myra. Our Egyptian vessel was loaded with grain for Rome. The pilot of the ship had sufficient room for our group and, because it was official business, he did not attempt to charge any fare to us. He was quite seasoned as a pilot and familiar with the winter storms of this sea.

"However, the stormy weather impeded the progress of the vessel and it took three times longer than normal to travel the one hundred thirty miles from Myra to Cnidus. The pilot informed me he needed to steer the ship to Crete. This added to our delay and we struggled getting to Fair Havens.

"Sailing was now a dangerous situation. In addition, the storms made Fair Havens undesirable as a refuge; it was too open to the weather. The pilot advised me that Phoenix would provide much better shelter for us and it wasn't that far away, only forty miles. I determined this was what had to be done."

Cleatus observed Julius' changing emotions. It was clear he was reliving every detail of his experience as he spoke. "The soft, southern breeze gave us hope the remainder of our journey would be calm. But it was false hope because the wind shifted, hitting us hard from the northeast. Very quickly we were in the clutches of Euroclydon!

"Because the storm originated from the northeast, its powerful winds, driving rain, and waves nearly 25 feet high pushed our vessel nearly 500 miles off its intended course! The pilot had his crew lash ropes around the hull of the ship to prevent it from coming apart. This was extremely difficult because the ship was rolling wildly from side to side. Had they not done this early in the storm, the ship would have fallen apart! The waves lifted the ship almost completely out of the water then crashed it down hard, as if the sea was made of stone!" He shook his head, remembering the terrifying force.

"They took down the sails, lest they tear from the force of the wind." Julius momentarily stopped. He shot a fleeting glance at the panel evaluating his story and saw that Seneca had lost some color in his face, no doubt based on visualizing the horrific effects of the massive typhoon.

"The force of the waves was so great the pilot had to change direction and allow the waves to push us in the direction the storm was going. It seemed as if Poseidon played with us, and was violently throwing the ship from side to side." The centurion stopped and looked at the set of eyes staring at him. He lowered his voice. "I truly believed we all would die. The prisoners cried out and several lost control of themselves because of the effects of the hurricane from hell."

Now even Cleatus and Flavius tensed their bodies at this depiction of uncontrolled winds and waves. Roman soldiers seldom traveled by sea. They preferred land and its solid footing. As Julius spoke in vivid detail, the two soldiers felt their stomachs levitate and twist.

"Citizen Paul was thrown from one side of the ship to the other, but made his way to us and said there would be no loss of life. He said an angel of his god appeared to him and said he should not be afraid because his god wanted him to be brought before Caesar."

The panel stared at Julius, but remained silent. "Citizen Paul plainly said the ship must run aground on a certain island. I was so sick, I did not pay much attention to his words.

"The sailors took soundings and discovered we were getting closer to land. Fearing we would hit rocks, they dropped four anchors. Then some of the sailors let down the skiff to escape the ship. Again, Citizen Paul came and informed me of their attempt and said that unless everyone remained onboard the ship, all would perish!"

Julius stopped and looked intently at the incredulous panel. Straightening his posture, he set his jaw, and raised his voice. "I ordered a couple of my men to cut the rope and let the skiff fall off. Several sailors initially sprang forward, but halted when my soldiers threatened them with their swords.

"At dawn, Citizen Paul encouraged us and insisted we should take food. We were weak. It had been fourteen days since we had eaten anything! Of a truth, the effect of the storm was such, no one could eat! Paul took bread and gave thanks to his god and began to eat heartily. Seeing his courage and confidence, we all ate, all 276 of us. He insisted that his god told him all would be well if we followed his instructions.

"The storm began to subside. Early in the new day, land was sighted on the horizon." Julius told them how the pilot attempted to maneuver the ship to a bay with a beach and hit ground. It ground its way into the sand and stuck on the sandbar. Soon the repeated force of the violent waves lashing against the ship broke up the stern. The pilot informed Julius the ship had to be abandoned.

"My men asked if they should kill the prisoners lest any of them escape. Since the prisoners, with the exception of Citizen Paul, were bound together at the wrist, I ordered the men not to kill them, for the storm would cause them to drown. The prisoners screamed with fright as they stared at the raging water." His audience remained riveted to his story.

Julius took another deep breath, and continued, "When the ship ran aground, I ordered everyone to leave ship and swim or float to shore with whatever they could find to support them. Citizen Paul, his companions, the crew, the soldiers, and I left the ship as it was being torn apart by the pounding waves. We jumped into the water and found pieces of the ship to keep us afloat. Some were able to swim ashore. We all survived! All 276! After 14 days of the typhoon! We all made it to the beach safely, just as Citizen Paul had predicted."

Julius straightened his arms and placed his hands on the table. "We were so exhausted we just lay on the beach, listening to the pounding of the waves and the ship shriek and snap as the timbers broke into pieces." He stood up and requested permission to go relieve himself. Cleatus and Flavius stood up to do likewise. It was time for a much needed break.

When they returned to Cleatus' office and sat back down to hear the rest of the lengthy debriefing, Julius picked up where he had left off in his narrative. "I learned we were on the island of Malta. During our stay there, things happened that are hard to believe." The centurion shifted in his seat and scanned the faces of the panel before he continued. In a halting voice, he said, "Citizen Paul received a death bite from a viper!" Then, he provided the shocking result, "And he did not die!" The members of the panel were incredulous, and reacted with signs of unbelief and amazement.

Cleatus was astounded. "Julius, how can this be? I know of no man who has survived the bite of a viper! Surely there is some explanation!"

Julius shook his head vehemently from side to side and insisted, "No! I assure you, General, I witnessed this with my own eyes!"

Julius explained how it had happened, that once on land, the natives of Malta came and greeted them. "We were in very bad condition, drenched, battered, cold, weak, and emotionally exhausted. The people showed us kindness, for they built a fire and made us feel welcome. The fire was just what we needed. It saved us from the cold and the rain. Citizen Paul went to gather wood for the fire. As soon as he placed it on the fire, a viper nearly five feet in length jumped out of the wood to avoid the fire." He shuddered involuntarily at the thought of it and swallowed hard before he continued, "The viper's fangs dug deep into Citizen Paul's hand. He could not immediately dislodge it. With his left hand he pried the snake loose and threw it back into the fire where it sizzled and died. We all sat transfixed, nobody could move or wanted to approach Paul for fear they too would get bitten.

"The natives all gasped and moaned and told me Citizen Paul would soon swell up and quickly die. His companion Luke, a physician, looked at his hand. The two said some kind of prayer and Luke sat back down. He made no attempt to put any herbs or ointment on the wound. We all waited and watched, expecting Paul to collapse. After a very long time of waiting with great dread, it did not happen. Citizen Paul continued to sit beside the fire."

Seneca leaned forward with his hands gripping his knees. He cocked his head sideways and demanded, "Julius, you said Paul did not swell up, and only continued sitting by the fire?"

"Oh, yes! The natives stared at Citizen Paul. Some began to wail a death song. After a long time, these natives began to sing a different song and they proclaimed him to be a god!"

Seneca was frozen, still leaning towards the centurion and concentrating on the storyteller. The two soldiers were motionless in their seats. But Julius had more that would astound them.

"The natives took us to one of their leading citizens, a man named Publius, who entertained us for three days. He was very interested in Citizen Paul's encounter with the viper. This man's father was very sick with a fever and dysentery. Citizen Paul went to the sick man and gently placed his hand on the dying man's head. He spoke some words over him. It was not long. The man opened his eyes, took a deep breath, and sat up. He was healed!"

The panel's eyes were wide and they gasped. They looked at one another with skepticism. Seneca exclaimed, "Julius, this indeed happened?"

Julius vigorously nodded his head. "Yes! You may seek verification from my men, the sailors, the prisoners, Citizen Paul's companions, and go to Malta for yourselves and inquire of the natives. You will learn it is all true!"

Seneca leaned back, slouched in his chair, struggling to absorb all he had just heard. He placed his left elbow on the arm of the chair and lowered his head onto his thumb and index finger once again. He tapped his finger slowly against his temple. He became silent and his concentration displayed deep lines across his forehead. Cleatus and Flavius exchanged baffled looks. Julius looked first at Seneca, then over to his comrades, but did not say anything, despite that he had much more to tell.

Finally, Seneca was the first to return from deep thought. In a contemplative voice, he inquired, "Julius. Is there any more that we should know?" Cleatus and Flavius turned their heads in unison towards the centurion.

Julius tightened his lips and nodded affirmatively, "When the natives heard of this healing, they brought many sick and dying to Citizen Paul. He healed them all. When it came time for us to leave, they honored us and provided the things we needed to continue towards Rome."

"Did Paul use any herbs or potions or anything else to cure the people?" asked Seneca.

"Nothing. We had no such things. All was lost in the shipwreck." Julius let this sink into the minds of his three interrogators. "Even the physician Luke did not minister to any of the sick, only Citizen Paul. Luke and Aristarchus lined the people up and Paul went to each one. He laid his hands on each person and they were immediately healed."

The three interrogators exchanged stunned looks of confusion. Julius summed up what each was thinking, "I've never known of such a thing and have never experienced anything like this before!"

The centurion looked at each man and quietly said, "But there is more to this story." All three cross-examiners waited in astonishment. "When we had traveled to Puteoli many people came forward, calling Citizen Paul and his companions 'brethren.' They are followers of 'The Way,' as it is called. They were very kind to us and we stayed with them seven days. There was much rejoicing among these people and Citizen Paul spoke to them as their teacher."

To emphasize his next statement, Julius leaned forward in his chair. "Twenty-five miles outside of Rome, many, many more of these 'brethren' met us from as far away as Appii Forum and Three Inns. There was much warmth and kindness extended to my men, and the prisoners, and I, as well. In fact, several of the prisoners openly wept at their kind treatment. Three of them requested Paul to pray for them. He spoke to them in a patient, loving way, explaining this god he called Jesus. Each prisoner then asked that this Jesus be their so-called savior."

With that, Julius indicated his tale of the incredible journey was complete. Feeling drained, he sat down, rotated his head in a circle to relieve the tension in his neck, and waited for the panel to continue their questioning.

Cleatus was the first member of the tribune to speak. "Julius, this has been an astounding description. Over four hours have elapsed since you first began. If you have nothing else to add, I declare this session over. Go to the private bathhouse and get a massage that you greatly deserve."

Julius welcomed the command for a soothing bath and a massage. He had no reason to linger and eagerly left for his reward.

With the centurion out of his office, Seneca stated, "Twenty-eight years ago in the province of Judea, the man-god these followers of 'The Way' call their Messiah did exactly what Citizen

Paul did on the island of Malta. The name of their Messiah was Jesus of Nazareth. He performed similar miracles throughout Judea. The Jewish religious leaders were fearful of this man-god's power and convinced Pilate to crucify him, which he did. The man's followers claim that three days later he came back to life and mingled with them for forty days, then disappeared. These followers claim he ascended to heaven. These are the ones they call 'The Way.'"

Cleatus and Flavius sat back down in their chairs. Just when they thought this unimaginable tale could not get more bizarre, they were wrong.

Seneca urged, "Julius' story must be believed. I feel it is the truth. The combination of the healings by both the man-god and now Citizen Paul are such, we need to obtain as much information as possible before this accused man's appeal before Caesar. There is much mystery involved with this man and we must learn what it is."

Cleatus concurred, "I agree, Seneca. There is much at stake here with this man and his case. Should we make any mistakes, it will not bode well for any of us! We must lay out a plan. Flavius will command the troops necessary to guard this man while he awaits his appeal before Caesar. Seneca, you must obtain much more information about this man. We must stay in communication with each other as this case progresses."

This was an intriguing case, with many questions in the minds of each participant. No one would allow it to be far from his mind; but for now, the astonishing meeting was over.

## Chapter 6

Seneca had traveled from his villa outside the northwest part of Rome for the meeting with Cleatus, Flavius, and the centurion who accompanied Paul from Caesarea. Now that the meeting was concluded, he opted to remain in Rome at his townhouse. It was time to implement the plan he had devised months ago when Nero first summoned him to the palace.

Standing in for Nero was not uncommon for Seneca. He had done so on several occasions shortly after Nero assumed the position of Caesar. He had spent six years as his teacher and mentor, and initially was glad to be of service to the new monarch. However, things were becoming different now that Nero was more accustomed to his duties as Caesar. He no longer sought Seneca's guidance as a mentor but retained him as one of two personal consuls. The other consul was Burris, whose debilitating illness had since forced him to refrain from being co-consul.

Now that Nero's mother was dead, Nero was changing almost daily. The mother-son duo had functioned well while Nero was young; but as Rome's supreme ruler, he began to hate her interference in governing Rome. She had repeatedly refused to stop her interference, so Nero had ordered her murdered. Rome suspected Nero was behind Agrippina's death, but took no action against the monarch. Nonetheless, Nero was distancing himself from everyone who had previously counseled him. Seneca was one of those.

Seneca often shared with his wife, Pompeia, how he lingered as consul mainly for the sake of Rome. He felt the Senate was appreciative of his involvement with the defiant and unpredictable Caesar. Seneca strongly believed now was a pivotal time that

Rome needed his services. The appeal case of the citizen named Paul could have major repercussions not only in Judea, but other parts of the empire. Seneca did not believe Nero was aware of these issues. His repeated absenteeism from Rome to pursue his artistic interests kept him isolated from pressing events in Rome.

Caesar had only one meeting with Seneca regarding turning over the appeal to the consul. Within one week following their encounter, Nero and his retinue blended in with a merchant caravan headed to Athens where they would spend the entire winter pursuing their individual frivolous pleasures. This was the second year Nero was choosing to stay away from Rome, neglecting his duties as monarch for over five complete months.

Seneca felt no need to have Caesar around as he chased after the facts of the case. In many ways, he felt more would be accomplished with Nero out of the picture, anyway.

Once inside his townhouse, Seneca sent a messenger to Pompeia requesting her to join him in Rome. Next, another messenger was sent to Aelia, one of Rome's leading businesswomen. Aelia owned many townhouses throughout the upper portion of the city. That evening, he opted to attend a party hosted by a trusted friend who also had a townhouse in Rome.

The friend was Cato, a renowned teacher, philosopher, and lawyer whose clientele consisted of many of Rome's major government and business leaders. Cato was instructor to their children and confidant to them in their official positions. Since he was alone in the city, Seneca looked forward to Cato's excellent company, and his guests would be interesting. He hoped to discover some valuable information from some of the guests that he possibly could use in Paul's appeal case.

The upper class of Rome thrived on dinner parties. It was their opportunity to showcase their townhouses or villas, network with the alliances they sought, and generally have a good time. Cato had a reputation for hosting excellent parties and this one would be no exception. But Seneca wanted to arrive early so that the two could discuss the citizen named Paul.

Cato had his servants prepare the evening's event so his time could be better spent with Seneca. When Cato first heard about potential involvement in this intriguing appeal, he had quickly agreed to be part of Seneca's team.

Seneca arrived somewhat earlier than expected. "My friend, welcome to my home!" Cato exclaimed ebulliently with a wide sweeping motion of his arm, inviting his friend to enter his townhouse. Cool marble floors, intricate murals, and high vaulted ceilings reflected Cato's wealth and status. The small rain pool in the atrium had a statue of Venus. Above the pool were murals of the goddess, surrounding the typical rectangular roof opening to catch the rainwater.

The evening's host escorted Seneca to a room that served as Cato's office. There was a handsomely carved desk with two thickly cushioned chairs, mirroring the noble bearing of their owner. Cato sat in the large chair behind the desk and his guest took the other. "Let's take full advantage of our time together, my friend! Please tell me about the meeting you had earlier today concerning our subject Paul."

Seneca began giving Cato the details of Julius' report. Cato showed deep concentration while he listened to the centurion's depiction. He sat transfixed with his right elbow on the arm of his chair throughout Seneca's report. His right hand supported his slightly tilted head. His eyes never left Seneca.

When Seneca got to the part about Paul being bitten by the viper and surviving, Cato sat upright, but his eyes remained fixed on Seneca. Though he made no comment, Cato's raised eyebrows or furrowed brow at various points in Seneca's narrative clearly indicated he was grasping the magnitude of the story.

Only when Caesar's consul had finished did Cato exclaim, "This is utterly amazing! I've heard stories about this man and what miracles he has performed throughout the empire. Frankly, I doubted the majority of them; but to have a sane centurion witness such a phenomenon gives credibility to these marvels. At this time, I really don't know what to think or to say about this matter."

"Do you remember the time when we met in Athens and this same Paul spoke before the finest thinkers of all Greece?"

Cato slightly turned his head, recalling, and nodded. "I do indeed. Paul was eloquent, confident, and not at all intimidated by all those great minds. As I recall, he even persuaded several in attendance to convert to believing in his god named Jesus."

Seneca chuckled. "Yes! One of the men close to me who was initially opposed to Paul's oratory, even verbally profane, ended up converting to that god named Jesus. At first, I was amused, but I also realized how powerful Paul was in his debate with these most learned Greeks. He certainly garnered my respect."

Cato extended his hand toward Seneca as a sign of agreement. "Mine also, dear friend. Now, after that time in Athens, here we are about to be a part of deciding this man's fate. I find this extraordinary, and if I believed in the gods, I would proclaim they were favoring us."

Seneca concurred, "My sentiments as well, my friend. At the same time, we must be very vigilant as we proceed. Our focus is to serve Rome and not placate any religious zealots who are out to murder him. Nor should we become enamored and taken in by his extraordinary ability to debate issues."

For a brief moment, the two comrades became lost in their own thoughts. Cato broke their silence. "Now that Paul and his companions have arrived in Rome, what happens next?"

Seneca stood up and began to move about Cato's office as he revealed his plan, "Because Paul initiated the appeal before Caesar, he is responsible to pay for his accommodations during his stay in Rome. With this in mind, I've arranged for him to rent a townhouse not far away from here. The owner is none other than Aelia, Rome's highly regarded female business owner. She is beyond reproach and completely neutral in this case."

Cato's head turned back and forth as he followed his friend's path around his office. As Seneca paced, he paused to emphasize a point about Aelia. At one juncture, the noted lawyer and philosopher interjected, "I have knowledge of this woman. She is as you say, Seneca; in addition, no doubt she is looking for a way to profit from this arrangement for more than just mere rent."

"I've thought about that, Cato. But whatever she gains monetarily from this is of no concern of ours. What matters is her discretion. She is one of the few people in Rome I trust in this matter. I fear we will not encounter many people trustworthy while Paul remains in Rome. We have much to do in determining who this man is and what the purpose behind his appeal is really about. What we don't need is to have people who cause us more worry and who will impede our investigations."

Cato placed his index fingers to his mouth, lowered his head, and pondered Seneca's words. A minute passed as each man envisioned possible scenarios. Cato looked up at his colleague and said, "There is also the matter of what these Jews will do while Paul awaits his appeal." He took some time to think, and said, "There are the unknowns. Potentially, other enemies of Paul who may step forward in some capacity during this time. We must always be on guard lest we become victims along with Paul. It's one thing to represent this man, but quite another to needlessly die with him over some petty religious issue," he added cynically.

Seneca returned to his chair and sat down to finish listing the details concerning what would transpire in the coming week. First, he would arrange for the assigned centurion guard to move Paul to Aelia's townhouse. Next, he would have Aelia come to Rome and meet her new tenant. Once this was taken care of, he would solicit reports about Paul from areas the accused man had dealings with. Seneca would contact friends located throughout the empire while Cleatus would concentrate on any military aspect of Paul's involvements.

He felt it necessary to clarify their tasks. "We must not get sidetracked in our research, Cato. The report from Festus is clear that the Tetrarch of Judea, Agrippa II, and Caesarea's most noted businessmen found no religious crime Paul has committed. Our focus is solely on the charge of treason and his intent, if any. This is how Caesar will judge this man. Religious disputes have no relevance in this appeal."

Cato listened carefully to Seneca's instruction. When the consul had finished, Cato asked, "When do we meet with this accused citizen?"

Seneca leaned back in his chair, placed his fingers under his chin, and smiled slightly. He looked steadily at Cato and said, "It is not *we,* my friend; it is *you.* I have other involvements to address for Nero. While I will assist you whenever I can, you will carry the brunt of the investigation and interviewing of our new client. My involvement will be to secure some information for you. As such, we will meet periodically to discuss the progress of the case."

Cato was taken aback at Seneca's words. "Well..., thank you, my friend, for trusting in my ability to handle this matter, which is quite serious. I do not shy away from this responsibility. Be assured, I will do all that I'm humanly capable of to make sure we don't miss anything in this case."

Seneca's face brightened. "That's why I selected you to assist me in this appeal. You are the perfect component in this puzzle that must be assembled. You have skill, cunning, the ability to vex, yet be charming, and that sense of curiosity—all of which will make you successful in this endeavor."

At first, Cato appeared embarrassed at the lavish praise. He was unaccustomed to hearing such affirmations among his colleagues. But, realizing the importance of his task, he collected himself and looked seriously at the man in charge of his assignment. "I fear there will be much intrigue involved in this case before it is finally resolved. Nonetheless, let us begin."

Paul, Luke, and Aristarchus quickly settled into their detention room in the west wing of the Palace. After joining hands in
prayer to Almighty God, each man sat on his cot to relax.

Soon, the door opened, and in walked a tall, imposing figure
dressed in full battle uniform. His armor had a shine to it that
normal field soldiers' armor lacked. The seated friends could tell
this figure was an officer in the Roman military. His attached red
cape and the helmet cradled in his forearm had the red plumage
that ran from the front all the way to the back. This indicated the
figure was a centurion, similar in stature to Julius.

Their assessments were quickly validated. "My name is Flavius, centurion to Commander Cleatus. I have been assigned to
guard you while you await your appeal before Caesar." The
guard's tone of voice was as imposing as his appearance. He was
young and brawny. His voice was low, firm, confident, and authoritative. His eyes were dark brown and the narrow valley formed
between his eyebrows gave notice he was serious and tolerated
no nonsense.

"I must inform you that Caesar has departed Rome to journey
throughout parts of the empire, inspecting our garrisons. This
requires him to be away throughout the entire forthcoming winter. Because of this, your appeal will not be heard until his return
next spring."

Flavius stopped to assess the impact of his announcement.
His eyes searched Paul for any sign of reaction and he was somewhat surprised Paul showed no emotion. The centurion's darting
eyes went first to Luke then to Aristarchus. It was the latter who
exhibited signs of shock about the announcement. "Isn't it customary for a close confidant of Caesar or a proconsul to hear this
man's appeal and as such not prolong his case?" Aristarchus questioned.

Flavius detected some concern and frustration in his tone. He
replied firmly, "Not in the case of treason, which this man is accused of committing. Only Caesar is authorized to decide for anyone accused of this, the most serious of crimes a Roman citizen
can commit."

Paul asked the centurion, "Since this is the case, will I be
housed here in the palace during this time of waiting?"

Flavius answered bluntly. "No. Because you initiated the appeal, you must secure housing yourself and a means to pay the
rent and your living expenses. This is Roman law." His words

came forth with strong emphasis. It was clear there would be no negotiation in this matter.

"This should be no problem. However, whom do I see about obtaining housing? And when will I be allowed to do this?"

Flavius flatly explained, "Seneca, Consul to Caesar, has arranged for you to rent a townhouse in the northwest sector of the city. It isn't far from here. You shall be transported there tomorrow." The centurion turned his attention to Paul's two companions and informed them, "Roman law does not allow anyone but the accused to reside in a dwelling. You both must seek accommodations elsewhere."

Flavius gestured toward Paul while speaking to both Luke and Aristarchus, "The citizen has unlimited freedom to receive visitors at the rented townhouse. He will not be allowed to leave the premises. However, you both—and any other companions or friends—may approach him during the day. But not the evening."

There was a long pause after Flavius finished giving the terms of Paul's detention. He scrutinized each man's face and their body language to assess the impact of his notification. Luke looked down and had one eyebrow arched, with his hands folded together on his lap. It was obvious he was pondering this development. Aristarchus sat nervously shifting from side to side on the cot. His lips were set in a slight frown.

Flavius glared at Paul whose face was serene, his eyes steady, and his body relaxed. The accused traitor calmly stood up, took a step towards Flavius, extended his arms, and opened his hands. "Thank you for notifying us of this development. I look forward to seeing the rental that has been arranged for me. I trust you will apprise me of how I can earn an income during my house arrest."

Flavius looked down at Paul, who was six inches shorter and forty years older. In a precise tone, he answered, "We have knowledge of your skill as a cobbler. You may use any tools brought with you and will be allowed to set aside a room in the townhouse for your work. Anyone seeking your services will be screened to make sure they are not intent on creating havoc to promote your cause."

"I assure you, Centurion Flavius, that havoc or any other disruption from myself or any of my brethren is not our intent."

Flavius merely looked coldly at Paul and the valley between his dark eyebrows seemed to deepen. "That remains to be seen. Rest assured, my men will be ready for any, as you say, disruption that might take place." With that, the centurion snappily turned and left the room with his red cape swirling behind him.

"Did you have any idea about Caesar leaving, or you having to earn a living to pay rent while you wait your appeal, Paul?"

The apostle of Christ answered Aristarchus, "You have been faithfully at my side for some time now, Aristarchus. Surely, you realize that the devil will throw any obstacle in my direction to prevent me from carrying out God's will. These obstacles are nothing to our heavenly Father. He will guide me, and us. He will open doors and close doors, that we can be His servants."

True to his word, Flavius had Paul transferred to his new lodging the next day. This time, only four soldiers, plus Flavius, escorted the missionary under the cloak of darkness to the townhouse that would be Paul's residence for the duration of his stay in Rome.

After making sure no spies had followed their path, Flavius led the way into the townhouse. Several members of the Praetorian Guard were waiting inside for the accused citizen. They had been chosen because of their loyalty to Rome and their battle-hardened experience. Flavius was also a member of the Guard and had hand-picked the soldiers needed for the assignment.

The first soldier was armed with the traditional two-foot wide by four-foot long combination of wood and leather shield. He carried the standard short sword hanging loosely at his left side. His body armor was shiny metal. Its protection consisted of a breastplate, forearm guards, knee to ankle protectors and a helmet. In addition to the short sword, this soldier had an eight-foot long thick-shafted lance with a sharpened metal point that was ten inches long. It all had a seriously imposing effect on any armed or unarmed man.

Flavius spoke quietly to the guard who stepped aside to allow the remainder of the group to enter the townhouse. The centurion then confronted three other Guard members. Lucilius was assigned to be Paul's shadow. Wherever Paul went, Lucilius was to always be at his side, even when the follower of Christ had visitors. There would be very little privacy for Paul during his house arrest.

Lucilius had the same armor as the door guard, but did not carry a lance. His only weapon was the short sword, but he was very adept at using it. He had a reputation, earned on the battlefield, of being able to draw the sword and thrust it deeply into the heart of an opponent within five seconds after first engaging the opposition in combat. His motion was smooth and quick, and he was accomplished at withdrawing the sword from one opposing combatant, and immediately using the butt end of the shaft to strike another opponent either between the eyes or in the temple area of the skull, eliminating two foes with what seemed to be one seamless stroke.

The other Guard member was named Marcus, a dog handler who was very proficient with a specially made mace that he had designed years earlier. The two dogs were massive. Their heads were nearly twice the size of other dogs' heads and had a somewhat boxy appearance. They had barrel chests and very strong legs capable of achieving a speed of thirty miles per hour. Their most valuable attribute was their powerful jaws that could break either a forearm or a leg in a single bite.

In addition to their speed, these military-bred dogs were very quick and agile with the ability to make quick turns and avoid a predator's weapon. The dogs were utilized in battle to tear open the belly of a horse as it raced towards the dog's handler. The dog would get very low and charge under the front legs of the horse, raise its head and bite the vulnerable belly, immediately incapacitating the animal. They were fearless animals, trained to obey only silent commands from their handler and no one else. Each dog usually weighed in at 150 pounds.

Flavius stopped and stepped aside to give Paul a good long look at the fearsome animals. The centurion mainly wanted the dogs to do a visual assessment of the man they were to deny escape. Flavius paid particular attention to Paul's reaction to the dogs. The accused citizen made no effort to befriend the animals, but neither did he show signs of fear of them. This impressed Flavius as well as the dog handler, Marcus. The dogs also sensed that Paul had no fear, but this would make no difference to them at all. They would carry out their intense training.

Paul glanced from the animals to their handler. Marcus stood 6' 2" tall, was fortyish, and stout. He had a massive chest that was accentuated by his chest armor. His hands were large and his fingers thick. His forearms were big and powerful enough to break an opponent's jaw or knock the breath out of them with a single blow. His legs were powerful, and had demonstrated extraordinary ability to retain balance and agility in hand-to-hand combat.

The apostle of Christ did not dwell on the man's solid, muscular frame. Instead, he studied the soldier's face. His eyes were blue, unusual for a Roman, his face chiseled, with a scar on his left cheek. No doubt, earned in a close-in skirmish years before. His dark hair was thick and curly. Paul thought he could see a deep sadness hidden in the soldier's eyes. The minister of Christ felt in his heart he would address this with the guard when the opportunity arose.

Paul's thoughts did not linger on the mace. Its leather shaft was nearly a foot long and weathered from hand oils. A metal chain linked the shaft to a solid sphere of metal only four inches in diameter. There were spikes of brass protruding from the sphere, each an inch-and-a-half long. The chain link was just under three feet long. Paul imagined how formidable it would be in personal combat situations. But it was of little interest to the missionary whose sole desire was to win spiritual battles, not hand-to-hand combat.

The third Guard member, named Draba, was nearly as tall as Marcus, muscular, athletic-looking, and obviously strong. His only weapon was the short sword. He had a swarthy complexion and a forbidding countenance. What most impressed Paul about Draba were his fiery eyes and unyielding expression of distaste. It was obvious he did not like Paul and that he would relish any opportunity to use his sword on the detainee if given the authorization, which was not to be the case. Roman citizens were due the utmost respect and consideration by all branches of the Roman military. Nonetheless, Draba could react emotionally at any perceived provocation.

Once Flavius had made his introductions and allowed Paul time to assess the protection that would be with him 24 hours each day, he dismissed Draba for his return to the Guard's barracks located in the west wing of Caesar's palace. He was due to return later that day to assume his evening shift, replacing Lucilius.

"Now that you have met those who will be protecting you during your house arrest, it is time I introduced you to the owner of the townhouse. She will take you on a tour of your rented house, as well as discuss the arrangements she insists on you observing."

On cue, a woman, tall by Roman standards, and dressed immaculately in a traditional gown favored by upper class Roman women, appeared from one of the rooms of the abode. Her dark hair was swept upward, befitting a woman of class. Her jewelry was minimal and tasteful, meant to enhance but not distract from her natural beauty. Purposefully, she strode directly toward the men who followed her every movement.

Her pace was casual, yet elegant. Her posture evoked sophistication, power, and authority. She stopped within two steps of Flavius and looked at him with calm respect. The centurion made a slight bow toward her and the assigned guards backed away. "Aelia, this is the citizen named Paul who will be your tenant while he awaits his appeal before Caesar. I will leave the two of you together for your private discussion." Flavius motioned for his men to return to where the door guard was positioned. He wanted to have one final meeting with them.

Aelia watched the soldiers' retreat toward the front door of the townhouse. Satisfied they were out of hearing range, she shifted her gaze to the new tenant. She was three inches taller than Paul, but what she noticed most about the man was his composed demeanor amidst the armed guards. His face exhibited no signs of stress or any indication of guilt that she could usually discern in an accused person's face.

In a business-like manner, she introduced herself. "Seneca approached me about the possibility of renting one of my townhouses while you are under house arrest. Let me state that I know you are accused of treason, but I have no opinions about this at all. I make it a point neither to learn details about any accused persons nor to intercede in any way on their behalf. I really abhor politics, as well as religion, although I've learned how to interact with them. Rest assured, I will not discuss either subject with you."

The feminine landlord stopped to give her new tenant the opportunity to express himself. Paul assured her, "I shall not bother you in any way, either to reveal details about what I'm alleged of committing or to involve you in any way regarding my case." Paul flashed an unexpected smile. "And we are similar concerning our views on politics and religion."

Aelia smiled back at her tenant, surprised at his response. She felt they would get along well together, but she carefully retained a business-like attitude. "Let me give you a tour of the townhouse. Feel free to ask questions as we proceed. Afterward, we shall discuss the payment terms that you must comply with during your stay here in Rome."

Because the soldiers remained in the front of the house, Aelia began her tour in the rear portion that contained the courtyard and small garden area. When they entered the courtyard, she stopped to allow Paul time to survey its picturesque tranquility.

The stucco walls were arched, and lined both sides of the

courtyard. Each archway led to a room. There were three bedrooms, an office, a dining room, and a kitchen. In the middle was a rectangular pool three feet deep. It was made of fine marble bordered by an intricate design of tile. "This pool is similar in purpose as the one in the front of the house. It collects rain water that comes through the opening in the roof." As she spoke, Aelia raised her hand towards the ceiling to show Paul the opening.

Paul was now familiar with the functional architecture of the rainwater roof. Surrounding the roof opening was marble that continued to the high ceiling, and walls that were adorned with murals depicting countryside scenes near Rome. Each mural was detailed and it was evident the artist was very skilled.

Aelia gestured to the other walls that also had frescos painted in similar fashion. Each arched doorway was visually tied to the other by a cantilevered covering. The support columns of the doorways were hewn from marble with typical Greek-inspired contours. The exquisite craftsmanship clearly indicated wealth and a demanding owner.

The landlord continued with Paul through each room to the kitchen, which was equipped for daily appetizers, regular dining, and frequent entertaining. Standing in the middle of the culinary room were three slave-staffers. Aelia briefly introduced each one to the new tenant. They had no reason to linger in the kitchen. Paul only needed to know that good food would be prepared there, with ample servants to deliver it. She was eager to spend more time in her favorite section of the residence, and gracefully turned towards the corridor that led back to the garden where they had begun the tour.

The garden was in the back portion of the townhouse, located beyond an opening in the rear wall that was tall and narrow. The short wall on the far side rose up three feet from the ground and had a single step to the opening. It led to the outside of the townhouse. Flanking this opening were several rows of garden herbs, vegetables, and fruits that Paul recognized as ones favored by Roman tastes.

The pair returned from the garden to the patio, and Aelia motioned for Paul to sit down in one of four pillowed chairs that surrounded a small table.

Aelia began, "While Flavius has discussions with his men, this will be a good time for us to discuss the financial side of our business arrangement." Paul agreed, and Aelia set forth her terms. "As you can see, my townhouse is prime property here in Rome. This is my personal dwelling when I must stay in the city." The adroit businesswoman gestured lightly with her hands toward both sides of the villa. "I own the adjoining townhouses on both sides of this residence. There are eight total. The one to the left is rented by my daughter and her husband. The others consist of businessmen and a couple of young government officials."

Aelia watched Paul's eyes for any kind of reaction. She knew her renter was a Jew and that peculiar race of people did not generally allow women to engage in commerce. She was thankful the Romans were not of that mindset. Paul exhibited no adverse reaction, so she continued.

"Normally, I charge two denarii per day rent for these units. The clientele I choose certainly can afford this amount. The location, relative safety, and quality is high, as you have seen." Paul's face showed interest, and Aelia was pleased to see he was listening carefully as she spoke.

"Seneca has informed me of the nature of your stay in Rome. He and the commander of the field military, General Cleatus, inquired of this location because it is close to the military barracks in the palace. It is also quiet and more secure than what an apartment would be. These factors do have a premium price that you alone are responsible for paying." She paused to determine the effect these terms had on her new tenant.

Now the shrewd businesswoman added firmness in her voice. "Your rent shall be two denarii per day for every day you reside here. This amount covers rent, food, and servants. Be assured, Paul, that since there will be many guards assigned to you throughout the day, they eat heartily. You won't be able to cook for them, and that's why I've assigned this task to my personal servants."

Aelia paused for Paul to make any comments or complaints over this arrangement. His courteous nod and contented silence prompted her to continue, "The monthly amount must be paid by the end of the first week of every month. There shall be no exceptions. Can you pay this amount? And how do you propose to meet this obligation?" Aelia sat back in her chair and folded her hands in her lap to receive Paul's answers to her questions.

The apostle of Jesus showed no signs of anxiety over the terms he would be obligated to meet. His head rested on the back cushion of his chair. He focused his eyes on Aelia's, and in a calm, reassuring voice said, "I was informed by Flavius I would be responsible for paying my own rent while I wait to appear before

Caesar. My trade is that of a tentmaker and cobbler, which I was taught during my training to become a Pharisee of the Jewish religion."

Aelia unfolded her hands and moved them to the arms of her chair, sensing potential conflict. Her eyes remained fixed on Paul's with unwavering attention as Paul continued, "In my travels throughout the empire, I've always earned my way, utilizing the craft God has blessed me in doing. I realize here in Rome the need for tents is highly unlikely. However, I perceive the demand for shoes, boots, and sandals is such there should be no problem in meeting your financial demands." Silently, he said a prayer, asking his Lord for provision of cobbler's tools to replace those that he had lost in the shipwreck.

Aelia's hands had been tightly gripping the chair. Her hands relaxed again. "Your perception about your craft is correct, Paul. Indeed, the demand for quality footwear is great in the city. The military alone would keep you quite busy. I have a contact here who owns a cobbler outlet. He does quite well, but can always use a skilled craftsman. I shall have him contact you within the next two days."

Once the financial uncertainty had been resolved, the pair resumed talking amiably about shared travels and nuances of the hubs of commerce each had frequented. Out of the corner of her eye, Aelia could see the group of military men had disbanded. Flavius was no longer present. It was time to go. The landlord then seemed to float up out of her chair in one fluid movement. Paul stood up with Aelia and followed her as she began walking toward the front part of the townhouse.

When they entered the atrium, Aelia paused by the rectangular pool in the middle of the room. At one end of the pool loomed a statue of the Roman god of business. It seemed very appropriate, considering Aelia's enterprises. The walls of the atrium consisted of marble panels; between each one there was a fresco of iconic Italian country scenes. The workmanship was evident and suggested it was made by the same artisan who had painted the frescos in the courtyard.

Wasting little time, Aelia escorted Paul to a room along the side of one wall. When they were inside, Paul noted the only furniture was a cushioned chair and a beautiful desk. He approached the desk and slowly moved the palm of his hand along its top, admiring the workmanship. The wood was a combination of olive wood and one of the indigenous pines of Italy.

He dropped to his knees to examine the highly detailed carvings of the legs and front panel of the desk. "This is exquisite, Aelia. Such talent and skill. Truly this person is blessed by Almighty God to be able to create such beauty." Paul looked admiringly at the desk, then stood up and looked at Aelia with a broad smile. "With such beauty as this desk, it is easier to understand why there are no other furnishings in this room."

Aelia chucked. "Yes, this is my personal office. When I'm in Rome and need to conduct business affairs, I utilize this room. All my personal records and effects have been removed. You may have full utilization for your purposes." The landlord tentatively asked, "Do you intend on conducting your cobbler duties from this room?"

Paul immediately responded, "Oh, no. I would not want to harm this exquisite desk. I respect the artisan too much to do such a thing. One of the vacant rooms in the courtyard portion of the house will do me well."

Aelia breathed a sigh of approval. The desk had been her gift to her now-deceased husband, and there were many memories associated with it she did not want to risk being destroyed. "Paul, I appreciate your sensitivity concerning this object. Whatever doubts or concerns I had earlier about you potentially causing harm or destruction to my city house are now gone. I'm confident you will treat my home as if it were your own."

When they left the office, they noticed there had been a change in the guard. The afternoon/evening shift had arrived. Paul recognized stormy Draba, who positioned himself close to the detainee after Paul left the office.

Realizing the hour, it was amazing to both landlord and tenant how quickly the amiable time had gone by. "Aelia, I had no idea of the hour. Do you have plans for dinner or could I persuade you to join me here?"

A warm smile spread over Aelia's face. "It would be a pleasure to share your first meal in your new abode." Of course, it would not be dinner for two. Draba would be present as well. The three proceeded to the dining room.

Aelia felt very comfortable in Paul's presence and took her time enjoying the evening, talking with him more. When Aelia heard about the shipwreck that Paul had survived on his way to Rome, she asked if he lost many possessions. Paul was honest. "All our possessions were swept away into the sea."

Aelia persisted, "But what about the tools of your trade? Your cobbler tools and other items?"

"Those, of course, are at the bottom of the sea," Paul answered simply.

Aelia wondered why this Jew seemed peaceful in spite of his dire pronouncement. She realized he needed to be able to work if she were to receive his rent. Having learned much about this man from their conversation, she believed her renter would be diligent and faithful to meet his obligations, so she boldly stated, "I will obtain the tools you need. You can pay me for them when you complete your first sets of soldiers' boots."

The topic shifted from travel experiences to Paul giving testimony about Christ. He could tell that Aelia was only mildly interested, and Draba simply turned off to the subject. Paul refrained from attempting to persuade them, but he praised Almighty God for the many blessings bestowed upon him, including the provision of the cobbler tools he needed.

Reluctantly, the landlord indicated she must go. "The good part is I do not have to travel far, only next door to my daughter's house. I shall stay with her and her husband on those occasions when I must be in Rome."

Paul walked her toward the front door. Per the terms of his house arrest, he could not venture beyond a boundary in the vestibule. He was not allowed to go outside the house, nor could he stand in the doorway. The Roman authorities were adamant about keeping firm control over any possible attempt that might do harm to Paul while he waited for his appearance before Caesar.

That night, as Aelia lay in her bed, thoughts about the day spent with her new tenant flooded her mind, causing her to remain awake longer than she expected. Paul was nothing she had envisioned. Yes, he was a Jew, but not uncouth like others she had met. He had a genuine appreciation for quality, artistry, and fine food. His engaging conversation was most gratifying.

Despite the difference in their ages—she was 49, and she speculated Paul to be in his late 50's—she felt a surprising attraction to this man accused of treason against Rome, whose fate could include execution. On that peculiar last thought, Aelia fell asleep.

## Chapter 7

Once the meeting with Julius, Seneca, and Flavius was over, Cleatus immediately began the process of obtaining as much information about Paul as possible. Treason was the most serious crime a Roman citizen could be accused of, but equally serious was the crime of intent. That also needed to be identified.

The general keenly felt his responsibility to unearth facts and evidence concerning these two issues. Cleatus wanted to know answers to these accusations against Paul. Whatever he obtained would be useful in handling the Jews and any dissidents Paul might be the leader of, or closely aligned with, in his personal quest, whatever it was.

Was this man instigating a future revolt? The Jews were known for this ever since Rome conquered them. Did he have political aspirations? Was he the leader of a band of marauders? These were important questions that needed answers as soon as possible.

It would take some time, but now that Paul was in Rome and under house arrest, Cleatus had the time. He needed to use it wisely. To do this, the general went to the location of the military's main intelligence unit, the pigeon farm.

Cleatus heard the carrier pigeons flutter their wings furiously, even while confined in their cages. It was as if they sensed being called to a mission and they were signaling their readiness. Each bird would be removed from its cage, a message in a capsule would be fastened to its leg, and the eager bird would be released. The general had prepared communiqués to be sent throughout the empire, wherever Paul had been. He watched his winged messengers with fascination. He was in awe of their speed, accuracy of flight, and determination, and was grateful for their amazing homing instincts. What they accomplished within a matter of hours or days would take weeks or months to achieve via human couriers.

After the last pigeon was out of sight, Cleatus returned to his office. Despite the fact his requests would be in the hands of the various governors within three days, even as far away as Syria, he knew the detailed accounts he requested in his messages would take much longer to complete. The intelligence reports he ordered would be thorough and too heavy for a pigeon to carry. They would have to make their way into his hands via human courier. It would be time-consuming and not without danger. In addition to potentially lethal winter storms, there were bandits who scoured the roads, seeking any potential source of bounty. A confiscated message such as what Cleatus sent could be deemed valuable and sold to people who had a great interest in Paul.

The assigned couriers traveling back to Rome would be disguised and would accompany a merchant caravan that had Roman military escorts. This usually was sufficient for matters requiring protection and secrecy.

Flavius left Cleatus' office and made his way to the Guard barracks where he knew Julius would be. There were several reasons for the centurion wanting to contact his friend and colleague.

It had been quite some time since they had last enjoyed each other's company, sharing stories, laughter, and their military career hopes. Flavius was several years younger than Julius, but they were like brothers, and brothers needed to stay connected with each other.

The centurion's second reason for meeting with Julius was based on the story of the journey made with Paul and the rest of the group. Indeed it was most unique, but knowing his fellow centurion the way he did, Flavius was sure there was much more that hadn't been revealed. These facts were what Flavius sought. They were important for him to successfully carry out his assignment of protecting and monitoring Paul.

Meanwhile, Julius was exhausted after the debriefing with his commander, his friend, and the civilian. He was glad it was over and urged his tired legs to take him quickly back to the barracks. His armor felt as if it weighed a ton, dragging him down.

It had been a long and, at times, very difficult journey but also life-changing, as well. He knew not many men had experienced what he had, and he sensed it was for a very important reason, but for now the reason remained shrouded in mystery.

When Julius first stepped into the bath, the warm water on his feet and ankles had an instantaneous effect on his entire body. His legs were weak and sluggish and it was with great effort that he wobbled deeper into the soothing water. Quickly he let himself go and sank down to cover his shoulders. The tired soldier let out a deep moan of relief. The slave girl assigned to give him the massage took his exhalation as a sign he was ready to have his muscles worked on.

The effect of the warm water and the gentle massaging made Julius relax to the point he almost fell asleep. Only the sound of his good friend's voice brought him back from near slumber. "I see you obeyed Cleatus' order to get a massage," laughed the voice Julius recognized.

"Ah, Flavius, it is always good to obey your commanding officer! That is the mark of a good soldier, is it not? But brothers stand together. Shouldn't you also be in the bath as my backup?" The two centurions laughed and Flavius began to undress.

Once in the warm water, Flavius realized how tense his muscles were. They began to relax as the water warmed and soothed the tissues. Another slave girl appeared and entered the water to massage his muscles. The only sounds heard were the sighing and moaning of the exhausted two soldiers and the soft giggling of the masseuses.

An hour passed by quickly and the two colleagues closed their eyes as they finished soaking. The therapeutic effect of the warm water and the massage had curtailed all meaningful conversation.

Completely relaxed and refreshed, Flavius suggested they have dinner together and chat some more about Julius' unique trip. "I would enjoy dining with you, my brother. In fact, I was hoping we could get together, as I have much to share with you. I don't know how long I will remain here in Rome. This may be the only opportunity I have to confide in you."

Instead of eating with the other officers, the two went to a restaurant nearby. The owners were fond of the Praetorian Guard and it was common practice that when any of its members came in, they received double portions. Julius and Flavius remembered this from previous visits. Both were ravenous, and the most pressing consideration of the night was whether to limit themselves to double portions.

When the appetizer of garum and fresh bread was served, Julius took two manic bites. He closed his eyes and breathed deeply, savoring the flavor of both the bread and the fish sauce. He chewed slowly, appreciating this delight that had not been available to him for over five months. With a mouthful of delicious sensations, Julius looked at Flavius. "Does this place still get their garum from Spain? It produces the best I've tasted anywhere!"

Flavius signaled for another bowl, and changed the subject to what was on his mind. "Julius, I was amazed at the events you spoke about during the debriefing. I sensed there was more than what you wanted to tell Cleatus. Am I correct?"

"Indeed you are, my brother." Julius began to explain between bites, "As you know, we of the Praetorian Guard are not real sailors. This is why I trusted the pilot of the ship. He is a good man and a very competent pilot. Yet, he was not only surprised by the force of Euroclydon, but feared for his life, as well. Paul sensed it and stepped forward to assist us both."

At this juncture, the second bowl of tantalizing sauce and more warm bread arrived, but this time the men were more subdued in their approach to the food. Julius said, "Paul, indeed, is a true leader. He assesses the situation correctly and makes sound decisions. I respect him greatly."

Flavius leaned forward and interrupted, "Do you believe, based on your time spent with Paul and his companions, he could be the leader of a sect that intends on rebelling against Rome?"

"Definitely not!" With a short laugh, Julius adamantly shook his head at the improbability. "There were too many opportunities for him to escape. Plus, when we reached Malta, he could have had the natives there turn against us, but he did not."

Flavius furrowed his brow and intently studied his friend's face and body language. Julius fidgeted in his seat, and his eyes darted back and forth as he lowered his voice to say, "I tell you my brother, the episode with the viper was such, the natives attempted to worship him as a *god*! In fact, my men and I had similar thoughts. Have you ever known *anyone* to *live* after being bitten by a viper?"

Flavius leaned back in his chair. Julius' words resonated in his thoughts like a loud clanging bell. "This is what is very perplexing to me, Julius. In fact, it unsettles me and I don't really know why."

Julius agreed, and proceeded, "Then there were the healings, none of which I've ever seen or known to take place. Why, even the Guard's own doctor, Dioscorides, would have been amazed at what we saw with our own eyes!"

Flavius nodded, "Your account gives me food for thought. In addition to providing basic security for Paul until his appeal to Nero, it is my assignment to obtain information about this man and his intentions. This is why I have chosen Guard members who have sharp memories and can accurately relay what he says and does with his visitors. These soldiers will be careful, discreet, and extremely observant while guarding Paul. Julius, I have never had an assignment quite like this one. I believe it will be challenging for you, but also, I hope, rewarding."

"Have no fear, my brother. What you are about to experience will change your life." Flavius was taken aback by his words. Julius leaned towards his fellow centurion and quietly confided, "Part of my duties in Caesarea was to monitor anyone thought to be a threat to Rome. There were repeated conflicts between the Jews throughout the region and members of this sect who call themselves members of The Way."

Julius paused to belch, a common custom of Romans. "It was, and remains, that the Jews are more of a threat than these 'Way' people. The issue is religious in nature. The Jews don't believe in the so-called Messiah that The Way members do. The Jewish leaders make every effort to demean and even persecute those of The Way, especially if they are Jewish."

Flavius briefly turned to fill their goblets and took a swallow from his own before responding, "My father has written me about this conflict. As Prefect to Tarsus, he has dealt with several such instances. The Jews have killed followers of The Way and Rome has relented in dealing with the killers. This is because the religion practiced by the Jews is accepted and authorized by Caesar and the Senate."

The centurion held his goblet just below his mouth and continued, "Governor Quadratus has multiple reports about similar hostilities between these two groups. In each and every one, it is the Jews who are the aggressors."

Julius placed his goblet on the table and looked directly at his friend. "During this time, I learned much about this man Paul. He has traveled to major cities throughout Judea and Asia, converting both Jews and others they call Gentiles to this new religion. He has been imprisoned, stoned, and driven out of these communities for what the Jews refer to as blasphemy."

Pulling at his ear, Julius thoughtfully stated, "The evidence is contrary to any sedition against Rome, but they definitely argue against the Jewish religion. My assignment of bringing Paul to Rome was an excellent opportunity for me to observe him. Many times along the way, I conversed in depth with him about The Messiah and what it means to be a member of The Way.

"I felt a very strong change within me as we traveled on land back to Rome. Experiencing how much the people loved Paul and his two companions and how they treated my men and I made a great impact on me."

Momentarily pausing, Julius chose his next words carefully. "All the events that happened—beginning with my involvement in Judea, my personal conversations with Paul, the shipwreck, the viper, and the actions of the people along the way—have led me to believe and to accept Jesus Christ as Messiah, my only true God."

Julius stopped, almost holding his breath, while he waited for his friend and colleague's reaction. Flavius remained silent. Julius added, "I know that Rome hasn't authorized this sect yet, and they possibly may not do so. It doesn't matter to me. I shall worship only Jesus."

Flavius recovered from the shock of his dear friend's words. "My brother, I have nothing negative to say about your decision. Only you know from your experiences what changes you want to make. Do you intend on remaining in the service of Rome as a member of the Guard, or are you going to follow this man Paul?"

"Paul and I have discussed this matter at great length. I have decided to continue my career in the Guard. I will pray to the Lord what it is He wants me to do. I believe He will use me during my remaining time with the Guard. I just have to wait for His orders."

Flavius was pensive as he studied his centurion brother. Mopping up the last of the garum sauce with a piece of bread, the centurion inquired, "I believe what you experienced and said about Paul must be shared with Cato. He will be spending considerable time with Paul, both as his attorney and to obtain any information to clarify the questions Seneca has, so that he may make a good recommendation to Nero. I can arrange a meeting between you and Cato for as soon as tomorrow."

"That would be fine with me. My body and mind are capable of any scrutiny that you or anyone else may seek."

Flavius raised his wine goblet, signaling Julius to do the same. "Here's to us, and to you, my brother. May your days be many and you be richly fulfilled." Julius smiled and the two men continued with their meal as their next course arrived.

Back at his residence, Flavius spent considerable time pondering the earlier conversation with his friend. He sent a messenger to Cato to interview Julius. Flavius' own adherence to the accepted Roman gods was weak and he simply did not understand the fervor Julius expressed for this so-called Messiah. This was very strange and perplexing.

His thoughts centered on Paul and his power of persuasion. He wrote out his thoughts, and when he had finished, he set aside the quill pen and just gazed at the parchment. His mind was in a daze. He was puzzled by Julius' statement telling him that involvement with Paul was going to change his life.

 Chapter 8

Lucilius had been briefed to expect Paul to have visitors, but he was startled by how quickly visitors came. The second day of his assignment to guard Paul, two of the citizen's companions came to meet with their associate. A third man was one Lucilius knew, and he was baffled by his request to meet with the detainee.

The member of the Praetorian Guard was pleased things were progressing at a pace that kept him from being bored. Flavius had informed all his men that the assignment would probably last until next spring. The time could feel like a very long winter or one that would seem to fly by like a passing flock of geese on their migratory journey. Lucilius much preferred the geese.

Paul greeted Luke and Aristarchus warmly with the traditional custom of a hug with a kiss on each side of their faces. The jubilant prisoner turned to introduce them to Lucilius. There was no tension in the air, but the Roman soldier remained within three paces of Paul and his visitors, as he had been instructed. His mannerisms silently made it obvious he would react with his sword should any one of the companions appear to do harm to the detainee.

The apostle led his friends and Lucilius to the garden for conversation. Both Luke and Aristarchus commented on its beauty. Roses were still in bloom and their intoxicating fragrance filled the area around the table. The three sat down and soon a manservant appeared with wine and snacks for the small group. Lucilius refrained from indulging. He let it be known it was not his role to be friendly with them.

When the manservant left the garden, Paul inquired of his

friends, "So, my brothers in Christ, have you secured comfortable accommodations here in Rome?" The two men answered that two different members of The Way had graciously taken them into their homes.

They informed Paul that the Jewish leaders, as well as the church leaders, appeared genuinely surprised that Paul was here in Rome and was accused of high treason. Aristarchus observed, "There is much confusion among the Jews here about your presence at this time. They appeared to be wary, although they were intensely curious."

Paul folded his hands together and quietly said, "My plan is to meet with both the Jewish leaders as well as Christ's church elders as soon as I'm allowed. I believe this will be within the next three days. I will be able to answer their concerns at that time."

Lucilius stood behind where Paul, Luke, and Aristarchus sat. From that vantage point he was able to hear every word. Thus far, there was nothing enticing to report to his commander, Flavius. However, the guard sensed that could change at any given moment.

Luke informed Paul the household where he was staying was owned by one of the church leaders, a man named Teman who was a converted Gentile, similar to himself. "Teman is quite eager to meet with you, Paul. He has questions to ask you that relate to the epistle you wrote to the church elders here."

Aristarchus echoed Luke's statement, "I'm residing with Hevel, a converted Jew. Because of your epistle to the church, he also has questions for you."

Paul's eyes seemed to twinkle. "I'm sure they do. I've expected this and am eager to discuss with them how they have understood and implemented the teaching written for them."

The missionary directed a question to Luke, "I would like to meet with the Jewish leaders first. As you know, wherever I travel, I first meet with the synagogue leaders to give them opportunity to repent and follow Christ. Can you ask them to meet with me as soon as it is possible?"

Realizing he first needed to ask if such a large group would be allowed in the townhouse at one time, Paul looked up at Lucilius.

The guard anticipated his assignee's unspoken question. "I'm sure that Flavius will grant your request, but I must get his permission first."

Paul chuckled, "Ah, Lucilius, you read my mind perfectly." He directed Luke, "You must wait until we do get this authorization."

The three Christ-followers conversed for an hour. Within a short time after their departure, someone Lucilius knew came to the townhouse to request a meeting with Paul. It was Antonius, a businessman who owned a cobbler shop that made boots for the military. Lucilius had used his services in the past and found the product sufficient. He was quite curious about why Antonius wanted to speak with Paul.

The mystified guard followed Paul as he led Antonius into the room Aelia utilized as her office. The landlord had added another chair for Paul's use. Paul sat behind the desk while Antonius sat in front of him. Lucilius stood behind Antonius, and was watchful while he speculated on the meaning of the visit.

Antonius wasted no time in revealing his purpose, "Aelia has informed me that you are a cobbler in need of work. If you meet my requirements, I shall make a pact with you to assist me in filling orders I receive from the military." The abruptness of his words implied he did not expect Paul to meet his demands. "Have you experience in cobbling? It requires certain skills mere tentmakers often do not possess." The inference was clear he disdained tentmakers, deeming them generally inferior to cobblers.

Paul remained relaxed as he listened to his prospective employer and simply stated, "I have been trained in the art of cobbling." With that, Paul removed one of his shoes and presented it to the skeptical businessman.

Antonius took it into his hands and carefully rotated it, giving it a thorough examination. He inspected the stitching and how the footwear was designed. Next he evaluated the type of leather used. Thick, stiff cowhide comprised the sole and goatskin had been used for the upper portion of the boot-like shoe. While conducting his investigation, Antonius had a fixed frown on his face. Periodically, he emitted a critical grunt.

Finally, Antonius gave the shoe back to Paul. "The shoe appears to be adequately made," he grudgingly admitted. "You have correctly chosen the right leathers for both durability and comfort. However, I must have you produce a pair to my liking before I make a decision."

Antonius started to stand up as his signal the meeting was over. He hesitated and sat back down, asking Paul, "Do you have proper tools with you or must you purchase them?" Lucilius could tell the cobbler would be greatly irritated if Paul answered he had no equipment. Should Paul answer he needed tools, Lucilius believed Antonius would not hire the detainee. After all, what kind of cobbler would not have the tools of his trade with him?

"I always carry my tools with me. In my travels, it is the only way I can support myself. Sometimes the need is for tents while other times it is footwear. My tools are of good quality and there should not be any need to purchase any from you." Paul sent up a silent prayer of thanks to Christ who had supplied them through Aelia. Lucilius was impressed with Paul's composure during this exchange. He knew Antonius to be a demanding cobbler businessman who didn't mind intimidating potential competition.

Antonius' skepticism was visible. He was rigid and defensive. "Very well, then. Tomorrow you shall have material for a single pair of military boots delivered here. There will be a template guide for you to follow. I expect the boots to be completed by the end of the week." Haughtily, he added, "If you cannot comply with that, I won't hire you."

Lucilius quickly turned his attention back to Paul who showed no sign of offense. The apostle replied in a calm, confident voice, "I do not foresee any problem meeting your schedule. Will you pick up the finished product? Or have one of your employees do so?"

Antonius thought carefully for a moment, then emphatically pronounced, "It will be I." With that statement, the businessman quickly stood up, turned away from Paul, and looked at Lucilius, signaling he was ready to leave.

After Lucilius escorted Antonius to the front door, he returned to the office where Paul remained seated behind Aelia's desk. He offered, "I know this man. He has a reputation for being stern and difficult. But I've purchased boots from him and they are of good quality. Naturally, the quality also comes with a higher price."

Breaking his official appearance of detachment, the curious guard asked Paul somewhat apprehensively, "Do you foresee any difficulty meeting Antonius' demands?"

The prospective employee shrugged his shoulders in an offhand way before he answered, "Lucilius, Almighty God has given me skill in this area. During one of my travels, I made boots for your fellow soldiers. I'm familiar with the pattern. The Holy Spirit gave me insight how to make them even better. I shall utilize what I learned in making this test pair. I do not think Antonius will be disappointed with my work."

When the morning guards appeared for their daily shift and

relieved the previous crew, the replacement guard assigned to remain close to Paul relayed Flavius' permission for a large group of Jewish leaders to meet with Paul. Ecstatic, Paul rubbed his hands together. This meeting had been foremost on the list of items he wanted to pursue from the time his desire to minister in Rome had first ignited in his heart.

The next day, when Luke came for his daily visit to his fellow servant of Christ, Paul quickly informed him of Flavius' favorable decision regarding a group of visitors. Luke was as elated as Paul. "I shall go this day and make your request known to them! I'm sure they will want to meet with you very soon."

Paul and Luke discussed other matters, and Lucilius was listening attentively to it all for his daily report to Flavius. The Roman guard had little knowledge about The Way followers, but he knew the main purpose of his report was to inform his commander of his observations and and let Flavius take it from there.

Two days later, ten Jewish leaders arrived at Paul's townhouse. Inside the vestibule, their heads moved from admiring the fabulous marble, to the frescos, to the arched ceilings. The coolness of the marble floor felt refreshing. The Roman guard stood with his back to the door, feet apart, shield ready, and his hand on the handle of his short sword. His eyes were narrowed and he purposely signaled his scorn for the Jews through his posturing. His behavior did not go unnoticed by the Jewish leaders.

Paul and Draba came to greet them. Genuinely pleased, Paul smiled as he spoke, "Welcome to my rented house. Follow me to the atrium." He led the way, and the Jewish leaders followed. Draba pushed his way between the Jews and Paul. When a few of the Jews murmured about his disrespect, the Roman guard turned his head and glared with fiery eyes and a curled lip, openly displaying his hatred towards them. His intimidation tactics were effective. They fell silent on their way to the meeting room.

As the group trailed the hostile Roman, their eyes took in the roof opening that brought in the sun and the rain. The water in the rectangular pool sparkled from the sun's rays. The movements of their robes and their feet created a slight echo in the room.

Paul continued past the atrium and into Aelia's vacated office. Chairs had earlier been removed from the office. The only furniture was the ornate desk and one chair behind it. The host went behind the desk, but remained standing out of courtesy to his guests who would need to stand in the sparsely furnished room.

The Jewish leaders remained expressionless during Paul's explanation of his current circumstances. Then, one of the Jews voiced the confusion that had led them to seek the morning's meeting with Paul. "We received no letters from Judea concerning you, nor have any of the brethren spoken evil about you. We don't understand why you are being detained."

Paul's face became thoughtful. Draba had positioned himself next to Paul and could hear perfectly every word spoken by everyone in the room. His head turned away from Paul to the left side of the room where one of the leaders inquired, "Tell us about this accusation of treason."

Paul carefully explained the details surrounding the false charge. He, and the searching eyes of Draba, could tell the Jewish leaders accepted his account of the issue.

Another of the Jews in the room spoke out, "We desire to hear from you what you think concerning this sect called 'The Way.' All that we know is it is spoken against everywhere."

Paul gave an impassioned explanation about the kingdom of God. As he did so, he moved among them, gesturing to emphasize certain important points. He referenced the Law of Moses and the Prophets, plus the personal experiences of the apostles concerning the deity of Christ Jesus.

Draba watched Paul's actions and observed how Christ's orator was captivating these men. He mentally promised himself he would not let this detained prisoner, a Jew, sway him in any way. In fact, he especially would make this point, about Paul's ability to influence, a strong part of his daily report for Flavius.

The meeting lasted much longer than Draba thought it would. At one point, a spokesman stepped forward to present the men's concerns. "Paul, many of us here were cast out of Rome by Claudius. We could not return for fear of our lives. It wasn't until he was deposed that we were allowed back to this city."

He glanced furtively at Draba who did not hide his contempt. The guard's face reflected his deep-rooted intolerance of Jews. The Jewish spokesperson swallowed hard but continued on, "Now things are better here for us and those who come here from Judea. We are able to conduct business and are free to worship in our synagogues. God is good to us here." At his words, the men murmured their agreement.

The spokesperson explained, "Ananias has repeatedly implored us to refrain from association with the Romans, to not pay their taxes, and to leave. We believe this is not what we ought to do. We are able to harmonize with these people and the foreigners who come from all over. We do not want to jeopardize what we have now, simply to obey Ananias whom we do not really follow. He has usurped both the position and its power from Ishmael ben Fabus who is old and seeks only his own decadent pleasures."

Draba was straining his ears and his mind to make sure he had not missed a single word among these leaders. Paul also listened attentively as the man spoke. At the conclusion of his statement, the disciple of Jesus looked into the eyes of each man present. He found nothing to indicate any disagreement with what had been explained.

"I do not want to harm you or otherwise cause you any problems with the Romans. My focus is on sharing Christ Jesus that all may receive His eternal salvation. Christ is the Messiah, the one sent to atone for man's sins, which He paid in full. His intention is to have a relationship with each of you and all who accept Him as Lord."

Although Paul had not addressed their concerns over Ananias, chaos erupted over his proclamation of Jesus as Messiah. Many of the Jewish leaders were persuaded, and openly stated they agreed with Paul concerning Jesus. Still other leaders ranted and raved their disagreement. At one point the men divided. One group stood to the left while the others went to the right side of the room. They glared at each other. Those who disagreed with Paul were angry and had their arms squarely folded across their chests.

Draba sensed this quarrel could escalate into a physical fight. He unsheathed his short sword and moved to a better position to protect Paul against any attack that might come. Paul stepped between the two groups and quoted words from a prophet named Isaiah, whom Draba knew nothing about.

But it became evident these Jewish leaders did know the prophet, and their reactions were varied. Some nodded their heads in agreement. The others threw their hands up in the air, made wailing noises, and some even bent over as if in great pain. Some of these put their hands to their ears, refusing to listen to Paul. Draba assumed his attack stance, hoping any one of these Jewish idiots would give him the opportunity to run his sword through their bellies. He would gladly do it.

In a voice loud enough to be heard throughout the townhouse, Paul firmly addressed the unbelievers, "Therefore, let it be known to you that the salvation of God has been sent to the Gentiles." The Jews ceased their wailings and focused on their host. With great emphasis, Christ's agent asserted, "And they will hear it!" The room immediately went silent except for the breathing of Paul and Draba.

One of the hostile Jewish leaders stepped away without looking at Paul, turned towards the door, and noisily made his way out of the room. As the others followed, the murmurings were mixed, those in agreement with his words and those adamantly opposed.

The guard at the main door heard the commotion emanating from the meeting room and prepared himself for battle. He unsheathed his sword at the sight of the first Jewish leader who came towards him with blazing eyes. When the startled leader saw the sword pointing directly at him, he stopped. The others did the same. Paul came around from behind the group and stretched out his arm toward the guard in a commanding signal to exercise restraint, "Let these men pass! There is no danger. Our meeting has been concluded."

The guard did not move, but surveyed the situation while still holding his sword in a threatening posture. Only when Draba explained to the guard everything was under control did the guard step aside. Paul motioned to the guard to open the front door. Drizzling rain had begun to fall. As the Jewish leaders hurriedly left Paul's shelter, their heated words of dispute could be heard down the street, becoming fainter and fainter.

Paul returned to the atrium and bent down. His left hand scooped up some water from the collecting pool and he washed his face with it. For a long time, he stared into the glimmering water, listening to the soft splashing and dribbling of the rain runoff.

When he finally straightened up, he returned to the office, followed by Draba. Distraught, Paul sat down heavily behind his desk. Draba remained silent, waiting for what Paul might do. After a short time, the follower of Christ looked up at his guard. In a disappointed voice, he informed Draba, "These men will not be returning to this townhouse." To Draba's great surprise, Paul's slumped shoulders demonstrated genuinely downcast emotions.

The troubled apostle sat at his desk for a while, brooding. Then, with a deep sigh, he stood up and strolled to the garden. He encountered Petronius, the morning dog handler who was a friend to Marcus. Petronius had heard the shouting, but dared not leave his post. His concern was that another group might possibly attempt to breach the short wall and do harm to Paul from the rear of the property. He and his trained canines were resolved to be ready for such a coup.

The sight of Paul coming towards him alone and physically unscathed gave him relief. Paul assured him, "Petronius, I'm sure you could hear the sounds coming from the meeting room. The men were leaders of the Jews here in Rome. Everything is well, they have gone, and I assure you they will not be returning here." Petronius elevated his gaze past Paul to Draba who stood in back of the detainee, signaling with a nod of his head and his steady eyes the truth of Paul's words.

Paul was obviously deep in thought. He turned away from Petronius and went to one of the patio chairs. The rain had stopped. He leaned back in the chair and gazed out through the roof opening to the heavens. Draba stood near Paul and waited anxiously for his shift to end. He was eager to make his report about these despicable Jews and their infuriating religion.

## Chapter 9

Paul repeatedly sought to approach his fellow Jews with the good news about Jesus Christ, giving them the opportunity to hear of His love, and receive forgiveness and eternal salvation. The minister of Christ was saddened by their tenacious clinging to man-made religion, and their disinterest in beginning a life-changing relationship with the Savior sent from God. The reaction by Rome's Jewish heads brought grief to Paul. His despondency lingered for a while.

It was relieved the day after, however, by his necessary attention to a new task when Antonius' messenger delivered the template and materials for the test pair of military boots. Paul took the items into the room designated to become his workshop. Aelia had taken the initiative to supply a cobbler's workbench for Paul's use. He was grateful to his new landlord, but even more appreciative to his Heavenly Father for providing what he needed. Immediately, he familiarized himself with the materials and the template. While beginning the process, friendly voices came from outside the new workshop.

It was Luke and Aristarchus making their daily visit to their fellow follower of Christ. Paul was glad to see his brethren. It would be refreshing. He stopped surveying the leather, and motioned for his guests to accompany him to the patio courtyard. Right away, in spite of Paul's attention to his friends, Aristarchus detected an underlying melancholy. "I take it, Paul, yesterday's gathering with the Jewish provosts did not go well."

Aristarchus and Luke studied Paul's face for the answer. The apostle of Christ closed his eyes and rubbed his hand across his forehead. Emitting a deep sigh, he uttered, "No. They still refuse to acknowledge that Christ is the Son of God and that He came to give eternal life. They are truly stiff-necked."

Draba listened intently to Paul's lamentation. The guard knew that Paul was a Jew, and to hear him speak out against his fellow Jews startled him. He attempted to subtly lean in to the conversation, not wanting to miss any of Paul's dialogue.

Luke came to Paul's side, quietly reminding him of their experiences elsewhere, "In the many travels Aristarchus and I have had with you, it has been the same everywhere we stopped. They listen and agree on a few things, but each time Jesus is spoken of as God, they become hostile."

Paul took time to reflect before he responded to Luke, "Our Lord God revealed this would be, and He commissioned me to speak to the Gentiles and minister to them." Paul looked through the roof opening into the endless azure sky. He sighed, "Yet, I cannot contain myself when we arrive at these different cities and meet Jews there and attempt to minister to them. Similar to yesterday, there are some who do accept the reality of Christ. But, unfortunately, most refuse to hear."

Aristarchus jumped into the conversation with a tone of finality, "What happened yesterday with the Jews is over. I have better news for you, Paul." Paul's head cocked and he looked inquisitively at his long-time friend and fellow minister. Aristarchus announced, "The elders of the followers of Christ request to meet with you at your convenience!"

Draba duly noted for his report how Paul's melancholy deportment immediately changed to happy interest. The Roman spy-guard was intrigued by this, and he hoped more would be revealed. He didn't have to wait long.

Paul smiled from ear to ear and emitted a pleased sigh. The widespread fingertips of his hands repeatedly came together as if bouncing off each other. Draba noticed the light in Paul's eyes. They seemed to sparkle like wintertime frost touched by the rays of the sun. "This is what I've been longing for since I wrote them from Corinth! It's now been over three years. At last we shall meet. Indeed, you bring me pleasing news, Aristarchus!"

They chatted about the church in Rome and how it had been thriving. They lamented, however, the false teachings that had tempted some of Christ's followers to return to their religious laws and rituals. Their deception was subtle and evil. Paul's look of concern clouded his momentary cheerfulness. "My main concern for the church here is how quickly and, in some cases, easily they have succumbed and fallen prey to these deceivers. They seem to have forgotten that Jesus came to set us free from man-made laws and rituals. I hope they have read and meditated on my epistle to them concerning these false teachers."

Aristarchus was the first to speak, "From inquiries I've made since our arrival here, it is mixed at best, Paul. Some locations here are doing better than others. It's reflective of their leadership."

Luke added, "I agree with Aristarchus. The leadership here is an assortment of teachings. What Aristarchus and I have done thus far is to contact the various leaders, inquiring about their practical implementation of your teaching, not just reading or hearing it. Now that they know you are here, they are eager to hear directly from you what you have to say to them."

It was difficult for Draba to control himself. This was valuable information that Flavius would want to know about! He was glad he would be the first to apprise his commander of this development. Inwardly, he felt this was exactly what he needed to secure the promotion he longed for. He was thankful to Mithras, the god of the Roman military, for making this assignment possible.

Paul interrupted Draba's thoughts, "Draba, for this proposed meeting with the elders of the followers of Christ Jesus, I must ask permission once again from Flavius. The group will range between twelve to sixteen men."

Draba listened carefully to the detainee's request and replied formally, "I shall relay your request when my shift is over." Paul indicated his appreciation and said goodbye to Luke and Aristarchus. He went to his new workshop to begin the test assignment from Antonius, relieved to have a project that would take his mind away from his disappointment and frustration over his fellow Jews.

Flavius gave permission for the large group meeting and instructed the men who would be on duty during that time to be vigilant. "It appears whenever our prisoner speaks to either Jews or so-called Gentiles about religious matters, there is always a near riot. I don't want this to happen. Draba, I want you to give Paul a written message from me concerning this matter."

Two days after permission was given for the meeting to take place, the various elders of the church locations throughout Rome came to Paul's rented townhouse. Most often, meetings were held in the early morning hours. Part of the reason was tradition. Mornings for both Jews and Romans began very early. The other reason was the elders of Christ's church had their normal work-day routines that needed to be followed.

Lucilius, Marcus, and Janus the door guard were on duty for this meeting. While they made their way to the townhouse, the three guards worked out their own plan for suppressing any disruption that might occur. They laughed amongst themselves at the thought of these foreigners reacting to the two ferocious dogs should they be unleashed to attack. "Both Brutus and Savas have not had any action for some time. They would enjoy even a light fight such as these foreigners are capable of providing." Their laughter stopped abruptly when they arrived at their assignment.

Shortly after Paul made his heart known to Almighty God, seeking His strength, wisdom, and gift of discerning spirits for the meeting with the church elders, Janus announced their arrival. Christ's apostle directed the group of fifteen elders of The Way into the office next to the atrium. Paul elected to stand again, as he had during the Jewish gathering.

This time, unlike the meeting with the Jewish leaders, there were warm greetings from the elders to Paul. The majority of the elders knew each other and had often met together to discuss Paul's epistles to them as well as God's teachings through His prophets.

After greetings were exchanged, Hevel stepped forward and addressed Paul. "We have waited patiently—well, mostly patient-ly—for this day." A few chuckles from the men underscored the elder's accurate description. "Your desire to visit us here in Rome is second only to our desire to meet with you and to discuss your epistle written to us. Please begin your teaching with what is foremost on your mind."

Lucilius was standing close to Paul, as he had been instructed to do. Looking out at the gathered men, he sensed a genuine desire on their part to hear Paul's words. Even so, the guard was ready for the first eruption that might take place. He looked back at Paul who was smiling.

Paul began, "When word reached me at Corinth about the influx of the false teachers, my heart sank. Your work for Christ here in Rome was flourishing and many had accepted Christ as Savior. I knew these deceivers might draw you away from following Christ and you could fall into the pit of religious legalism."

As he spoke, Christ's ambassador began to move about the

cramped room. The assembled men crunched together to give Paul room to move, as well as to better see and hear what their mentor said. Lucilius opted not to follow Paul. The guard was confident he could spring forth against any attempt to assault Paul. He discreetly moved more to the center of the room and in front of Aelia's desk as Paul continued to speak.

"My concern for you is how these deceivers have persuaded many to reject the teaching of Jesus. To reject Christ is to reject God the Father! Almighty God had his prophets give advance notice of this to us through what is written in Scripture. It is foolish to cast off God for the deception perpetuated by these agents of the devil."

Paul paused and slowly made his way back to the center of the room. Lucilius could see Paul's concentration and hear his careful choice of words. Paul turned to face his congregation. "Brethren, Israel continues to suppress the good news about Christ. I bear them witness that they have a zeal for God, but *not* according to right thinking. Right standing with God is not achieved by attempts to perfectly fulfill religious laws by human effort! This cannot be achieved. Right standing with God, our righteousness, comes only through Christ Jesus, who forgives the sins of those who truly repent, and freely bestows His righteousness on all who believe."

As Paul was about to continue, four of the church elders pushed their way to the front and stood before Paul. A man named Anat became their spokesperson, "We have read your epistle sent to us while you were in Corinth and discussed it at length among ourselves." At that, Anat drew himself up to his full height, thrust his chin forward, and challenged in a loud voice, "We do not agree with your epistle. And those whom you call false teachers have come to us from Jerusalem to rebuke you and your sayings." Lucilius' abruptly came to attention, ready for action.

A deathly quiet took control of the room. No one voiced any disagreement with Anat. Another of the four, Gershom, added, "These learned men, sent from Jerusalem, have opened our eyes to your disobedience to the ancient ways given by God to acknowledge that we are His own. It is by His command of circumcision that we are Jews. What you profess is against God's command. As Jews we cannot purvey that to our congregants."

One of the remaining two men decided to censure Christ's envoy. Itamar was older than the other two men. His face was flushed, his eyes blazing with anger. He pointed his finger in

Paul's face. Loudly, he proclaimed, "Israel does not need this pretended good news you profess! Israel has Scripture that has been written by Moses, who received it directly from God! We need no man such as you to interpret Scripture for us!"

Lucilius noticed how the eyes of the other men in the room were all focused on Paul. They were waiting tensely for his reply, but before he was allowed to speak, the final of the four men burst forth with his condemnation of Paul. Daryawesh was the tallest of the four and stout. Imperiously, he looked down at Paul.

In a calmer voice than Itamar's, but still full of anger, the Jew hissed, "I agree with the teachers from Jerusalem who are wise in restating to us that our works are essential for salvation from God. We are respected by the Romans and have their consent to recognize Judaism as a favored religion. Without this approval we would be persecuted, and possibly executed. The Romans are very tolerant of our religion and we do not want to jeopardize our good fortune for one such as you. Claudius exiled us from Rome, but now mighty Nero has allowed us to return. We will not forsake his kindness."

When Itamar finished his spiel, he looked at his cohorts and together they officiously turned and headed towards the door of the office. The remaining men readily opened a path for them, like the parting of the Red Sea. The angry four religious zealots did not exchange looks with anyone as they marched out.

When the furious four had departed, the rest of the assembly looked at one another with mixed dismay, disregard, and shock. Their murmuring began immediately; but soon they settled down, and turned their focus on Paul. Lucilius also looked attentively at Paul. He was eager to hear a heated retort to the men's accusations. But Paul's mannerisms remained composed. Christ's calm ambassador gestured with extended arms, palms down, to soothe the emotions of the gathering.

Confidently, he addressed the issues brought forth by the combatants. "Truly, I say to you, these men have succumbed to the Judaizers who are intent on keeping all Jews in bondage. Was it not the prophet Isaiah who said, 'Lord, who has believed our report?' Those who have believed have done so by faith. Faith comes by hearing, and hearing by the word of God."

When Paul finished this part of his rebuttal, he paused to reflect on the truth of the Scriptures he had just quoted for them all. The men nodded their heads in thoughtful assent. Paul's eyes moved from man to man, meeting each man's gaze in a personal acknowledgment of their presence. "Moses has written in Deuteronomy, 'I will move you to anger by a foolish nation.' And to Israel He says through His prophet Isaiah, 'All day long I have stretched out My hands to a disobedient and contrary people.'

"My Jewish brethren, I say, has God cast away His people? Certainly not! For I also am an Israelite, of the seed of Abraham, of the tribe of Benjamin. God has not cast away His people whom He foreknew!"

Paul held out his hand to the Gentile elders and succinctly boomed, "Through the stumbling of the Jews, salvation has come to the Gentiles! Because of this stumbling you have been grafted like an olive branch into the tree. Now stand by faith! And do not get haughty over your blessing. Continue in His goodness. Otherwise you will be cut off. Do not be ignorant of God's mystery."

The ambassador paused and swallowed hard before he finished. "I beseech you, brethren, that you present your bodies as a living sacrifice; holy, acceptable to God, which is your reasonable service. Do not be conformed to this world, but be transformed by the renewing of your mind, that you may prove what is that good and acceptable and perfect will of God."

Christ's chosen mentor gave out a long, soft sigh. Everyone present could hear it, and they felt the genuine desperate imploring of his heart. Lucilius saw more. He saw a fatigued man, and grabbed the apostle gently by the arm, guiding him to sit on the corner of the desk. Hevel took notice of Paul's condition and addressed his colleagues, "We have much to contemplate and to meditate on. It is time we return to our homes."

That concluded the meeting, but everyone knew in their hearts they would return for more mentoring. Probably not in a large group, but certainly individually. This unpleasant confrontation had solidified in their hearts their need to diligently implement the teaching Paul gave through his epistles, as well as their need for his personal admonishment now that he was in Rome.

Hevel and Teman remained behind after the other church elders left. Paul addressed them in a soft voice, "I'm grateful you have remained, my brethren. I wish to speak with you about these four critics who are following perdition. The issue of their leadership is most important."

Teman jumped in with his commentary, "I've known two of these men for quite some time. Itamar has made no attempt to silence the Judaizers when they first infiltrated his group. He has aligned with Gershom, and together they both have openly chastised the converted Gentiles for not becoming circumcised. In addition, they rebuke these same Gentiles for eating pork."

Paul had moved around his desk to sit down in his chair. As Teman spoke, God's ambassador placed his elbows on the desk and rested his chin on his clasped hands.

Teman regarded the intensity in Paul's eyes as he spoke to him, "Several of these Gentiles have approached me about this false teaching. They are quite concerned and confused about their salvation in Christ." Teman's voice clearly conveyed sadness and frustration.

Hevel looked at Teman, and when he realized the converted Gentile was finished, he addressed Paul, "I've had experience with Anat and Daryawesh, also, as they are close to my group. I have personally met with them and pleaded that they would banish these Judaizers from spreading filth to their groups. They cursed and scolded me, then dusted their sandals in front of me."

Fire began emanating from their mentor's eyes. Lucilius also took notice of Paul's unhappy demeanor. He was very curious how the detainee could get so worked up about gods and religion. As a Roman, there were many gods to worship. He carefully inched his way closer to Paul's side. He did not want to miss anything—not only for his own benefit, but also for an accurate report to Flavius.

Paul waited a moment after hearing the testimony of his two brothers in Christ. He arched an eyebrow and quietly said, "We all must give an account of ourselves to God. Therefore, let us not condemn these men; but rather resolve this issue to the glory of God."

Hevel and Teman received the caution against condemnation, and agreed with their mentor to commit the issue and their actions to a resolution that would be in harmony with God's way.

Paul grasped his outer garment's shoulder with his hand and solemnly declared, "It is obvious these four men must be removed from the position of authority that they hold in the church. They are not worthy to be Christ's shepherds. Their faith has been eroded by their greater desire to hold Rome's favor. I would personally go to each of these men's group meetings and settle this matter, just as was done five years ago with the church in Galatia. Because of my confinement here I cannot do this. This needs to be addressed before each man's entire group."

Again, Hevel and Teman were in agreement with Paul's words. Both moved closer to Paul in anticipation of hearing his plan. "Therefore, Hevel, you must go to Anat and Daryawesh's next group meeting. Teman, you do the same with Itamar and Gershom. Be bold. State these men have been removed from their leadership position by the authority given me from Christ Jesus."

Hevel and Teman's eyes widened as they heard Paul's decision. "Take Luke or Aristarchus with you," he continued. "Tell the group that this is not a dictate from me, a mere man, but is instruction from God's Holy Spirit, who guides according to His truth, not according to the preferences and whims of men. Warn them. Should anyone continue to follow these men, they will be disobedient to God and subject to His correction. They will suffer consequences as our forefathers did during their journey to the Promised Land."

This time, Hevel and Teman looked at each other. They realized the severity of the problem with the purveyors of falsehood and deceit. They kept silent, waiting for Paul to finish his instructions to them.

"No doubt, there will be some who choose to follow these deceivers. Do them no harm and let them go. I turn them over to themselves and the devil. Choose replacements for these four men and have each one visit me here that I may instruct them."

Paul stood and leaned across the desk to give his final words, "Should no replacement be found, combine the groups with your own. Address this issue with your people and make sure they understand the truth. We cannot let the devil gain a foothold here. God's work is being done and it must continue."

The dedicated ambassador of Christ walked around his desk and gave each man a traditional blessing with a kiss on each cheek. Hevel and Teman thanked Paul for his guidance and assured him they would carry out his directive. Together they left with an increased desire to protect the faith and teachings of Jesus, their Messiah and Lord.

Lucilius watched Paul after the men had departed. The detainee's fire and intensity became concentration, then showed a sense of peace. He informed his guard he wanted some time alone in his bedroom to pray. This was the one room in the entire townhouse where Paul could enjoy privacy. Lucilius did not object. He was glad for the interlude. It would give him time to collect his thoughts for Flavius.

Chapter 10

While Paul remained secluded in his bedroom, praying and meditating, the normal afternoon shift change took place and an eager Lucilius quickly moved toward Flavius' office in Caesar's palace. In the same wing of the palace was the Praetorian Guard's barracks. This was very convenient for the loyal guard because he did not have to waste time traveling to give his daily reports. It also allowed him to report more accurately while the events of his shift were still fresh in his mind.

He felt confident about the details of his daily report, and strode purposefully into Flavius' outer office to announce his presence to the seated secretary.

Flavius employed a scribe to attend the debriefing with Lucilius. Having scribes take down the reports was Flavius' idea. He knew full well the frailties of the human mind. One of his concerns was keeping his soldiers from becoming emotionally involved with the detainee. When giving their respective reports, the guards focused more on factual details and less on emotions.

The scribe was accurate and quick about writing down what was important pertaining to Paul's case. "Lucilius, have a seat and we can begin while the events of your shift are fresh in your mind," said Flavius as he gestured toward a chair near the scribe. The scribe had parchment and quill pen ready.

The centurion commander let Lucilius tell without interruption what he had witnessed throughout his shift. Despite remaining silent, Flavius at times reacted to portions of Lucilius' depiction. It was obvious to the guard his commander was mentally analyzing the events of the day. Observing Flavius' mannerisms did not deter him from focusing on his assignment.

"Your report is well done, Lucilius," stated the centurion from his seat behind his small desk. "You are sure that during this meeting Paul made no mention of any action on the part of these so-called church elders that would fall within the definition of treason or intent to incite sedition?"

"I'm quite sure, Commander. It was obvious Paul was at times very angry with the actions of the four men who opposed him. Yet he remained in control of himself. Afterwards, he was very direct about what Hevel and Teman were to do. The main effect of this surprise development seemed to make Paul down-hearted more than anything."

Flavius arched an eyebrow. "Was there any mention of how long before these replacement elders would be selected?"

Lucilius shrugged his shoulders, "There was nothing said by anyone, but I'm confident in saying this process will begin very soon."

Flavius stood up and slowly walked about his office. Lucilius sat and watched every movement the commander made. It wasn't long before the superior centurion stood in front of Lucilius' chair and looked down his long torso at the guard. "Go, and have your meal, and then relax. We are done here." Lucilius quickly got up from his chair and left to do as instructed. He realized how hungry he was. The scribe informed Flavius he would make copies of the report and Flavius would receive his copy the next day.

At the initial meeting of Flavius, Cleatus, and Seneca, it was decided that daily reports from the guards would be copied in triplicate. It could be time-consuming, but Seneca secured the services of Rome's most qualified scribes to do the transcribing. Normally, official reports were not long, only a single page. In Paul's case, the high crime of treason and intent meant some reports could be two pages.

In this way, everyone would be well informed of all that transpired with the prisoner of Rome. It would also allow each main decision-maker to devise his own plan and strategy for determining if Paul was guilty of treason or the intent of treason. This would afford the tribunes the proper usage of time to complete their report for Nero when he returned from Athens in the spring.

Flavius watched the scribe leave his office. Deep in thought, the centurion began to pace. He knew there would be a meeting with the other tribunes and he wanted to be well prepared.

As the centurion paced like a lion, Paul emerged from his bedroom and went directly into his workshop. There, he surveyed the template given him by Antonius. He closely examined and felt the different leathers to be used in the test pair of military boots. The skilled cobbler quickly set about creating his assigned project.

Draba carefully observed Paul's actions. He was curious about this Jew and his ability to produce a quality pair of boots. Halfway through the project, Paul stopped and looked up at his inquisitive guard. "Draba, how inconsiderate of me. I've been absorbed in this project and I've forgotten the time. We must share our evening meal. I'm sure you and the other guards are famished. I know I'm ready for nourishment."

Draba wondered if the engrossed cobbler had heard his stomach rumbling like a storm beyond the horizon. Indeed, he was hungry. When the meal was served in the dining room, Draba took advantage of the situation to inquire how Paul came to be a skilled cobbler. The guard was personally curious, but mainly was seeking information he could pass on to Flavius.

Paul described how, as a young Pharisee in training under the guidance of the eminent Gamaliel, he learned the craft of both tent making and cobbling. It was part of the requirement for all Pharisees that they be able to support themselves whenever the need arose. "There were several options available to me, but after experimenting with a few, I chose what I believed God gave me the talent to do. Years of practice have allowed me to turn this talent into a skill by which I can better serve Almighty God," the prisoner explained.

Draba was pleased with himself for obtaining this detail and felt Flavius would appreciate his thoroughness. He thought again that perhaps it would aid his chances for a promotion.

Satisfied with the meal, Paul announced, "Draba, it is time I finished my endeavor. The meetings have taken up much of my time, and I know Antonius will expect the boots to be completed when he comes tomorrow. I know you must remain close to my side, so bring with you any food you wish to eat."

Draba grabbed a piece of bread and a few dates in his large hands and followed Paul back to the converted workshop. He was very interested to find out how long it would take this Jew to complete the boots. The dubious guard was surprised how quickly and efficiently Paul's hands maneuvered the leather. Within two hours the boots were completed.

Paul handed the finished pair to his guard. "Here, Draba, inspect these boots and please tell me how they match up to your expectations." Draba carefully inspected the boots. To his shock, they were far better than he expected. The stitching was tight and close. The leathers were intermingled in a functional and effective manner.

The guard was well aware how important boots were to the foot soldier. Personally, Draba had cursed many a cobbler for the inferior work he was forced to wear, especially in battle. These boots were vastly better than those he currently wore. "These would do well for any infantryman. He could march in them and effectively battle an enemy," he admitted.

Paul beamed as Draba returned the new boots. He noticed Draba comparing the new footwear to the template given by Antonius. "I cannot help but notice that you have changed the design from the one created by Antonius. Why did you do this? Antonius expects you to make them just like his template indicates."

With a twinkle in his eye, Paul answered, "During my journeys, I've made boots for Roman soldiers. They informed me of issues with what they wore and I took their input and devised a different template. The soldiers received them well, so I retained that process."

Draba looked up from the template and warned him, "Still, Paul, I tend to believe Antonius will not be pleased with this change. He is prideful of his work and probably will be jealous of what you have done. It may not go well for you and he will reject employing you."

Paul acknowledged this possibility and did not create an argument with the guard. "You could be right, Draba. In any event, we will find out Antonius' reaction tomorrow."

Draba countered, "Should Antonius reject you, I still would like you to make a pair of your boots for me. I am in need of sturdy footwear."

God's cobbler looked down at how Draba was shod. He could see loose stitching and heavy wear and knew the guard was not comfortable in his boots. "It would be my pleasure to make you a new pair. After Antonius' inspection, you may be my first customer."

The next day Antonius personally arrived to deal with the Jew and to see if his confident claims of being a cobbler were legitimate. Antonius had twenty years in the craft and had a solid reputation with both military men and civilians living in Rome. He was the main supplier of boots and tents for Rome's army. This, and his affiliation with Aelia exporting boots, sandals, and leisure footwear throughout the empire, had made him wealthy.

Aelia had become his benefactor shortly after he opened for business. Her astute business sense led to their partnership, without which he probably would not have attained his current status. He was indeed grateful to her, but also arrogantly prideful, believing that he could sustain and grow his business without her intervention. He felt he was doing Aelia a favor in dealing with her new tenant—this accused Jew.

Antonius did not like Jews, and viewed them as imitators of work initiated by Romans. He would be open-minded about Paul, but at the same time very critical of his work. He wanted only qualified cobblers working for him.

He walked the entire distance from his shop to Aelia's rented townhouse to see Paul. He enjoyed the exercise and the opportunity to use muscles he ordinarily did not use while working in his trade. The fall air was pleasant and he breathed deeply. The soft cool breeze relaxed him. Arriving at the front door of the townhouse, Antonius took in one final deep breath of fresh air and knocked on the door.

Junus recognized the cobbler from his previous visit, and announced his arrival. Both Paul and Lucilius came to greet the visitor. Draba was disappointed he would not be on shift when this important meeting would take place. He would have to wait for his rotated shift to learn the outcome.

Antonius looked skeptical as he met Paul. He had no smile of greeting; in fact, his mouth was tightly closed in a deliberate effort to intimidate. He was all business and did not want to waste his time on friendly conversation, especially with a man he did not believe capable of meeting his standards of work.

Even Lucilius detected Antonius' attitude and was impressed that it did not affect Paul's response. The prisoner led his prospective employer to the makeshift workshop.

Without a word, Paul handed Antonius the finished pair of boots. Lucilius noticed an immediate change in Antonius' attitude. The cobbler businessman was impressed. His eyes widened as he inspected the boots. He scrutinized the stitching and ran his fingers around the stitches and the transitions from one type of leather to another.

He opened the boots as much as possible and visually dissected the inner portions of the boots. He then compared them to

112

determine how well they matched each other. Next he evaluated the difference between his original template and Paul's design. His back stiffened. Coldly, the cobbler stated the obvious, "Your design does not match that of my template." Turning to face Paul, Antonius squared his shoulders and crossed his arms across his puffed up chest. "Why did you deviate from my design? I specifically stated you were to follow my design only."

Lucilius was taken aback at Antonius' reaction. Earlier, the guard had viewed Paul's finished product and could determine how well made they were. He even lauded Paul for constructing a boot that was better than what currently was available from Antonius and other cobblers in Rome. He was anxious for Paul's answer.

"There is nothing wrong with your design, Antonius. In my experience, making boots for Roman soldiers during my travels, I took their complaints and requests and ended up with what you have in your hands."

Paul's answer did not suggest conceit or insult, but were merely the facts presented in a quiet voice. He added, "I believe my design will be well received by your clients and enable you to sell more product than other cobblers."

Lucilius scrutinized Antonius' changing demeanor. His lips seemed to pucker and one eye closed as he contemplated Paul's words. As he thought about Paul's assessment, he slowly ran his finger around the boots he still held in his hands. Lucilius could only wonder what was about to come forth from Antonius.

"Your point is well made, Jew. Truly, I did not expect you to create this type of quality work. You are an exception to what I've experienced with other Jews who say they are cobblers. My irritation at your deviation from my instructions is appeased by your work and your words. I am not opposed to your design, because I agree with your assessment that it will result in more work and will profit my business."

Antonius placed the boots down on Paul's workbench with a solid thump. Lucilius refrained from revealing his amusement by moistening his lips and affecting an unconcerned attitude. He was pleased that the obstinate businessman could see value in aligning with the house prisoner. With a changed attitude, Antonius began to discuss the terms he would make with Paul, "It is customary that my employees receive two denarii per day. In addition, they are required to complete four pairs of boots per week. Should either their production or the quality of their work not meet my standard, they are terminated. This is my offer to you."

Lucilius noted the sternness in Antonius and his resolute demeanor. His eyes shifted to see how Paul would respond. God's cobbler looked directly at Antonius and countered with equal resolve, "Your terms are not acceptable to me, Antonius. I have knowledge that skilled craftsmen in Rome receive three denarii per day for their accomplishments. Further, I do not desire to be your employee but an affiliate assigned to produce product for you."

Antonius could not help but cough at Paul's refusal. He listened stiffly while Paul finished his negotiation, "My proposal to you is that we agree upon a certain number of finished boots to be in your possession at the end of each week. So long as the quality meets the expectations of the customer, we shall continue. As payment, you will render to me three denarii per completed pair of boots. This still allows you to charge sufficiently to make a profit."

Lucilius had not expected Paul to make such an offer. The guard knew Antonius was not accustomed to being treated in this manner. But Paul was a skilled cobbler who would bring plenty of business into Antonius' shop, especially from the military. Lucilius also believed any member of Rome's army would pay additional denarii for such quality as Paul made. He held his breath, waiting for Antonius' answer to Paul's proposal.

In a tone of rejection, Antonius mocked, "Surely, you are not serious, Jew! My offer to you is well within the guidelines of being fair. You are wrongheaded in your demands!" The defiant businessman waved a hand, pretending to be insulted. He scoffed, "How do you propose to acquire customers while you are confined to this townhouse? You cannot leave, set up a shop, or otherwise make yourself known here in Rome." He snorted, "Without my assistance you will fail."

Paul remained placid. He tranquilly sat down in his work chair and patiently looked up at the flushed Roman businessman. Coolly, he again countered Antonius' assessment, "Antonius, while it is true I must remain confined solely inside this townhouse while I await my appeal to Caesar, I am not without resources. Already, guards assigned here have requested boots similar to these. They have stated my work exceeds what you offer them. In addition, my brethren can solicit business for me. It will not take long for word of my handiwork to spread and there will be sufficient business for me to pay my rent to Aelia. In fact, once

114

she becomes aware of my ability, she will offer my services to her clients. You do not hold the exclusive position you perceive."

Lucilius was impressed with Paul's response and how he was firm without being angry with Antonius. Without turning his head, the guard moved his eyes to see the effect of Paul's response on Antonius.

The overconfident Roman's face had paled. He no longer moved with swagger. His face revealed the setback he was feeling. He glared at Paul, looked aside for a brief moment, then looked again at his competitor.

In a reluctant, conciliatory admission that to Lucilius sounded almost like a complaint, Antonius avoided admitting the defeat he keenly felt. "Rather than fight you, Paul, I shall agree to your terms." Seizing the offer Paul originally made, Antonius added, "I shall require a minimum of five completed pairs of boots per week. More would be appreciated, if you can handle such a workload." He paused to judge whether this would be adequate to seal the deal. Then, to soothe his wounded pride, he warned, "And mind you, Paul, there shall be no drop in quality, otherwise our agreement is void."

The amused guard looked quickly at Paul who remained placidly seated behind his workbench. In an undisturbed voice, God's cobbler proclaimed his agreement to the terms. To seal the agreement, Paul stood up and approached his new business partner.

They grabbed each other's hands and placed their other arms around each other, coming together in a brief embrace. This sealed the contract. Each man stood by his word. This was a show of honor and respect.

"I shall have one of my assistants bring you materials tomorrow. There is much demand and we must not squander this opportunity."

With that, Antonius quickly turned and left Paul alone with Lucilius who said, "I'm glad you two were able to settle your differences. Do you really believe you can develop your cobbling business in Rome while confined to this house?"

Paul casually responded, "Lucilius, it was Almighty God who has blessed me with the ability to be a cobbler. My faith and trust is in Him. He provides all my needs. He has blessed me in the past and I am humbled to know that He will provide for me while I'm detained here in Rome."

Lucilius tilted his head to one side with a wondering expression. He could not understand Paul's adamant loyalty and worship for this god he often referenced. But that was of less interest to him at the moment. He surveyed the wear on his boots, and wiggled his toes, noting the tender spots in his feet that were beginning to protest the age of his footwear. He looked forward to having a new comfortable, stout pair of boots from the skilled prisoner he was guarding and spying on.

## Chapter 11

When Draba returned for his adjusted afternoon shift, he found the detainee diligently working on a pair of boots in his makeshift workshop. In his mind, Draba bemoaned how the Jews' adherence to their confusing religion had created such difficulties between them and Rome. Despite his dislike for Jews, Draba respected Paul's cobbler skills. The Roman guard was pleased an agreement had been reached between Paul and Antonius.

Christ's cobbler greeted him cheerfully, "Ah, Draba, it's good to see you again. As you can see, Antonius sent over a supply of work to be done. It feels good to use the skills Almighty God has blessed me with." Draba noted the pile of different leathers surrounding Paul. He was surprised at how jovial and genuinely happy this prisoner of Rome seemed.

"I shall remain by the doorway so as not to disturb your work," Draba said. His statement was short and unemotional. Humming, Paul looked down at his work and set about creating a product that would glorify Christ Jesus. Having learned that his prisoner was not at risk for escape, Draba sat in a chair and observed the detainee's focus as he worked the different leathers. It was clear to Draba that Paul was enjoying his task.

An hour later, Junus announced to Paul that he had a couple of visitors. Draba immediately stood at attention and assumed his defensive alert status. Paul looked up from his work to see Luke and Aristarchus standing in the doorway of his converted workshop.

"My brethren, welcome to my dwelling! It is a pleasure to see you both!" Paul rose from his work chair and went around to greet his spiritual colleagues, "Come, let us go onto the patio and have some afternoon refreshment. I'm eager to hear what you are doing."

Once they were seated and offered some wine, Aristarchus was the first to tell Paul of the developments in replacing the four false teachers, "I've assisted Hevel, and we believe there are two fine men worthy of the responsibilities of being elders to their groups. Is it possible for you to meet with them tomorrow?"

Paul thought briefly and replied, "Tomorrow afternoon will be fine for me. As you can see, my leatherwork is demanding and I must devote the morning hours to accomplishing my projects."

Aristarchus was delighted. "I shall notify Hevel as soon as we leave here. These men are anxious to meet with you."

Aristarchus nodded at Luke, inviting the doctor to inform Paul of his news, "My brother Teman and I have also interviewed several men who meet the requirements of being a church elder. Similar to Aristarchus, we have decided on two men we believe you should question. Since tomorrow is taken, can our men come here the next day?"

Paul was pleased. "Yes, they can, but again it must be in the afternoon." Draba became very alert. This was exactly what he had been instructed to notify his superiors about. Inwardly, the guard was elated to relay this development. Unfortunately, he would be on the morning shift and unable to overhear the proceedings on either day. He would have to confer with Lucilius to obtain the details of the two meetings.

Luke informed his ministry companion his days were full of attending to the needs of the church members in the northern part of the city. "Word has funneled to the brethren about our arrival here, and many requests are coming to me for medical needs. This also gives me an opportunity to canvass the attitudes of the people concerning the impact of your epistle."

Paul listened intently and asked Luke questions pertaining to the people's reaction to his epistle. Draba strained to remember all the details he was hearing as he made mental notes about the epistle and its contents. No doubt, this could provide valuable information concerning the investigation into the prisoner's charge of treason and intent.

After discussing at length, Aristarchus brought the encounter to a close, "Paul, it is getting late, and I must return to my family. We have made great progress here today. I must hurry to Hevel to ensure there is ample time to notify our candidates of their appointment time with you tomorrow."

They stood up together, and Luke and Aristarchus left. Paul returned to his workshop along with his constant shadow, Draba.

Conforming to Paul's request, Aristarchus and Hevel arrived at mid-afternoon with their two candidates, Ehud and Benaiah. Despite reassurances from Aristarchus and Luke, the two candidates were noticeably nervous. They knew about Christ's emissary, including his unwavering high standards.

The Roman officials dutifully carried out their communications with one another. Junus allowed the group into the house and announced their arrival to Lucilius who was expecting them. Draba had informed his Guard cohort about the meeting and Flavius had given Lucilius specific instructions concerning this conference.

Paul took his four guests into the dining room where five chairs were arranged in a semi-circle. Lucilius stood close to his assigned detainee. To reduce the nervousness of the two candidates, Paul had requested some refreshment—sweetened wine, fruit, and honey, with bread for dipping.

Christ's apostle initiated the meeting by cordially asking general questions of each candidate before officially interviewing them. He did not want to frighten them unnecessarily. Paul's sociable demeanor quickly relaxed the nervous men as they chatted together. With a congenial atmosphere achieved, Paul began his questioning in earnest. He chose to interview Ehud first and requested Benaiah to wait in the courtyard until it was his turn. Confused, Benaiah did as instructed.

"Ehud, please tell me, who is Christ Jesus to you?" Ehud was an older man, born a Jew, and converted to following Christ while in Jerusalem during Pentecost. He quickly responded, "Christ is my personal Savior and is my all-in-all. My entire life is devoted first to Him."

Lucilius was listening carefully and making mental notes as Flavius expected of him. The spy-guard closely observed Ehud's body language and Paul's. "Thank you, Ehud. Tell me about your experience on the day of Pentecost in Jerusalem."

Ehud beamed at the request. He loved telling about his experience. "I'd heard about this Nazarene, Jesus, his teachings and miraculous healings. I was curious. When I heard one of his disciples named Peter address the large crowd, I was riveted on every word. Here was an uneducated fisherman saying things about Jesus that amazed me. I couldn't explain it at the time, but I felt a strong inner desire to say yes to Peter's appeal to acknowledge Jesus as my Lord and Savior."

Lucilius found it easy to concentrate on Ehud's explanation and could picture the size of the crowd and the impassioned speech of the man named Peter. It revived the guard's memory of a time when he had heard a stirring speech by Cleatus before a major battle.

"The more Peter talked, the stronger these inner promptings became, until I found myself earnestly desiring all he spoke of. Immediately, I felt something come over me. It was a peaceful sensation, but also exhilarating, and I found myself weeping unexplainable tears of joy! I felt embarrassed until I looked around and saw others were doing the same."

The presenter paused, and swept away the dampness in his eyes as he relived his tale. He took a sip of the sweetened wine to wash down the lump in his throat before he continued, "For a while afterward, this extraordinary feeling of joy and exhilaration remained in me. One of Peter's assistants talked to me about it and said it was God's Holy Spirit letting me know I was a new creation in Christ. I realized I needed more of his teaching, so I stayed an extra day talking with him."

Ehud looked at Paul who showed keen interest in what the converted Jew had to say. Feeling comfortable with Paul's attentive silence, Ehud continued, "When I returned to Rome, I meditated on this teaching. Once back here, I spoke with the rabbi of my synagogue. He surprised me by becoming very angry! He told me that Jesus was a blasphemer against Jewish law and tradition and that I should not follow any of his teaching."

Paul then injected a comment. "Obviously, you did not heed the rabbi's plea," he smiled. "What did you then do?"

Ehud briefly looked at Hevel who also smiled as he went on, "I told the rabbi I must follow Jesus. So he removed me from participation in the synagogue! Soon, I heard about Hevel and his group of Christ followers. I went to him and he introduced me to Anat and his group. Anat was closer to where I live, so I joined his group of Christ followers."

Christ's emissary leaned slightly forward and with an intense look for his next question, "What was your reaction to the false teachers who infiltrated Anat's assembly?"

Without hesitation, Ehud sadly shook his head and replied, "At first I was shocked. Then I became angry because Anat promoted these men and their teaching. When I questioned Anat and these teachers about their deviance, I was rebuked. I went to Hevel, and since then I have attended his assembly."

Leaning on his knees, Paul put his fingers to his lips and surveyed Ehud's face. He softly asked, "Do you believe you have the spiritual wisdom and ability to get Anat's assembly back to following only Christ Jesus' teachings?"

All eyes in the room focused on Ehud and waited for his reply. Almost before Paul had finished his question, the converted Jew pronounced, "Absolutely. I've maintained contact with many in Anat's assembly and they are ready to take whatever steps are necessary to eliminate all the false teachers from the assembly, including Anat.

"I've met with many of these people and stressed that as new creations in Christ, we don't need rigid law-following to be one of His followers. All we need to do is follow His clear guidance and live our lives obediently as He directs."

Paul exhibited no signs of agreement or disagreement with Ehud's commentary. Instead, Christ's ambassador gave a challenging question to the candidate, "Tell me Ehud, as a converted Jew, do you believe Gentiles who accept Christ as Savior should become circumcised?"

Again the candidate did not hesitate in his answer, "Absolutely not. To do so would relegate personal relationship with Christ to mere observance of Jewish tradition—which rejects Jesus as Lord. Neither circumcision nor uncircumcision has anything to do with faith and following Christ. He has made us free from the laws and observances of our forefathers. Christ Himself taught this."

Hevel was pleased with Ehud's definitive answer. His posture relaxed when he heard his important statement; it revealed Ehud's clear understanding of the new life that his faith in Jesus had brought to him. The senior elder of the church in Rome fixed his eyes on his mentor Paul who decided to ask another question regarding the practice of faith. "One last question, Ehud. If you were invited to a Gentile's home to eat and this person was not saved by God's grace and mercy, would you eat pork if it were served?"

This time, Hevel's eyes quickly darted back to Ehud. "Again I say, Paul, this would take following Christ's precepts and not necessarily aligning with Jewish tradition. It is far better for me to show this seeker Christ's love and compassion than to adhere to man's rules of religion."

Paul lifted his elbows from his knees and leaned back in his chair. He continued looking at Ehud and smiled happily. Then he said to Hevel, "My brother in Christ, I find no reason why Ehud should not become the elder of Anat's assembly. It is clear that Ehud has received the new life Christ Jesus promised to those who put their trust in Him and forsake man's ideas of religious observances and rules. However, I believe it is necessary for Ehud to receive further training both from you as well as myself."

Ehud was pleased. He grinned with pure joy and let out an audible sigh of relief. Paul and Hevel chuckled quietly, understanding the release of his tension. His earlier nervousness about answering Paul's questions honestly and in a forthright manner had been left behind as he answered with deep conviction. After his interview, Ehud felt the tightness in his body relax; but his earnest considerations during the interview left him feeling oddly fatigued now that it was over.

"Would you wait in the courtyard and have Benaiah come for his session?" Ehud nodded and left the dining room a bit wobbly. Before Benaiah entered the room, Paul quickly stated to Hevel, "You have done well in selecting this candidate. We shall see how Benaiah answers my probes."

Benaiah was nearly fifteen years younger than Ehud, yet had exhibited leadership traits that inspired Hevel to list him as a candidate for the important position of replacement leader of Daryawesh's assembly. Since Benaiah was also a converted Jew, Paul asked him the same questions he had asked Ehud.

The candidate indicated he had accepted Christ as his Savior based on initial discussions with a member of Hevel's assembly. "I witnessed a difference in these men, how they conducted themselves, as well as their attitudes." At that point, Benaiah looked at Hevel. "I sought out Hevel, who answered more of my questions. I decided to accept Christ as Lord and was directed to Daryawesh's assembly because it was within the boundaries of my home."

Paul became concerned with several of Benaiah's answers as well as non-answers to the remaining questions. In response to the circumcision issue, the candidate was firm in saying that anyone who accepts Christ as Savior must be circumcised because Jesus was a Jew and had been circumcised. "How else can you truly follow your Lord if you don't do as He did?"

Lucilius was confused by the different answers given to Paul's question. Since he did not understand the issue, the guard paid more attention to what Paul said. Lucilius felt this was the best way to sort through the information needed for his report.

Benaiah was also adamant about not eating pork under any circumstances. "To do so would violate my family history. I must honor their memory and keep the long-standing laws of our forefathers."

With that answer, Paul ended the discussion. He looked at Benaiah and softly rendered his decision, "At this time, Benaiah, I do not believe you are the right person to lead Daryawesh's assembly." The candidate was stunned by Paul's rejection. Quickly, his eyes darted towards Hevel seeking assistance. Hevel did not return the candidate's glance. Benaiah remained a moment, staring blankly down at the floor. Silently, he got up and left the room.

Hevel was first to comment on the rejection, "Paul, I am surprised at what we just heard, and I certainly concur with your decision. Benaiah has hidden his inner feelings about these issues from myself and others, as well. I do have a third candidate I can bring to you later this week."

Paul's face showed disappointment, but his words to Hevel were reassuring. "Deception is often difficult to discern, Hevel. It takes some time to let go of long-held beliefs, even if they are wrong ones. It is good that Benaiah's error came out during this time with him. Bring your other candidate here within the next three days. We must not tarry in replacing Daryawesh."

The elder statesmen for Christ exchanged farewell embraces with Paul and left the townhouse. Lucilius took the opportunity to ask Paul for clarification on questions he had concerning the two interrogations. Paul was patient in answering his questions. Lucilius found himself unexpectedly being drawn closer to the man he was assigned to guard and possibly kill should he make any attempt to escape or cause sedition.

The next day, Teman brought his two candidates Gallus and Nonus to the townhouse for Paul's scrutiny. Each was a converted Gentile and very active in giving the gospel of life and doing good works. Teman was confident Paul would find both men suitable for the vacated leadership positions.

Again, the meeting was held in Paul's dining room. The host-inquisitor did his best to make the two men feel at ease for the process of selecting replacements for Gershom and Itamar.

Paul selected Gallus for the first interview. The converted Gentile had moved with his family while he was a youth. They came from Britannia to Rome where his father could more successfully operate his business as a blacksmith. Gallus had initially accepted the Roman culture and its belief in many gods.

The first question posed to the husky blacksmith was the same Paul had asked the previous candidates, "Who is Christ Jesus to you?"

To Paul's surprise, Gallus hung his head as he responded, "I was a heathen on the path to hell when Christ convicted me of my errant ways. He revealed to me my dark heart. I felt dirty. I was cheating customers and being volatile towards my wife and children."

Gallus lifted his head and looked at Paul earnestly, "How I thank Christ every day for His compassion towards me! His love for my soul created a yearning so deep within me that I cried out to Him and asked Him to be my Savior. Christ is the Son of Almighty God! I have surrendered my heart to Him alone. I am a changed man."

Paul showed no emotion after hearing Gallus' life-changing testimony, although he was already feeling a spiritual kinship with this ardent believer. He proceeded with the remainder of his inquiries. "At any time have you felt the need or the desire to attend a synagogue or to adhere to Jewish mandates?"

"The Jews do not like Gentiles, especially those who claim Christ as Lord and Savior! Jews who know that I'm a follower of Christ turn their backs on me and will have nothing to do with me. I'm not angry towards them for this. I'm only sad they let religious traditions get in the way of living their life as Christ desires them to do."

Paul continued to be unreadable by his onlookers, showing no reaction or expectation. He placed his elbow on the arm of his chair and rested his head on his thumb and index finger. He posed a new question, "You are a blacksmith carrying on a successful business as your father did. Would you create any kind of idol for a customer to worship?"

Lucilius was startled by this question and became even more attentive. As a soldier, he had worshiped Mithras, the so-called god of the military and protector in battle. Roman soldiers often had carvings of the mythical god in their rooms. Sometimes they would carry small carvings of Mithras attached to their body, even in battle situations.

With a firm voice, Gallus stated, "I would not. I would merely tell the person I don't make things of religious nature. I know there is great risk in doing this because that individual could accuse me of violating Roman law. Despite any potential punishment, I cannot, in my conscience before Christ, build an idol for anyone. I have rid myself of all idols, and it would grieve me to contribute to someone else's deception and sin against God."

The Roman guard's eyes widened at this response. Rome accepted many religions and carvings and statues of their multitude of gods. They were not only common in the city, but among cultures that extended beyond Rome to all parts of the empire.

Rome required allegiance from those under its rule, including observation of their religious beliefs. Unwillingness to honor Rome's gods could be physically and economically painful for any violator. Lucilius was impressed with Gallus' resolve and wondered if he would have the same courage if he were in Gallus' position.

Paul again refrained from showing any kind of personal reaction to Gallus' statement of faith. Instead, he asked the candidate another question, "Gallus, how would you lead the assembly whose leadership has been removed?"

The heavy-set blacksmith scratched his head of thick, dark hair. He stroked his chin while he pensively sorted through the many responsibilities and challenges he knew he would face. Then he looked directly into his inquisitor's eyes and said with a shrug, "I would do what I am already doing—working with each man to encourage and help him personally to obey Christ's teachings in every aspect of his life, both at home and in his chosen work. Be fair, compassionate, showing kindness, and letting everyone see that he is a follower of Christ."

Gallus paused to consider one more element before he continued, "I would personally hold each man accountable for his actions and would not be afraid to confront him on any issue. And like them, I would be held accountable for my own teaching, attitudes, and behavior, as well."

Paul let his hand drop to his side, thankful for the mature insightfulness of this candidate. He stood up from the table and approached the stout Gentile convert, opening his arms widely. He firmly embraced Gallus and declared, "I believe you can lead this group and keep them grounded in following Christ's direction."

Christ's ambassador put his hand on Gallus' strong muscled back. "Go now, and be about your business, Gallus. God bless you! Return soon, so we can discuss your leadership."

The blacksmith gave Paul his thanks for approving him for the elder position, and left with a heart full of joy. Paul smiled at Teman. "*This* man has the heart to serve Christ as elder of the assembly! But you must confer with him and teach him, as will I, while I'm here in Rome. Now, usher in Nonus."

Nonus was a short man with very strong arms and hands from years of working as a baker. A former slave from Gaul, his master granted his freedom just before his master died from complications associated with lung disease. As a freed slave, Nonus had remained in Rome where he met Teman. Within a year after their friendship began, Nonus accepted Christ as Savior. Repeatedly, he had exhibited a heart for helping others and often took freed slaves into his home to assist them in adjusting to life on their own.

In response to Paul's question about who Jesus was, to him, Nonus joyfully declared that Christ was His king and ruler of his heart. Contritely, he also admitted, "I mocked Him and persecuted those who claimed to be His followers. There was anger in my heart and I didn't really know the reason for it."

Nonus' head dropped a little, with his eyes still looking at Paul, searching for Paul's reaction. The apostle's kind face showed his understanding. He reassured the humbled convert, "I, too, persecuted Christ's followers and had a religious zealot's anger towards them. We share deep thankfulness for Christ's compassion and love for us."

The short, balding baker lifted his head and a smile lit up his round face. He nodded his acknowledgement of Paul's statement. "Every day, I remember Christ's grace in saving me and I sing a song of praise and thanksgiving for His mercy."

Lucilius noticed how all the candidates except Benaiah had the same positive, even joyful, tone of voice and their faces glowed as they spoke about this god named Jesus whom they revered. This was unusual to the guard. Normally in Roman conversations, they seldom spoke about their gods in this manner.

Paul continued with his interrogation of Nonus, "You are a freedman and a new creation in Christ Jesus. How would you deal with a situation should Rome require you to state where your allegance lies?"

Without any hesitation, Nonus replied, "I would clearly say that Christ is my King and as a follower of Him, I obey His commands first and Rome's second. I will adhere to Rome's laws so long as they do not conflict with Christ's teachings. I would do this even if it resulted in punishment to me, which would be likely. But Jesus Christ has given me everything! How can I deny Him to others?"

Lucilius was not prepared for this question or Nonus' answer. He knew this would be very important to Flavius and he was determined not to forget it. He realized his thoughts had been lulled into complacency by the long question and answer time in the interviews, and that he must be alert to such unexpected developments.

Paul asked another question, "Would you require your assembly to do the same?"

Nonus straightened in his chair before replying, "I would strongly remind the assembly that it is Christ Jesus who saved them from eternal damnation, and not Rome. They must focus on where they will spend eternity first. This life on earth is but a brief prelude to our eternal living. I see this as a test of faith and it is important not to fail Christ!"

Lucilius recoiled at Nonus' answer. Such fervent behavior was quite unusual for civilians. He felt he was learning much about these followers of this Christ. His interest was growing and he knew he would consult with Paul about this when they were alone.

The prisoner of Rome reached over the table, clasped Nonus' hands, and fervently pronounced, "Nonus, I believe you will serve our Lord well and with all your heart! Take over this assembly."

Nonus' eyes widened in surprise and he humbly thanked Paul for approving his position in the assembly, adding, "But Paul, I realize that it is Christ who has given me this position."

Teman realized the interview was over and the time was getting late, so he rose from his chair and said, "Nonus, congratulations! But it is now time for us to leave." Nonus turned his head to Teman and reluctantly stood up. Paul followed suit and hugged each man. Then the two newly appointed leaders left the townhouse with Teman, knowing they had been given an important responsibility to help further the kingdom of God.

Stretching his arms out wide, Paul grinned at his guard. "Lucilius, I'm sure you agree with me that it is time we had our evening meal. This has been a long but productive day, and I'm hungry!" The Roman guard completely agreed as he returned Paul's grin.

The two men had their meal in the courtyard patio. Later, Lucilius would give a most interesting report to his commander.

Chapter 12

The onset of autumn hit Rome with a cold rain on the day Hevel took Ahron to be interviewed by Paul. The dark, foreboding weather added to Ahron's uneasiness about meeting with the man who had rejected Benaiah. Ahron and Benaiah were friends and had often teamed with each other in spreading the good news about Christ. After Benaiah's rejection by Paul, Ahron was dubious concerning his own interview with Paul.

The apostle of Christ was consistent with his earlier efforts to help the candidate feel comfortable about the meeting. Ahron quickly relaxed, and the more he conversed with his interrogator, the more he respected and liked Christ's emissary.

When Paul asked Ahron who Christ was to him, the candidate joyfully proclaimed that Jesus was his Lord and Savior. Both Hevel and Paul could see and hear the level of his enthusiasm for his salvation and for the privilege he felt for being a servant to the Son of God.

Ahron earnestly explained how in every given situation, be it with a fellow follower of Christ or a lost soul, his focus was to carry out God's will and to let the other person see Christ through his words and actions. Ahron gave several examples of the impact and effect this had, and how in several cases it factored into a lost soul asking Christ to be his Savior.

Hevel was pleased to see that Ahron had overcome his anxiety towards Paul and the meeting. When Paul asked a key question concerning Ahron's approach to dealing with issues that would arise within his assembly, Hevel paid particular attention to Ahron's answer, "There is absolutely no place in any assembly for those who desire to instill legalism into Christ's teachings. Be they Jew or Gentile, the focus should be on serving Christ and not man or impersonal institutions. We must do all as unto the Lord, and not as men pleasers."

A deep sensation of relief came over Hevel. He felt that Paul would accept this man to be the replacement leader of one of the growing assemblies in Rome. Ahron had strong character, discernment and wisdom, and would not back away from any issue. He would confront any contention directly and without delay. Hevel was pleased how the Lord had guided him to select this younger man for the position of responsibility in God's church.

During the interview, Lucilius was focused more on Ahron's answers than on Paul's questions. It was clear that Paul had a pattern and the Roman guard could understand the reasoning behind Paul's methodology. When the examination was completed, Lucilius predicted that Ahron would be acceptable to his assigned detainee.

Lucilius was correct. Paul did approve Ahron and similar to the other chosen leaders, stated he wanted to meet periodically with Ahron to help him in his leadership role in the church. Lucilius knew these seminars would be important to Flavius and he hoped to be on duty when they occurred. He had no doubt that Draba would attentively glean all information from these discussions, but Lucilius was becoming very interested in Paul's teachings and wanted to personally hear them for his own benefit.

One week after Paul approved Ahron as leader of his assembly, Aelia came to Rome to meet with her renter. The occasion marked Paul's first full month of renting her townhouse and she personally wanted to collect the rent and to obtain answers to questions that plagued her mind.

Junus announced her arrival and Paul eagerly came out of his devised workshop to greet his landlord. The fall day was crisp yet sunny, and they opted to sit in the courtyard for their discussion. "How are you adapting to your surroundings and your tasks, working with Antonius?" Aelia asked.

"Your townhouse is very comfortable and exceeds my expectations or needs. I particularly enjoy the magnificent frescos throughout the rooms."

Aelia slightly smiled at Paul's comment. She did not want Paul to know how much she appreciated his compliments. At this juncture, her focus was strictly on business, so she avoided further discussion about the beauty of her city home. She inquired, "Do you have any finished product that I can examine?"

Paul got up from his chair and went to his workshop, returning with a newly completed pair of military boots. He handed them to his inquisitor and sat down to watch her study his work.

Carefully, the businesswoman went over each boot with her long elegant fingers, touching and looking closely at the stitching. She held up one boot to analyze the design and the use of the different leathers. Finally, her inspection was complete, and she handed the leather goods back to her renter. "Your work is very good, Paul. I'm particularly impressed with your design. I can see how it would be more comfortable to a soldier. Your choice of leathers is influenced by Antonius, but how you combine them is vastly different than what he normally produces."

Aelia kept her eyes on Paul and continued with her assessment, "Your work will be very much sought after by both the Praetorian Guard members and field soldiers. They are always wanting a better boot. Tell me, what's been Antonius' reaction to your handiwork?"

Paul clasped his hands together, pleased to have a chance to demonstrate to his landlord that there would be no lack for the rent he would pay. He felt a brief chill from the breeze that funneled through the courtyard, but he ignored it. "Antonius has made no complaints about my labor. Initially, he was upset that I deviated from his design; but once he reviewed the boots, he could see the improvement."

Aelia momentarily shook from the chilly breeze and Paul suggested they continue their discussion inside the townhouse in her office. Lucilius was glad for the change as he also felt the change and believed it was the initial wave of a stronger storm.

In the office, Aelia had Paul continue his tale of Antonius' reaction to the new boot design. "Evidently, Antonius has received favorable comments from some of the soldiers who have purchased the new boot. He usually sends raw leather to me by one of his workers. I haven't met with him in several weeks."

The astute businesswoman asked her renter how much he was being compensated by Antonius. "He pays me by the completed pair." Paul chuckled as he detailed the entertaining negotiation that went on between them.

Aelia let out a musical laugh, "I can imagine the expression on the man's face as you presented your demands. He isn't used to someone like you, Paul. He does value quality work, and despite being reluctant to pay the price, he will grudgingly do so. How much did you negotiate for a completed pair?"

Paul's answer impressed the businesswoman, but she extended her arm in his direction with a slight wave of her hand. "I believe you can get another denarius for each completed pair. Antonius would easily triple the price he pays you. At four denarii a completed pair, Antonius will charge twelve denarii to the buyer, who won't quibble about the price because of the quality."

Lucilius listened attentively to this portion of the discussion. Aelia then directed her attention to the guard, "Lucilius, you have purchased boots many times from Antonius as well as other cobbler's. Am I correct in stating your willingness to pay such a price?"

Pleased to become a part of the conversation, the guard answered, "Absolutely, Aelia. Comfortable, strong boots are vital to soldiers. In battle, lives can be lost over a faulty pair of boots. In long marches, a bad pair of footwear can cause extreme pain in the legs and feet and will limit the distance traveled."

The guard looked briefly at Paul, then refocused on Aelia. "Members of the Praetorian Guard get paid twice the amount of regular soldiers, so we can easily afford twelve denarii for a quality pair of boots. Regular soldiers will pay the price as well."

Aelia beamed at Lucilius' confirmation of her judgment. She turned back to look at Paul and strongly suggested, "You really should charge four denarii for your labor. In fact, if Antonius is not willing to pay that price, I will contract with you to sell them directly to me."

She paused and straightened her back to its full height and raised her arched eyebrows. "I have outlets throughout the empire that, once the field soldiers learn of your work, they will eagerly request a pair from you. In addition, you can fabricate civilian shoes, sandals, and winter protection for Rome's populace and keep quite busy."

Paul sat motionless as Aelia made her proposal. He clarified his intent, "My main motivation is to use God's blessing of talent and skill to honor Him. I do not foresee any problem with securing an added denarius for my effort. It will make available that much more to use for His purposes. So, I will agree to charge Antonius the extra denarii and should he refuse, you and I have an agreement."

Aelia let out a delighted laugh, "Paul, I shall enjoy doing business with you. It will be very profitable for both of us." The shrewd merchant of commerce then changed the topic. "Since it is the first of the month, do you have the rent that we agreed upon?"

Paul produced a small pouch, withdrew the agreed amount, and handed it to his landlord. Aelia placed the money in a larger bag without counting to see if it was all there. "Thank you, Paul. Now I must go to conduct other business before I return to my villa. I look forward to our time together next month." She giggled with a slightly suppressed smile, "Who knows, maybe at that time we shall forge our business relationship."

She rose from her chair, and smiled at Paul with a twinkle in her dark eyes that even Lucilius could see from his vantage point. Elegantly, she glided out of the townhouse. The guard and the detainee watched her leave. Then, Lucilius made a personal request of the detainee, "How soon can you make me a pair of boots? What I now wear are getting worn and will not do well with the approaching winter."

Paul assured Lucilius with a smile, "I shall send a message to Antonius for extra leather and get started on your pair at once when the new delivery arrives. "

On that same beautiful crisp fall day, a meeting was convening between Cleatus, Seneca, and Flavius. It had been decided that a regular get-together was necessary to review events concerning the prisoner of Rome they had been assigned to monitor. To avoid suspicion from anyone intent on either harming Paul or interfering with his appeal before Caesar, the clandestine conferences would take place at Seneca's townhouse. Flavius would arrive at the front entrance while Cleatus would ride his beloved warhorse and enter through the rear opening common to all townhouses.

Cleatus arrived first and made sure his steed was well taken care of. He easily climbed over the short wall and was escorted by a servant to Seneca's office. He appreciated the warmth of the room and that his host had provided hot soup to combat the chilly weather. Soon after Cleatus' arrival, Flavius was ushered into the office and also was immediately tempted by the soup's irresistible aroma.

Seneca cordially greeted them, "My colleagues, please indulge yourselves with this soup and fresh warm bread. Alas, this chilly day brings notice of worse weather to come this winter. Let us warm our chilly insides as we discuss the first month of our prisoner's activities."

They sat around a table Seneca had made. It was a combination of olive wood and myrtle wood. Seneca was a fine craftsman, one of the best in Italy, in fact. By Roman standards, the six-foot table was long. Seneca purposefully had designed it that way with very detailed carving on the legs and around the top edge. It was one of over five hundred different sized tables the consul to Caesar had fabricated. The ones which had not yet been sold to discerning buyers were used throughout both his residences. Seneca preferred longer dining tables which allowed for more dinner guests than the traditional Roman custom of three to four reclining lounges. Seneca and his wife enjoyed bigger parties and the tables suited their desire to have many guests.

Seneca officiated at the clandestine gathering and asked Flavius to give his account first. "Over this first month my men have been diligent and thorough in their duties. The majority of information was derived from the morning and the afternoon shifts. The late night crew has fewer opportunities to obtain information since Paul retires to his bedroom earlier than most Romans."

The centurion paused in his account to slurp the hot, flavorful soup, before continuing, "The evidence secured by the guards indicates Paul is considered one of the main leaders of a religious sect here in Rome which claims a man-god named Jesus is their savior. The advocates of this sect heed his directives.

"He rebukes all attempts by anyone who strays from what he refers to as the teachings of this Jesus. Two weeks ago, four leaders of groups here in Rome were ousted by Paul's command. He personally chose replacements and has directed these men to confer with him periodically for advanced training."

Seneca interrupted Flavius. "This sounds suspicious. Do you have any information about these four new sub-leaders?"

The centurion shook his head. "Not yet. At this time spies that I've assigned to obtain more information have not completed their tasks."

The host waved at Flavius to proceed. "My analysis of the daily reports from the guards suggests this sect is in opposition to the Jews."

Seneca again interrupted to ask, "This sect is, therefore, a new religion that has separated from that of the Jews?"

Before Flavius could answer, his commander, Cleatus, responded, "Yes, that appears to be the case, Seneca. My reports reveal this sect began shortly after this so-called Jesus was crucified by Pilate. The followers of this man-god call themselves 'The Way', but throughout the empire our province commanders refer to them as 'Christians' because that is the name of the god these people worship."

Flavius was thankful for the interruption because it allowed him to take in some more of the warming soup and fresh bread. He had to wolf down the food hurriedly before Cleatus finished. The centurion looked intently at his commanding general to determine if more facts about Paul were to be revealed. There were none.

Seneca eyed Cleatus thoughtfully and decided to add his commentary, "I know this prisoner." His guests were caught by surprise over this piece of information. Seneca leaned towards them to ensure he had their attention, "Some years ago he was in Athens at the same time I was. He spoke before the Greek Senate. I was able to listen to his teaching and... he was quite persuasive."

Cleatus exhibited his surprise at Seneca's revelation by tilting his head back against the padded back of his chair. Flavius's surprised movement was just the opposite. He leaned forward with interest, grasping the arms of his chair and shifting his position. Both men showed great interest.

The consul to Caesar feigned unawareness of their reactions, not wanting to be deterred in his description. He studied his audience and continued, "His words were so eloquent they caused some of the Greek Senators to argue among themselves, very similar to what he does when speaking to the Jews he encounters on his travels.

"This Paul is shrewd and very intelligent. Even cunning, in several ways. My belief is he does not seek political power. He gave up that aspiration when he chose to follow this Jesus. His main focus is evangelical, which can be a danger to Rome."

Both Cleatus and Flavius were transfixed during Seneca's unexpected narrative. Flavius looked at his superiors and detected that neither man was going to continue, so he quickly spoke up, "There are many aspects about this prisoner that remain unknown. Based on what you have said, Seneca, how do you want us to proceed?"

Seneca, the consul to Caesar, had a habit of resting his forearm on the table and moving his hand back and forth. A slow movement meant he was deeply pondering the commentary. A rapid movement indicated he was anxious or irritated. No movement meant he was either not interested or was about to announce his thoughts. At Flavius' question, Seneca's hand was moving slowly. "You are quite right, Flavius, about the detainee

Paul. We must acquire as many pertinent facts as we can about him and his involvements throughout the empire. What we obtain will determine how we proceed in counseling Caesar prior to this man's appeal."

Seneca's face hardened. His hand was no longer moving back and forth. With steely eyes directed at both Cleatus and Flavius, he instructed, "We cannot fail in this assignment. Quite literally, our lives are at stake here." He tapped the table for emphasis and his voice rose with an ominous tone, "Should we give Nero the wrong information, he will become angry and we shall pay a heavy price for our incompetence."

Seneca's other forearm rested on the table. Leaning heavily on both arms, he gave his plan to his colleagues. "Cleatus, we need those reports from your field commanders in the provinces Paul has traveled. They must tell us of any political sedition he caused and also how these Christian followers are heeding his directives. Have you received anything from these inquiries?"

Rome's top-ranked general squared his shoulders and re-minded his comrades, "It has been slow because of the onset of the stormy season. Land travel is the only way possible at this time of the year. Thus far, three reports have arrived. I'm in the process of reviewing them."

The chief strategist remained silent, then focused his atten-tion on the centurion assigned to guard the prisoner. "Flavius, instruct your men to continue being alert and wise in their deal-ings with the detainee. Don't let them become lax in their obser-vations! This can occur over time, should they become too friend-ly with him."

Flavius took the opportunity to interject his strategy and demonstrate his leadership, "Based on the two big group meet-ings that have occurred, I've decided to limit the number of peo-ple to visit Paul at a given time. I've already instructed the guards there shall be no more than two people allowed to be with Paul at at the same time. Secondly, these visitors can only visit for one hour at a time; then they must leave. Thirdly, visitors will be al-lowed only from mid-morning to mid-afternoon."

The centurion looked for his superiors' approval before he finished revealing his strategy. "Finally, I've chosen several youths to be at the townhouse as messengers during each shift. Should anything out of the ordinary occur, these messengers are instructed to immediately come to my office so I can direct how to handle the situation."

Cleatus' eyes shone and a small smile of admiration crept into the corners of his mouth. The commanding general felt his choice of Flavius for commanding the guards assigned to Paul had been a good one. Flavius' strategy reassured the general his confidence had not been misplaced. "I agree with your plan of action, Flavius," he commended. "You have assessed these early developments well. I personally would do the same as you have chosen."

Flavius was embarrassed by the accolades given him by his commanding general. He fought to hide his delight and bowed to his commander. Seneca, too, was impressed by the young centurion. He knew Flavius' father, Marius, and what an intelligent soldier he was. Flavius was obviously from the same mold.

To ease Flavius' awkwardness, the consul took control. "I have one final detail for each of you." Both Cleatus and Flavius listened attentively. "I've enlisted the services of a friend of mine named Cato to interrogate Paul. On the surface, Cato will appear to be Paul's attorney to assist him with his appeal before Caesar. In reality, he will be our extra eyes and ears to gather whatever is pertinent for our final report to Nero."

Flavius could not stifle a small chuckle and gave the reason for his reaction. "I know Cato. He was my mentor growing up. My father hired him to prepare me for my service to Rome. He is quite knowledgeable, and loyal to Rome."

Seneca tilted his head and stated without hesitation, "This is the same Cato, Flavius. We studied the Greek philosophy of stoicism together and shared several assignments in the past. I have great confidence in his ability to manipulate Paul to get what we want."

The host of the clandestine meeting was pleased and stood up to conclude the meeting, "Our time together has been well spent. We shall meet again at this time next month. I'm sure there will be much to discuss." The three laughed at what they believed to be a great understatement. Flavius left first through the front door. Cleatus moved quickly through the townhouse's courtyard and stepped over the short wall opening to his waiting and eager steed.

As the covert gathering dispersed, Aelia was discussing her new renter with his supervisor, Antonius. As benefactor to Antonius, the opportunistic businesswoman owned sixty-five percent of his cobbler business. She regularly discussed business matters with her manager to keep things in order and profitable.

Aelia surveyed the surroundings of the shop and could tell business was quite brisk. This was pleasing to her and confirmed that her initial assessment of both Antonius and the cobbler niche were profitable enterprises. The majority owner carefully walked throughout the shop with Antonius following her. The cobbler was a nervous individual by nature, which he worked hard to cover up. But whenever his benefactor arrived at the shop his nerves churned his stomach into a knot.

Aware of his discomfort and with precision, Aelia inspected the finished product made by Antonius and his four assistants. She picked up one pair of military boots in her left hand and another pair in her right hand. "Antonius, do you see the difference in these boots?"

Antonius moved closer to see the objects of her inquiry. Haltingly, he said yes, he saw a difference. "The pair in your left hand was made by one of my assistants and the pair in your right hand was made by the Jew, Paul."

Aelia knew Paul had made the one pair of boots but pretended ignorance. She looked innocently at Antonius. "Why the difference in the quality? I know you require all your workers to utilize the template you have devised."

Antonius shifted his weight from one foot to the other, and a concerned expression developed on his thin narrow face. "The Jew, Paul, has his own style and method. The soldiers who have purchased his boots laud their comfort, durability, and strength." Antonius hung his head as if in shame and very quietly admitted, "They prefer his boots over mine, and want only him to create their footwear."

This was the very opening Aelia sought, to seal her directive to her manager, "Can your new subcontractor produce sufficient quantity to meet the demand?"

Antonius was quick to answer, which he did in the same low voice, "No. There is a backlog developing that will be difficult to fulfill."

"What do you propose to do about this situation, Antonius?"

Aelia had no hint of accusation in her question, but in spite of her inoffensive tone, the uncertain cobbler began to sweat. His moist forehead betrayed his attempt to appear nonchalant as he tossed his response to Aelia, "I wanted to see if you might have some idea what can be done to meet this demand."

Inwardly, Aelia was ecstatic over Antonius' answer. This was proceeding more smoothly than she had anticipated. "It is quite obvious, Antonius, that you have Paul who can teach his technique to you and your assistants. Demands can be met and a better quality product will be made available. It will increase our business quite handsomely."

Antonius' body language demonstrated his relief at her solution. Aelia cleared her throat for emphasis, "I strongly suggest you first get Paul to teach you how to imitate his technique, and then you teach your assistants." Aelia paused, but Antonius realized she wasn't finished with her thoughts. He nervously waited to hear the rest.

"Under no circumstances, Antonius, do I want your personal feelings about his being a Jew to interfere with your ability to learn his better technique. The success of our business depends on you controlling your emotions."

Antonius closed his eyes in submission to his benefactor's demand. Seizing her advantage, Aelia finished, "If you do not adhere to my demand, I shall personally contract with Paul and oust you from the business. In addition, expect this subcontractor to require four denarii for each pair of completed boots he produces. This is well worth the money because we can charge much more. People will pay extra for the additional quality."

Antonius sighed deeply. He did not like the fact a Jew was capable of producing better quality work than his. And he cringed at having to pay this Jew more than what he paid his assistants, but because it was coming from the sale of the boots and not his own pocket, he acquiesced.

"It's possible, Antonius, that Paul may hesitate to ask for the extra denarii. If he delays, you take the initiative and offer it to him. Do you understand?" Antonius slowly shrugged his shoulders and said yes.

Relieved at how well this had gone, Aelia softened the impact by giving Antonius some money for him to have a fine meal with his assistants in appreciation for their diligence in their work. "Enjoy yourself, Antonius. You are doing well and I foresee much profit from our association with this prisoner."

Antonius was mollified by her kind words, and Aelia left. She had one final important meeting to attend before returning to her villa. Thus far, it had been a very productive day for her.

The cunning businesswoman met with the chief house servant assigned to cater to her new renter. The two convened at one of Rome's respected restaurants, which Aelia also happened to own. Over a sumptuous meal, the chief house servant relayed everything that had transpired with Paul over the first month of his house arrest.

Several times, Aelia's surprise was evident through her reactions and her questions. When the house spy had finished, Aelia thanked him for his observations, "As always, you have exceeded my expectations. What you have relayed to me is very valuable for my purposes. Please continue and, obviously, don't let anyone know what you are doing."

The combination of worthwhile information and a fine meal satisfied Aelia. During her short trip back to her villa, the businesswoman pondered her dual role of landlord and spy, mulling over what she had learned and how she would use these new insights to her advantage.

## Chapter 13

Draba was worried. He had been summoned to appear before Flavius before assuming his regular shift to guard Paul. The conniving guard thought he had done well by informing Flavius about Paul's epistle to his followers in Rome several days earlier. By his optimistic estimation, he believed this information would surely boost his chance of being promoted, potentially to a centurion.

Now all that appeared doubtful. Usually, when a soldier was summoned to appear before his commander, it wasn't good. He was unsettled as he announced his presence to Flavius' secretary. Luckily, he did not have to wait any time before learning what infraction he might have violated.

"Come in, Draba," summoned Flavius in a normal tone that took Draba by surprise. He had been prepared to meet an irate commander. "I want to discuss the information you gave in your report about an epistle Paul wrote to his followers here in Rome."

Draba impatiently waited for his commander's next words. Flavius sat in his chair and picked up a piece of parchment, which he smoothed and silently read. When he was finished, he looked up at the guard standing anxiously before him. The centurion was unaware of his guard's emotional state as he began to question him, "In your report, Draba, there were no names of Paul's followers who might have received this epistle. Do you remember the names?"

The agonized guard scowled as he attempted to remember the details Flavius expected. He shifted from one foot to the other and put a hand to his chin as if he could stroke out the information. He began to sweat, struggling desperately to recall those elusive names. After a few miserable moments, he remembered and blurted out, "Hevel and Teman."

His announcement sounded more like a dog's bark. Flavius ignored the staccato delivery and asked another question, "Were there any other names, or even leaders, who might have received this epistle?"

Eager to please his commander, Draba unhesitatingly shook his head, and in a calmer voice said, "There were approximately ten more men there, but these two definitely were the main leaders. The others allowed these two men to speak for them."

Satisfied, Flavius changed the topic. "Do you know if there was more than one epistle written by Paul to this group of followers?" Draba's nerves were settling down and in a more natural voice he stated there was only the one letter. Flavius wanted to be certain of this. "Draba, when you arrive for your next duty shift, attempt to find out if there might be more than one letter. If so, be sure to make it part of your next daily report."

Draba snapped to attention and acknowledged he would carry out his commander's order. Flavius' face softened a little and he smiled at the soldier, recognizing it had been an ordeal for his loyal guard. "Draba, you are doing a fine job. Your reports indicate a keen sense of observation and good memory skills. There has been much activity already in Paul's detention here and you have performed your duties as expected."

Flavius' accolade was a welcome finish in Draba's ears. He was greatly relieved his initial fear had been misguided. "Thank you, Commander. I shall obtain the information you request." With the meeting complete, Draba saluted and withdrew to his quarters.

Meanwhile, Cato had arrived at the detainee's townhouse for his first meeting with his new client. Under normal circumstances, an assigned attorney met with his client just before the trial. The attorney would advise the client how to present his case before the judge or magistrate and would be at his side during the proceedings. This case involving Paul was vastly different because of Nero's absence and delayed return to Rome. Once an accused man petitioned to be heard by Caesar, no other judge could intervene or substitute.

Cato didn't mind the unavoidable delay. It afforded him more opportunity to learn about Paul and his adherence to this Jesus sect that was gaining popularity. As a Stoic, Cato had little use for any religion, and believed politics was like the ocean tide. It was constantly on the move and there was always more than one wave. As a result, thus far in his life, he had learned to adjust to the fickleness of politics and use it to his advantage in whatever way possible.

The Stoic philosopher stood on the step to the townhouse front door. He made sure his new toga revealed the distinctive bluish purple stripe that indicated his illustrious position in Roman society. The marking was evident on the right shoulder of his undergarment tunic and also at the bottom of the toga. Taking a deep breath, Cato knocked on the front door.

Junus opened the door and bowed in respect to the Roman official. He ushered him into the atrium of the townhouse to wait for Paul. Cato stood very straight, held his head high, and displayed an official appearance as he waited for his client to appear. Lucilius and Paul came out of the makeshift workshop and walked towards the visitor. Lucilius recognized the stripe on the toga and realized he needed to be mentally sharp for what was about to take place.

Paul looked curiously at his visitor but did not know who the man was or his purpose. He stopped two paces in front of the important-looking stranger and waited for the visitor to identify himself.

Cato's voice was low, firm, and brusque. "My name is Cato, your assigned attorney to prepare you for the appeal before Caesar whom you have petitioned. Where can we talk about your appeal?"

Casually, Paul motioned towards the main office and began walking in that direction. Lucilius stood to the side and allowed Cato to accompany the detainee. It would not have been proper for the guard to put himself between his assigned detainee and the Roman official. Nonetheless, Lucilius was close enough behind the two men that should Cato make any combative move towards Paul, Lucilius would be able to easily thwart the attack.

Inside the office, Paul sat in the chair behind the desk, as was his custom. Cato sat facing him, while Lucilius stood at the ready behind the attorney, where he could hear and observe the interchange.

Cato took the initiative. "I've studied the report Festus sent Caesar concerning your appeal before Nero on a charge of treason and intent." Cato's penetrating eyes were locked onto Paul's. The attorney gave every indication through his impersonal voice and mannerisms that Paul should expect no wavering or compromise.

The counselor let his words resonate with his new client as he waited for a reaction.

Evenly, Paul invited the attorney to continue, "Go on, Cato. Please tell me your opinion of this report."

For a brief second, Cato's eyes scanned Paul's face, assessing his statement. In a very official voice, he answered, "It's clear your case has definite religious overtones. Your accusers, Ananias and Tertullus, were adamant you should stand trial before your Sanhedrin for your religious crimes. Yet, Festus, Aprippa II, and the prominent businessmen of Caesarea found you innocent of these crimes." His remark ended in an ever so slight questioning tone to invite Paul's comment before he continued.

Paul nodded his agreement with his attorney's summary. It was quite accurate. Lucilius' gaze drifted between Paul to Cato, anticipating some conflict to develop between the two men. The guard wondered if Cato's antagonism would interfere with his representation of Paul's defense. Cato obviously believed he was wasting his time on this prisoner Paul.

Cato puffed out his chest and in a sharp voice announced, "I do not engage in petty religious disputes or debates. Give me reason why I should represent you in this appeal. Remember that Rome has approved the Jewish religion. As such, religious disputes are handled on site where they occur."

Startled by the outburst, Lucilius shifted his gaze back to Paul. The curious guard not only was personally interested in this dialog; he also was fully aware he must grasp what was being said and intimated, in order to give a complete and accurate report to Flavius later in the day. The Praetorian Guard member was intrigued with Paul's surprisingly placid demeanor, especially in the face of such an unwarranted harsh affront.

Calmly, Paul explained, "The report should include that the Sanhedrin's hired attorney, Tertullus, accused me of treason against Rome. Despite this charge, Tertullus presented no evidence to substantiate his accusation."

Cato squinted and pursed his lips. He had not paid attention to this detail. He resolved to review this aspect of the report when he returned to his townhouse after this meeting. As he made this mental note, his client offered his own knowledgable insight.

"Of course, I knew I would be found innocent of the religious charges. Bear in mind, Cato, I was under detention by Felix for two years in Caesarea. During this time, Felix found no guilt, but detained me—for extortion. I am sure you are aware of this practice of his. But neither the Sanhedrin nor I would pay. When he was recalled to Rome for his failures, he left my case to be decided by the next procurator—who is now Festus."

Paul sat forward in his chair and leaned his elbows on the polished desktop. He looked steadily at his prospective attorney and went on, "I was the one who brought up the false charge of treason to Festus. He realized the serious nature of the accusation as well as my right as a Roman citizen to appeal to Caesar. He had no choice but to honor my request. In fact, I believe he was relieved to have me and the Jewish leaders out of his hair, if even for a brief period of time."

Lucilius' eyes darted back to Cato. The attorney cleared his throat and in a milder tone said, "Your account coincides with Festus' report. You are astute in your reasoning, Paul. I might add, you also are very clever and cunning in how you manipulated this charge."

Paul's voice raised slightly as he corrected the attorney, "I did not manipulate anyone. I merely confronted the emotional reaction of Tertullus by claiming my right as a Roman citizen. Wouldn't you have done the same?"

Lucilius detected a slight flush on Cato's face. "Under the circumstances, Paul, I would have invoked my citizenship rights," Cato admitted. The Roman official leaned back in his chair with his head on the padded back. "These Jewish leaders have not softened their attitude towards you in any way, Paul. Because of the delay in Nero hearing your appeal, they can come to Rome for your appeal and present their evidence corroborating this charge by Tertullus."

Paul countered Cato's assumption, "I find this very doubtful for several reasons. First, any so-called evidence would be false fabrications. This requires an elaborate effort on their part and one that first would have to be submitted to Festus, according to Roman law. He would not entertain such falsification lightly. Second, any witnesses would have to be bribed. Should they make a false charge to Caesar and be discovered, he would have them executed because they are non-citizens attempting to levy a serious charge against a Roman citizen. No man would put his life on the line for those Jewish leaders."

The detainee let his words sink in before he finished, "Lastly, Cato, Ananias has usurped the authority of the real high priest, Ishmael ben Fabus. The Jewish people are not happy with this. Ananias is very disliked by the Jews. The Roman authorities, especially in Judea, are waiting for an opportunity to arrest Ananias because he is inciting unrest between the Jews and the Romans. He has much to lose."

Now Paul spoke more slowly to emphasize his final point. "For these reasons, I do not believe Ananias, Tertullus, or any other member of the Sanhedrin will oppose me here in Rome. It is left to you, and whoever else is assigned to my case, to determine if I've committed treason or intent against Rome." After his last words, Paul deliberately waited for the Roman official's reply, wondering how he would argue. He watched Cato without blinking.

Cato was silent, exchanging stares with his client. Finally, he let out a laugh and clapped his hands together, startling both Paul and Lucilius. The attorney commended Paul with a grand gesture, "You have assessed your situation correctly. I admire how you have maneuvered the events and the people involved thus far in your case. Not many men have the ability you have just demonstrated. I'm relieved I don't have to be an adversary to *you*. It would not be pleasant!"

This time it was Paul's turn to laugh heartily and ask, "So, Cato, does this mean you will proceed as my attorney?"

The Roman official chuckled, "This will be very interesting, Paul, possibly even challenging. I look forward to interacting with you on this appeal. Let us take some time to establish how this will work."

Paul raised his hand to interrupt, "Before getting into the details of my appeal, let us enjoy a good midday meal." Smiling, Paul looked up at the stunned Lucilius and said, "I'm sure Lucilius and the other guards are ready for some nourishment. I know I am. Come, let us partake of the bounty Almighty God has provided for us."

With that, the detainee stood up, walked around to the front of Aelia's treasured desk and gestured toward the dining room. With a dignified nod, Cato joined him. During their amiable meal, Paul and Cato hashed out the plan that would assist them in proving Paul innocent of treason.

When his shift was over, Lucilius nearly ran back to the palace to give his report to Flavius. Several times during his recitation, Flavius held up his hand to slow down the guard's animated report. "Lucilius, your eagerness and enthusiasm is making it difficult for the scribe to accurately note your words. Please calm down. We have plenty of time for you to relay the events between Paul and Cato."

Lucilius mustered his self-control and succinctly finished his detailed depiction of the events. These same events had also impacted him, although that would not be in his report. After he left, Flavius pondered the meeting. He was impressed with this Jewish prisoner, yet at the same time, wary. He wondered if Paul's shrewdness could cause him trouble during the interim while he waited to appear before Caesar.

Early the next morning, Antonius arrived early at Paul's townhouse. He brought along with him his cobbler tools and some extra leather in a bag that was so loaded he needed to use a leather strap over one shoulder to assist carrying the items.

Once inside the townhouse, the Roman cobbler was led to Paul's workshop in the rear portion of the dwelling. Paul was already at work, studiously fabricating a pair of boots. Antonius stood in the door for a moment, watching Paul at the workbench Aelia had supplied.

In a stumbling voice, Antonius called to his fellow cobbler, "I've come for you to teach me your technique in making boots." Awkwardly, he fiddled with his bag.

Paul looked up at Antonius' strained face. "I shall enjoy sharing what Almighty God has blessed me to do." Looking around, Paul surveyed the workshop. He called for help and requested a chair be brought into the shop for Antonius.

Once he was able to sit down, Antonius spread out his leather, arranged his cobbler tools at one side and, with new humility, stated, "I'm ready, Paul." For most of the day, Paul patiently guided Antonius through the process he had devised to produce high quality boots for military and civilians.

Draba looked on, in awe of how smoothly Paul controlled each phase of creating the boots and how patiently he taught. The guard watched with fascination as Antonius and Paul interacted. He paid particular attention to the change in Antonius' demeanor, evolving from rigid and tense to amiable and joking. Most surprising of all was his apparent acceptance of the Jew.

Just before the daily shift change, Paul called a halt to his teaching. "Antonius, this has been a full day. You have progressed well in learning this new technique, but it is time to cease. We will continue tomorrow."

Antonius realized how fatigued he was from the combined

physical exertion and mental concentration while following Paul's instructions. He was ready to cease for the day and did not argue. After he returned to his home, the cobbler contemplated the day's events. He was quite impressed with Paul's new method, but even more impressed by the Jewish cobbler's patience with him. The Roman was beginning to think differently about Jews in general. Certainly, his attitude had softened towards Paul.

The next day was actually enjoyable for Antonius. In fact, he was disappointed at how rapidly the time went by. At the end of the day, the Jewish cobbler proclaimed to his Roman counterpart, "Antonius, you finished your first set of boots with this new method. Do you feel ready to take this technique and teach it to your assistants?"

Antonius replied honestly, "Not quite, Paul. I feel several more productions are needed before I'm comfortable enough to teach others."

Paul smiled, "Then I look forward to spending more time with you."

Each day that Antonius returned to Paul's townhouse, he felt his spirit lift while he was around the prisoner. Inwardly, he liked the Jew, but he certainly would not share those feelings with any of his fellow Romans.

After making several more pairs of boots, Antonius approached Paul. "I believe I'm now adequately prepared to teach my assistants your technique. But there is something else I want to discuss with you."

Draba looked inquisitively at the Roman cobbler who was still talking, "I feel your technique will allow us to charge more for these completed military boots as well as civilian ones. I must admit your method is superior to that of mine."

Paul chortled, "I see, Antonius, that Aelia has spoken to you about paying me an extra denarius for each pair of boots I make."

Antonius blushed at the exposure. "She has, but now that I've learned your process and see the potential, I agree wholeheartedly with her. People will easily see the difference in the quality and will not object to paying more for our work." Antonius measured Paul's agreeable countenance, and concluded, "I take it, you do not object to this increase?"

The servant of Christ replied, "No, I do not Antonius. We have an agreement." With that, the two cobblers signified their pact with an embrace and a thump on the back. Antonius packed his tools in his bag and left the townhouse, reveling in his newly acquired skills and several exceptional pairs of boots ready to sell at a premium price. He felt a smug satisfaction, congratulating himself on the way home.

Later in the day, a weary traveler arrived in Rome. His sole purpose was to engage the prisoner prior to his appeal before Caesar. The traveler desperately wanted to meet with Paul that same day, but extreme fatigue from his journey had robbed him of his energy to find the detainee.

Reluctantly, he made his way to the house where he would be staying during his short time in Rome. There, he would once again go over the plan he had hatched out earlier before he began his long trek to Rome. It was vitally important he meet with Paul.

Wearily, he knocked on the door of the house of his hosts. The owner opened the door and viewed the haggard visitor who was having obvious difficulty standing upright in the doorway. "Epaphroditus, you have made it safely here from Philippi! I have been greatly concerned. Come in, my friend!"

The owner helped his exhausted friend into his home.

## Chapter 14

Epaphroditus was so worn from his difficult journey that he slept a full twelve hours after his friend Quantus helped him to bed. Shortly after his replenishing sleep, Epaphroditus eagerly met with his friend. He had much to tell him.

"How do you feel now, my friend?" asked a concerned Quantus. Somewhat groggily, Epaphroditus thanked his hosts for their kindness and provision and apologized for his inability to converse at the time of his arrival.

Quantus's wife, Pricilia, was on hand with fresh, hearty broth to nourish him, and Epaphroditus began to relay the events of his trek. He had been chosen by the church at Philippi to deliver gifts for Paul. They had been informed, via carrier pigeon, of his plight and the loss of his possessions during the shipwreck.

The gifts consisted of money, an outer robe for the winter weather, scrolls, and additional cobbler tools. "The church knows that Paul must support himself while waiting for his appeal before Caesar and they want to provide what they can for him."

Quantus listened carefully. "Paul has been here in Rome over a month. When did you leave Philippi?"

Epaphroditus swallowed the warm, nourishing broth, then replied, "Nearly two months ago. I joined a merchant caravan in Philippi, but soon after our departure, we encountered a fierce winter storm. The cold was intense and several of the animals died. Four of the merchant's slaves got very ill. I also succumbed to winter's bite, incurring a fever."

Epaphroditus stopped to sip more of the warming broth. Quantus looked at his friend and could see the effects of the journey had been severe. He had lost weight, he had dark circles under his eyes, and he obviously was very weak. The retired Roman soldier was concerned about his friend. He was a former member of the Praetorian Guard, and Quantus was accustomed to seeing him strong and energetic.

"You were delirious on your arrival here. We put blankets over you and warm rocks under your bed. Do you still feel chilled?"

The gaunt-looking traveler shook his head. "No, your kindness and God's grace has saved me for what I must do while here in Rome."

Quantus remained focused on the frail appearance of the former strapping Guard centurion, and warned him, "You are still weak and must curtail your activities until such time as your strength returns. It will be several months before Paul's appearance before Nero, so you have time to meet with him."

"But I must get the church gifts to Paul as soon as possible and then return to let them know how Paul is doing. In addition, the church is having issues that Paul must know about as soon as possible," Epaphroditus wanly insisted.

Quantus put his hand on his friend's shoulder. "I will personally deliver the gifts for you and inform Paul about your condition. He will not want you to further weaken yourself."

Epaphroditus continued to disagree with Quantus until exhaustion persuaded him to retire to his bed. A deep sleep came quickly to the devoted traveler.

Quantus instructed Pricilia, "While he sleeps, I will deliver the gifts to Paul for him. Please watch over Epaphroditus. If he should awake during my absence, comfort him as best you can." He gathered up the gifts and headed for Paul's townhouse north of where he and his wife lived.

Paul was both glad and concerned to hear from Quantus about the arrival of Epaphroditus. "You did right, not letting him come here in his condition! I shall have Luke go to your home and examine our brother. Luke will visit me later today and I'm sure he will be able to assess Epaphroditus' condition before you partake of your evening meal."

Quantus bade Paul farewell and hastened back to his sick colleague. Along the way, he was comforted to know that Luke would determine the severity of his Christian brother's physical condition. As Quantus walked the mile and a half back to his home, he reflected on the flow of events that had led to how he and Epaphroditus had become friends.

Each had become soldiers, joining the army in their youth from different towns. Quantus was from Rome, while Epaphroditus was from Cyprus. He chuckled at the memory of first seeing the tall, slim, handsome man with the mischievous blue eyes and commanding voice. Quantus and several of the other soldiers laughed when they heard his name, which was derived from the goddess of beauty named Aphrodite.

Soon, these soldiers became impressed with Epaphroditus' valor and physical strength that were repeatedly manifested on the battlefield. His valor inspired those around him, and three years after entering Rome's army, Epaphroditus and Quantus were elevated to the rank of centurion. After this, they were assigned to different units, yet they had maintained their friendship as best they could. The times they reunited by plan or by coincidence were always as if they had never been apart.

Pulling his robe tighter against his body to ward off the winter chill, Quantus smiled at the thought of their respective retirements, twenty-five years after first enlisting in the army. Epaphroditus had announced he was going to take advantage of Rome's retirement policy of giving former soldiers land or a business in one of the colonies established by the empire. Philippi was one of the more desirable locations for Epaphroditus and he had eagerly established himself in the hub of commerce.

Quantus had opted to return to Rome and was able to use his retirement benefit to purchase a restaurant on the southern edge of the city. They both had married around the same time but had not communicated until they learned of each other's conversion to following Christ Jesus.

Quantus kept apprised of Epaphroditus' activities as a servant of Christ in Philippi. The once fierce warrior on the battlefield applied his steadfast attitude now to battle persecution from the Jews, who opposed the teachings of Christ and His followers.

The apostle Paul referred to Epaphroditus as a brother in Christ, a fellow co-worker for their shared ministry of bringing the gospel to the Gentiles. He also referred to him as a fellow soldier for the many battles each faced with the Jews, and at times with the Romans. Their efforts were as tireless and tenacious as on the battlefield, now advancing God's kingdom on earth.

As Quantus finished his thoughts about Epaphroditus, he realized the cold walk was over and he was home. Shivering, he shut the front door behind him. The warm house felt good and he immediately sought out his wife for some of her excellent broth and any news about their sick boarder. Epaphroditus still lay asleep in bed. Quantus prepared more warm rocks to slide under his cot for the heat to radiate through the combined straw and wool mattress and warm his body.

Soon after his arrival back home, Quantus let Luke in to observe their beloved sick warrior for Christ. Luke sat on the bed and began to examine his new patient. There was a fever, and Epaphroditus' breathing was weak. The physician probed his patient's body, but found no signs that suggested issues with any internal organs.

Luke made a paste of several herbs he had brought with him. He combined marigold, garlic, and fenugreek to combat the fever. He also added ground ginger, turmeric, basil, oregano, pepper and pumpkin seeds, all of which were ground into a powder. Finally, Luke made the concoction into a poultice and applied it to different parts of Epaphroditus' body.

The remainder was stirred into the broth, which was force-fed to the sick man. After this treatment was administered, the physician looked gravely at Quantus. "Keep giving him small amounts of the broth and make sure the paste is covered and secured against his body. That is all we can do at this time. I shall come by tomorrow and see how he fares."

The physician shuddered when he stepped out into the late afternoon wintry air. Wind that swept through the city buffeted his body. He lowered his head and gathered his cloak tightly around him. He made his way to his own residence, admiring Epaphroditus' strength and determination to journey so far.

Early the next morning, Luke ventured out just as the sun was heralding a new day. The physician was relieved the harsh winter wind had subsided and the rain had ceased. Despite this interlude, the air remained damp, very cold, and unpleasant to all who ventured out.

Luke was able to make his way to Quantus' home faster than he had on the previous blustery day. Inside the warm, inviting home, the worried hosts told Luke there had been no change in Epaphroditus' condition. The physician wasn't overly concerned yet because of the lingering nature of fevers he had encountered in patients over the years with similar ills.

However, when he entered the room, the doctor was taken aback at the sight of his fellow follower of Christ. The patient's eyes were sunken, his facial color was pallid, and his breathing more shallow and rapid. Luke could see that Quantus and Pricilia had followed his instructions and had kept a fresh poultice on Epaphroditus' chest and in his armpits. Gently, he placed his hand on the sleeping man's forehead. It was alarmingly hot to the touch.

He looked up at the two concerned caregivers, somberly remarking, "Our friend has a high fever. It is vital to watch him closely. I fear his condition is deteriorating to the point he may not survive." Quantus and Pricilia held each other's hand and immediately went to the Lord in prayer. Luke stood up from the patient's bed and joined them. Medical science could only do so much; the rest was in God's hands.

Quantus quickly left to inform Paul of Epaphroditus' precarious condition. The host also made sure there were plenty of supplies for their needs. During this period of time, winter's heavy hand continued to assail Rome and all its inhabitants. It was proving to be one of the most severe winters known to those who had lived in the city for many years.

Paul sent a messenger to the church leaders who convened at Paul's townhouse. There they joined in communal prayer for Epaphroditus as well as for other followers of Christ who had succumbed to winter's onslaught. Fortunately, another doctor was available to substitute for Luke. The assigned guards were impressed with the action and the compassion exhibited by these peculiar people whom Rome generally disliked. Their non-compliance with Rome's religious beliefs obviously did not preclude a fervent belief in their own god.

Two-and-a-half weeks into his deathly illness, Epaphroditus slowly opened his eyes. He felt woozy and very weak. Carefully, he turned his head to survey his surroundings and barely recognized the bedroom Quantus had provided for him.

The man who was at death's door suddenly noticed Luke sleeping on the floor next to his bed. With extreme effort, Epaphroditus raised up on his elbows, looked down at his physician and hoarsely called out Luke's name. Luke did not respond, and Epaphroditus persisted, but could not call any louder. He felt as if he were shouting although it was only a desperate whisper.

Luke heard the soft pleading and sprang awake, quickly getting up to attend to his patient. Epaphroditus was leaning on his elbows and was exhausted, but managed a weak grin. Luke sat on the edge of the bed, and urged the feeble man to lie back down.

He felt Epaphroditus' brow and was relieved the debilitating fever no longer had a grip on his friend. He also took note that natural color was returning to the patient's face. "You have overcome the fever, Epaphroditus, much to the praise of God. Let me get you some nourishment."

Quantus and Pricilia were ecstatic at the news their house guest was returning to life. Pricilia made a bowl of the broth with the added anti-inflammatory ingredients and took it along with fresh bread into the sick man's bedroom. Quantus and Luke followed closely behind.

"It is good to have you return to the ranks of the living," said Quantus, whose eyes brimmed with rejoicing. Epaphroditus was barely able to nod his head. Pricilia held him upright to help him consume the food, and Luke paid close attention to how his patient responded to the provisions. Epaphroditus steadily ate all the sustenance, giving glad confirmation to his attendees that the sickness was leaving his body.

Another week elapsed before Epaphroditus felt strong enough to leave the house and continue with his mission. "It is time that I go to Paul with my message about the church at Philippi. It is most urgent that I inform him of the issues taking place there," Epaphroditus insisted to his host.

"Very well, my friend, but I shall accompany you in case you flounder along the way. You are not as strong as you think," cautioned Quantus.

Together, the two friends traveled the distance to Paul's townhouse. Quantus was concerned about Epaphroditus' ability to complete the mile journey and was relieved when they stood before the front door of their destination.

Their arrival was announced. Paul stopped work on his military boot project and rushed to greet his fellow warriors for Christ. Draba was close behind Paul, and was eager to meet the man who had been a role model for him.

Paul welcomed Quantus and the recovered traveler. Gazing at Epaphroditus, he exclaimed, "My dear brother in Christ! At last we are together! God had mercy on us both and spared you, lest I have sorrow upon sorrow. It has been quite a time for you, and I praise God for His healing grace to us both!"

As he spoke, Paul embraced Epaphroditus with a heartfelt hug and then extended his greeting to Quantus. Draba looked on, and at hearing Quantus' name, realized he also was a former centurion and member of the Praetorian Guard. He felt honored to be in the presence of these two highly admired former military stalwarts, known and revered throughout Rome's military.

"You look hungry, my friends," said Paul, nodding toward Epaphroditus, and Quantus. "The cook has prepared an excellent meal and there is plenty to share with both of you. Come, let us partake of God's provision." The apostle of Christ grabbed his fellow warrior's arm and gently guided him to the dining room.

After refueling himself, Epaphroditus wasted no time in relaying to Paul the issues taking place within the church at Philippi. Paul listened raptly until everything was revealed. "You have done well as leader of the Philippians, my friend. The Holy Spirit has empowered you to see the subtle deception of the false teachers. Your actions honor our heavenly Father."

Epaphroditus showed no pride over Paul's affirmation, but he also did not feign false humility. Instead, he uttered, "It is what has to be done to combat the deception of the enemy. You have encountered this, as well, during your Christ-assigned ministry. Christ blesses us with His discernment and discerning spirits. Then we merely have to follow His direction."

Hearing these words, Draba learned first-hand the character of one of Rome's more valiant warriors. At the same time, he was disappointed his role model had fallen victim to being a religious zealot in a cause that Rome did not officially recognize. A sense of fear engulfed the guard as he briefly thought of what might happen to this highly esteemed man should Rome declare his religious sect a threat.

Draba's wandering thoughts were brought back to present reality when Epaphroditus mentioned gifts for Paul. "Quantus has informed me you received the gifts presented by the Philippians. Since I must remain here in Rome until winter releases its stranglehold, tell me, my brother, what I can do to assist you." Epaphroditus waved his hand, indicating their surroundings, and noted, "Your house arrest curtails your outside undertakings, but I can be your voice and vessel in whatever capacity you believe is necessary."

Paul beamed. "Epaphroditus, your resoluteness to serve our Lord is clearly evident. Wait, my brother, until you are sufficiently recovered from the fever before launching into our shared ministry. You were close to death, and still are weak, and strenuous activity will only cause you to relapse. Be patient, my friend."

Epaphroditus dropped his head at Paul's caution. Draba imagined how Paul's words affected his role model. He knew how it felt to have a fervent heart and to be denied an assignment that has meaning and purpose. Even delays are hard to bear in such instances.

Taking a deep breath and sighing, the deflated warrior replied in a subdued voice, "You are correct, Paul. Your assessment of my strength is true, though I wish it were not so." Raising his head and peering directly into Paul's eyes, he found some optimism, "It shall not be long before I return to discuss what action is required of me while I remain in Rome."

Paul rose from his chair and walked to Epaphroditus. He placed his hands on his shoulders with a warm smile. "In my heart, I believe you will recover quickly. But now, return with Quantus and fortify yourself." Both Quantus and Epaphroditus rose up and, with embraces, bade Paul farewell. Draba followed Paul back to his workshop, pondering the conversation and his own thoughts. He mentally began preparing for the report he would need to give within the next two hours.

Flavius interrupted Draba's recital of the news, waving his hand for him to cease his narrative. "What you are telling me, Draba, is noteworthy. I must send a messenger immediately to Cleatus about this development. He will want to know about Epaphroditus and his arrival here in Rome. We will wait until he arrives before you continue."

Draba was taken aback by his commander's directive. He had no idea this retired centurion from Philippi had such status with Rome's chief military general. He was both impressed and wary of the situation.

Upon hearing the name of Epaphroditus, Cleatus wasted no time in hurrying to Flavius' office. He acknowledged both soldiers' salute to him and got directly to the point, "Flavius, what is this situation about Epaphroditus?"

The centurion slightly bowed his head towards Draba and gestured for him to restate his report. The nervous guard was very careful to include everything that transpired during the meeting between Christ's two warriors. During his narrative, Cleatus sat without moving a muscle. His breathing was barely perceptible, his eyes narrowed and seemed to pierce right through Draba. The general didn't have to say a word to be intimidating.

When Draba finished giving his report, Flavius broke the tension. "You have done an excellent job in your observation of what took place at the townhouse and also in recounting this event for us." Then the centurion turned his head to face his commander and asked, "Would you like to ask Draba any questions, General?"

Cleatus looked up at the ceiling in Flavius' office and closed his eyes, considering what he had just heard. After a brief moment, the general lowered his head and looked at the uneasy guard. "I have no questions, Draba. I commend you on your ability to report this event in the manner you have done."

Draba noticeably relaxed, but did not speak. Flavius then dismissed his personally chosen trooper and Draba left quickly. Once Draba was gone, Cleatus verbalized a request to his centurion, "Flavius, I want to be kept aware of Epaphroditus' recovery. If necessary, have Dioscorides personally examine this man and make sure he is well taken care of. When he is sufficiently able, I want him brought to my office that I might interview him personally."

Flavius was surprised by his commander's request, but indicated he would do as instructed. He reminded Cleatus that Paul's personal physician had taken care of Epaphroditus through his ordeal. "This doctor named Luke was a protégé to Dioscorides and employed techniques he learned from Dioscorides during the time he cared for Epaphroditus."

Cleatus grunted and said, "In that case, I don't believe we need to take Dioscorides away from his other duties." The general paused and added, "Unless, of course, Epaphroditus relapses; then I want our main doctor to care for him." Flavius agreed to the command. Cleatus finished with a commendation, "Flavius, you are doing even more than I expected in this case involving this Jew Paul. Continue with whatever you decide is most effective."

Cleatus accepted Flavius' proud salute and returned to his office.

## Chapter 15

Ten more days elapsed before Epaphroditus was back to his full strength. During that time, Marcus and Lucilius visited the former Roman soldier at Quantus' home every day after their daily report to Flavius and his scribe. Draba secretly wanted to do the same, but refrained from engaging his role model due to his stubbornness over their differing religious grounds. The obstinate guard was distraught over Epaphroditus' conversion to Christ, and he wanted nothing to do with his kind, regardless of his status as one of Rome's premier soldiers.

However, both Marcus and Lucilius relished the opportunity to get to know Epaphroditus. Their conversations with the recovering Philippian were congenial, and they were gratified Epaphroditus always seemed pleased when they visited him.

After several visits and in-depth conversations, Marcus felt compelled to ask, "Epaphroditus, how is it that a man of your reputation and position has converted to this sect called The Way?"

Epaphoroditus' heart leaped. It was the opportunity Epaphroditus hoped for, to present the gospel to these younger soldiers. He knew that God in His perfect timing would open the door for him to speak about the power of His Son, Christ Jesus.

"Marcus, it's very simple. There was a huge void in my heart that I couldn't explain. This emptiness kept nagging at me, no matter what I engaged in doing. I sought relief, but none came. One day, while I was tending to my business of buying sheep for shearing and butchering, I felt a strong urge to go to the nearby stream from which we obtain water for the animals. I was tired and thirsty, so I sat by the water for a short while."

Epaphroditus' listeners were intrigued by his account. His words softly blanketed the younger men. "When I took a drink from the stream, a voice from out of nowhere clearly spoke to me saying, 'Epaphroditus, I offer you not this refreshing water but the everlasting water of eternal life. Follow Me.' I had never heard such a loving command."

Marcus and Lucilius leaned forward with their chins on their hands and their elbows on their knees. Epaphroditus continued, "The voice directed me a second time to 'Follow Him,' and I found my heart welling up and I knew it was Someone good and that I would do well to follow. I had heard of Jesus…, somehow I knew it was He. I don't know how. I looked around, and saw no one, but I felt His presence. I don't know how to explain it. I said, 'Yes, I will follow You!' At that very moment, I felt a cleansing deep within me and tears flowed down my cheeks for no reason. I felt more than happiness—I felt something much stronger. It was pure joy. I didn't understand it, but I knew it was real!"

Quantus was discreetly standing by, listening to his guest. He intently watched the two soldiers as they listened to Epaphroditus' story of his conversion. His heart began to pound and he felt the power of the Holy Spirit in his home. Inwardly, he shouted praise to God.

Epaphroditus finished by telling how, after that momentous occasion, he sought out a person he knew was a member of The Way. They talked, and Epaphroditus was drawn to hear more; he began to visit his home to learn more about Christ Jesus. Of course, the Holy Spirit also counseled and directed him, he said. "Since then," he added, "Christ has drawn me ever closer to Him and directed my ways."

Sensing his listeners were becoming overwhelmed by his testimony, Epaphroditus shortened the story of his personal salvation. Astonished, both Marcus and Lucilius had very little to say. Quantus stepped forward and offered the men refreshment, which they consumed with only minimal conversation.

"Epaphroditus, your story is very unique, the likes of which we have never heard before. There is much for us to ponder. Please bear with us during this time of thought," requested Lucilius. The evangelist agreed that is what they should do. The two soldiers then left to return to their barracks.

Afterwards, Quantus smiled at his houseguest. "Epaphroditus, you have definitely planted a spiritual seed in the hearts of these two lost souls. Let us pray that your words will have power and that God's will and plan for these two men will be carried out." Eagerly, Epaphroditus agreed and Quantus led the prayer.

Later that night, Epaphroditus lay in bed and thought about his earlier conversation with Quantus. He sensed in his heart God's direction for him while in Rome. With great joy and a sense of peace, he fell into a sound sleep.

The next morning, he insisted he needed to meet again with Paul. As always, Paul was delighted to visit with Epaphroditus. They shared so much in the way of attitude, thought, and purpose in their passionate desire to be a servant to their Savior. Epaphroditus got right to the purpose of his visit as he and Paul sat in the office just inside the townhouse. "My brother, last night our Lord God gave me direction for this time I will spend in Rome."

Paul became alert to his spiritual brother's announcement. He had encountered many such directives from God and he knew it was of great importance for his brother in Christ to reveal God's message. Epaphroditus was eager and buoyant as he spoke.

Before he disclosed his proclamation, Epaphroditus looked up at Lucilius who was standing close to Paul. He smiled and said, "Last night, God urged me to concentrate my efforts on teaching both Lucilius and Marcus about His ways and mysteries." Lucilius was astounded. He and Marcus had agreed to seek out Epaphroditus' thoughts concerning his being a follower of this new god Jesus.

Paul watched his guard's reaction to this revelation, and Lucilius spoke, "Aah..., Epaphroditus, I'm glad for your words. Indeed, Marcus and I had agreed to ask you to teach us about your belief in this god Jesus." The guard relaxed his official posture and shuffled his feet a bit as he searched for more words.

Realizing how startled the Roman soldier was, Paul smoothed over his awkwardness, saying, "This is very good news! Lucilius, you and Marcus will be well taught by my brother."

The brief conversation ended with Epaphroditus cheerfully stating that he would convene with his new mentees after their normal shifts. They would meet whenever the two soldiers wanted. To his surprise, the guards chose their first session for later that day.

The two Roman seekers of truth did not speak to anyone about their meetings with Epaphroditus. Although Rome was lenient about religions, this new sect called The Way had political overtones, they thought, and unanswered questions. As such, Cleatus had instructed his field commanders and Flavius to warn their men against becoming involved in this religion.

Two days later, the wheels of progress began turning for Cleatus. He invited Epaphroditus to his home, and the former Roman soldier agreed to meet with him. Cleatus was looking forward to renewing his relationship with this man from his past.

Despite their friendship, the Roman general had to adhere to his sworn duty of protecting Rome's interests. In this particular case, he had hidden his personal scribe in a small room adjacent to the townhouse's dining room. This room could not be easily detected by guests. Special sound funnels were secretly installed in the dining room that connected to the small listening room.

General Cleatus had learned about this technology after capturing a Persian general's stronghold. He had the technology copied and later installed it in his townhouse. He had utilized it many times, especially when holding private meetings such as would be the case with Epaphroditus. Limited sounds and distractions in a private gathering enabled sound funnels to relay the conversation to the listening room where his scribe made notes of it all.

This clandestine technique had paid dividends for Cleatus many times and added to his aura of mystery and intimidation in both military and political circles. The general had no remorse for using the secret method against his friend and former army colleague. His overriding concern was that it would prove effective and meet his desired need.

Cleatus made sure the dinner menu was excellent. He wanted his guest to feel comfortable and at ease. The general did not want to alienate Epaphroditus, whom he feared might reveal details about his involvement with these Christians that were becoming a growing concern to Rome's politicians and military.

Dinner was over and it was time to begin the surreptitious conversation, "Epaphroditus, it has been too long since we last saw each other! I believe our last visit was when you retired from Rome's service."

The guest smiled at his host. He had speculated before his arrival that Cleatus would inquire about his retirement life and in particular his conversion to being a follower of Christ. So he expected Cleatus' next probe, "My friend, when you decided to retire to Philippi and become a businessman there, I was greatly pleased. You deserved this opportunity after your many years of service to Rome."

Epaphroditus returned the compliment, "We shared much

during our time together in the army. You were an excellent commander. I've followed your rise in the military since my retirement and know you have served Rome beyond what any other soldier would."

"You flatter me unnecessarily, Epaphroditus. I merely did what needed to be done. Rome's continued glory has always been foremost in my decisions."

Epaphroditus raised his goblet of wine in the direction of his host and reasserted, "You have done well, and I salute you. Now, my friend, I sense you have questions you want to ask me. Let us begin."

Cleatus was only mildly surprised at the directness of his esteemed guest. During their time together, Cleatus had promoted Epaphroditus to the position of centurion, based on his bravery and intelligence. He expected Epaphroditus to have guessed part of his intent in inviting him to dinner.

"I do not intend on deceiving you, Epaphroditus. We have been through too much together. I'm genuinely pleased we can meet again. Because of the nature and seriousness of the case involving Paul, your association with him and this Jesus Christ are very important to me. Paul's life is at stake here, and you can shed light on questions we have."

"I do not take offense at your desire to probe about my involvement with Paul or with my relationship with Christ Jesus. It is a pleasure to talk about Christ with you or anyone, for that matter. Of course, I want to help my brother Paul, but more importantly, I want to speak the truth."

Cleatus was relieved at Epaphroditus' relaxed openness. He knew that despite their previous relationship during their tenure in the military, people can change, and he had worried that Epaphroditus' radical turn of belief might have negatively impacted their friendship. He was greatly comforted by his friend's reassurance.

The ensuing discussion between the two men continued long into the night. One question and answer volley led to another, and the interrogating general felt he was getting greater insight into his past friend's newfound belief as well as that of his assignment, Paul. It was probably enough for now. "My friend, it is very late and I've taken up much of your time. I appreciate your answers to my many questions. There is no doubt in my mind about your sincerity and passion. You have given me much to think about. But, now, it is time to escort you back to Quantus' home."

During the carriage ride to Quantus' house, talk shifted to their past military experiences. After Epaphroditus entered his residence, Cleatus had much on his mind concerning his long-time friend Epaphroditus, and Paul's man-god Jesus who was captivating so many people. He was deeply concerned about the potential consequences of this new belief. It was even more important that he, Seneca, and Flavius obtain the truth about this growing religious phenomenon. Paul's life was at stake; but more importantly, Rome's future actions towards these unique people had significant ramifications.

The spy-minded general instructed his carriage driver to hurry back to his townhouse. Cleatus wanted to waste no time in conferring with his scribe to ensure the evening's conversation was duly recorded.

Once inside the townhouse, Cleatus encountered the scribe dutifully transcribing the conversation's important points onto parchment. The scribe looked up from his work into the concerned and inquisitive face of his commander. "Everything worked well, Cleatus. I shall finish here within a respectable time so as not to disturb your sleep."

Cleatus leaned over the seated scribe and inspected the transcript. "This recording is vitally important. I must go over what you have written and compare it to my own mental notes to add any more insight. Once this is accomplished, we both can get our needed sleep."

The two toiled several hours before the general was satisfied the transcription was complete. "You have done well, and the new day soon arrives. Go home and get your rest. Bring me the original, plus two copies, of your transcript to my office in two days." With that, the fatigued yet gratified servant of Rome lumbered off to bed.

Three days later, Cleatus met with Seneca and Flavius for their agreed monthly meeting to discuss developments and progress in Paul's case. The commanding general was pleased with the scribe's report and felt it would be very beneficial and enlightening to his cohorts, so he carried it with him.

Seneca hosted the secretive gathering in his townhouse. Outside his home, several Praetorian Guard members, dressed in civilian clothes and impersonating street vendors, carefully watched for any sign of spies or potential assailants. The main concern was not over the Jews who despised Paul and wanted his death, but over Nero's political enemies seeking any possible advantage to dethrone Rome's current Caesar. Nero's downward spiral of focusing mainly on his own frivolous pleasures was causing growing unrest among Rome's ruling elite.

As the men sat in Seneca's dining room at one of his ornate tables, Cleatus wondered if Caesar's counsel employed the same monitoring system utilized by the general. He doubted such was the case and deduced it wouldn't make any difference so long as he did not incriminate himself, which he had no intention of doing. However, he resolved to be very careful with what he said in front of his fellow investigators.

"Gentlemen, it is now December and time once again to discuss Paul," opened Seneca, as he looked at his allies with a warm smile. "I see we have a report from you, Cleatus, concerning a friend and former military colleague, Epaphroditus. What is the significance of this man to our involvement with Paul?"

Cleatus was delighted to be the center of interest, and seemed to puff out his chest like a pigeon. As he began to speak, he stroked the report as if to draw out points he felt were important. "I won't waste time explaining about Epaphroditus' relationship with me. You both know this, and also about his valiant service to Rome. The report you see before you reveals his current mindset with this religious sect we call Christians. It parallels the thinking of Paul. The two have much in common."

Flavius briefly glanced at his written document while Cleatus spoke. He realized he would be spending considerable time after the meeting analyzing both the report and Cleatus' additional information. The centurion looked up from the report when Seneca asked, "Cleatus, what are the main similarities?"

The general was eager to answer, "Their fervor for this man-god Jesus is such that he is preeminent in their thinking and their actions. It is suprising, considering Paul is a Jew and Epaphroditus a so-called Gentile. Despite such diverse backgrounds, they have a very strong common bond. So strong all other allegiances are held inferior to following the dictates of this man-god."

Flavius then interjected a question that was supremely pertinent to their case, "Is this shared allegiance of concern to *Rome*, and does it impact Paul's appeal before Caesar on the charge of treason and intent?"

Cleatus looked admiringly at his centurion, and answered, "Their mindset is to convert so-called 'lost souls' to becoming followers of this Jesus. They are not intent on overthrowing any government, nor do they espouse causing riots or breaking Rome's laws. In many ways this is opposite the actions of the Jews, especially those in Judea."

When Cleatus finished, Flavius quickly asked for verification, "Are you saying, General, that we should not dare to associate these Christian advocates with the actions of the Jews?"

Cleatus blurted, "Exactly, Flavius. The teachings of this man-god Jesus infuriates the Jews and their religious mantra. And the so-called Gentiles don't care because many of them revere many gods. One more is of no consequence to them."

Again the centurion questioned, "Since Rome and the Greeks have a shared religious belief system, are you saying that Rome should accept this Christian belief and that it poses no threat to the empire?"

Cleatus carefully formulated his response. "Flavius, Rome must always be vigilant against any form of insurrection. At the present time, these Christians are a small sect at war with the Jewish religion. Should this escalate and disrupt Rome's ability to rule, then they must be dealt with and restrained."

Seneca entered the conversation with a self-assured observation, "Gentlemen. If I may add, all religious beliefs at a certain point in time come into conflict with one another. This leads to combative mindsets and it becomes a matter of control. Thus far, Rome has avoided such a situation by authorization of different religions and whenever possible incorporating them into their own belief system. However, this is proving not to be the case with the Jews. They are most obstinate."

The host paused to ensure the others understood the issue at hand before he continued, "We are finding Paul, Epaphroditus, and the many others who subscribe to this Christian belief system are focused on the afterlife. They evangelize conversion to this new Jesus even while they advocate obeying government laws. They claim not to be religious. They describe it as a relationship with their god. The evidence thus far indicates that neither Paul, nor the other Christians, including Epaphroditus, is intent on treason."

Flavius took the initiative to clarify Seneca's conclusion, "If, as you say, Paul and Epaphroditus and the other Christians are not treasonous,... then there is no case against Paul?" His quizzical expression looked for confirmation from the others.

Seneca nodded his agreement, "Exactly, Flavius."

Cleatus looked disturbed. There were so many unanswered

questions. "This may be so, Seneca. However, it behooves us to not jump to hasty conclusions. We have several months before Nero returns from Athens. Our time should be spent continuing to observe, investigate, and analyze Paul and his fellow Christians to make sure our final report to Nero will not get us afoul with him."

"I agree with you, Cleatus," said Seneca. "It seems Paul's case isn't as simple as it should be. There is still much to learn and many questions to answer." The chief Roman consul waved his hand in a haphazard way, demonstrating his vexation over all the complicating factors. "Nevertheless, we must continue our course."

The collaborators looked silently at one another, each man wondering what the next few months had in store for him. There was a mixture of excitement and worry over the uncertainty of the situation. The results could be far reaching.

## Chapter 16

Throughout the winter months of December through February, Epaphroditus continued to meet regularly with his two new mentees, Marcus and Lucilius. The almost daily interactions with the two soldiers buoyed Epaphroditus' spirits, giving him renewed energy and strength. The Gentile evangelist responded to the guiding of the Holy Spirit and gave Marcus and Lucilius deeper insight into what it meant to be followers of Christ Jesus.

The pair of lost souls were mesmerized by their mentor's words and passion for his new belief. Romans weren't known for relationships, especially with their idol gods. Hearing Epaphroditus speak of an endearing relationship with this Christ was a new and stimulating thought that especially appealed to Marcus.

Epaphroditus was aware of the dark secret Marcus had locked deep within his heart. Shortly after retiring to Philippi, Epaphroditus had encountered Marcus who also had retired there after his twenty-five years of service in Rome's army. He had married and the couple had a boy who took after Marcus. When the boy was five, he and his mother came down with the deadly fever which ran rampant throughout Philippi and the surrounding region. The fever showed no mercy, killing many in its terminal path. Among the hundreds who succumbed to its lethal tentacles were both Marcus' son and wife. The combined loss had devastated Marcus.

Epaphroditus had gone to his fellow army colleague and attempted to console him as best he could. He was limited by his own adherence to Rome's cultural and religious beliefs—which also limited his effectiveness. Nonetheless, Marcus had greatly appreciated his former colleague's attempt.

A few years later, Epaphroditus surrendered his life to Christ and reached out to Marcus without success. He learned that Marcus had re-enlisted in the army and had been made a member of the Praetorian Guard. His assignment was to instruct the field soldiers in the techniques of being dog handlers and taught proficiency in the use of the mace.

Marcus utilized his battlefield experience and developed a twist on the standard mace that was used primarily by some cavalry units. He replaced the stiff shaft with a flexible chain that was secured to a leather handle. The spiked ball was reduced to half the size and weight. When swung in either an arc or a circle, the speed generated a much more lethal blow, yet it was safer for the user. The shaft of the standard mace was nearly four feet long while the chain attachment to Marcus' innovation was only two-and-a-half-feet long.

When Cleatus took particular note of this innovative development, he was eager to have Marcus instruct new soldiers in the technique. It coordinated well with being a dog handler because it made the soldier more mobile and able to perform as if he were four soldiers, rather than just one. Cleatus was also pleased to be reunited with his former trooper. When Cleatus was a centurion, Marcus was assigned to his century group and proved himself not only loyal to Rome but a fierce and inspiring combatant.

When Epaphroditus had learned of Marcus' new course in life, he lamented not being able to speak with him. He wanted to give him the good news about Christ. Now, after twelve years of separation, God's grace had brought the two men together again. Epaphroditus was excited and humbled by this opportunity, and was careful to follow the guidance of the Holy Spirit in ministering to his mentee.

January was normally the peak of the winter season, a time when seasonal illnesses were at their highest. More deaths occurred during the month of January than at other times during the year. January was also a time of anguish for Marcus. It brought back memories of his wife and son's deaths. For him it was a time he dreaded and loathed.

Marcus felt compelled to reveal his gut-wrenching emotions to his friend and new mentor. One of his free days coincided with the anniversary of his family's demise. Marcus departed from his usual custom of making offerings to his pagan idol, Mithras, and instead asked to speak privately with Epaphroditus. "My friend, you know the sadness that comes to my heart on this dark day," groaned Marcus whose whole being reflected his state of mind. "Based on our recent conversations, I must have your counsel."

Epaphroditus reached out and grabbed Marcus' hand and directed him to the private room he used in Quantus' home. "Sit down in this chair and tell me what concerns your heart, my friend," said Epaphroditus with an unspoken quick prayer for wisdom. He saw it was going to be a serious conversation.

"This is a dreaded day for me, one that causes me great turmoil. Based on your teaching of your relationship with your god, this Christ Jesus, I am wondering. Is it possible he can cure my heart and remove this wretched turmoil from my mind and body?"

With gentle compassion, God's ready servant replied, "Christ Jesus is always at the door of your heart waiting for you to invite Him into your life, that He may forgive your sins, give you eternal life, and take away bondage that chains your heart and mind."

Marcus looked pleadingly at his friend. "I'm very tired of this torment. It has been with me such a long time. I ask, how can Christ Jesus remove this dark cloud that hangs in my heart?"

Epaphroditus assured him, "It is what He wants to do! He came to give life, and give it abundantly! It is easy, Marcus. Simply ask him with a sincere heart to come into your life. Tell Him you want to know Him, and to worship Him every day of life He gives you. Do this with all sincerity and He will hear the cries of your heart and transform you into His new creation."

The depressed soldier stared at Epaphroditus, still wondering. It didn't make sense to him, but he longed for it to be true. Finally, he bobbed his head and begged, "Epaphroditus, help me with this plea." Epaphroditus went to where Marcus was sitting and placed his hand on his friend's despondent head. Gently, he told his friend, "Say these words after me. 'Christ Jesus, I ache for the comfort only You can give my soul. I need you. I ask that You come into my life and be my Lord for now and forever, that I may know You, follow You, and have eternal life with You.'"

Marcus repeated what Epaphroditus instructed him to say. There was no holding back on his part. He was broken, and no longer willing to put up any pretense. God read his heart and just as immediately sent his Holy Spirit to indwell the soul of His now redeemed child.

The newly saved man let out a sigh of relief as the Holy Spirit laid claim over his soul. Marcus felt a rush of comfort. It was as if a great and heavy weight had been removed from his shoulders. Relief flooded his body and mind. He suddenly found himself weeping tears of release. The doubts he had felt just a few moments before were replaced by joyful faith.

As he looked up at God's servant-evangelist, Marcus witnessed joy on Epaphroditus' face, too, who beamed and smiled back at his new brother in Christ. "My friend, welcome to the family of Almighty God! All the angels in heaven sing, rejoicing over this moment—and the devil gnashes his teeth in anguish."

Marcus didn't quite understand Epaphroditus' words, but felt in time he would come to know their meaning. His tears of joy and relief continued unabated, cleansing his tortured soul of all the guilt, anger, bitterness, and grief that had held him in a death grip for years since the passing of his wife and son.

Within a short time his tears were dried, and Marcus asked his new brother in Christ, "Epaphroditus, you speak about being a new creation and having eternal life with Jesus. But I ask, what about my wife and my son? Is it possible for my family to have such a relationship, or is it too late for them?"

This was a question that God's servant evangelist was prepared to answer. He had been asked it many times by souls longing for the salvation of their loved ones. "It is so, my friend. God's fervent desire is to have eternal relationship with *all* his creation. Your young son is in heaven with Almighty God. God's faithfulness and desire for all to find eternal life with Him is your assurance that your wife also had opportunity to know and accept Christ as her Savior for eternal life with Him and you and your son."

Marcus was somewhat perplexed. "How can she have had this opportunity? I was at her side when she died. No one was there to help her say the words you said with me."

Epaphroditus gently and lovingly explained, "The words aren't a magic incantation. God knows the heart of all His created ones, whether words are spoken or not. He doesn't always reveal how He works or when He works. But in His sovereignty, He makes His salvation available to all those who desire Him. He is not willing for any to die without Him. Even His creation displays His beauty, so no one can honestly plead ignorance of Him; there is no excuse. Even at the very moment of death, one may ask for forgiveness, or reject Him. He allows all to have a chance to make their own decision. Jesus told his disciples this with certainty."

Marcus relaxed, closed his eyes for a brief moment, then looked at Epaphroditus. "In my heart, I believe she said yes to

Christ's invitation."

Epaphroditus was serious with his reply, neither denying it nor affirming it. "You know your wife better than I or any other human could have known her. Rest assured, God will give you comfort in this matter and should it be His will, He will confirm your hope to you."

Marcus accepted his friend's reassurance with a hopeful smile. "I eagerly await His confirmation."

At that moment, Quantus appeared in the doorway of the guest's bedroom to inquire if Marcus would stay for dinner. Epaphroditus excitedly announced the momentous transformation of Marcus. Quantus' eyes sparkled, and he ran to Marcus, grabbed him by the arm, and gave him a tight hug. "My heart shouts for joy that your name is now written in God's book of life! Come! Let us tell Pricilia the good news. We must have a celebration."

Though confused about what had exactly taken place, Marcus knew this moment had changed his life forever. He felt so different! He just wanted to take it all in and see what developed.

After an enjoyable evening with his new family in Christ, the Roman soldier indicated it was time for him to return to his barracks. Epaphroditus walked the short distance with him despite the cold nighttime air. Marcus purposely walked slowly, making sure they were alone to speak. "My friend, I don't really know what to do now, but I know you will assist me in this new journey. Please don't say anything to Lucilius or to anyone else, except Paul. I need time to understand what is happening."

"Of course, my friend, I shall honor your request. In fact, I was about to tell you we should meet privately so that I can teach you what to expect, now that you are a member of God's family. Do not stress or be worrisome about anything. Christ is in control and will not abandon you or lead you down a false, deceiving trail. Give all your concerns to Him now. He will show you the way."

Marcus was relieved to hear these words. He stopped, looked thankfully at his friend, and softly said, "I appreciate hearing this. I'm eager and excited about this new journey." With that, the two separated. Marcus shook off the cold breeze and strode towards the palace barracks. Epaphroditus quickly returned to the warmth of Quantus' home where he blissfully joined Quantus and Pricilia in praising Almighty God for His grace towards Marcus.

Following his recovery, Epaphroditus made regular visits to Paul, which was a delight to Lucilius and Marcus, but of concern to Draba. Marcus and Lucilius enjoyed being present when Paul and his fellow warrior for Christ were together, discussing concerns over the Jewish false teachers and Gentiles whose businesses were negatively impacted by the beliefs of the followers of Christ.

On one occasion, Draba was close to chastising Epaphroditus for his close association with Paul. The Roman guard found it difficult to accept that a Macedonian and former Roman advocate would consider this Jew as a brother. Draba was very uncomfortable that Paul, a Jew, was also a Roman citizen. It was definitely out of the ordinary.

Draba believed Paul should be incarcerated in the palace prison, chained to the wall, instead of being under house arrest with limited freedoms. It was Draba's contention that Paul was taking undue advantage of Rome's civility towards its citizens accused of crimes, especially when it was high treason. In his mind, there was no doubt that Paul, as a leader in this religious sect, was advocating sedition against Rome. Draba's emotional reaction and imagination was further influenced by those who came to visit Paul on any given day.

Draba strongly hoped for the possibility that one day while he was on duty, Paul would reveal his true nature; then Draba could report his findings to Flavius and change Paul's treatment. When Epaphroditus visited Paul with Draba on duty, the guard became acutely observant of the dialogue between the two warriors for Christ, hoping to achieve that end.

Draba's wish almost came true for him on a rainy day in January. Paul warmly greeted his fellow evangelist, "Epaphroditus, you are wet. Come by the fire in the dining room and warm yourself. We can have some warm liquid."

The two godly warriors sat near the open fireplace and Epaphroditus was the first to speak, "Now that I'm sufficiently recovered from the fever, I want to talk with you concerning the church in Philippi." Draba inched closer to avoid missing any important exchange between the two brothers in Christ. Epaphroditus took a sip of his warm drink. "Although the church is doing well, the Judaizers continue to barrage church members with their false teaching. They also attempt to get the business owners to refuse to do business with Christ's servants."

Paul asked, "Are the elders engaging the church to rebuke these Judaizers?"

Epaphroditus took another quick sip before answering, "Yes, but it often requires considerable time and effort to confront all the church members who are swayed by the false teachers."

Paul clasped a knee with his interlocked fingers and leaned back in his chair. He scowled a bit with concern over those suffering under these difficulties. "I'm gratified the elders are remaining steadfast. What about the Roman authorities? How do the Roman authorities react to this interference with their businessmen?"

Draba's heart began to pound. This was what he had hoped for, and he relished what he might hear in Epaphroditus' reply.

As he spoke, the Macedonian appeared unemotional regarding the conflict, "Of course, the Romans favor their own, especially those former soldiers who have retired to Philippi and have their own businesses. The garrison commander follows Rome's dictates to allow business to flourish. It remains one of the hubs for Rome to receive many highly desirable items that are not available in Italy."

At that point, Epaphroditus turned his head and looked at Draba. He knew that the guard would be reporting the contents of this conversation to his superiors. His acknowledgment of Draba conveyed his understanding of the command and also that he had nothing to hide in his comments to Paul.

Epaphroditus kept his eyes on Draba. "Our brothers in Philippi know that to truly follow Christ, they must not impede the work of others, but show them, through Christ, how to do business ethically." Draba understood what was being said and he bristled slightly that it was directed to him as well as to Paul.

The Macedonian looked toward the fire. The crackling wood held his attention as he resumed speaking to Paul, "I have sessions not only with our brothers who own businesses in Philippi, but also with the Roman garrison commander. It is important to resolve any differences amicably, and before the false teachers are able to incite any riots."

Paul remained still, with his hands folded around one knee. His thumbs tapped together slightly as he thought. Without looking at Draba, he answered Epaphroditus, "You are doing the work of Christ Jesus, my brother. I can tell how you yearn to return to Philippi and be with our brothers and sisters there. Each day that you grow physically stronger is a day you are closer to returning to your home and your business." He smiled his encouragement.

The apostle of Christ reached for his beverage and revealed, "I have thought and prayed about the church in Philippi and their love in sending you and their gifts to me while I'm detained here in Rome. I've written a letter to the church, which I would like you to deliver. I've also instructed our brother Timothy to accompany you on your return journey. The church at Philippi needs both Timothy and your spiritual wisdom and strength during this time."

Paul stood up and told Draba he needed to get his finished letter from the office next to the dining room. The surprised guard allowed Paul to retrieve the letter alone. When Paul returned with letter in hand, he gave it to Draba. "I know that all correspondence must first be approved by Seneca and Cleatus. Give this to Flavius that he may copy it. When it is duplicated, please return it to me."

Draba looked at the letter, then at Paul. "Flavius will have this in hand as soon as my shift ends this day." The guard was too dumbfounded to add anything to his brief statement.

Paul explained to Epaphroditus, "Flavius won't tarry in having copies of this letter made. It should be back in my hands within a few days, my brother. I'm sure you desire to prepare for your journey back home."

Epaphroditus confided to Paul, "I've learned about a caravan that will depart for Philippi and other cities within the next week. I'm glad you agree with my desire to return home. There is much work to do there for Christ Jesus, and I long to be His servant in Philippi." He and Paul embraced, and Epaphroditus wrapped his body in the warm cloak that had dried while he sat near the fire. He proceeded back to Quantus' home, enjoying its residual warmth.

Neither Paul nor Draba discussed the letter to the Philippians as Draba tucked it under his cloak to keep it dry. Draba dashed through the rain to make his report to Flavius with his valuable treasure. He knew the document would be important to those who would be involved with Paul's appeal.

Flavius was startled when Draba presented the epistle. At first, he looked silently at the letter. Draba stood in front of Flavius' desk, studying the centurion's reactions as he skipped over the writing.

Then Flavius put the paper aside and glanced at the seated scribe who was waiting to take dictation. He nodded to the guard, "Let us not waste any time with today's report. Proceed as you normally have, Draba. I shall not interrupt until after you have finished. I'm sure there will be questions for clarification afterwards. Now, begin."

Draba was proud of how well he remembered the conversation between Paul and Epaphroditus. He gave a fluid report concerning the two subjects of interest. True to his word, Flavius did not interrupt, and when Draba was finished, Flavius threw a barrage of questions at him.

The report lasted nearly one and a half hours, roughly four times longer than usual. Draba was weary when Flavius finally said he was finished, "Go eat some food, Draba, and of course make no mention of this report to anyone. Relax and enjoy your evening, for tomorrow is another day of uncertainty."

Flavius was pleased when the scribe told him copies of Paul's epistle to the Philippians would be available within the next two days. The centurion knew full well that both Cleatus and Seneca would want the report as soon as possible. Five months had transpired since Paul's arrival under guard from Caesarea. They believed the letter would shed light on much of the speculation over this Roman citizen accused of treason.

The young centurion commander was content to wait for the completed copies of Paul's essay; he had plenty of duties to attend to that kept his mind occupied.

When the scribe presented him with the completed copies two days later, Flavius immediately had messengers deliver individual copies to Seneca and to Cleatus. As he expected would happen, Seneca requested a special meeting to discuss the contents of the epistle with Flavius and Cleatus. The chief consul gave himself and his two military cohorts two days to evaluate Paul's writing before their special conclave.

Seneca arrived late in the afternoon on the day of the scheduled meeting with Cleatus and Flavius. It was a short distance from his villa to the townhouse in Rome, but seemed much too long for Rome's senior consul to Caesar. The month of January was noted for its foul air in the capital city and Seneca detested breathing in the heavy smell of the wood smoke.

The slim Roman moved nimbly and rapidly to ensure the dining room would be ready for his guests. Seneca had ordered one of his own hand-carved tables to be delivered to the townhouse. Today's meeting would give him an opportunity not only to professionally impress his guests, but also to observe their favorable reactions to his beautifully crafted wood. He and Pompeia loved to entertain, and this rectangular table could accommodate more than the traditional small couches. He would not need room for six today, but enjoyed knowing there would be luxurious spaciousness at the table. Seneca walked around the table, evaluating it from various angles. Satisfied with its appearance, the host entered the kitchen to inspect the food he had requested. He barely finished this task when a house servant announced the first arrival.

As usual, Flavius appeared in his crimson cape with the matching crimson horsehair-festooned helmet, flaunting his rank as centurion. His armor glistened in the late afternoon sun. He was easily recognizable. Hidden in the dark recesses of several nearby buildings were Praetorian Guard spies dressed in commoner attire. Each disguised soldier nonchalantly watched the centurion enter the townhouse.

Once the door closed behind Flavius, the spies outside looked in all directions for a sign of anyone intent on either barging into the townhouse or waiting for a potential victim to emerge later.

Within minutes following Flavius' entrance, Cleatus dismounted his black stallion at the rear of the townhouse. He studiously surveyed the surroundings to make sure he wasn't followed, then entered through the back kitchen door.

Seneca guided his guests to the carefully prepared dining room. He was anxious to see their reaction to his new table. Flavius stood gazing with admiration at the waxed top and the ornately carved legs and rails. Cleatus ran his hand along the top of the table as he slowly walked around its perimeter. "You have outdone yourself with this table, Seneca," commented Cleatus. He had been to many of Seneca's previous house parties and was aware of the Roman's vanity in showing off his talent and vast wealth.

Flavius was just learning about Seneca's desire to exhibit his possessions and was startled at the beauty of the workmanship. "Very talented hands have worked on this table, Seneca. It is more like a work of art." With these comments, Seneca's ego was massaged and he felt the meeting would proceed nicely. He gestured for his guests to take a seat in one of the three chairs spaced around the table.

"I trust each of you has had sufficient time to analyze the essay composed by our detainee," said the host as he held up his copy of Paul's letter and waved it back and forth. The two guests acknowledged they had.

"Cleatus, tell me your impressions after reading this letter," requested Seneca in a searching voice. The head field general squared his massive shoulders. The oil lamp's light made Cleatus appear sinister as it cast undulating light and shadows on his black armor. The general placed his copy of the letter on the table and rested his thick-fingered hand on it.

"My findings are that Paul is addressing this so-called church of Christians to encourage them in their mission to follow this god named Jesus. I found no cause for alarm or intent of sedition in its contents." Cleatus stretched his neck and commented, "However, Paul's words are such anyone who listens to them will be motivated to carry out his instructions. He is showing himself to be a strong leader of these people."

He turned his head toward his centurion subordinate, signaling it was his turn to comment. Flavius nodded to his commander, cleared his throat, and explained, "I once was stationed at Philippi. It is a very diverse city with, interestingly, only a handful of Jews. I find it impressive. Paul is able to not only encourage various ones, but also is able to unite Asians, Greeks, Persians, Romans and other nationalities for their common cause." His confidence grew as he spoke, even though he was the youngest of the trio. He added, "And I agree with you, General, that Paul is a strong leader and would even make an excellent commander in Rome's military."

It was Cleatus' turn to nod his respect for the energetic young centurion. A slight smile formed at one corner of his mouth. He was pleased that Flavius wasn't afraid to express his opinions before Rome's supreme field general.

Seneca wasn't surprised at the brevity of the two military officer's assessments. Roman communication was noted for being brief, often curt, without preliminaries. But, it was a trait that Seneca disliked. He much more preferred the Greek style of expansion and poetic aspects of speaking and writing.

"Thank you, both, for your input. In studying Paul's manuscript to these Philippians, I detect his love for them, and his desire they remain united in the face of bickering among their members. He attempts to relay a sense of peace and contentment to them in all their pursuits, and warns them to rebuke false teachers who attempt to infiltrate their ranks."

Seneca spoke in a respectful and admiring voice that both Cleatus and Flavius noticed and filed in their memory banks. The Roman consul and philosopher gently placed his copy of Paul's writing on the gleaming tabletop and quietly laid his hands on it. He peered down at the work, then slowly lifted his head to address the anxious men, "What is prominent in this epistle is Paul's expressions to the Philippians of his adulation for this god Jesus!

He truly reveres him and guides his followers to do the same."

Cleatus wasn't prone to the emotion that Seneca had just displayed, and he brought up a question that deflated the Roman consul's moment of admiration for Paul. "Seneca, do you foresee the probability that at a given time, Paul's influence on these Christians in Philippi and other parts of the empire could result in an uprising against Rome?"

Seneca's posture drooped at the question. He rubbed the back of his neck while he considered. Sitting upright again, he answered, "No, I do not. This epistle is clear about Paul's intent. There is no hidden message, meaning, or admonition to revolt against Rome." Sensing their acceptance of his answer, Seneca returned to his earlier thought, "Paul is most adamant about following this god Jesus first. However, it is quite within the realm of reason that perhaps a portion of these Christians, even without Paul's approval, may become overzealous and revolt."

Flavius picked up on this theme. "Seneca, based on what you have told us, do you believe this epistle should not be allowed to get into the hands of the Philippian Christian leaders?"

Cleatus admired Flavius' insight and was unsure how Seneca would answer. His eyes squinted as he waited for Seneca's reply to the younger officer. "Flavius, knowing what I do about this peculiar sect and its advocates, I do not see any reason to withhold this letter from them." With a slight smile, Seneca leaned forward to clarify his reasoning, "Remember, gentlemen, Epaphroditus is now a convert to this sect and is very influential among them. He is a wise leader, trained well by Rome, and quite capable of diffusing any insurrection attempt."

Cleatus swiftly agreed, "You are right, Seneca. Epaphroditus will keep a cool head. And he certainly has never been afraid to thwart anyone who desires to rise up against Rome!"

Flavius looked at both men to ascertain a consensus. "Then, are we agreed that this epistle will be allowed delivery to the Philippians and we shall monitor what happens after it is dispersed among these Christians?"

Seneca and Cleatus concurred with their younger colleague. Paul would be given back his original letter, and when Epaphroditus returned to Philippi, a secret agent would tag along in the same caravan to monitor what ensued.

That ended their official business, and the host happily began entertaining and impressing his guests with a fine meal.

 Chapter 17

The next day, Seneca summoned Cato to his townhouse. The assigned attorney-spy needed to be briefed before he appeared before his client. Seneca relished the thought of showcasing his exquisite table to his colleague. There was no doubt in his mind that it would lead Cato to desire to have a similar one constructed for his own purchase.

Cato's physical characteristics were the kind that naturally drew attention. He was tall and handsome, with angular facial features that reminded one of a Greek statue. He conveyed a strong sense of dignity, almost regality, with his long strides, purposeful gestures, and measured words. His intellect and philosophical conversations elicited admiration from his colleagues, and awe mixed with intimidation among his rivals.

Cato was courteously prompt, as always, in his arrival at Seneca's townhouse and indeed was impressed by the new piece of furniture. Seneca saw his admiration but, to his dismay, his accomplice did not plead for information concerning the crafting or the craftsman of the table. Instead, Cato was more concerned about the development of Paul's case and wanted to get down to business as soon as possible. Seneca was slightly irritated by this, but he consoled himself with the thought that a succinct updating with Cato would allow him to return sooner to his villa where he could breathe clean air again.

Food was always a focal point in Roman business meetings or social gatherings. Although this particular get-together was limited to two people, Seneca nonetheless provided ample cuisine for the affair. As they dipped fresh, warm flatbread into a garum sauce bowl, and snacked on fruit delicacies, Seneca opened the conversation, "Cato, your client recently composed an epistle for his fellow Christian sect members in Philippi. Cleatus, Flavius, and I reviewed his essay at length and discussed whether or not to allow its distribution to the Philippians' leaders." Wiping his hands on a new hand cloth, Seneca presented Cato with a copy of the Philippians' letter.

Cato carefully handled the manuscript, but did not take the time to read it. "I look forward to reviewing this when I return to my townhouse. What is your assessment of its contents?" As Cato listened, his thoughts went briefly to the time he and Seneca had attended Paul's oratory before the Greek Senate some years earlier. He remembered being very impressed with the man's eloquence and persuasiveness.

Seneca gave his synopsis, and Cato ate the last bite of bread. He wiped his mouth, and addressed his compatriot, "This is most interesting, my friend. I shall be sure to review this document very closely. Based on your words, I believe we now have something more interesting concerning our assignee. We go beyond the political, criminal, aspect into the philosophical. This is more to our interest, seeing that we adhere to Stoicism. My questions will address the philosophical facets of this letter."

Seneca put down a piece of the sauce-flavored bread and cautioned his collaborator, "I know you will enjoy engaging Paul over his writing, but do not lose sight of our main purpose of determining the treason and intent portions of this case. Nero will not listen to anything pertaining to Paul's philosophy. The Cretan favors his own pathetic attempts at music and poetry over more intellectual pursuits." Cato accepted Seneca's advice with grace, acknowledging its truth.

After their meal, Seneca noted with disappointment that Cato still had not commented or inquired about his beautiful table. Instead, Cato had focused their discourse entirely on their earlier exchanges about Paul, and now he indicated he must leave for his home. Seneca asked him if he enjoyed sitting at the table. "It was very pleasant," Cato responded, eager to be on with his task. Seneca realized there was no opening for further conversation as Cato continued, "I must thank you for the fine meal, Seneca, but now I must not dawdle. It is time for me to leave, for I have the privilege and duty to analyze this epistle. The sooner I evaluate its contents, the sooner I will be able to discuss it with our assignee." With his usual efficiency, Cato took the writings, bowed politely to his host, and headed for the door.

As Cato's carriage made its way to his townhouse, Seneca

scurried into his own waiting carriage for his long-awaited ride to his luxurious villa.

When Draba returned the letter Paul had written to the church in Philippi, the guard was keen on obtaining any useful information the detainee might reveal that would influence the opinion of the tribunal in dealing with this Jew. Paul thanked Draba for returning the epistle, and requested the waiting messenger boy to fetch Epaphroditus. Draba was pleased this meeting would take place while he was on duty and he waited impatiently for Paul's friend to arrive at the townhouse.

Soon, Epaphroditus was announced by the front door guard. Paul put down his cobbling work and went to greet his friend. Draba was close behind Paul, with his senses on high alert for this much-anticipated meeting. Due to the inclement weather, they opted for the main office rather than the courtyard patio normally favored by Romans for such occasions.

Paul immediately gave the Philippian letter to Epaphroditus. "My brother, the authorities have sufficiently examined my letter to the church at Philippi and now I entrust it to you! Are you returning to Philippi as you earlier indicated?"

The Macedonian briefly glanced at the guard, who obviously was hanging on every word to report to his superiors, before he answered Paul, "The caravan shall leave day after tomorrow. I am ready for the trip, and will safeguard your epistle in this special pouch. It will keep it dry from the weather."

Epaphroditus sorely wanted to discuss Marcus' conversion with Paul, but knew he could not do so because of the presence of Draba. Christ's servant had pledged not to reveal his life-changing event until Marcus was comfortable for it to be known. Now that he would be leaving Rome within the next 48 hours, there was no time to inform Paul of his conversion. Epaphroditus knew, however, that God's perfect timing would make it known.

Paul and his fellow warrior for Christ spent their remaining time together discussing Epaphroditus' business and what he intended to do, once the church elders had the opportunity to read Paul's teaching to them. "I want to make sure they understand your words, my brother, and assist them in ways to implement your teaching so the church can continue to prosper, grow, and carry out God's plan."

After the allocated visiting time was used up, Paul and his special brother in Christ reluctantly bid each other farewell, and Epaphroditus placed the epistle in the pouch. There was both sadness and joy in each man's heart after Epaphroditus left. Sadness at not having more time together, yet joy that each warrior had the same passion. They would continue battling for lost souls and God would be with them.

After thanking Quantus and Pricilia for their hospitality, Epaphroditus stepped out of the warm house into the cold, rainy, early morning. He ducked his head with a shiver in the pelting rain and headed to where the caravan was located. Sabine was the leader of the merchant train and was supervising the last minute preparations for their departure.

There would be 79 camels returning to Philippi and one horse-drawn wagon that contained several cages of homing pigeons destined for the Roman garrison located just outside the city. The pigeons were valuable cargo, and great care was taken to ensure their safe arrival. When communication with Rome was necessary, a pigeon would be released to return to its home nest in Rome.

Sabine made sure the cages were adequately secured with protective coverings placed over them to protect the birds from the harsh weather. Should the pigeons become injured or die, Sabine would be held personally accountable and the penalty would be severe. In certain ways, the pigeons were the most valuable cargo to make the long trek to Philippi.

The merchant train captain was informed by the Roman military superior that the infantry contingent would be the only protection unit for the trip. Due to the relatively small size of the caravan, the cavalry would not be part of the armed unit. This did not cause Sabine alarm because he knew from experience Rome's infantry was quite capable of dealing with any marauders they might encounter along the way.

What was of greater concern to the merchant captain was the presence of a late addition to the group. A man who sought passage because he was to conduct business in Philippi. Sabine knew the regular businessmen who made routine trips to that huge city of commerce, but this man was unknown to him.

At the same time that the military superior returned to his unit, Epaphroditus arrived and stood before the merchant captain. "Ah, Epaphroditus, you are here! We are almost ready to depart on our journey despite this foul weather. I have a surprise for you, my friend." Sabine led the Macedonian businessman to another part of the caravan and produced a fine horse for him.

"This animal is part of our cargo and I want you to ride it. It is far better than letting it walk behind one of the camels and possibly breaking loose and running away." As Epaphroditus inspected his new steed, Sabine drew closer to his fellow businessman and furtively whispered, "There is a new passenger with us and I do not trust him. I tell you that you should be wary of this man. I fear he may be something other than who he says he is."

Epaphroditus listened carefully to Sabine's warning. "Thank you, Sabine. I shall be aware of this man and observe him closely. I will inform you of anything I learn about him that could cause you problems."

Three weeks into the journey, the caravan stopped at one of the many waystations that popped up with the advent of heavy winter caravan traffic to Rome. It was a place to rest and obtain water and food supplies, and valuable information. Travelers eagerly sought news about what lay ahead, and especially if any marauders were lurking.

The new passenger had not drawn attention to himself during the early part of the journey. He was taking some water when Epaphroditus quietly approached him. He had his back to him, and when he put down his water goblet and turned around, he was startled at the steely-eyed presence of Epaphroditus. Wasting no time on idle conversation, Christ's warrior confronted the man in a soft voice, "Who has ordered you to spy on me and make this trip to Philippi? It is obvious you have no ties to the city or to any businesses there."

Before the traveler could answer, Sabine suddenly appeared from nowhere and stood beside Epaphroditus. "I would like an answer to that question, myself! As captain of this caravan, I have the authority to remove you!" Sabine then motioned with his head towards the Roman army unit over his shoulder. "At my word, the army will detain you here and when they return to Rome take you with them. You will answer to Rome about your activities."

The traveler's eyes shot back and forth from Sabine, to Epaphroditus, to the nearby army unit. He saw he was caught, and he confessed, "I am under orders by Cleatus and Seneca to follow this man to Philippi." He pointed to Epaphroditus. "I am to report on his activities." He looked pleadingly at his questioners. "If I'm not allowed to continue, I will be punished on my return to Rome. I'm not here to harm you in any way, only to observe and report."

Epaphroditus looked at Sabine. Both believed the fearful man's answer. Christ's warrior studied the pale countenance of the traveler. "I believe what you say, and therefore do not have any objection to you continuing this journey." He turned to Sabine and said, "Let him remain with us. I'm not surprised that Cleatus and Seneca have taken this action. My association with a man who awaits his appeal before Caesar is the reason for this espionage. They seek information that could determine his guilt or innocence."

Sabine relaxed and redirected his eyes to the traveler. "It shall be as Epaphroditus wishes. You may continue with us, but I will watch you closely," he warned in a menacing voice. "If things are not as you say they are, I shall personally run my knife through your belly and end this on my terms!"

After that private confrontation, the caravan proceeded on to its far-off destination. The only interferences came from repeated storms and cold winds that made the shaken traveler wonder why he had taken on his failing assignment. Finally, upon the safe arrival of the merchant train in Philippi, the evangelist Epaphroditus took him to his home and arranged for him to stay with one of the church members while he carried out his duties.

The spy stayed one month, growing in curiosity while observing Epaphroditus, and inquiring about his Jesus. With his duty completed, the traveler thanked Epaphroditus for allowing him to complete his assignment. The irony of being a discovered spy and yet being able to carry back a report which was facilitated by Epaphroditus was not lost on either of them as they parted.

The now-not-so-secret-agent joined another caravan taking its much-needed cargo to Rome. When he gave his report to Cleatus, he wisely left out the portion of having been discovered in the caravan. Neither did he tell about being spared by the unexpected warmth and compassion of Epaphroditus and members of The Way during his stay in Philippi.

Cleatus and Seneca were pleased with the spy's report, never suspecting how easily all the information had been obtained. The supreme Roman military general was greatly relieved to learn that his former trusted centurion, Epaphroditus, was not part of any insurrection plot against Rome. "Seneca, our agent has been very factual. His report coincides with what I've received from the garrison commander in Philippi about the followers of this god named Jesus. I see no reason to believe that this epistle Paul wrote to his so-called church in any way promotes a plot against Rome."

The chief consul to Caesar agreed. "I concur with you, Cleatus, and I am equally sure you are greatly relieved to know that one of your valiant warriors remains loyal to Rome."

With a smile, Cleatus spoke a reminder, "But—his loyalty to Rome is superseded by his passion and loyalty to this god both he and Paul worship. This does not detract from our duty to continue securing evidence for Nero about the religious zealot under our detention."

On the day that Paul had to bid farewell to Epaphroditus, his trusted fellow warrior for Christ, Cato was about to pay him a visit. Since Cato was part of the official team to represent Paul, there was no time restriction on his visits. Cato was appreciative of this allowance. Not only did he believe extra time was necessary to prepare Paul for his appeal, Cato was delighted the time extension permitted him to discuss philosophical matters with a man who had impressed the Greek Senate with his wit, wisdom, and intelligence.

The dreary, overcast sky did not depress Cato's spirits in the least as he proceeded to Paul's townhouse. Lucilius noted, as always, Cato's confidence when he and Paul escorted the attorney into Paul's office for their discussion. Two chairs were arranged as usual for the pair, while Lucilius remained standing, in case he needed to intervene in any physical assault against Paul.

Cato had a copy of Paul's epistle to the Philippians in his hand and held it up to Paul. "As you know, Paul, the state makes copies of all your correspondence for our records, as well as for your defense in your appeal. I've read and analyzed this essay to your people in Philippi,...and I find it intriguing."

Paul was surprised by his lawyer's unexpected jolliness. Lucilius made sure he was close to the participants, determined not to miss any of the important and intriguing conversation that he knew would be forthcoming.

Cato immediately launched into his assessment of Paul's teaching meant for the Philippians, "The same elements you employed during your oratory with the Greek Senate are clearly evident in this essay. I must say, as I read your manuscript, I found myself being uplifted and encouraged. And I'm certainly not one of your religious converts."

Paul was patient, but his steady gaze conveyed that he was dissecting Cato's comments. Cato maintained his cheery demeanor to veil his close observation of his client. He continued his façade, "Several questions come to mind that, hopefully, you can clarify for me." This time, Cato changed his jovial manner for a moment of more seriousness. He shot a penetrating look at Paul.

Paul was keenly aware of this courtroom tactic, but was not perturbed. Cato queried, "Please explain why you refer to both knowledge and discernment in your admonishment to these Philippians?"

Paul had his elbow on the desktop and supported his head with his hand and fingers while Cato spoke. He held his casual position while replying, "I chose the Greek words because knowledge refers to each individual's personal relationship with Almighty God. Discernment points to a person-to-person relationship. A true follower of Christ Jesus will seek to grow in his personal relationship with his Savior first. We are to grow in the knowledge and grace of Christ. As these flourish, so do our relationships with other individuals, both those who are saved as well as those who remain lost souls."

Lucilius was surprised that he was able to understand what Paul was talking about, despite the fact he had not had the opportunity to read the letter before giving it to Flavius. His thoughts were interrupted by the persistent attorney who was asking, "How can one have a *personal* relationship with a *god*, and why is that of any importance?" Lucilius was startled by Cato's question and eager for Paul's answer.

"Personal relationship is important to God. He has chosen mankind for this. Each of his creation has unique personality traits. Having a growing relationship with man, God is able to teach, grow, and enlighten man, so that man is better able to carry out His plan and purpose for his life."

Paul paused for both Cato and Lucilius to process his words. Then he leaned back in his chair and continued, "Man is estranged from his Creator because of his sin. God is grieved by the separation sin causes. He sent His Son Jesus to die for us, to pay the penalty for *our* sin, the penalty *we* deserve. Anyone who repents and asks for His forgiveness will receive it and becomes reconnected with Almighty God. A personal relationship with Christ allows man to experience God and learn His ways and His thoughts, to better obey His commands."

Christ's evangelist detected that Lucilius was mulling over Paul's words, but Cato was processing them for a more intellectual discourse. Paul was focused on Lucilius more than on his attorney. "Lucilius, if I may ask you, do you have a personal relationship with any of your gods?"

Lucilius was startled again by Paul's question. The guard did not suspect he would become an object of this conversation. It took him some time to evaluate Paul's question. He wanted to give him an honest answer, mainly because of his growing interest in this topic. Romans had no personal relationship with any of their gods or those they chose to revere after inheriting them through their conquests. Cato, too, was startled by Paul's unexpected move, and expected to be entertained by Lucilius' forthcoming answer. He was all ears.

The guard cleared his throat, and directed his answer to Paul. "My whole adult life has been as a soldier serving Rome. As a soldier, I've been taught that the god Mithras is the one assigned to the military. Before entering into battle, afterwards, and in enjoying the bounty of the conquest, we give thanks to Mithras." Lucilius concluded, believing this was the best answer to the question.

"Now, Lucilius, do you ever go to Mithras for any other reason or on any other occasions?" Paul asked.

Lucilius did not have to contemplate Paul's question. His answer came quickly and definitively, "No. When I'm not engaged in battle I have no need to address Mithras."

"How about any of the other Roman gods? Do you revere them or have a personal relationship with any of them?"

Feeling confident in himself, Lucilius confided to Paul and to Cato, "No, I do not. I go about my everyday duties based on my ability to handle different situations. The only time I've ever gone to any god is to Mithras and only to plead for his help in battle."

Cato's astuteness caused him to grasp Paul's approach to his earlier questions. Rather than interrupt, the philosopher-attorney opted to let Paul continue with his premise.

"Do you have personal relationships with, say, other soldiers or civilians?"

Lucilius replied, "With a few other soldiers. Mainly, those who are in the same unit as I. We talk about a lot of things. We share our opinions and some of our feelings, but still there are some personal things that impact us emotionally that we keep to ourselves."

The guard hesitated and actually flushed as he continued, "There have been times I've become involved with women, but mainly for sex because being married is frowned upon for infantrymen such as myself. But I do not discuss my inner feelings with them," he asserted.

Paul sensed that further questioning would make Lucilius embarrassed or possibly irritated, so he shifted his gaze back to his attorney. "It is part of our human nature to seek out relationships, at whatever level, with our fellow humans. Our emotions and feelings dictate how much of a relationship we have with each other or our god. What is unique about having a personal relationship with Jesus is that He initiates the relationship and guides us so that we grow in this relationship and He draws us closer to Him. It is a manifestation of His love for His creation."

Cato remained still, waiting for Paul's focal point. "You see, Cato and Lucilius, Jesus Christ blesses us with love that transcends all other relationships and makes it possible for us to have an enduring relationship with other humans and treat them as God wants us to. When we experience God's love, we can love others as He loves us."

Lucilius was astounded at Paul's contention. It never occurred to him before that it was possible to have a relationship with any god, or that a god would want a relationship with a human. This was completely opposite to what he had been taught and what was foundational to Roman polytheism. Yet, Lucilius could envision the reward of having a growing relationship with anyone—god or human. It was the security of trust. The guard was changing his opinion of this Jew he thought he did not really care about.

Cato sought to regain control of the interrogation. "I understand what you are saying here, and what you contend in your epistle to the Philippians. What I want to know, Paul, is to what extent does your teaching reach? What are the political motives behind your admonition to these Philippians who follow you?"

Paul did not move, except to slightly shake his head. He answered simply, "There are no political motives. The focus is on understanding Christ, for each person to better obey Him and carry out His plan and purpose for their lives. He is not interested in man's politics and power maneuverings. He is far greater than anything man can devise. God is concerned that His created ones focus on Him, because their eternal lives are at stake. Our life on earth is but a vapor, but eternal life lasts forever and that is where our thoughts and efforts should be."

Again, Cato sidestepped Paul's reference to eternity, "Yet, Paul, in your writings and your speeches, some of which I've personally heard, you advocate putting this god, this Christ Jesus, before Caesar. Isn't this fanning the flame of sedition?"

Paul frowned at the suggestion, "Most certainly not, Cato. You misunderstand the meaning and power of having an eternal relationship with Jesus. By putting Him first, He empowers us to deal with our earthly issues. By following the commands of Christ Jesus, we are able to let this world see Christ through us, by His love and compassion that the world does not understand—but gladly receives."

"Yet, did not this Jesus proclaim before Pilate that he was the king of the Jews? If so, isn't it reasonable to assume all kings are interested in power, control, and eliminating their enemies?" Cato needed to press his point to see if he could flush out any underlying motivations of sedition or treason.

Paul didn't flinch. "Earthly kings, yes! It is as you say, Cato. But Christ Jesus is the heavenly king of the Jews, and to all who freely choose to proclaim He is the Son of God, man's Savior, and deliverer. His love is unlike any human form of love. When we sincerely, with all of our hearts, worship only Him and follow only Him, He gives us discernment, wisdom, and discerning spirits to handle what the world puts in our path!" It was clear Paul had lived every word he spoke with such conviction.

Lucilius was impressed with Paul. He was able to answer Cato's questions, and he did not back down or manifest any uncertainty or weakness in his answers. Lucilius now understood that Paul was saying the same thing that Epaphroditus had taught him and Marcus during the days they spent together. Lucilius felt a strange, enlightening curiosity overtaking him. He could not explain it, but while it wasn't causing him distress or anxiety, it was driving him. He wanted to hear more of what Paul had to say.

Cato, too, felt power in Paul's explanation. He realized his client's attitude and behavior was in complete harmony with his words. He was impressed by the ardor Paul had for this Christ Jesus. He realized that Paul was not guilty of treason against Caesar or Rome. At the same time, he grasped that Paul's words and teaching could be interpreted as intent for sedition, and that he must gather more evidence to prove Paul's innocence of treason at all costs. He was convinced Paul was completely innocent of the highest crime against Rome.

With new respect for his client, Cato needed to get to work on his defense. "Paul, you have given me valuable insight for preparing your defense before Caesar! I must conclude our conversation. It is getting late and I want to process what you have given me." Cato grandly rose up from his chair, bowed to his client, and stated, "We shall meet again for more discussions." Deeply engrossed in his thoughts, he headed to the vestibule, donned his cloak, and swiftly entered his waiting carriage.

# Chapter 18

After Cato left the townhouse, Lucilius tentatively asked Paul if he could speak with him about a personal matter. Paul readily agreed, and the two men stayed in the office to talk. "Paul, I found your words to Cato about your Christ Jesus to be very thought-provoking. What you said is very close to what Epaphroditus taught both Marcus and myself while he was in Rome."

The guard shifted his posture, searching for the right words to convey to Christ's evangelist. "I'm struggling inside, Paul. Your words, as well as those of Epaphroditus, have caused me to wonder. I can't really explain this feeling but it is strong, compelling, ...and I find myself thinking about it at different times. Can you enlighten me about what is happening inside me?"

Paul knew this was an individual issue and he must be careful not to antagonize Lucilius or cause him more confusion. Since Paul had encountered this before, he was comfortable with the question, knowing God's Holy Spirit was in control and would guide his words and give him the boldness he needed.

"Lucilius, you are evaluating your past beliefs alongside those that are new and foreign to you, and it is causing you to think about making a dramatic change in your life." Paul spoke softly and saw that Lucilius was not rejecting his explanation. "Tell me, what stands out in your mind about Christ Jesus?"

"How compassionate he is, and that he cares so deeply about me. I've never experienced this, and didn't know it was possible for someone like me. As you know Paul, we Romans are not the type of people to show love or to give our emotions much place in our culture."

Paul smiled understandingly at his distraught guard. "The first step is just what you are encountering, learning about a love that goes beyond what the world knows. The second step is to personally experience Christ and His love through your actions. Once you do, floodgates open and you are blessed with His discernment and wisdom. The more you experience His love, the more you cherish it and strive to follow Him. He opens the doors of your heart to things that only He can provide for you. In essence, Lucilius, you retain the same body, but your spirit transforms and you become a *new creation* in Him."

Lucilius stared at Paul, straining to understand. Paul waited, his eyes searching the guard's face, letting the Holy Spirit work in the guard's heart and mind. After several moments, Lucilius let out a heavy exhalation, "If I understand you correctly, Paul, you are telling me to give in to this new feeling and to trust this God, Jesus." Lucilius looked deeply into Paul's eyes, seeking approval of his statement.

Paul came around to Lucilius, and placed his hand gently on Lucilius' sturdy shoulder. "Yes, Lucilius. Christ has said that if you have faith as small as that of a mustard seed, and place it in Christ, that is sufficient for Him to bless you with eternal life."

Lucilius looked away from Paul who felt the guard's body relax. The guard looked at Paul with searching eyes, and made a short, definitive statement, "Paul, I want to experience Jesus."

Paul kept his hand on Lucilius' shoulder, and asked, "Do you seek Christ Jesus with all your heart?"

Lucilius spoke slowly and seriously, "Yes, I do. I feel He is the only one I can turn to at this time in my life."

Paul nodded and responded, "Then, Lucilius, simply ask Christ to forgive your unbelief. Ask Him into your heart that He may lift your burdens and help you, and give you eternal life with Him."

Lucilius stared at Paul. "Is that all I have to do? I don't have to make any public declaration or pay for this eternal life?"

Paul smiled broadly. "No, Lucilius. Christ's salvation is free, based on a sincere and humble heart—not on rituals, payments, or any good works!"

Lucilius left his hesitation and questions behind, and spoke aloud, asking Christ into his life in his own simple, sincere words. It was his very first prayer to mankind's Redeemer.

When Lucilius finished, Paul saw quiet tears beginning to trickle down his cheeks. The Roman guard used his hands to quickly wipe them away. "I don't know what these foolish tears are all about." He was embarrassed at his uncharacteristic show of emotion.

Paul joyfully explained, "Don't worry. It is God's Holy Spirit now indwelling your heart and spirit. Whether you have tears or no tears, He is with you. He will be with you until you are called to heaven. He will comfort you, guide you, teach you, and be your counselor. He is God's first and greatest gift and blessing to you. His presence within you is the permanent seal He places on you, just as we seal an official document. It signifies that you belong to Him! No man, circumstance, or principality can steal this from you, Lucilius. Christ will never forsake, nor abandon you throughout the course of your earthly life."

As Lucilius listened to Paul, he beamed in wonder, "I feel as if a great weight and burden has been lifted from me. I don't know how to explain it."

Paul beamed back at the new convert, "There is no need to attempt any explanation. You are now a brother in Christ to me and to all those who have come before you, accepting Christ as Lord and Savior. We understand because we, too, have experienced His forgiveness and love. It is a life-changing event."

Suddenly Lucilius became concerned. "What must I do now? Do I tell my friends, especially Marcus, or even Flavius?"

Paul was still smiling. "Just dwell in the joy and the peace Christ is blessing you with at this time. There is no hurry to inform others of your decision. The Holy Spirit will give you guidance on what to say, when to say it, and who to tell about your life-changing decision."

Paul then prayed with him a prayer of thanksgiving to Christ Jesus for the grace given to His new creation. When Paul finished, Lucilius said, "Your words were very touching. Is it possible I, too, will be able to pray as you do?"

Paul gently chuckled, "Yes, my brother, you already have! You say your own words right from your heart, and God hears every word exactly as you mean them. Just obey the prompting of the Holy Spirit and obey Christ's commands."

Lucilius asked, "When? When do I start this process?"

Paul chuckled again, "It has already begun." Lucilius looked baffled, so Paul added, "Do not stress, worry, or become anxious about this. The Holy Spirit is guiding you. Just listen for His still, small voice of prompting and direction. You may not hear it with your ears. More often you will feel it strongly in your heart and spirit. But you will know. God knows how to direct us on our paths and make His will known to us."

Lucilius' heavy eyebrows lifted, wrinkling his brow as he tried to imagine what it would be like now. This was all new to him. But he was excited. "I shall do as you say, Paul."

Later that same day, Cato stopped in front of Seneca's townhouse. The two had agreed that after Cato completed his first interrogation of Paul, they would meet and discuss what had transpired.

Seneca was ready for this meeting and instructed his house servant to usher the attorney into his office. "Your time with Paul did not last as long as I thought it might, Cato. Are you ready to give me details of your interrogation? We can do this while we have lunch. Everything is ready. Come, let us go to the dining room."

Cato enjoyed sharing meals with his colleague. Seneca had an appreciation for fine food and wanted his guests to revel in his culinary delights. Rarely did he disappoint his guests who anticipated satisfying their tastebuds and their bellies.

By the time the entrée was completed, Cato had relayed the details of the interrogation to Seneca, who sat comfortably satiated from the excellent food prepared by his servants. Seneca took a sip of the Spanish wine. He looked at the goblet, then at his guest, and boasted, "I recently received this batch of wine from my supplier in Spain. Do you find it tantalizing and smooth?"

Cato quickly agreed with his host's description, knowing that to say otherwise would be an affront and disrespectful. Fortunately for them both, the fact was, the wine was very good. Wishing to return to their earlier topic of conversation, Cato asked, "What are your thoughts about my interrogation of Paul, Seneca?"

The amiable host placed his goblet down on the table, puckered his lips, and set forth his honest opinion. "Our subject, indeed, is not guilty of treason. The fact that his accusers have not come forward is a clear indication they won't. Besides, they are not Roman citizens and, as we both know, only a Roman citizen can accuse another Roman of treason. To do so and be found liars would mean their immediate death. We can eliminate this accusation from further investigation."

Cato briefly looked away from Seneca and poured himself more wine. Watching the rich red liquid running into the goblet, he probed, "Do you agree with my assessment that we still must determine Paul's intent?"

Seneca maintained a resolute attitude. "Most certainly. We know little about this new religious sect Paul has such zeal in espousing. There are elements that require more clarification. This epistle he wrote to the Philippians is simple enough to understand. What we need to assess is the impact his writing has on the people and what it causes them to do. Hopefully, their actions will manifest before Nero returns. If not, we then must inform Caesar of this and recommend a delay in the appeal."

Cato disclosed his eager thoughts at this, "And in the process, my good friend, we shall have an opportunity to delve more into Paul's mind and thinking."

Seneca's expression grew more serious as he heard Cato's comment. "I must remind you, Cato, to be very careful in your grilling of our captive. Zealots such as Paul can be very convincing. In addition, we know Paul to be shrewd, intelligent, and cunning. Do not take him lightly or think you can easily control him, otherwise he will own you."

Cato's reverie subsided with the chiding from Seneca. "You caution me wisely, my friend. It is easy for me to become sidetracked. Having these debriefings will be most valuable for me. I do realize I must remind myself prior to examining Paul about the possibilities of being duped by him."

The two agents of intrigue then toasted each other with their goblets and the house servant served them their dessert.

Several days elapsed before Lucilius confronted Paul in the confines of his townhouse workshop. Again, the guard requested a conference with the cobbler evangelist, "Paul, may I speak with you concerning revealing my salvation to others?"

Paul laid down his cobbling tools on the workbench and gave the new convert his full attention. There was nothing in the guard's demeanor that indicated trouble. "Go ahead, Lucilius. I am eager to hear what you have to say."

"After yesterday's shift, while Marcus and I were heading back to our barracks, I told him of my accepting Christ as Lord and Savior." Lucilius' face showed heightened happiness. "To my surprise, Marcus informed me that he, too, had accepted Christ's invitation and became a follower while Epaphroditus was here in Rome. We both were dumbfounded, and so joyful in our hearts that the other was no longer lost to the world."

Paul's head tilted back as he began to laugh, exclaiming, "This is indeed joyful news! It is so reflective of how God works in His perfect timing. He surprises us in ways we do not anticipate!" Lucilius also began to laugh as he left the in-house workshop. He stepped to the edge of the courtyard and called for Marcus.

The dog handler quickly looked over his shoulder toward the sound of the voice. He could tell there was no cause for alarm—it was only the giddiness of his fellow Guard member. Marcus gave a silent hand signal for his two dogs to remain on guard, and he traversed the courtyard to his waiting companion. "What is of such importance, Lucilius, that you summon me away from my post?"

Suddenly, Paul appeared from the workshop and answered Marcus' uncertainty. "Marcus, Lucilius has just informed me about your acceptance of Christ's eternal life with Him. I'm exceedingly pleased and sing a song of halleluiah and praise to the Lord!" Paul's joy was sincere and exuberant.

Marcus stood speechless, looking dazed for a few moments, as his eyes went first to Paul, then to Lucilius. "I'm very relieved that you know, Paul. I've been waiting for just the right moment to share this with you. When Lucilius disclosed his conversion to me yesterday, I knew the time had come to tell you."

Paul stepped forward and gave each of the converts a tight hug and proclaimed, "Welcome to the family of Holy and Sovereign Lord." His joy was overflowing.

Lucilius looked at Marcus, signaling him with his eyes to make the request of Paul they had earlier agreed to. Marcus boldly revealed, "We would like for you to instruct us on what we need to know and to do now that we are Christ's. This is completely new to us and we don't want to displease our Lord."

The two converts were surprised by Paul's reaction. It was the first time either of them had witnessed Rome's prisoner almost dancing. In a bubbly tone, Paul said, "It would be an honor for me to assist you in your walk with Christ Jesus!"

Then Paul's tone became more serious. "You are correct—there is much to learn to become a true follower of Christ. The devil will thrust deceivers at you to weaken your resolve for Christ. I, and other followers, can give you each insight; but it is only the Holy Spirit who gives you spiritual discernment and discerning spirits to rebuke lackeys of the devil. He will do this on a personal basis as you reach out to Him and ask for His wisdom and rely on His grace."

Over the course of the next few weeks, Paul met with both men while they were on duty. During the day shift, Paul adjusted his work schedule to spend time instructing the pair. When their day shift was completed, Paul resumed his cobbler duties and worked until late into the night.

When both were on the afternoon shift, Paul mentored them during their dinnertime, making allowances for Marcus to inspect the rear wall opening for signs of intruders. It was easy to discern the two Roman soldiers were like sponges, soaking up all that Paul had to offer.

In between sessions with his new mentees, Paul also held court with Hevel, Teman, and the four replacement church elders. Since these visitors were limited to one hour each per orders of Flavius, Paul routinely received repeated visits from these men to complete the counseling and tutoring.

Paul regularly gave praise and thanksgiving to Christ for the many opportunities he had to work out the desire of his heart. For several years he had yearned to do this—teach the Roman church to be more effective in their obedience to Christ. Now it was happening. With devoted zeal for Christ, he felt humbled by His abundant blessings.

The Roman authorities had great interest as they took note of the many people who frequented Paul's townhouse. Secret agents were kept busy following these visitors and observing their actions, looking for any indication of intended rebellion against Rome. The voluminous files submitted by these spies strained Flavius. It was all part of Rome's diligence in learning not just about Paul, but about this odd sect, as well. It was all very puzzling to them and was becoming a larger force to reckon with than had first been thought.

The magnitude of Rome's involvement with Paul involved nearly 200 Praetorian Guard members serving in daily shifts of eight hours each. There was a guard at the front door, a second one to shadow Paul, and a third assigned to the rear of the townhouse courtyard where the wall opening could allow escape or entry to intruders. In addition, there were the many spies who shadowed Luke, Timothy, Aristarchus, and, of course, the church elders who routinely met with Christ's evangelist. There were the proficient scribes who transcribed Paul's epistles for the Roman authorities to analyze. The townhouse also had a shift of messenger boys, whose sole purpose was to take messages to Caesar's palace, to notify Flavius of unpredicted events.

Paul was one of only a handful of Roman citizens detained under house arrest to have this many soldiers involved in his protection and surveillance. Part of the reason for the abundance of personnel was the Roman desire to know about its people. To do this required detailed organization with a finely-tuned sense of timing to make sure everything functioned smoothly.

Rome's need for organization and attention to detail came into play late in the month of January. The winter created havoc that extended into the northern regions of the empire including Gaul, Britannia, and Germania. The economies of these wintry regions slowed to a snail's pace and food became scarce.

The winter's impact caused a band of Germanic bandits to form a single force that totaled 225 violent criminals. This horde believed that going south to the richer confines of Rome would provide them the food and the wealth they greedily desired.

Two strong leaders kept this sinister force intact and fixed on the waiting prize to be found in Rome. The wealthy landowners and businessmen who owned villas outside of Rome would be their targets. At the same time the villas were robbed, the second part of the horde would plunder the many townhouses that extended from the northwest to the northeast sections of the city.

Because the townhouses also were owned by the rich and elite of Rome, they represented a second source of great bounty. In the winter, they usually were unoccupied because the foul air from the wood-fueled stoves drove the elite to their villas. Robbing these townhouses would be easy and quick. The size of their force would allow them to strike all the townhomes almost simultaneously.

Their plan was to start in the northwest and end in the northeast all in one night. When the bounty was seized, the horde would escape east to the mountains and disperse back to their respective home countries. The blueprint was clear and readily accepted by the members of the horde. They assembled their weapons and headed south.

The one element they did not account for was Paul. These criminals did not know about Paul or the extreme measures the Romans were taking to ensure his safety as he waited to appear before Caesar. Ironically, a true criminal element was about to encounter an imagined criminal element—with the latter being fiercely guarded by alert and formidable Roman soldiers.

The advancing pack of human wolves was not the most inconspicuous. Roman outposts soon learned of the moving human storm and utilized their most effective communication weapon, the homing pigeon, to warn Rome of the molten flow of thieves and murderers.

Cleatus sat at his desk and reread the brief message brought to him earlier that morning. It was the third time he went over words that warned of death, destruction, and general mayhem that was about to strike Rome, similar to one of the many winter storms that generated out of the east.

The Roman general was not distressed by the news—quite the contrary. Cleatus basked in the knowledge a battle was about to rage on the northern parts of the city and that he would be the chief strategist assigned to decide the outcome of the deadly conflict. It was a position Cleatus had experienced many times in his career. The ability to strategize and to get men to carry out plans they may not agree with, were attributes that had elevated Cleatus to the rank of general. He was not worrisome about the outcome; he was anxious for it to begin.

Flavius was perplexed at being called to Cleatus' office. They had just met with Seneca during their regular monthly meeting to discuss the situation concerning their prisoner Paul. Since this was his only assigned duty, he could not imagine what was on his general's mind.

"Thank you for coming so soon, Flavius. Please sit down. We have a dangerous impending event you must prepare for." Flavius sensed the excitement in Cleatus' voice. The general's eyes glistened, his face was flushed, and his body language radiated power and strength.

"General, is this something that I know nothing about, concerning Paul?"

Cleatus nodded his head and added, "In a manner of speaking it is, Flavius, but it really goes beyond the scope of Paul's situation."

Flavius waited for his commander to continue, and Cleatus' excitement generated eagerness to release his information, "I have just received word that a horde of criminal bandits is advancing on Rome from out of the northern regions. Our informants state the size of this force to be over 200 men, well-armed, with wagons. It is obvious they intend to attack and plunder Rome for their personal gain."

The announcement affected Flavius as if he had received a jolt of lightning. He sat up straight, his eyebrows shot upward, his eyes widened, and his mind began to race as it processed this breaking news. The centurion interrupted his commander, "If this gang of thieves is heading towards Rome, the probability is they will attack the villas and townhouses in the northern sector. Paul's townhouse will certainly be one of the targets. He and our guards will be in harm's way. These townhouses must be extra fortified against these marauders."

The general seemed to relax. He sat back in his chair and placed his folded hands in his lap. He looked directly into Flavius' eyes and softly said, "Yes, they will. And we will be well prepared to defend them and the rest of Rome." Cleatus beamed his approval at how quickly his centurion had analyzed the situation. "You see this in the same manner as I do, Flavius."

Flavius remained rigid, his lips clamped tightly together. His eyes darted back and forth, trying to visualize the scenario. His mind was racing with the many possibilities that could occur.

Sensing his confusion, Cleatus eased the centurion's emotions, "I have already begun the preparations to welcome our forthcoming 'guests.' We will only require the services of two centuries to adequately fortify the villas located in the northern parts of the city. A total of five soldiers will be hidden in each villa. In addition, a special camp of our finest cavalry will be positioned more to the west between the villas and the townhouses. They will be able to engage these criminals quickly once the attack begins."

Flavius was tracking with the general's plan and could see how the trap would ensnare the pack of marauders. Cleatus disclosed more of his strategy, "As the unsuspecting thieves encounter our troops, some will fight while others will scatter to escape. No matter what they do, we will annihilate them. Our forces are sufficient to prevent any survivors from making their way to the townhouses to join up with their other attackers."

Cleatus paused to savor his vision. "Our cavalry will be out of sight and come forth on a signal from a flaming arrow shot into the night sky. Our mounted archers will attack the vagabonds who are positioned to raid the row of townhouses that line the northern part of Rome."

Retaining a quiet, matter-of-fact tone, the general continued to divulge his grand plans, "These archers will have a well-lit playground provided by stationary archers positioned on the roofs of the townhouses. There will be two waves using the longbow to rain down torch arrows on the grassy plain behind the townhouses. They will create sufficient lighting that the archers will easily be able to pick out their targets."

The general looked at Flavius to make sure the centurion was mentally following the plan. Satisfied by the attentive expression on the younger soldier's face, the master military strategist revealed more. "This lighting will also allow the troops situated in each townhouse to better see their targets as they attempt to enter the rear courtyards."

Cleatus then let out a hearty laugh that surprised Flavius. "These despicable dogs will be in a death vise. There will be no escape." Savoring the depiction, the general nodded and confirmed, "There shall also be no mercy."

Flavius asked clarification from his commander, "General, what is it you specifically want me to do?"

Cleatus remained seated, completely relaxed. He lifted his chin and chimed, "Inform your guards of the impending ruckus. They are adequately trained for such an occasion as this. In fact, I surmise they will be eager to break the monotonous routine they have been subjected to these past few months."

Flavius audibly chuckled in agreement with Cleatus' speculation. Cleatus continued, "You also will direct the infantrymen comprised of lancers and swordsmen that will line the row of townhouses under attack. Should any of these dogs make it past our inside force, the outside throng of Praetorian Guard members will destroy them!"

Cleatus rose up from his chair, gathered his full height, and looked down at the seated centurion with pride. "Men such as Marcus, trained with the mace and the use of the dogs, are equivalent to ten Roman infantrymen. We will have men like Marcus in each of the townhouses with their twin dogs." The general pounded his right hand against the armor of his left shoulder and stated with a stern voice, "We will unleash a fury that sends these vagabonds directly to the River Styx."

Flavius found himself perspiring and his throat was dry. He was certainly accustomed to battle and hand-to-hand combat, yet he was concerned about the surprise element associated with battles. Cleatus' plan was perfect for the situation, but there could be additional factors that would require changes. Flavius did not want any surprise factors to harm his prisoner. The centurion was thinking beyond the mere joy of demolishing one of Rome's enemies. "What do you propose I do with our prisoner Paul? We must ensure his safety; otherwise, Nero will have our heads."

Cleatus showed no signs of surprise at Flavius' question. He looked calmly at his centurion and directed, "You shall place Paul and Aelia's house servants in her office. Should the need arise, have the front door guard usher them out of the townhouse. The force of infantry is there to protect them. But quite frankly, Flavius, I do not foresee this happening. I really do not."

Flavius took a deep breath and exhaled slowly. He fired a final question to his commander-in-chief, "How much time do you think we have before this conflict occurs?"

Cleatus placed his left hand on the top of his desk and moved his fingers back and forth on its surface. "At the most, four days. Predators such as these are being slowed by their wagons intended for carrying their ill-gained rewards. Once here, they will scout for signs that we are waiting for them. The moment they think all is well, they will deploy and attack under the cover of the night, just as wolves do."

Cleatus automatically anticipated one of Flavius' thoughts and addressed it. "I will be with the cavalry and direct their charge. When the ground archers send us a signal that it has begun, I will send forth the cavalry of mounted archers."

"Flavius, I must go and finalize with our mounted archers. We will maintain our presence at the garrison located near the port of Ostia. The marauders will not detect us there, yet we will be close to the villas to participate in this hunt."

The centurion knew it had been a long time since the commander-in-chief had experienced a battle, and Flavius could see Cleatus was looking forward to this clash of human and animal flesh.

## Chapter 19

When Flavius returned to his office, he summoned subordinates who would direct the activities of the rooftop archers and those in charge of the platoons of Praetorian Guard members stationed in the palace. Other guards were ready at the garrison located just outside the city.

He ordered that each rooftop archer have an assistant to supply him with a torch arrow. These highly skilled bowmen could fire three flaming arrows per minute, as long as an able assistant handed the next arrow to the archer. In line with Cleatus' vision, Flavius instructed one row of archers to be positioned low on the rooftop to aim their arrows to no more than thirty yards beyond the rear walls of the townhouses. The purpose was to saturate the townhouse area that was at greatest risk of being overrun by the enemy.

The second row of archers would concentrate on the section of the grassy plain from thirty-five yards away from the townhouse to sixty yards out. The longbows were quite capable of reaching these distances. When the sergeants were adequately versed in their duties, they were released to direct their men.

Flavius then met with the sergeants of the infantry units. The first wave of soldiers would be the highly skilled lancers who were capable of incapacitating a foe up to fifty yards away. Behind the lancers would be the short sword infantrymen who would advance on the remnant attackers.

Once this unit was advised of their roles, Flavius met with the guards assigned to Paul. The majority of his men were happy at the prospect of engaging an enemy in hand-to-hand battle. The quiet exceptions were Marcus and Lucilius. They obviously wanted to protect Paul at all costs, but experienced mixed emotions and concern based on their newfound faith.

Neither convert wanted to disobey Christ Jesus by taking a human life. Compounding their internal conflict was that they could not seek Paul's advice beforehand. Flavius had strict instructions neither Paul nor anyone else was to know of the plan to thwart the oncoming assault. Both guards felt like islands about to be bombarded by a hurricane. They could only wait and pray.

Cleatus' stallion, Nike, sensed something was in the air. The magnificent Nicean warhorse's ears were alert, and his eyes glimmered, as the master began to saddle him for the trip to the Ostia port compound. "Aah, Nike. Despite your age, you have not forgotten our destiny. You show signs of age, but your heart is alive and on fire. You have the eagerness of youth." Cleatus gave his tall black stallion a carrot and patted his gleaming neck.

The majority of the Roman populace located in the northern section of the city did not know tension was in the air. The sequestered soldiers were careful not to suggest any impending disaster. Neither Marcus nor Lucilius betrayed their oath to Flavius by revealing the secret that had been forced upon them.

As part of his personal preparation, Flavius toured the northern sector of the city, beginning in the east and proceeding west, ending at Paul's townhouse. The centurion scoured the area with his eyes for details that could factor into the deployment of the infantrymen and the rooftop archers.

He saw how the townhouses were interspersed among the apartment houses. Each sector of Rome, in essence, was a small city of its own. As such, the residents lived among the elites. Many of the renters were slaves who served Rome's prominent businessmen. At night and during their time off, these slaves lived close to where their master resided, or close to the industry they worked.

Unlike the ones in the interior of Rome, these apartment buildings were better constructed. They had running water and sanitation, and each apartment was able to accommodate up to eight slaves. One of the recent innovations was the use of semi-translucent glass in the two windows of the apartment.

Flavius looked up at the well-maintained structures and admired the glass in the windows. He was relieved the tenants could not see out of the windows which only allowed light to enter the premises, but provided no view. Their lack of transparency was a good thing, in that no tenant would panic at the sight of the battlers, and none would attempt to interfere with the soldiers.

As the centurion walked slowly and surveyed the upcoming battleground, he calculated that nearly 10,000 of Rome's approximately 160,000 slaves lived in this section of the city. It was densely populated, but Flavius did not fear a corresponding uprising from the slaves once the attack began. The mindset of Rome's slaves abhorred foreign attackers disrupting their lives and their employment. Rome's elite had a reputation of benevolency towards their property—human and otherwise. The slaves knew that should their master be killed, they would be resold and there was no guarantee the next owner would be as gracious as Rome's.

When Flavius arrived at Paul's townhouse, he did not enter the abode. He stood in the center of the street and surveyed 360 degrees. The apartments that butted next to the townhouse were four stories tall. Their dimensions were sufficient for the two rows of archers assigned to provide illumination for the defenders. This section was similar to a cul-de-sac with no entrance from the grassy plains that bordered the area.

The street was cobblestone, but the soldiers would have solid footing to battle any attacker who might escape the special armed forces inside the townhouse. The apartments did not have open courtyard areas in the rear of the buildings, so they would be easier to defend than the townhouses.

Flavius let out a grunt of satisfaction as he finished his visual inspection of the surroundings. He was confident no intruder would survive the superior army personnel of Rome. He looked at the door to Paul's rented residence and chuckled wryly. He found it somewhat ironic that this prisoner would survive the forthcoming deadly attack only to be at the mercy of Caesar. He turned and headed back to his office.

At the Ostia compound, Cleatus enjoyed his time with the mounted archers. Their sense of enthusiasm and prebattle banter took him back to his own youthful days, and he reveled in the victories that came to his mind. He knew these dedicated archers would have practiced their riding skills during the day, and at night would silently make their way towards the villas that lay a few miles northeast of them.

Cleatus closely observed the practice sessions, but did not interfere with the unit officers. He did not want to disrupt the teamwork established by their supervisors. He was pleased with the discipline that had produced the skill and competency of the mounted warriors. Rome had incorporated mounted archers after suffering severe losses in previous wars, notably against the Persians and the Carthaginians. In true Roman fashion, they had taken what they learned and innovated the tactics to the extent that Roman cavalry was now the most feared in the empire.

The preparation pattern repeated itself for three days, but the men did not become anxious. They knew it was a matter of time before the death wave announced its arrival.

Its stealthy appearance came on the fourth night. As the horse warriors silently made their way to the appointed waiting area, Cleatus looked towards the heavens. The moon was a partial orb, shining minimal light onto the ground. There were numerous stars that provided weak illumination. What encouraged the general were the encroaching clouds. Wispy and thin at first, they began to grow pillowy, thick and bunched together, eventually blocking the stars.

Watching them, Cleatus became excited. These developing conditions were exactly what would be needed for the intruders to initiate their attack. By the time the cavalry unit reached its destination, the cloud cover blocked out all traces of the moon and its light. The general approached the unit leaders to alert them in a low voice that the attack would begin fairly soon. The cavalry leaders and the horsemen also took note of the moon's disappearance and their senses heightened. They were eager for the human wolf pack to begin their ill-conceived plan.

Within a half hour of the moon's disappearance behind the clouds, a lone, flaming arrow spiraled its way upward in the black sky like a missile sent to assist the stars. This was the signal to the cavalry. The battle had begun. Cleatus remained at the rear of the cavalry unit. Part of the mounted merchants of death headed towards the villas that were strung out ahead of them. The remainder turned and headed east toward the townhouses and apartments. Each unit had to travel one and a quarter miles to join in the skirmish. The distance was easily covered and allowed the infantrymen and the dogs to engage the main thrust of attackers. There was no need to hurry.

After the lone fiery signal, torches within and surrounding the villas exploded in light. The rooftop archers shot their cascade of fire into the grassy plain. Because the grass was relatively dry due to the winter, some of the grass ignited, adding more light to the area.

From his vantage point, Cleatus could clearly see the fires, but not any of the action taking place. All he could do was wait.

His completely black uniform and black stallion in the darkness would only be an impediment to his own troops. A collision with any one of his cavalrymen would be deadly to all. It was imperative he remain out of the way. He accepted his role, but certainly did not like being barred from participation in the deadly pandemonium.

Nike smelled the aroma of battle, the sweat and blood of the combatants, and the smell of horse sweat and manure. The tall stallion's head repeatedly pulled at the reins, wanting his master to release the power that churned deep within his body. Cleatus would not allow it, and the high-spirited stallion made small circles to entice his rider to let him fly towards the action.

Finally, after an hour, the proud specimen of muscle and power got his wish. Cleatus urged him toward the villas, though not at the breakneck speed they once enjoyed together. The general cautiously crept up on the battlefield. His main concern was the potential sweep by the mounted archers against possible escapees. By his estimates, he thought the battle should be over, but combat could still continue if the earlier intelligence reports had underestimated the size of the attacking force,

Cleatus drew his sword in case the action sucked him into its nucleus. Nike arched his neck and his fiery eyes darted back and forth, searching for an enemy, as they slowly advanced. Out of the dim light, a figure approached the aging pair of warriors. "Hail, General!" called the dark figure. It was one of the unit commanders.

"Hail!" responded Cleatus, and the figure advanced in the general's direction.

"General, we have successfully engaged the raiders and repelled their attempt to wreak havoc." Nike turned his trained body that the two riders could communicate better.

Cleatus asked, "Does this apply to the other villas that proceed north?"

The unit commander stated that messengers sent from other units announced all the attacking force had been vanquished. "You may begin your inspection here, General. I'm sure our results will coincide with what you encounter at the other villas."

Cleatus dismounted and began scrutinizing the landscape. The dead and wounded insurgents lay in a pile in front of the villa. As Cleatus walked the premises, the evidence indicated initial contact had been made at the rear of the property where it was easier. The blood on the ground marked where each assailant had met his ultimate destiny.

The unit commander proudly stated that Roman soldiers were relatively unscathed. None had been seriously wounded or killed in the melee. In addition, the inhabitants of the estate were unharmed—shaken by the events, but able to resume their normal activities.

The commanding general carefully inspected the bodies that were piled in front of the villa. Cleatus could tell they were from three different northern regions. These men clearly were not trained soldiers. "How do you propose we dispose of these dogs, General?"

Cleatus rose up from his kneeling position to look at the dead and wounded and softly said, "When it becomes light, we can load them onto a wagon I shall send from Rome."

Cleatus then mounted Nike, and addressed the unit commander, "I shall return tomorrow morning for a full inspection." The general proceeded down the line to each villa. Each stop revealed a picture similar to the first battle site.

When he finished, he turned toward the townhouses and let Nike gallop a short distance to release the horse's frustration and pent-up energy. It was a release for the general, as well, and the action steadied him before his next encounter with the second battle site.

The jaunt was too short for Nike's liking when Cleatus reined in his steed to a stop. They had arrived at the first townhouse located in the far northeast section of the robber's route. The result was similar to what had taken place at the villas. There were ample signs of combat, some destruction of property, and a heap of dead and wounded assailants piled against the back of the townhouse wall.

Paul's rented townhouse was the final stop on Cleatus' victory tour. Flavius greeted him in back of the property and accompanied the general for his inspection. Cleatus surveyed the flaming torch arrows strung out on the grassy plain. He was very pleased with how well they still lighted the area, after enabling the cavalry archers and infantrymen to detect their targets. Hundreds of flaming arrows formed a ribbon of light that meandered along the row of townhouses and apartments. It was as if an artist had used a brightly colored paintbrush to highlight the curve of the layout of townhouses and apartments.

Cleatus briefly looked up at the top edge of the apartments. He could see details of the rooftops and a few shadows of occupants inside. The general returned his gaze to Flavius. "Is our prisoner unharmed?" Flavius proudly replied that Paul and the house servants were safe and no intruder had made it past Marcus and Lucilius to inflict harm. The same was true of the other townhouses along the targeted area.

Flavius reported that he had already sent the lancers and swordsmen back to the barracks. "I saw no need to keep the men here. I thought that should any of the apartment renters come out and see the number of our force, they would be curious and interfere with our plan. Of course, they also could be mistaken for the enemy and be harmed in the process."

The centurion was taken aback by his commander's reaction. Cleatus showed no signs of emotion. He slowly turned his head from side to side. Flavius could see the general's eyes through his black helmet. They did not sparkle from the victory that had just been won. Instead they were resigned, even sad looking. In a tired voice, Cleatus said, "The sun is beginning to rise. I must send out the wagon to pick up the bodies of these dogs—these human wolves—and dispose of them. This must be done before residents of this area become aroused at what took place. We do not want to disrupt normal activities."

Flavius nodded his acceptance of the general's statement. Cleatus then mounted his eager Nike. Before leaving, he gave Flavius one final command, "Come to my office later this morning and give your completed report. I will combine this with what took place at the villas and make my appearance before the Senate later today."

Cleatus rode off. At the mid-point between the villas and the row of townhouses and apartments, he encountered two of the cavalry commanders. They were inspecting two abandoned wagons that obviously had been used by the invaders. Each wagon had a lone horse grazing on the short grass. One of the cavalry commanders informed Cleatus, "These wagons were surely intended to carry the bounty from the raids. As you can see, General, the two men assigned to these wagons have each taken a horse and escaped. Do you want me to send troops in search of them?"

Wearily, Cleatus said, "No, let them go. They will make their way back to their homeland and relay the events that have taken place here. Their stories will reflect how mightily they were defeated." The subdued general walked Nike around each wagon and ordered the cavalry commanders, "Have the bodies loaded onto the wagons. Head north and dispose of them in a manner which they deserve."

Cleatus then urged Nike back to Rome. It was a slow ride, during which Cleatus reflected soberly on the battle. He did not lament the taking of human life or any destruction of Roman citizen property. His melancholy was the result of the fact he was too old to physically engage in the rigors of combat. This he could live with as a part of life, but what disturbed him even more was that his mental alertness was waning. This was a definite sign he was losing an emotional tie to the involvements of military life.

During the invasion, Aelia and her house slaves had been sequestered in her office outside the city. Normally, it was suitably spacious for all her needs, but with the addition of the house slaves, it was cramped. No one complained. A soldier had been positioned outside her office to protect the owner and her property. No marauder had been able to come close enough to the villa to harm the inhabitants.

Aelia had thought repeatedly of Paul and his safety. This was an odd experience for her. Since the demise of her husband some years previously, she had felt no real emotions towards any man. Now the preeminent businesswoman was aware of her growing feelings towards the prisoner who occupied her city townhouse. Inwardly, she smiled at the improbability.

In Rome, Paul and the house slaves Aelia had assigned to serve and spy on her renter had also been taken into the safer office location near the front portion of the townhouse. Junus was assigned to protect the occupants. Marcus and Lucilius manned the rear of the townhouse where the point of attack would likely take place. Marcus' dogs would play a key role in thwarting the attackers.

In addition, Draba and the other guards assigned to protect and to monitor Paul had been called back to duty. Despite their readiness and eagerness for combat, Draba and the other guards could only watch Marcus and Lucilius destroy the intruders one by one as they attempted to enter the residence. Draba, especially, was disappointed. He wanted to engage as many infidels as possible in hopes it would factor into his promotion. Instead, he mourned how efficiently Marcus and Lucilius had slain the raiders from the northern regions.

The hostilities within the townhouses had not lasted long. The time from when the assailants were first confronted until the end of the conflict was only a half hour. When the eerie silence of death signaled the end of the hostilities, Draba counted six dregs of humanity dead. Marcus and Lucilius each had killed two, and the attack dogs had each killed one.

Draba had to admit that Marcus was poetry in motion as he flung his barbed one and three-quarter pound mace. Each swing required a minimum of effort, yet was highly accurate in finding the vulnerable skull of the attacker. Draba had attempted to learn the skill of using this mighty weapon, but could not master the snapping of the wrist. He simply wasn't strong enough to get the ball of death to work properly.

Marcus had taken the traditional solid shaft mace used by the cavalry, and adapted it with a twelve-inch leather handle attached to a two-and-a-half-foot, small linked chain. The weight did not impede the launch of the deadly ball secured at the opposite end of the handle.

After the snap of the wrist, the death ball quickly sped to its target. Once the chain snapped, the full force and energy of the man and metal combination carried the barbed ball. The result was instantaneous death when colliding with a human skull. Should the ball contact a shoulder, forearm or ribs, the bones would be crushed, disabling the victim.

The targeted prowler might have heard the sound of death as it whizzed towards him but he never felt any pain upon its impact. Before the body slumped to the ground, Marcus had been quick to drive the short sword in his left hand into the deceased lungs.

Lucilius had used only his short sword, but his movements were quick and efficient. The highly skilled and battle-seasoned Roman had knocked his opponent back with the curved wooden shield used by Roman infantry. As the adversary stumbled backward, Lucilius immediately drove the short sword deep into the man's heart. It did not require a second effort to send the interloper to meet the caretaker of the River Styx.

After the fray, Draba was highly surprised at the reaction of both Marcus and Lucilius. Normally, the victor would shout the name of the war god Mars or Mithras and raise his weapon in a salute of honor. Instead, the two long-time soldiers looked at each other, knelt down, and began to sob.

Draba, was shocked at what he saw as a sign of weakness. He wondered what caused this from loyal Roman soldiers and members of the Praetorian Guard. He made a mental note of it and speculated it had something to do with the prisoner they were assigned to watch.

Flavius was exhausted from the night's ordeal with the insurgents. Over all, he was quite pleased with the performance of his men, especially Marcus and Lucilius. The centurion shuddered when he thought about two of the enemy marauders being eviscerated by the attack dogs trained and handled by Marcus.

He paused before entering Cleatus' office and took a deep breath to steel himself and to get more oxygen to his brain. He needed to give his commanding general an accurate and detailed report.

General Cleatus was seated behind his wooden desk. To his right and in front of the desk sat Seneca. The chief Roman consul to Caesar looked haggard, no doubt from the unprovoked attack. Flavius sat next to Seneca. "It was quite a night, and now we must finalize, and analyze, the events that will be presented to the Senate," opened Cleatus. He was known to get meetings started without fanfare. The general focused on his younger centurion and asked, "Flavius, what's the status of the townhouses and apartments that were targeted by these scum?"

"A total of 120 perpetrators were eliminated, General. None were able to get past the dog handlers and the other guards positioned at the rear opening of the townhouses. No guards were seriously injured during the battle and no inhabitants of the townhouses were harmed. Property loss was minimal."

Flavius paused to give his commander the opportunity to ask any questions. Cleatus remained mum, so the centurion continued, "The aggressors were lightly armed, with only knives. None wore any type of armor. There's no indication any of these foes were part of an organized army."

Seneca was silent, closely watching the two military personnel. This was his first time to be part of a battleground debriefing. What shocked him most was how callous the two militarists seemed in their attitudes toward dehumanizing those who were killed. The dead were merely objects in a death game that was won, this time, by Rome's superior forces.

Cleatus interrupted with his first question, one that was on Seneca's mind, as well. "What's the status of our prisoner Paul?"

Seneca leaned slightly forward in his chair, anxious to hear about Paul. Flavius quickly told them, "Paul and the house slaves were isolated in what is normally Aelia's office. Junus stood outside the door and Draba was there also. No insurgent was able to get past either Marcus or Lucilius. In my observations, Paul did not appear to be rattled by the battle. He and the house slaves were calm and offered prayers to their god Jesus. After the hostilities ceased, Paul asked if there was anything he could do to assist our guards. I said no, and our men began to remove the corpses from the property. The house slaves then proceeded to clean the blood off the rear walls."

Cleatus looked at Seneca and invited him to ask Flavius any questions, but the chief consul declined. The general concluded the brief meeting, "Your men did an excellent job, Flavius. In addition, you handled the troops stationed in the street very well. This will be mentioned when I appear before the Senate. I see no further need to continue. I must prepare my presentation that will be given within the next hour to Rome's governing body. I will consult your reports as I do so."

Flavius and Seneca rose up simultaneously from their chairs as if choreographed, and left Cleatus' office. Neither man spoke in the palace corridor. The centurion returned to his office, and Seneca hastened back to his townhouse.

Seneca was anxious to get back to his townhouse to receive the message he hoped would be waiting for him regarding Pompeia. In addition, Cato was to meet him at the townhouse for an important meeting.

As he had anticipated, both the messenger and Cato were already there when he arrived at his townhouse. Seneca's worried face caused Cato to defer to the messenger. Seneca could not contain his anxiety and was about to bellow his orders to find out about Pompeia, but the alert messenger broke protocol. Before Seneca demanded information, he quickly assured him his wife and the house slaves were unharmed and in good spirits.

The shaken Roman official sent a return message of greeting and notification of his safety to Pompeia. Seneca then ushered his colleague into the dining room. "Cato, let us have some wine. I believe the circumstances of last night allow us this indulgence. Good wine will soothe our nerves." The wine was poured and they collapsed into the cushioned chairs to relax their churning thoughts.

The adrenalin rush Seneca had felt needed time to settle back into normality. After some slow, deep breaths, they compared notes on the night's upheaval. "Cato, did you have any doubts or concerns about your safety during the attack?"

"Very minor, Seneca. My familiarity with Rome's military tactics did not allow me to worry. However, I can understand your opposite perspective, with Pompeia away from your personal protection. But all is well, and now we must continue with our assignment concerning our prisoner client."

Seneca's thoughts shifted to Flavius' report. "I'm not surprised about Paul appearing very self-possessed during the events or his petition to his god Jesus. And I surmise Cleatus and Flavius determined the insurgents were not associated with Paul. T hey gave no indication to me they thought Paul was involved."

Cato had taken a short sip of his wine while he listened to Seneca. He had been rolling it around his mouth, and now he quickly swallowed in order to corroborate Cleatus and Flavius' important statement. "Nor should they, Seneca. It's obvious that Paul had no connection with this offscouring. He wants and anticipates his appeal before Caesar. Even if he were connected with these raiders, they would bide their time until after his appeal before inflicting any harm to Rome's inhabitants. Paul is intelligent, and he would not resort to anything such as this."

"I concur, Cato. Nonetheless, we should not overlook any opportunity this incident affords us to obtain evidence of any treasonous intent on Paul's part. When do you intend to meet again with your client?"

Cato hastily swallowed his wine and said, "Day after tomorrow. I must complete some research that ties in with this incident. The questions I form based on this research will assist our cause."

"Very well, then. We shall meet again, prior to our regularly scheduled meeting with Cleatus." Seneca was ready to retire.

Cato savored his last swallow of the excellent wine before going to his carriage. On the journey home, the businessman-attorney's sharp mind was already formulating new questions for his prisoner client.

## Chapter 20

Cleatus finished reviewing the assessments by Flavius and the unit commanders quelling the raid. He stood up from behind his desk, grabbed his helmet, and proceeded to the palace where the Senate was awaiting his arrival.

Rome's commanding general did not carry any papers with him and had no subordinates to accompany him. He didn't need anyone to assist him in chronicling the attack for Rome's ruling body.

His walk to the Senate chamber was a short one. He was immediately ushered in to address the ruling assembly. All conversation ceased as he powerfully strode to the area designated for presentations made to Rome's dignitaries. Cleatus was a stunning figure. He was the only individual dressed in black among the several hundred senators. The senators wore their traditional white togas with blue stripe and a gold ring on their index fingers. Cleatus stood at his full height of six feet three inches. His burly build was enhanced by the black armor and its minimally-outlined details in dull brass, in stark contrast to the white togas in the rest of the assembly.

His cloak was dark maroon with hints of dark blue. It was secured to his massive shoulders by two brass buttons. His black helmet remained on his head. Its side face panels were outlined with brass. The dyed horsehair atop the helmet rose up eight inches, adding impressive height to his already imposing appearance.

Cleatus looked over the assembled senators, but made no greeting. He waited for the rustling of clothing and shifting feet to quiet down as he surveyed all the senators seated before him. There were two rows of elaborate, cushioned chairs. One row of seats was slightly elevated, allowing senators there a perfect view of whomever would address them.

When his visual survey was completed, Cleatus unhurriedly removed his helmet and held it tightly against his side. In a robust voice, he began his narrative. As he spoke, the marbled walls and floors of the meeting chamber added import to his words with their reverberations.

"As each of you is aware, raiders from the northern regions of the empire attempted to wreak havoc with Rome's citizenry who have villas and townhouses in the north section of the city. This force of human wolves totaled just under 300 men equipped with knives and some swords. Their plan was to simultaneously strike the villas and the townhouses and steal anything of value, including citizens or their slaves."

Some of the senators leaned forward in concentration. Their eyes were riveted on the commanding figure. Cleatus had made previous accounts before these men and he knew when to pause to add drama to his words. This he did with ease by emphasizing certain words that he knew would be fixed in each senator's mind.

"They did not succeed." Cleatus stopped and the words echoed throughout the assembly hall. "Our forces annihilated these despicable dogs, and no citizens or any of their property were harmed."

The general's pause at that point was very brief. "We utilized both our infantry and the cavalry to squeeze these marauders' positions tightly so that there was no escape for them. Our efforts were thorough and no Roman soldier was seriously injured during the brief conflict."

Cleatus waited to give the senators time to appreciate the thorough victory and to ask questions. One senator wanted to know, "How did you learn these attackers were going to strike the northern section of Rome?"

Casually, Cleatus turned toward the voice that came from the back row of togas. He replied, "A combination of scouts and informants gave us ample warning for us to put together a sufficient force to thwart their efforts."

Another question shot forth, "Did the battle last long?"

Again, Cleatus turned toward the questioner to make personal contact with the senator. "Thirty to forty minutes, total. Our cavalry was swift and their arrows accurate in finding their targets, which were on foot. Our infantry was stationed within the villas and the townhouses. They used their superior skills to kill the interlopers."

The senators were aware of how efficient and effective Rome's army could be. Each man had his own mental picture of the battle taking place and they entertained their visions during a brief silent period. Cleatus remained rigidly at attention. He enjoyed observing the expressions on the senators' faces. Finally, another question came from a senator seated in the front row, "General, were there any survivors, and what has happened to these insurgents?"

Raising his voice, Cleatus pronounced, "Survivors as well as the dead were placed together in three wagons. They were transported back to the northern regions where they were hung on poles for the inhabitants to see." This was common practice by the Roman military.

There was no need for the customary crucifixion because the majority of them were already dead. The remaining few wounded would soon die, thus robbing the Romans of their cruel enjoyment of watching human suffering. This delivered the message Rome wanted to convey to any rebel; when you choose to fight Rome, be prepared to die. However, even this did not always prove to be a deterrent, which the Roman military was glad didn't take place. They preferred to satisfy their brutal lust for savagery by acts of violence against their enemies.

The meeting hall remained silent after Cleatus concluded his depiction of the attack. Then the senior member of the Senate stood up and moved beside Cleatus. He extended his arm toward him, saying, "My fellow senators, we all should be grateful for Cleatus and his masterful strategy in dealing with these vermin." Then he turned and lauded the general face to face, "General Cleatus, you have a long and notable career in Rome's military and have distinguished yourself on many occasions. Once again, you have served Rome admirably and we extend our sincere gratitude to you." The entire Senate rose up and clapped their appreciation.

Cleatus showed no signs of emotion hearing the accolades. He knew this same ruling body could turn on him at any moment, for any perceived provocation. Nevertheless, the general gave a slight bow towards the senior senator, and then another to the senate body. He placed his impressive helmet firmly on his head, turned snappily, and exited the Senate chamber.

As he walked back to his office, Cleatus' troubled thoughts

were dominated by the realization of how numb he had become to the different affairs of state. In his heart, he knew the day of his retirement must come soon.

During Cleatus' address to the Senate, Aelia was returning to the city to anxiously inspect her townhouse. She needed to see for herself how her slave servants and renter had fared during the skirmish.

Paul and Lucilius answered her questions as she toured the courtyard to determine the damage. Once the landlord's inspection was complete, she looked directly toward Lucilius, then to Marcus who was positioned at his normal station close to the rear opening of the townhouse. "Thank you both for your efforts. I expected to see more damage than what has occurred. I—and Rome—are proud of your efforts!"

The two guards made a tight fist and thumped their respective armored breastplates. As they did so, they bowed to Aelia in the official manner of responding to one of Rome's elite class. Aelia looked at Paul and a smile formed on her angelic face, "I'm glad you were not harmed in any way, Paul." In an effort to mask her growing emotions for her renter, she then jokingly added, "It would not be good for my bank account had you died."

Paul laughed, and agreed, "Nor mine! Plus, I would have been deprived of establishing my innocence before Caesar." The two carried on their light-hearted conversation in the dining room along with the ever-present Lucilius.

Aelia enjoyed the times she spent with Paul and was touched by the kindness and respect he showed her. His intelligence and passion for what he believed were traits she admired. Roman men were not known for kindness, respect, and compassion, thus Paul nobly distinguished himself in Aelia's mind. After a half hour of jovial discussion, the landlord realized she had to leave to attend to other business.

Lucilius breathed a sigh of relief when the front door closed behind Aelia. The guard felt the time was right that both he and Marcus could consult their mentor about their acts during the hostile engagement, and they were anxious to do so, "Paul, before you return to your cobbler work, Marcus and I are wondering if we may speak with you concerning last night's raid."

"Most certainly, my brother. I was expecting this to happen and had you not initiated this request, I would have suggested it. Come, let us enjoy a good lunch and we can talk while we eat."

Marcus could not leave his post, so their lunch was served on the patio where the guards could maintain their duties and have a mentoring session at the same time.

When the meal arrived, it was Marcus who opened the discussion, "Paul, Lucilius and I are deeply disturbed by our actions against the intruders."

Lucilius quickly jumped in with a hoarse voice, "We are struggling to reconcile our new faith and belief in Christ Jesus with the taking of human life. We are in turmoil, and need your counsel in this matter."

Marcus resumed control of the conversation. "Our main question to you is, were we disobedient to Christ in the taking of those lives? And what should we do now?"

Paul pushed his plate of food aside and looked kindly into the eyes of his troubled mentees. "This indeed is a serious matter and worthy of discussion. Being a follower of Christ and becoming a new creation means leaving the old self behind and embracing our new relationship with our Savior. We have a new view of people and the world, and it raises questions that need answers. This often means foregoing our earthly ways for the ways of our Lord."

The two converts ate sparingly as they concentrated on Paul's words. They knew their mentor would not attempt to give them encouragement at the expense of compromising Christ's precepts and commands. "First, let me assure you there was no disobedience to Christ's commands. You did not provoke or otherwise initiate conflict with any of these assailants. Your main intent was protecting the lives of Aelia's servant slaves, myself, and the city of Rome."

Marcus and Lucilius glanced at one another, wondering what the other's response would be. Paul could see their earnest desire to understand and to be relieved of guilt. "I know this is a difficult situation for you. It is common for questions to arise for those who come to Christ Jesus with a sincere heart and want to follow Him. It is good you are thinking about these things." The distressed converts retained their anxious expressions. Paul saw they were deeply hurting, and suggested, "Allow me to give you three illustrations that pertain to your current situation."

The apostle of Christ then launched into the story of Joseph, the betrayal by his older brothers, being sold to traveling vendors, imprisonment due to the lies of Potiphar's wife, and the broken promises of two of his fellow inmates.

As Paul detailed Joseph's biography in the Jewish writings, the two guards were mesmerized by Paul's story; it was one they had not heard before. Paul recounted how Joseph throughout each ordeal had remained steadfast to his belief in Almighty God and His principles, obeying His commandments. He then told how the head jailer witnessed Joseph's godly character through his actions and blessed him with a leadership position, even while he was imprisoned.

Finally, Paul described how God rewarded Joseph's obedience by giving him the interpretation of Pharaoh's dream, all of which led to Joseph becoming heir to Pharaoh's throne.

Paul leaned forward and placed his elbows on his knees with his hands clasped. He then expounded the surprising main point of the true story, "It was only after experiencing hardship and remaining steadfast to God's precepts that Joseph received spiritual wisdom. He was guided by the Holy Spirit and carried out Almighty God's plan. It blessed him, it blessed his family, and it blessed all of Egypt. He demonstrated what it means to walk by faith and not by sight. Too often, new converts to Christ grow discouraged with the trials and battles because of what they see around them, and they lose sight of God's rewards of victory that lie ahead."

Paul stopped to refresh his throat with some wine and a bite of crisp apple. As he ate, he studied the body language of his mentees. Both Marcus and Lucilius sat still, deep in thought. They were noticeably serious about this account of God's mysterious ways with one of His faithful servants.

Paul began his next chronicle, about the life of God's warrior king, David.

The new believers were amazed as Paul wove together meaningful details of David's history. His emphasis was on how God first revealed his plan for David at a youthful age when the diminutive warrior killed the giant Goliath. "It was God who chose David over grown men who were paralyzed by their unrighteous fears, because David had a heart willing to serve Almighty God. David's actions of mighty faith inspired the Jewish leaders for action, and God's chosen people were protected from destruction by their enemies."

Paul continued the story of David, telling how David fought thirty-nine wars as God's warrior king. "King David lived out the strengths God blessed him with and developed his God-given talents into highly refined skills. He refused to let his human emotions and feelings interfere with being God's servant to carry out His grand plan."

Both Marcus and Lucilius were fascinated by the stories, receiving the godly blitz of divine teaching. When Paul finished the example of David, he paused again to refresh his palate. He drank and ate slowly, all the while evaluating his mentees' concentration. He did not want to undermine this opportunity for God's teaching and His blessings of discernment and wisdom to His followers. Jesus' new followers showed they were thirsty for more— thirsty in their new spiritual lives.

"Now, my brothers, my third example to you is about myself." Paul's candid revelation of his own experiences held the two mentees spellbound. They ate and drank, without noticing the passing time, while Paul gave his personal testimony. Paul held nothing back, emphasizing how his religious zealotry had deceived him and caused God grief, "I was blindly immersed in Jewish religion, adamant that Christ's followers were dangerous heretics who must be punished and eliminated. Religious fervor took control of my emotions and contributed to my being an enemy of Almighty God."

Lucilius was deeply affected by Paul's teary eyes and change of tone as he spoke softly, humbly, and thankfully about his personal encounter with Christ. The guard was moved by Paul's description of his subsequent conversion and how Christ had to temper his zealous servitude by taking him into the desert of Arabia and there teach him what it meant to be His follower.

When his early personal testimony was finished, Paul sat back. He looked compassionately at his mentees and said, "I wish to convey to you, my brothers, how important it is to understand that God's ways are not man's ways and His thoughts are not man's thoughts. His ways and thoughts are far higher than anything man can conceive.

"Now that you have accepted Christ's salvation and lordship, you must be mindful that your faith will be tested at different times and in many ways. This is Christ's way of refining your faith just as gold is refined into a precious metal. It is an arduous process! His greatest blessing to you for your steadfastness is being drawn closer to Him. He also gifts you with His wisdom and discerning spirits to equip you to thwart the fiery arrows of the devil, and at the same time manifest Christ in all your works."

Marcus was the first to respond to his mentor's teaching, "I perceive through your stories that each man, including yourself,

Paul, had personal struggles to overcome to be obedient to Christ." Paul did not deny this, and Marcus continued, "It seems these struggles came early in each one's relationship with Christ and they had to rely on whatever amount of faith they had to press through the struggle."

Paul was quick to affirm him, "Marcus, you perceive correctly! Christ has said that the faith of a mustard seed is sufficient to establish a relationship with Him and He will cause it to grow into a tree that bears much fruit. A mustard seed is quite small, but God acknowledges even a very small thing that is authentic. A mustard seed of faith may be powerful when He blesses it!"

The husky guard sat back in his chair, contemplating this new teaching. Lucilius picked up where Marcus' question left off. "Paul, you are telling us that we must manifest our loyalty and trust in Christ—and not in man, religion, or governments."

Paul shook his clasped hands in excitement as he answered, "Yes, Lucilius, you are correct! When you obey Christ first, He guides you how and to what extent you obey man's institutions. If your action is against His will, the Holy Spirit will instruct you by impressing upon you that what you are asked to do will either glorify Almighty God or elevate the devil. When you profess God with your mouth but your actions follow the devil, you are a hypocrite and a deceiver."

Marcus coughed and cleared his throat, having choked on Paul's blunt description, and said, "Am I correct then, that I must totally surrender my will to Christ's will?"

His mentor clapped his hands together with a single, exuberant exclamation, thrilled at Marcus' succinct summary. "Yes, Marcus! It is only by total surrender to Christ that He can mold you into the new creation He wants you to become. In the process, Christ builds His personal relationship with you. This is how much Christ loves you, cares for you, and why He sacrificed His life for you, giving you eternal life with Him."

Unexpectedly, Marcus slumped and hung his head, drinking in the impact of Paul's words. Lucilius also was very sobered. He observed the angst of his colleague and looked at Paul. "Am I correct in stating that the common thread in these three biographies is that to be a follower of Christ we must pray and obey only His commands?"

Smiling joyfully, Paul bobbed his head and exclaimed, "Absolutely, Lucilius! Don't make this process and your new life journey harder than what Christ wants it to be. Pray. Obey. And trust Him in all things, especially your very life! Let Him reveal the plan and purpose He has for you. A plan and a purpose that is designed especially for you. Remain humbled, always seeking His face, alone. By professing and elevating Christ to the lost world, He proudly professes you to our Heavenly Father,... and the heavens rejoice!"

Lucilius choked up and could not hold back his tears of relief, nor did he feel it necessary to contain them. Paul let his mentees enjoy comfort from the Holy Spirit. The two converts to Christ warmly thanked their mentor. Then all three resumed their lunch with improved appetites while contemplating God's mysterious ways. They had just finished when Draba and the other guards arrived for the shift change.

As Marcus and Lucilius slowly walked towards the palace and their barracks, Lucilius laughed softly.

Marcus looked at him curiously, "What makes you so jovial, my friend?"

"I was thinking, Marcus, about Paul's teaching. As I look down the street that leads to our barracks, we also are walking down a path with much uncertainty to become true followers of Christ Jesus."

Marcus quoted what their mentor had spoken to them earlier, "'Yea, though I walk through the valley of the shadow of death, I will fear no evil, for You are with me, Your rod and Your staff will comfort me.' Lucilius, I am no longer afraid to die!"

Lucilius agreed with his fellow warrior. He finished the thought with the other words that were still resonating with him, "'Surely goodness and mercy shall follow me all the days of my life; and I will dwell in the house of the Lord forever.' Forever, Marcus! Think of that!"

## Chapter 21

Cato finished his research into Paul's activities and compiled a list of questions to ask his client. With winter's grip on Rome lessening each day, it wouldn't be long before Nero returned to the capital city to resume his empirical duties. It was imperative that Cato and Seneca had the necessary evidence and clarifications to present to Caesar. Their input would influence Nero's decision concerning Paul's fate. The attorney wanted to be fair to his client and present only the facts of the case.

It was clear that Paul had not committed a crime of treason, but Cato knew that Caesar and the Senate would then focus on the issue of intent. This was the stumbling block for Cato, a famed mentor to Rome's elite and one of its prominent businessmen. Cato's and Seneca's personal reputations were on the line with this case. Should they falter in obtaining all the facts and evidence required under Roman law, they would suffer dire consequences.

Rome's official stepped out of his carriage and was met by yet another cold blast of winter wind. He shivered. He did not like winter, especially in Rome. With his cloak, he covered his nose, shielding it from the sooty residue that hung in the air from all the wood burning stoves in the city's residences. Hastily, he went to the front door of the townhouse and was grateful to be admitted without delay.

Paul came out of his workshop and greeted his dignified attorney. Draba accompanied Paul and followed Cato and Paul into Aelia's office sanctuary. Before they were seated, Cato directed his attention to the Roman guard and spoke authoritatively, "Draba, I request that you allow Paul and me to confer about his appeal in private. It is necessary for us to discuss his case without any interference or impedance."

The Roman guard was taken aback at the counselor's request. Initially, he had nothing to say, but quickly composed himself. "Flavius indeed has instructed us about this possibility and that we must comply with your request. I will wait outside until you are finished."

The Praetorian Guard member clenched his fist and brought it against the breastplate armor of his chest in the traditional salute of obedience to a higher authority. He turned and left the office. Satisfied, Cato directed his efforts towards his client. He scanned Paul's surprised reaction and decided to give his client a brief explanation.

"Roman law ensures an attorney and his client privacy, especially in a case of this magnitude. Fairness is a prerequisite to maintain honesty for everyone involved in the case. It would be a grave injustice should any aspect of your case leak out to someone capable of taking advantage of this information." Cato straightened in his chair and finished his preamble, "Rome seeks justice in your case and does not want to be swayed by lies or false evidence."

Paul believed that Cato could be trusted with any pertinent facts he wished to give his attorney of record. "Thank you for enlightening me on this facet of Roman law, Cato. My intention is to work with you in an honest and forthright manner. Now, what is on your mind that you seek my presence this day?"

Paul sat down in the chair behind his desk and gestured for his attorney to also be seated across from him. Cato came straight to the point, "Seneca and I have been confronted by Cleatus and members of the ruling Senate about your case. Of great concern to them is that you are using your Roman citizenship as a ruse for your own nefarious purposes. As such, I must ask you questions that will ease their anxieties."

Cato allowed Paul sufficient time to digest the information presented to him. He saw that his client was weighing his statement, but also that he was unruffled by its implications. "I understand what you are saying, Cato. Proceed with your questions, and be assured I shall answer you truthfully."

The first question came at Paul as swiftly as a crossbow arrow fired by one of Rome's cavalry archers. "Why did you wait to assert your citizenship when you were arrested by the garrison centurion in Jerusalem? Was it because you wished to avoid a scourging from Rome's soldiers?" Cato sat back, ready to hear Paul's answer.

"It was the Jewish leaders that falsely accused me of sedition against Rome. This ploy on their part was meant to have me arrested and scourged, and to stand trial before Felix, whom they planned to bribe."

Cato rested his hands in his lap, but his mind was on full alert. "Go on with your explanation, Paul."

Christ's servant maintained his soft-spoken manner and added, "Knowing they intended to assassinate me, I had no choice but to declare my citizenship to the centurion and the garrison commander. It was the only way to obtain a safe Roman trial. What caught both Ananias and Tertullus off guard was Felix being replaced by Festus. They could not bribe the new procurator, so they demanded I be released to them for a religious trial."

Paul's interrogator then took up the story and confirmed Paul's statements, "You are correct with this. Festus has sent a detailed report about it. He lauded you for your quick thinking and understanding of Roman citizenship." Cato then asked a point of great significance for Paul, "Do you really grasp the magnitude of the value of being a Roman citizen?"

Paul did not hesitate. "My father was fully aware of the importance and the value of such an affiliation. That is why he did what was necessary that I could be born a Roman citizen."

The Roman interrogator sat relaxed and kept his hands neatly placed on his lap, as he pressed the point, "You say this, yet your actions and the history surrounding you suggests differently. First, you aligned with the Jewish religion, became a rising Pharisee within their organization, switched affiliation to this Christian sect, and established your cells of followers in some of Rome's major commerce colonies." Cato let his knowledge of these things sink in before he continued, "This depicts you as a rebel, seeking ways to overthrow both the Jewish leaders, as well as Rome, for your own power and advancement."

If Cato was attempting to upset Paul, it failed. Paul was unperturbed. But he challenged his attorney's suggestion, "You are leaving out certain unshakable facts, Cato, in your attempt to discredit me." Paul stared unblinkingly at his attorney and firmly refuted his false assumptions, "While you are correct that I became a Pharisee, it was due to my father's urging that I become a leader of the Jewish faith and assist in their survival against the likes of Roman oppression. I was a religious zealot and, notably, I arrested, imprisoned, and executed followers of Christ Jesus."

Cato immediately jumped in to say, "As I remember, you executed a man named Stephen for his public demonstration of his faith in this Jesus."

Paul closed his eyes against the painful memory and confessed, "That is correct. Afterward, the risen Christ personally convicted me of my crime against Him, Jesus, and blinded me for three days, during which He revealed Himself to me. It was at that time I fully surrendered myself to Him."

"So, indeed, you did switch affiliation from one religion to another?"

Paul shook his head negatively, "That is not the case, Cato. In surrendering to Christ Jesus, I forsook all religion. Instead, I asked forgiveness from Christ and received a personal relationship with Him that lasts forever. It is not religion. Christ is the antithesis of religion. He is above all religion."

"Then explain these cells of your followers located in so many of Rome's major hubs of commerce."

Paul placed his arms on the polished desktop and folded his hands together as he quietly answered, "I have no followers, Cato, nor do I seek any. My sole purpose is to speak about the deity of Christ Jesus to all who are lost. I tell them that He is truly God, the Savior of mankind, and that He wants them to admit and confess their sins, have a personal relationship with Him, and receive His free gift of eternal life."

"If what you say is true, why do this recruiting in Rome's major sites of commerce? Why not in Jerusalem and to the Jews—the people that you are part of?"

"At first, I did exactly that, Cato. I tried to evangelize the Jews—you are aware of how they reject not just me, but the message about Christ Jesus."

Cato chuckled and said, "That is an understatement, Paul. The Jews truly hate you and would do anything to have you executed."

Paul opened his hand in a concurring gesture. "Exactly. That's why any contention that I am allied with the Jews is completely and logically false."

"That may be the case; but it remains you now are targeting so-called Gentiles, many of whom are residents of Rome's major colonies and even citizens here in Rome. Can't this be construed to be actions of a rebel intent on overthrowing Rome and establishing his own government?"

"I can see your logic, Cato, yet it remains far from the truth. God fully convinced me that my efforts to evangelize the Jews are *not* part of His purpose for me. His Holy Spirit is the one who directed me to these different communities. I went to each one because God, in His all-knowing power, had me speak to those whose hearts were ready to receive His word and act on His invitation to follow Him."

Cato stared broodingly at his client. Guessing at his contemplation, Paul turned the tables and asked his own important question for evidence, "In each of Rome's colonies where Christ's churches have been established, have there been any incidents to suggest His followers have tried to overthrow the Roman government?"

The interrogating attorney's concentration created a deep furrow between his eyes. Paul's question struck him by surprise. Rapidly, he assessed the question and came out of his concentration with a response, "Your followers thus far have not taken any action against Rome, but that doesn't mean they won't. Isn't it quite possible they are waiting for your appeal before Caesar to be completed before they rise up against Rome, especially if you are found guilty of treason and its accompanying crime of intent?" The inquisitor was proud of his counterclaim and his confident smugness showed. With one eyebrow quizzically raised, he waited for Paul's counter.

The apostle of Christ was not irritated by the question. Calmly he replied, "As I have stated before, Cato," he paused before continuing, "I really have no followers. My purpose is to make followers of Christ *alone* and instruct them about their personal relationship with Him. Verily I say to you, Cato, no true follower of Christ will rebel against the Roman government." He stressed the words, "true follower of Christ" by lightly tapping the desk in cadence with each word.

To seal his defense against Cato's accusatory question, Paul then struck a heavy blow to his attorney's hypothesis, "Cato, you question my motive, suggesting I am utilizing my Roman citizen for my personal gain. Have you not also used your Roman citizenship to further your purposes?" Before Cato could reply, Paul continued, "You have acquired substantial wealth and prestige as well as position among Rome's elites by means of your Roman citizenship. Why is it not wrong for you or Seneca or others in your position to capitalize on your Roman citizenship, yet I must defend the use of mine?"

Paul then finished his defense, "Maybe you should reread the letter I wrote to the church in Philippi. Is that the work of a traitor? My letter urges the church to be content in all things, and to rejoice always. Is there anything contained within that letter that espouses sedition, now or in the future? If so, then cease being my attorney. For I know you do not wish to represent a guilty man before Caesar."

Cato's eyes widened at Paul's discourse. He was motionless, impressed, unable to refute his logic. Finally, he conceded, "You are quite correct in your argument, Paul. I commend you on your defense. You handle cross-examination well." His earlier smirk was now an admiring smile. "However, this session between us does not eliminate the perception and the doubts that Cleatus and members of the Senate may retain. It is my duty to compile suffi-cient evidence to sway their opinion."

The attorney pressed on, "It is now February. In another month, possibly a month and a half, Caesar will return to Rome. All investigation into your case must be completed by that time. I will continue to assist Seneca; but be mindful that Cleatus is also doing a separate probe into your affairs."

Cato waved a hand and sighed, "There remain aspects of your case for which I must secure evidence in order to verify your in-nocence. We need something of substance." The Roman counselor pantomimed a snatch. "Substance—to combat whatever the op-position may present against you. Hopefully, what we need will come soon. I will be diligent in my efforts on your behalf."

The assigned attorney gripped the edge of the desk that sep-arated him from his client. In a firm voice, he insisted, "The evi-dence we need must not be related to religion. Already, Caesar, prominent businessmen, and the majority of the Senate believe the Jews and your sect are peculiar people with strange supersti-tions! One of the big questions in the minds of Romans is why the Jews and your sect refuse to align with Rome's gods. Rejecting this opportunity to accept Rome's gods is a sign of an unpatriotic attitude."

The attorney sat back again, but retained his steady gaze. "Religious observation is an exercise in loyalty," he remarked. "The actions of the Jews, and now you and your so-called Chris-tians, manifest disloyalty. This will impact the *intent* portion of your case."

Cato stood up to leave. He paused, facing his client. "I espouse Stoicism; as such, I despise all aspects of religion. I fear religion will be your downfall in your upcoming appeal." His handsome face scowled, showing his distaste. "It is such a waste."

He started to leave, but stopped in his tracks at Paul's response, "It appears, Cato, that we are in agreement concerning the futility of religion. We must continue communicating for better understanding of God's truth and His plan, and not man's."

Cato revealed a momentary perplexed expression, then regained his composure and took a few more steps. He paused at the office's closed door and slowly opened it, fully expecting to find Draba eavesdropping on their conversation. The guard was standing a few feet away from the door looking into the vestibule of the townhouse.

Nonetheless, Cato wondered how much the Roman guard and spy had heard and would relay to his superiors. He thought to himself this case was becoming more complex than he had anticipated. The whole case was a challenge and a test of his intellect. However, this pleased him considerably because he always was most stimulated when satisfying his intellect and matching wits.

He was surprised to realize he was developing an appreciation and admiration for his prisoner client. He certainly believed him. His initial reluctance and suspicion had been replaced by a passionate commitment to find ways to prove Paul's innocence and to influence Nero's decision in favor of Paul. It was going to be extremely tough to accomplish this, a real challenge.

The worried attorney entered his waiting carriage and sank heavily into the cushioned seat, pulling his cloak around him. As the driver began the short trek to Cato's townhouse, the melancholy attorney whispered to himself, "Maybe one of the other worldly miracles that seem to accompany Paul will occur again on his behalf, ...maybe this god of his has a plan, ...it would have to be a grand one."

Cato found relief from his whirling thoughts by listening to the clopping hooves and the grinding carriage wheels as they moved in the dark.

 Chapter 22

The camel caravan of goods destined for Rome that began its arduous journey in Ephesus was about to enter the empire's capital city. In addition to goods from Ephesus, merchants from Colosse, Laodicea, and Hierapolis brought their coveted wares that complemented the Ephesus goods.

One traveler with this merchant train was pleased that the trip was nearly over. Once in Rome, he could secure both lodging and employment, then melt into anonymity in the city of nearly 400,000 residents. Its size and capacity to absorb newcomers made the capital city a haven for individuals seeking to escape their past and to start life anew.

Such was the goal for the weary, anxious traveler named Onesimus. The youthful single man had devised a plan to leave behind Colosse and all the tribulations he had dealt with for so long a time. Now his plan was very close to becoming reality. His heart was jubilant! He became less agitated and more excited as the camel train came within sight of Rome.

Onesimus felt he had nothing to lose by casting his fate into the lap of his new location. He was a runaway slave. By running away from his master in Colosse, Onesimus knew he had already created a situation of potential peril for himself. Runaway slaves who were caught were severely punished and sometimes executed for their transgression.

The escapee's daring crime had been catapulted by his festering frustration over a blatant wrong. A fair resolution could have declared him a free man. But because the legal authorities refused to honor their own rules, Onesimus took it upon himself to become his own judge and render a decision in his case. He felt justified in leaving Colosse and joining the merchant caravan.

He looked forward to a fresh, free life in this hub of opportunity, and vowed never to return to what was now hundreds of miles away in his past. The young slave fought to contain his enthusiasm lest any other traveler notice him and become suspicious of his demeanor, especially the Roman troops that provided protection for the camel train. They were always watchful for passengers who possibly could be spies from the many clans of bandits who frequented the trade route in search of unwary prey.

Finally, the caravan reached the main marketplace's clearinghouse for goods, and the runaway slave surveyed the environment. There were many tents with vendors offering goods from countries throughout the Middle East. Off to one side were rows of warehouses where prominent Roman businessmen stored their imports. Goods would be distributed from there to the waiting citizenry with their insatiable appetites for new things.

With camel caravans arriving almost on a daily basis, the marketplace was a congested hub of activity heightened by shrill noises, sights, and foreign smells. Onesimus casually began walking down a path that separated the rows of tent vendors. Barkers shouted out their offerings to him and some even held up their products for his inspection. He ignored them, but secretly enjoyed the atmosphere that represented his new life.

Soon the new arrival stopped at a tent that displayed a variety of leather goods. Onesimus stepped up to the vendor and asked, "Can you direct me to one of the better cobbler shops? I seek employment."

The vendor looked at the youthful immigrant closely and delayed answering his inquiry. He slightly turned his head and spat on the ground beside him, then wiped his mouth and snarled, "How good are your cobbler skills?"

Onesimus took off one of his boots and presented it to the vendor. "This is an example of my workmanship."

The vendor examined the boot thoroughly and handed it back to its owner. "Go to the northern district of Rome and seek a man named Antonius. Tell him that Gladius has sent you to him." He gave the runaway slave some general directions, and Onesimus felt a surge of hope rise in his heart as he thanked him.

The seeker of new life immediately began walking to the northern district, as instructed by the vendor. Along the way, he recoiled from the rank smells and squalor that surrounded him in this southern part of Rome. The rows of shabby apartment buildings, many in disrepair, contradicted what he had imagined for his future. The stench of garbage and human waste permeated the air. Onesimus at one point took to holding the sleeve of his cloak to his nose to lessen the smell. This was far different than Colosse.

As the would-be colonist continued on his journey north, the sordidness gave way to better apartment buildings. At the base of each one was a well-maintained business. The streets were cleaner and the air void of the disgusting reek in the southeast part of the city. Onesimus began to feel better about his decision to escape to Rome. He had not been prepared for his initial experience, but in this improved part of the city his confidence began to grow that this man Antonius would be the type of employer he sought.

It was mid-afternoon when Onesimus finally arrived at his destination. He stopped short of the cobbler's domain to survey his surroundings. The streets were clean, and he gladly noted exquisite townhouses intermingled with apartments that were pristine in appearance. The businesses on the bottom floor of each of the apartment buildings were well cared for, inviting, and attractive.

His spirit was encouraged by what he saw, and his thoughts became euphoric. This area manifested what he had hoped would be the case—the presence of money, and lots of it! He had thought about how he must present himself to convince those he met that he was more than a slave. With renewed bravado, Onesimus strode into Antonius' leather goods shop.

The runaway slave stood inside the shop and cheerfully announced his presence. Soon a man approached him with a curious expression on his face, "Welcome to my cobbler shop. What type of footgear do you desire?"

Onesimus was pleased that his first contact was the owner. In reply, he said with studied poise, "I seek Antonius. Gladius has referred me to him because of my cobbler skills."

Antonius' expression changed from curiosity to dubiousness. "I know this man Gladius. Sometimes he refers good people to me and other times he does not. How do I know you have the skills I require?" he inquired gruffly.

Smiling, Onesimus took off the same boot he had shown to Gladius. Confidently, he bestowed his product into the hands of Antonius. The cobbler looked at the boot, then at Onesimus, and back again at the boot. He inspected every part of the footgear and rubbed his hands on the stitching, especially where the top of the boot attached to the sole. He looked inside the boot and held it away from him to peer at its symmetry.

Onesimus was pleased at the close scrutiny Antonius gave to his product. He knew this man could tell quality workmanship. Antonius handed the boot back to the runaway slave and squinted into the young man's face as if trying to read his mind. "You have skills. I can use you in my business, but be mindful that I'm a difficult man to please. My clientele expect high quality at all times. I do not allow shoddy work to leave my shop. You will start on a probation basis. Should you falter, you will immediately be dismissed." Onesimus was ecstatic.

Antonius showed his new employee where his workstation would be and told him how much he would earn from the completion of each pair of footgear he produced. Finally, Antonius asked, "Since you just arrived in the city, have you secured a place to stay?" When Onesimus indicated he had not had time to search the area for available housing, Antonius proffered, "You can stay with another of my employees. He resides in one of the apartments above this shop."

Onesimus was beside himself with his good fortune. In Rome less than five hours, and already he had both a job and housing! He began to believe good fortune was finally coming his way. He did not yet know his new job and residence was within one mile of Paul's rented townhouse, nor did he know what this would mean for his future.

Three weeks later, when Aelia made her customary rounds to the businesses she had dealings with, Antonius took it upon himself to show her the excellent workmanship by his newest employee. Aelia took hold of a pair of military boots fashioned by Onesimus and admired his advanced skill level.

"This underling is improving your product offering, Antonius. He is good, but not as good as the Jew I aligned you with. What is his name and how did he come under your employ?" Antonius briefly explained how it came about for his windfall. "We shall find out if he stays in Rome or decides to wander elsewhere," said Aelia, who then concluded her usual business with Antonius.

Aelia's mind was processing the possibilities available with the new cobbler Antonius hired. When her driver stopped the carriage in front of her rented townhouse, the smart businesswoman made it a point to consult Paul about some of the possibilities. His input would be very valuable.

After the landlord procured the monthly rent from Paul, she presented him with a pair of military field boots made by Onesimus. "I would appreciate your comments on the workmanship of these boots." Christ's servant agreed, and inspected them in the same manner in which Antonius had done.

"This cobbler indeed has good skills. He has followed the template favored by Antonius, which indicates he adapts quickly to new techniques. There are a few areas of improvement needed, but overall, Antonius should be pleased to have him as an employee."

This was exactly what Aelia was hoping to hear from her renter. "I'm pleased to hear this, Paul, because I would like for you to train this man in your technique, which is better than Antonius'. It is my contention once this man learns your method, he will produce better quality merchandise and also within a faster time frame. Would you agree to tutor this new man?"

"Of course I would," said Paul agreeably. He waved his arm about the improvised workshop and noted, "As you can see, space is quite limited here, but I obviously cannot leave your abode. The man will have to come here. Would Flavius allow such an arrangement?"

Aelia smiled and replied in a confident light-hearted tone, "There shall be no problem obtaining approval from Flavius. This I assure you. When can you begin tutoring the new cobbler?"

Paul shrugged his shoulders. "Once he is approved, send him my way immediately."

The clever business magnate's eyes sparkled, "Expect him within the next two days."

The landlord and her renter then shared the evening meal together and enjoyed animated conversation. Aelia was reluctant to end the pleasant interlude, but needed to spend the night with her daughter and her husband who lived next to Paul. It was not socially acceptable for single women to be out alone at night after a certain hour.

Early the next morning, Aelia met with both Antonius and Flavius and divulged her plan to them. Antonius was startled, but could see the benefit of her scheme and easily agreed. Flavius hesitated as he considered such an arrangement from as many different angles as possible. Finding no impediments, he gave authorization and said he would inform the day guards. The centurion cautioned his petitioners, "Be mindful, both of you, that this

Onesimus must leave at the afternoon shift change."

Two days later, the immigrant from Colosse was introduced to his new tutor by an enthusiastic Antonius. The dubious Onesimus found Paul to be accommodating and easy to be around. He was quite impressed with Paul's cobbler skills and realized he could learn valuable techniques from this man under house arrest. The runaway slave certainly could relate with Paul's situation and found himself willing to be more trusting of this detainee than he otherwise would be. However, Onesimus still did not feel relaxed enough to share his true circumstances with the amiable Jew.

The next three weeks went by quickly for the runaway slave. Each day spent with Paul was enjoyable, and he could see his skill level was improving under Paul's tutelage. Antonius and Aelia were happy with the arrangement because of the increased revenue and growing demand for their products. The quality of work produced by these two odd characters was definitely paying off.

Onesimus was becoming less apprehensive about being discovered as a runaway slave. Without that worry, his relaxed emotions allowed him to feel a youthful fondness for Paul; he considered him not only as his tutor, but now a valuable friend. The Roman guards were vigilant in their observations of the two cobblers, and their daily reports indicated there were no signs of any intrigue involved between the two. Nonetheless, Flavius still had Onesimus' activities closely monitored.

One pleasant morning in February, Onesimus was particularly enjoying his walk to Paul's workshop. He breathed in the air deeply. It was a clear morning, crisp, with blue sky. Thankfully, it was a respite from the foul smoky air that sporadically settled over the neighborhood. As he approached the front door to Paul's townhouse, he stopped abruptly and stood frozen, terrified by the sudden interruption of his happy thoughts.

Coming out of the residence was a familiar face he had not expected to see again. It was Epaphras, a good friend and business associate of Philemon, the slave master Onesimus had bolted from weeks earlier. There was no avenue of escape for the young runaway. He attempted to cover as much of his face as possible with the sleeve of his outer cloak, as if he were protecting himself from smoke.

Trying hard to exhibit no sign of recognition or anxiety, Onesimus neither spoke nor looked at his potential nemesis. He side-stepped Paul's visitor and fellow servant to Christ, and hastily entered the townhouse. His heart was pounding and his breathing quickened. He felt weak with anxiety. His vocal cords were constricted so that he could only grunt a greeting to the front door guard. He dared not reopen the door for a second look down the street to verify it was Epaphras.

Epaphras at first had calmly moved past the young man who obviously was attempting to hide his identity. As he began to walk down the street, Epaphras puzzled over the man's behavior. Suddenly, he stopped and spoke aloud, "Onesimus!" It was a startling realization. He knew Onesimus had run away from Philemon and that great efforts had been made by the slave master to retrieve his property, but to no avail. He was sure the person he had just encountered was his friend's runaway slave.

Onesimus was shaking as he sat down to begin the day's work projects. He felt overwhelmed by the sudden unwelcome encounter. Paul could tell something was amiss with his young protégé, but opted to wait until the young man decided to share what was bothering him.

Outside, Epaphras stroked his full-face beard several times as he pondered what to do. Finally, he decided to return to Paul's townhouse to make sure his speculation was accurate. He turned around and hurried back to the townhouse where the surprised guard allowed him reentrance to the residence. The guards were fully aware that visitors could only be with the detainee one at a time and one hour per day. Junus saw by the concern on Epaphras' face that an exception should be made this time. It was obvious something was out of the ordinary and could be significant to their observations of the prisoner. Junus knew Draba was on duty and could easily handle any potential conflict that might arise.

When Epaphras stood in the doorway of Paul's workshop, Onesimus nearly fainted. He dropped his cobbling tool and sighed heavily. Epaphras stared at the young man and confirmed his identification of the young cobbler. Paul looked up from his leather project and was baffled at the sight of his fellow warrior for Christ, "Epaphras, what brings you back here?"

Draba looked on and he, too, was very curious about the reemergence of Paul's friend. He was poised for action in case of any wrongdoing on the part of the Colossian. Epaphras turned from the runaway slave and softly said to Paul, "My friend, I recognize your apprentice here as one called Onesimus, a runaway slave of Philemon. I was unsure until now that this young man is the same person sought by Philemon. Indeed, he is Onesimus."

Paul and Draba focused their attention on the pale-faced cobbler who was in obvious anguish. Onesimus sat at his workstation without speaking, only furtively glancing back and forth between Draba and Paul. Draba prepared himself for the runaway to attempt an escape.

Paul could see the torture on his protégé's face and in his cowering body language. He asked, "Onesimus, is it true what Epaphras says about you being a runaway slave?" The distressed escapee initially could not speak, only nodded his head that he was the offender. Slowly, he regained enough composure to painfully state the truth. He leaned forward in his chair and put his hand over his face as he began to sink into the pit of his most dreaded imaginations.

Draba was highly charged! A runaway slave could be very dangerous, and the guard called for his colleague, the dog handler Petronius. Onesimus continued to sit limply at his workstation. Epaphras moved aside to allow Petronius to enter the room. Paul got up from his workstation and moved toward the panic-stricken young man to reassure him, "Do not fear, Onesimus. No one is going to hurt you. Please tell us the truth. It is only when we know the truth that we can assist you."

Onesimus did not move. Finally, he took a deep breath and raised his head to look up at Paul. "Everything Epaphras has said is true," he confessed. Beginning to sob, the young man relayed how he escaped to Rome in the camel caravan. At the end of his narration he asked Paul, "What's going to happen to me, now?"

Christ's disciple placed his hand on the slave's trembling back and quietly said, "You must go with Draba to his commander Flavius. I will speak with Epaphras for more details. I know Philemon, who is doing God's work in Colosse. He is a devoted follower of Jesus and a godly leader in his home church. Once I know the details, I will confer with Flavius and attempt to intervene on your behalf in whatever way I can. But now, do not be anxious or worrisome and especially do not attempt to escape. Draba will surely kill you should you attempt to take such action."

Draba listened attentively to the detainee's words and was self-congratulatory that Paul gave credit to his authorized power, cautioning the runaway slave not to escape. The Roman guard was well-instructed in the procedure for handling such situations, and indeed would run his short sword into the slave. Draba's report to Flavius concerning this particular situation would include how Paul had instructed Onesimus to respect the Roman law.

The Roman guard stepped aside and spoke with Petronius about the timing of the event. There remained several hours until their shift change and they needed to decide how they would proceed. They conferred for several minutes before Draba announced, "Paul, it has been decided that this runaway slave shall remain here until our shift change. At that time, we both shall escort him to Flavius. He must remain in this room. Petronius and his dogs will stand guard outside in the courtyard. Any attempt to escape—and the dogs will be turned loose on him."

This was the same as announcing a death sentence. Onesimus knew about the viciousness of the attack dogs. Paul and Epaphras looked down at the flustered slave who sat wilted, barely breathing. "You have my personal guarantee Onesimus will not create any conflict for you," said Paul. The compassionate follower of Christ requested some water for the distraught slave.

When Marcus and Lucilius arrived for their afternoon/evening shift, they were startled to hear what had taken place. Draba met them outside the townhouse entrance to tell them he and Petronius had custody of the likeable young man whom Paul had been training in cobbler skills. Draba announced the man was a runaway slave and that he and Petronius would transport the slave to Flavius.

The Roman guard confidentially recommended to his counterparts that they should closely observe Paul and Epaphras to obtain any information that Flavius would need in this developing case. The shift replacements were stunned at this latest development, but agreed to do as Draba suggested.

The new converts to Christ briefly talked with each other before confronting Paul and his fellow soldier for Christ. "We have a serious situation here, Marcus. Our duties to Rome are obvious, yet we also are now servants to Christ who wants us to be different. What are your thoughts about this?"

Marcus scratched his head while his right hand began to unconsciously rotate the ball of death that was attached to his wrist. He looked earnestly into Lucilius' face and said, "At this point, it is not our decision to make. We must go about our duty as Roman soldiers and let Paul make the bigger decision on how to deal with this runaway slave. We know nothing about this other than what Draba has told us. He always hides details that will allow him to better portray himself to our superiors. Let us observe

Paul and follow his direction."

With that settled, they entered the domus. Immediately, they were met by Paul who filled them in on the developing situation. Paul was succinct and careful in his complete depiction of how Onesimus had been revealed to be a runaway slave. Epaphras explained the background of Onesimus.

Lucilius and Marcus were greatly affected, hearing Epaphras' and Paul's tale that was truthful, yet completely devoid of criticism, sarcasm or condemnation. When the narrative was completed, both Roman guards felt compassion for the slave. But they also felt confident that Paul and Epaphras were fully capable of dealing effectively and rightly with this calamity.

## Chapter 23

Flavius was taken aback when Draba and Petronius declared that Onesimus was a runaway slave, even though it was not unusual for runaways to seek asylum in Rome because of the city's capacity to swallow up a single soul in its sea of humanity and prevent his discovery. Rome was always on the lookout for such criminals. Rarely did runaways enjoy their freedom beyond six months.

The centurion summoned two new guards and had the panic-stricken slave removed to one of the prison cells located within the palace. Once he was alone with Draba and Petronius, he listened to their report of how this predicament had come about.

When their report was finished, Flavius shook his head, then looked at his chosen guards, "You have done well here. It always amazes me how runaways believe they can escape and survive within the city. It's almost as if they have an unspoken desire to get caught."

The centurion commander released the two guards and instructed the scribe to make copies of the report as soon as possible. Flavius grabbed his helmet and made his way to Cleatus' office. This matter was one the military general needed to know of immediately.

Cleatus initially showed no signs of emotion upon learning of the runaway slave. "This ordinary event is today extraordinary, a potential crisis because of the involvement with our prisoner Paul," he remarked. The general began a slow, measured pacing in his office, thinking beyond what he spoke to his centurion, "We have a watershed here for us. There are many new elements that must be addressed. For your part, Flavius, continue to have your daily guards closely observe Paul and his visitors. At this point, we do not want to disrupt the prisoner's normal routine. This could ruin our chance to learn more of his plans."

Cleatus stopped his pacing and pointed at Flavius, "Your actions will provide much needed information that will factor significantly into what we report to Nero when he finally returns from Athens."

The general resumed his seat behind his desk and looked towards his subordinate centurion. Cleatus' jaw was firmly set, but he spoke softly to Flavius, "Do not tell your men more than they need to know. Admit that this Onesimus is a runaway slave, but do not attempt to implicate Paul with him. It would taint how your men operate." Cleatus tapped his fingers on his desk, planning his next action, "I will relay this development to Seneca. He will react to this according to the political aspect, but we must focus on the military protection of Rome."

The impromptu meeting ended, and Flavius returned to his office with clear understanding of his continued role in this developing dilemma. He silently admitted to himself he felt excitement over this new development. The intrigue stirred his emotions and made his assignment of guarding a prisoner into something bigger and more challenging. He knew he would be successful in guiding his men to the conclusion of this fascinating case.

After his meeting with Flavius, Cleatus sent a messenger to Seneca's villa outside Rome. The message was brief. It stated the need for an emergency meeting with the Roman consul. While the general waited to receive a reply from Seneca, he had time to mentally create his plan for dealing with this twist in Paul's case. Similar to Flavius, Cleatus found himself becoming more energized and invigorated for dealing with what was normally a mundane criminal procedure.

Word came to Cleatus that Seneca would receive him the next morning after 10 a.m. The general was pleased at this arrangement. It coincided with the visit of the garrison commander in Rome, away from his assigned tri-city area that comprised Colosse, Laodicea, and Hierapolis. It was perfect timing. The garrison commander had finished his visit and was scheduled to return to his post the next day. Cleatus intercepted him and learned valuable information concerning the runaway slave's background. This would be shared with the Roman consul Seneca, and no doubt would play a major part in their strategic planning.

That evening, the general took his wife to dinner at one of

Rome's finer restaurants to enjoy a private celebration. He was very pleased at the recent turning point in his involvement with the alleged traitor to Rome.

While Cleatus was having a pleasant and relaxed evening, the detained Onesimus was experiencing an exact opposite range of emotions. He sat chained by his feet to one wall of the cell. The chain was heavy and the iron clasps secured to his ankles chafed his skin and caused blood to ooze around the edges. The cell was becoming dark as the sun dropped below the horizon. Along with the darkness came a cold dampness, causing him to chill physically and tremble emotionally.

The darkness was an ominous vehicle propelling his thoughts into a wilderness of hopelessness. As a runaway slave, he knew his future was bleak. In addition to being scourged by the Roman army, his fate rested with Philemon. As his owner, Philemon could put him to death, or reject his return and have him sold at auction. He could even allow the Romans to crucify him as an example to other runaway slaves.

Onesimus held his head in his hands. The young man's body shook with inner wailing, and soon released tears of despair that ran down his face and solidified into a salty crust. In his desolation, he could not believe that his tutor and friend would betray him into the hands of his enemy. He was confused and angry because Paul, too, was a prisoner of Rome. He thought his mentor, of all people, would understand his plight. Onesimus slumped over onto the bed for a tormented sleep.

The following morning, Cleatus arose, refreshed for his meeting with Seneca. He ate a hearty breakfast and went to the palace stables to ready Nike for the day's outing. The mighty warhorse instinctively picked up on his master's emotions and kicked his hind legs out to show he, too, was eager for an outing. The aging horse surrendered to the polished saddle, and soon they were heading toward Rome's outlying grasslands.

Seneca and his gardening slave were in the front portion of the villa. They were surveying the landscape in preparation for a promising spring that was about to spread color and life over drab empty spaces. As they talked, the landowner noticed his slave glancing inquisitively over his shoulder. Seneca turned to find out what was distracting his slave, and saw a lone figure approaching from the east.

The dark, indistinguishable silhouette was a strange contrast against the blue sky with white wispy clouds, and the tan winter grass waving in the cool breeze. As the dark mass drew closer, Seneca recognized the form as Cleatus and his famous steed, Nike. The landowner continued to watch the arrival of his guest, wondering at the surprise visit. Cleatus rode like a king, upright and noble. His black attire declared the magnificent image he liked to portray.

Nike did his part, as well. The horse, black as night, pranced toward his objective, lifting his forelegs high in his warlike training that showed his strength and agility. He could easily strike out with his strong hooves. The stallion seemed to send a message he was ready for whatever action might be required.

Seneca found himself mesmerized by the powerful combination of man and beast, and failed to hear his slave's words. He suddenly realized his gardener had spoken to him. "What did you say?" he asked, as he redirected his attention. The slave repeated his request to continue the landscape review after his guest departed. "That would be excellent," the consul replied. "Now go and inform Pompeia that our guest has arrived."

The host ordered another slave to care for Nike, and Seneca took Cleatus into his office where they could have their tête-à-tête without interruption. "Your message of urgency has my interest, Cleatus. What is of such importance that requires such a drastic change in our routines?"

Without any preliminaries, the guest revealed the cause of urgency. As Cleatus spoke in his deep voice, his words bounced off the walls of the office like thunder to Seneca's ears. The host was flabbergasted and his face showed it as he reacted, "This indeed is worthy of an impromptu meeting, and you are correct—we must address this issue immediately!" Immediately, Seneca's office transformed into a war room, similar in atmosphere to the military high command space they used when formulating strategies against their enemies.

"There are many facets involved now. We must agree on what each of us will do to resolve this issue quickly. It is imperative that this does not grow from a nuisance into a major dispute." Seneca's mind was reeling with the possible scenarios.

Cleatus was in complete agreement with the Roman consul. "I don't believe it will be that difficult for us, Seneca. I shall concentrate on the military and law enforcement portion, while you focus your efforts on the political."

"You are correct, Cleatus; but remember, there will be instances we cross over in our labors. As such, it is vital we do not impede each other or give any suspect the opportunity to identify our strategy or to alter theirs."

Cleatus nodded and smiled slightly, adding, "Yes! Unfortunately, Seneca, this very thing has occurred in the past. Rome has experienced three different major slave uprisings. Our might and the slaves' lack of true leadership and strategy have allowed us to suppress these rebels of the past. My concern is that this Paul and the runaway slave Onesimus could be harbingers of another revolution."

Seneca admired Rome's leading general. He rubbed his hands on the padded armchair as he contemplated. General Cleatus was loyal to Rome, battle-tested, intelligent, and savvy in strategy formulation. His persistence and determination were valuable assets for dealing with this new facet in Paul's case. The consul was relieved he could depend on Cleatus to thoroughly demolish any rebellion. Seneca was aware the general would also serve his interests to quell other issues involving Paul and his followers.

"What do you intend to do to fulfill your part in this mission, Cleatus?" Seneca knew that Rome's leading militarist had already implemented aspects of his strategy and he knew that using physical force was necessary at this time. Cleatus was not one to vacillate or wait for direction, especially in matters involving military policing.

Cleatus' low voice added a somber effect as he revealed his initial actions, "I have discussed the circumstances involving Colosse with my garrison commander stationed there. He has been quite informative. It appears our runaway salve is the property of a man named Philemon, who is a prominent businessman in Colosse and owns many slaves." The general suspended his narrative and leaned on one arm of his chair. His eyebrows were raised in anticipation of Seneca's response to the next detail, "Philemon was converted by our detainee to this new religious superstition we call Christians when Paul recruited many to his cause."

Seneca sat back in his chair with surprise and heightened interest. "This is most interesting, General, most interesting. Has our detainee also recruited this Onesimus slave?"

Cleatus was quick with his reply, "Apparently not. Paul focused his efforts on freemen, which I would have done were I in his shoes. As you know, converting the freemen will lead to converting their property."

"Do you know why this Onesimus elected to run away from his master?"

Cleatus, perturbed at the uncertainty, drummed his fingers on Seneca's desktop and answered, "I do not at this time; but this information will be forthcoming."

Seneca's brow furrowed. "Unfortunately, due to the hazardous sea conditions, this information will have to come via the camel caravans and will take much longer. We may not get this information until after Nero returns to Rome."

It was Cleatus' turn to frown, acknowledging this unacceptable possibility, before addressing it, "My operatives will send a brief summary of their findings to me via carrier pigeon. This will ease our concern and allow us to confer with Nero." Cleatus needed further reassurance and asked Seneca, "Are your agents capable of doing the same thing?"

Seneca confirmed it as he casually repositioned himself in his chair, "Most certainly, Cleatus. You assess the communication factor well. Getting this summary will allow us to obtain an extension on Nero's hearing of Paul's appeal." With a sly, knowing smile, he reminded his colleague, "Nero Claudius Caesar will grant us extra time because he does not want either embarrassment or punitive action by the Senate over his handling of this case."

Seneca, Nero's chief consul, clasped his hands together and rested them on his ample chest. He also smiled slyly as he shared his thoughts with his guest, "Cleatus, we have an excellent opportunity before us, right here in Rome, to gather sufficient evidence as to the guilt or innocence of these two men."

Cleatus heard the delight in his host's gleeful pronouncement. Seneca had a reputation for shrewdness and cunning, so the general listened carefully as his host revealed the reasoning behind his excitement, "We can take immediate action by having Onesimus' trial held at Paul's rented townhouse. The grilling of the runaway slave will induce both the slave and Paul to reveal any concealed schemes they have. This will be our foundation to assist Nero in deciding the fate of our detainee."

Now the general moved his fingers in a circular motion on his desktop. His eyes looked away at nothing in particular as he pondered the suggestion. Seneca's folded hands waited for Cleatus' response. Finally, Cleatus spoke, "There is merit to your plot, Seneca. Keeping the two separated until those proceedings will cause their minds to speculate tirelessly. This will benefit us and speed up what they expose during the trial. Of course we shall have a scribe in attendance to verify what is revealed."

Seneca was relieved that Cleatus approved of his plot. He suggested a delayed time frame, "I propose we wait two weeks before conducting the trial. This will serve us well in several areas. The detainees will have more time to stew in their thoughts! And we can explore other avenues for more information that will benefit us."

"You are devious-minded, Seneca—just what is needed at this time!" Cleatus' callous baritone laughter filled the office. "Of course, it goes without saying, our respective agents will overlap their efforts as we scour Rome for insight into any nefarious schemes our targets may desire to hatch."

Seneca shared his collaborator's perspective and joined his laughter. "Come, Cleatus! It is time for lunch and I believe our meeting can be concluded." The host escorted his guest to the dining room where Pompeia waited their arrival. Their jovial attitudes placated her worry over their emergency summit.

After an amiable lunch, Seneca ordered a slave to bring Nike from the stable to the front of the villa. Cleatus thanked his host for an enjoyable time, and mounted his steed. Seneca watched the black-clad powerbroker move eastward toward Rome.

Cleatus prodded Nike to proceed at a quick pace, which caused the deep crimson and Prussian blue cape to rise and ride the breeze. Cleatus felt the flapping and fluttering and enjoyed the vision of his cape waving a victorious farewell.

Still feeling buoyed up by the meeting with Flavius, as soon as he was out of sight of the villa, Cleatus stopped. He relished the blue sky and sunshine, and took advantage of the beautiful weather to indulge in trained maneuvers he had long enjoyed with his stallion. He pulled the reins to the right and Nike immediately responded. Combining his use of the reins with that of his feet, Cleatus signaled his warhorse it was time for action. With each gesture from his master, the mighty black warhorse sidestepped, rose up on its hind legs and pawed the air with his forelegs. He snorted his lust for using these battle techniques.

Nike's master led him through the maneuvers that were once common to them during battle. Finally, Cleatus instructed his aging companion it was time to run like the wind, exactly what the mighty horse craved. Instantly, he became a black comet racing across the golden grassy plain with his rider, resembling a specter of death racing to destroy its opposition.

## Chapter 24

The day after Onesimus was taken into custody and placed in a cell, Epaphras visited Paul to update him about the situation. Paul took a break from his bootmaking projects and the two followers of Christ sat in Aelia's office along with the ever-present Praetorian Guard member in attendance, which this time was Lucilius.

Epaphras asked Paul, "Is it possible we can discuss the matter concerning Onesimus alone?"

Paul shook his head and explained, "This matter concerns Roman law and, as such, my house guards must be present to hear and report to Flavius. Rome's concern is to learn as much about Onesimus and our involvement together as they can, to determine if we are conspirators." Paul looked up at Lucilius for confirmation, "Is this not so, Lucilius?" The guard's steadfast gaze met Paul's eyes as he softly answered yes. Paul noted the angst on Lucilius' face and tightness in his stance. He made a mental note to ask him about his discomfort later, after Epaphras' departure.

"Besides, Epaphras, I have nothing to hide. I welcome the presence of Lucilius and the other guards. They will see for themselves I do not intend to overthrow Rome." Uncertain, Epaphras rubbed his forehead with his hand, thinking over Paul's reasoning. But he could see there was no alternative.

"Now, Epaphras, it is vital you tell as much about Onesimus as you can, so I can determine what course of action to take to assist him—if indeed I can do such a thing."

Slowly, Epaphras began to explain what he knew about the runaway slave, "Before you came to know Philemon and led him to Christ's salvation, he was a hard man, especially to his many slaves. After he purchased Onesimus, Philemon determined the young slave needed to be broken to prevent rebellion, his own, as well as influencing other slaves to do the same. A series of punishments and beatings followed. Apparently, young Onesimus had taken enough abuse. He stole money to finance his escape and planned how to carry out such a risky undertaking."

Lucilius was very observant of Paul's demeanor and facial expressions as he listened to Epaphras tell his story. The guard noted that Paul was attentive to every word. When the Colossian finished, Lucilius became impatient, anxiously waiting for Paul's reaction.

"You say, Epaphras, that Philemon came to own Onesimus *after* accepting Christ as his Savior?" Epaphras affirmed it without hesitation. Paul pressed, "Did you have cause to observe Philemon's treatment of his slaves *after* he accepted Christ into his heart?"

Epaphras stroked his beard with his hand as he thought seriously about Paul's question. "He did relent in many ways; but still, on occasion, he did beat some slaves, including Onesimus." Epaphras paused, thought more about his answer, then amended, "But he never beat anyone as severely as he did before his conversion to Christ Jesus."

Paul looked up at the ceiling of the office and kept his gaze on the beautiful fresco Aelia had commissioned for her enjoyment. After a few moments, the apostle of Christ asked Epaphras, "Did you or any other church member confront Philemon about his treatment of his slaves, including Onesimus?"

Again Epaphras stroked his beard heavily has he contemplated the question, "I did, and I was told that another church elder did, also."

Lucilius was curious and perplexed at Paul's line of questioning and could not understand what his assigned detainee's purpose was. He looked quizzically at Paul, hoping for an explanation. However, Paul's eyes were fixed on Epaphras as he explained, "Epaphras, you are quite aware that once a person accepts Christ, he becomes a new creation and Christ begins His transforming work in His creation by having the Holy Spirit direct them away from the ways of the world. Sometimes it is a lengthy process. It appears Philemon remains under his earlier attitudes and actions concerning the treatment of slaves."

Lucilius' listened attentively. Meanwhile, his heart was open to receive his mentor's teaching. Epaphras, too, wanted more from Paul on this topic, and asked, "What do you propose should be done concerning Onesimus, Paul?"

Paul took his eyes away from the artistic ceiling fresco and focused on Epaphras. "I will pray, seeking the direction God wants me to take. Until He answers my petition, I shall do nothing. You should also pray and seek God's direction, lest you become disobedient to Him. Remember, my brother, that God's will, plan, and purpose should not be interfered with by mortal man. Our duty is to follow Christ Jesus in whatever manner He wants, and not be slaves to the emotions of our human hearts."

Lucilius was grateful to Christ, knowing it was He who provided him with this valuable teaching through his mentor Paul. Both he and Marcus were eager students to learn the ways of the Lord, and this was something they needed to know. He leaned forward to hear Epaphras' reply. "Thank you, Paul, for this reminder. I do have kindheartedness for this young man and believe he was wronged by Philemon. Sometimes it's difficult to wait for God's intervention in a matter such as this."

Lucilius was deeply moved by Epaphras' statement. It added to his emotional conflict that he intended to share with his mentor at his first available moment. The guard suddenly realized that the time limit of visitation with Paul had expired. He cleared his throat and reluctantly spoke, "I'm sorry to inform you that the time of this visit has expired and now it must end."

Paul lightly pressed his lips, dropped his hands in his lap, and said, "Thank you, Lucilius, for your reminder. I've learned much about the relationship between Philemon and Onesimus. It is sufficient for me to take it to the Lord God in prayer." He stood up, gently took Epaphras by his elbow, and led his valued colleague to the vestibule.

When Paul returned to his workshop, he hesitated to sit down to resume his boot project. Instead, he looked at Lucilius with concern and softly asked, "My brother, I could not help but notice the concern you showed during my conversation with Epaphras. Please tell me what troubles you so much?"

Lucilius requested they go into the courtyard where Marcus could become a part of the discussion as well. Paul readily agreed. Once in the courtyard, Lucilius motioned for Marcus to join them. When the three were together, Paul inquired what concerned them so much. "We are spiritually torn, Paul. Flavius has instructed us to continue closely monitoring you and the many visitors who approach you. We know he seeks any information that might pertain to your relationship with Onesimus," lamented the conflicted guard.

Marcus quickly interjected, "The circumstances involving this runaway slave are serious, and we are limited in our knowledge of what is going to happen with this man, and possibly with you."

Paul gratefully received what his two mentees were considering. He consoled them, "Do not be dismayed at what is happening or what could happen. Once your superiors reach a decision on what action to take, rest assured it will be in accordance with Roman law. I do not know the mind of God in his matter, but I know He will reveal what He wants me to do, if anything, in His perfect timing."

Marcus fidgeted with the hanging ball of death that was at his side. Lines at the corners of his eyes tightened and deep wrinkles formed. "Is this a part of learning how to follow Christ Jesus?"

Paul touched his young mentee's muscular shoulder. "It is, my brother. Remember, God will always test your faith at different times and in different ways. This is part of His process of refining you to carry out His purpose for you. As you remain steadfast in your obedience to God, He will bless you with His wisdom and discerning of spirits to give His comfort and insight."

The tension surrounding the mentees dissipated, but Lucilius had to admit, "Patience is not an easy attribute of mine. I fear our Lord has His work cut out to transform me on this."

Paul chuckled, "Lucilius, we all have our afflictions. Some are so deeply ingrained within us it takes a combination of time and events for Christ to achieve the cleansing He desires for us." To ease the moment, Paul changed the subject, "Come, it is time we dined together. I'm hungry and I know you are, as well." They made their way to the dining room, ready to exchange their worry for thoughts and conversation about other things.

That same day, Cato met with Seneca at the Roman consul's villa. He always enjoyed the brief journey to the countryside and the fact that Seneca's villa was not far from his own. Their meeting would still allow him to spend time at his own villa. He had plenty of research to analyze that pertained to Paul's case.

Cato knew something had happened for Seneca to request an emergency conference with him. He guessed it centered on Paul or Nero. As such, he attempted to prepare himself for the unfolding of his suppositions. But he wasn't prepared for the topic Seneca had on his mind.

When he sat down with his colleague in the comfort of his office, he saw that Seneca exhibited no signs of distress or panic. Instead, the consul began to relay the circumstances developing now between Paul and the runaway slave named Onesimus.

While Cato listened attentively to the sequence of events, his outward composure was inwardly becoming shards of turmoil. The situation involving the young runaway slave brought back painful memories of his own experience when he was seized by sea pirates while he assisted in his father's exporting business. On one of the seafaring trips from Ephesus to Rome, his father died at the hands of the ruthless pirates. Cato, the youngest son, was also onboard and was captured and sold like an animal at auction.

There had been no rescue available for Cato, and the young man had encountered years of bondage, being sold from one owner to the next. It was his education and intellectual abilities which saved him from hard labor and a shortened life. His various owners quickly saw his worth, and exploited it to their advantage.

During this process, Cato had learned a great deal about Romans, survival, and how to manipulate those who considered themselves superior. It was during this period that the young man became enamored with Stoicism. It became a mental shield for coping with his dehumanizing plight.

Seneca was speaking continually during the parade of Cato's troubling memories. When Seneca finished his depiction of events, Cato sat motionless. His stomach ached from the emotions his memories had just discharged. Remembering the days of his youth, he wanted to scream, to vomit, to run away and purge himself of those horrific memories. Because this was not a viable option for him and would not rectify the past, Cato stoically suppressed his emotions, feigning consideration of Falvius' words. He willed his emotions to recede as his colleague discussed their approach to the new developments.

Taking a deep breath to collect himself, Cato stated, "I am in agreement with your plan for the delayed trial of this Onesimus. It will be insightful to learn how Paul responds to this trial. We have discussed the need for some kind of breakthrough on this case, and I believe it is now being presented to us." Cato had to take another deep breath before he asked, "What do you want me to do?"

Seneca tugged at his earlobe a brief moment, then announced his directives. "I want you in attendance at the trial to keenly observe Paul. Depending on what takes place during the hearing, I want you to apply pressure on Paul to disclose any hidden agenda he might have."

Cato looked at Seneca without any outward reaction to the consul's strategy. He braced himself for the answer to his next question, "Do you also want me to grill this runaway slave?"

Seneca was aware of Cato's past and did not want to subject his fellow collaborator to undue emotional pain. "No, I do not. Cleatus and I will take care of that portion of the case."

The relief Cato felt was briefly displayed on his face, which Seneca was quick to pick up on. "Enough of this. You have time to prepare for this trial; but let us have some refreshment and you can inform me about your findings concerning our prisoner client."

Seneca was impressed by his associate's research and assessment of Paul's epistle to the Philippians, as well as other reports about activities Paul was involved in prior to being arrested by Felix in Caesarea. "This is valuable information for us, my friend, now and going forward, especially when you continue to probe Paul's mind," he commended.

Much took place during the lull leading up to the runaway slave's trial. For Onesimus, it was a daily descent into deeper misery. He was allowed no visitors, was not permitted the use of an attorney, and was not spoken to by any of the guards. In essence, the young slave was in solitary confinement, as if being a prisoner of his own thoughts was not enough. He was repeatedly plagued by thoughts of how his regarded friend Paul had betrayed him.

At times, he envisioned striking back at Paul in retribution for his perceived betrayal. Other times, he focused on the probability he would either be executed or resold. In his mind, there was very little difference between the two deaths. His mental and emotional turmoil was creating weight loss—fifteen pounds, so far—as he awaited his fate.

Via carrier pigeon, Cleatus sent notification to Philemon of Onesimus' arrest. A second message was a simple request: Would the slave owner take back the runaway slave? Philemon also received a single message from Epaphras, also by carrier pigeon, informing him that Paul was involved in the issue concerning Onesimus. Philemon was astonished at that, wondering what the connection was, but knew more information would be forthcoming. He had time to deliberate his decision about Onesimus.

Paul received several visitors from the church in Rome, expressing their concern that his involvement with Onesimus could taint his appeal before Caesar. The apostle of Christ had to assure them that God was in control and they should not let their emotions lead them into disobedience to their heavenly Father, or untoward behavior of any kind. With each visitor, the vigilant guards had more data to submit to Flavius.

As each day drew closer to the fateful trial, everyone involved, with the exception of Paul, became more tense and, in some instances, irritable. When the trial day finally arrived, it was met with great relief. For Paul, there was an eagerness to step onto the battlefield and engage the spiritual enemy who was the instigator of these events to rob, kill, and destroy God's work. Paul had no idea if God planned on using him during the trial, but he was spiritually and emotionally prepared to be his heavenly Father's vessel.

Normally, runaway slaves appeared before a mid-level judge who sentenced the already-determined-guilty rebel. Options rested with the decision made by the slave owner. If the owner elected to receive the slave back, there would be a brutal scourging of the offender. Onesimus would also be branded with the letters FUG, short for fugitive; a lifelong reminder of his offense.

Should the slave owner reject the return, the slave was sold at auction. Rome retained a commission on the sale and the balance was given to the former owner who did not have to pay any tax on his subsequent purchase of a replacement slave. In the majority of cases, the slave master chose to sell the offending slave lest the slave instigate a future revolt. If a slave engaged in sedition during his runaway time period, crucifixion was automatic.

There were several dramatic changes prepared for Onesimus' trial. Instead of the mid-level judge, it would be Seneca and Cleatus, the two titans of power in the Roman governmental system who would decide the slave's destiny. Crucifixion was ruled out because there was no overt rebellion on the slave's part. The influencing issue would be the decision from the slave's owner.

Neither Seneca nor Cleatus divulged the time Onesimus' future would be decreed. It wasn't until the actual day that those involved would learn of the event. All players in the life drama would be equally unprepared for their impromptu performance.

Flavius was instructed to remain at his duty post and make sure the proceedings were not interrupted by any dissidents. He would not be a part of the trial. The guards retained their normal shifts, and both Marcus and Lucilius were on duty during the time of the trial. They would not be allowed inside the makeshift judicial chamber, but would be assigned duty outside the improvised courtroom. Cato would be in attendance as Seneca had instructed.

The Roman consul and his co-conspirator, Cleatus, arrived unannounced at the door of Paul's townhouse. The guards were shaken by their surprise appearance. The sight of two of Rome's highest ranking officials led them to believe this ordinary slave trial was much more complex than they first had thought.

Paul wondered why this trial was being held in his confines. When he walked into the dining room where the trial was to take place, his heart filled with compassion. The young slave stood shackled by heavy chains, including an iron neck collar that restricted his head movement. Onesimus would not acknowledge Paul, and did not see his tutor's effort to convey his compassion and encouragement to him.

Seneca and Cleatus were seated on one side of the dining room table, and Paul was instructed to sit opposite them and next to Onesimus, who was required to stand. Cleatus opened the proceedings, "This trial is to determine the punishment for a runaway slave named Onesimus who is the possession of a man named Philemon of Colosse." Cleatus focused his eyes on Paul. "It is also purposed to determine if Rome's prisoner, Paul, has any involvement in the activities of this runaway slave; and if so, to what extent."

Paul remained composed. Onesimus turned his head as much as the iron collar would allow, and peered angrily down at his betrayer. Cato's eyes darted back and forth between Paul and Onesimus. Each time Cato looked at the shaken slave, his muscles tightened. It took great effort to appear neutral in this matter. He wanted desperately to defend this young man with whom he had so much in common.

Satisfied with his opening statement, Cleatus took the next step in the proceedings. He hoped what he was about to reveal could cause Paul to react, "In accordance with Roman law, the slave owner Philemon was informed of the arrest of his property."

Purposely, Cleatus looked quickly toward Paul and Onesimus for any reaction. Seeing none, he continued, "Philemon had the option to appear in person at this trial, or he could relay his decision to this court via carrier pigeon."

Again, the chief judge paused for effect, creating agonizing suspense. Cato's attention was locked on Paul, as was Seneca's. Paul was serene. Onesimus' head hung in hopeless resignation.

Up to that point, Cleatus had spoken in a monotone. Now, in a strong authoritative voice, he announced, "Philemon has decided to let this court determine the fate of his slave." He paused. "As such, Seneca and I have agreed that the runaway slave, Onesimus, shall remain in Rome and continue to work for Antonius and keep his apprenticeship with Paul. This apprenticeship shall not be lengthy because the slave has demonstrated competent skills. Once the slave's apprenticeship is completed, Philemon will be notified and he can elect to receive his property back or put him up for auction.

"This is in accordance with Roman law which gives the slave owner more time to determine his desire to retain the slave and not incur economic damages. Since Philemon has given this court his permission, it shall be acted upon. Because Onesimus has not behaved in a rebellious manner against Rome, we give him opportunity to redeem himself and make himself more profitable."

No one in the room was more astounded at Cleatus' and Seneca's decision than Cato. He had not had an inkling this was about to take place; but he knew there was much more to this decision than the fate of a lowly slave who could easily be replaced by Philemon. He surmised it was to test Paul and entice him to unravel his secret intentions. Cato knew in his heart that Paul also was aware of this ploy.

Cato also realized his own perceived role in the maneuver, but was not offended. On the contrary, he was eager to untangle the speculation concerning Paul. Cato changed his focus to Cleatus who boomed out more of the decision. "Onesimus." At the sound of his name, the bewildered slave lifted his head and looked at his judge, enduring the chafing of the iron collar around his neck.

"You will continue to work with Paul, here in his residence, but only during the established work day. At the end of the day, you shall be remanded to an apartment next to this residence under guard. Further, should you make any attempt to escape, the guard is directed to execute you." Cleatus waited for the echoes of his booming decree to dwindle down before he demanded, "Do you understand what I've said?"

Softly and with difficulty due to the discomfort of the iron collar, Onesimus replied, "It is as you deem." Despite his quiet verbal acquiescence, Onesimus' anger seethed against Paul.

Cleatus declared the trial over. Guards from the palace who had accompanied Onesimus to the trial were summoned to escort him to his new accommodations. Onesimus lowered his head and exited the judicial chamber without looking at anyone.

After the trial, Seneca and Cleatus held a private meeting at the general's townhouse. Both titans of Roman justice were relaxed, even jubilant, over how the trial had played out. As the judicial conspirators enjoyed wine, honey cakes, and dates, Cleatus remarked, "Rome's history with slave rebellions requires us to be vigilant. Our forced arrangement between these two prisoners hopefully will enlighten us about any proposed uprising Paul may be planning. Onesimus will be our bait!"

"I agree with you, Cleatus. The evidence we have compiled thus far does not entirely establish Paul's innocence. We need more evidence, but we do not have the luxury of unlimited time to secure such proof. When Nero returns from Athens, I must obtain an extension in Caesar's hearing of Paul's appeal."

"We are under no time restrictions, because this is a case of intent to incite rebellion," the general corrected. He reminded Seneca, "To a degree, that is what Felix did by detaining Paul for two years in Caesarea. We cannot overlook the fact that Felix also attempted to bribe both Paul and the Jews. We can hold Paul, or Onesimus for that matter, until we are satisfied Rome is under no danger from them."

Cleatus ran his fingers through his graying hair and confidentially revealed the recent decision he had made, "I must confide to you that this involvement will be my last duty for Rome. When this case is concluded, I shall retire. For this reason, I do not want to make any hasty judgments involving our prisoner. My duty remains the same now as when I first entered the military—to protect Rome at all costs. I will utilize time as my main weapon against these prisoners."

Seneca raised his eyebrows at the general's announcement. He was surprised. He took a morsel of food and studied his host's face while he slowly chewed. Cleatus did not exhibit any remorse attached to his decree, but fatigue was visible in his countenance.

The Roman consul then brought his own revelation, "I, too, will be retiring from service to Rome and this will be my last endeavor. Nero is becoming a tyrant, rather than a true leader of Rome. My influence with him is lessening. He is growing more unpredictable and unstable. I fear bad developments will take place in the near future, possibly involving our prisoner."

Having revealed truth to one another, both men relaxed their official appearances, and exchanged candid expressions of mental, emotional, and physical fatigue derived from many years of battling diverse enemies.

Seneca sighed, "This case is more far reaching than what it should be."

Cleatus admitted, "It has potential to cause the demise of many people, ourselves included."

The champions lifted their wine goblets in a toast to their common bond.

## Chapter 25

At the conclusion of the trial, Cato left the townhouse rapidly, without conferring with Paul or anyone else. He needed fresh air to calm himself. Viewing the chained young man, and remembering his own time of being a slave, triggered a wretched queasiness in his stomach. He stepped into his waiting carriage and had his driver mercifully take him away.

A short time later, the more composed Roman official returned to the site of the trial, feeling prepared to begin his role in this subterfuge. Resolutely, he entered the apartment building next to Paul's rented townhouse and began the long ascent to the top of the four-story building. The closer he got to his destination, the more difficult it was for him to breathe, due to his emotional strugglse with what he was about to do.

When he arrived at his objective, he heaved a deep breath and approached the wary guard, "I am Cato, assigned to meet with the slave prisoner. Allow me to speak with him."

The guard visually inspected the toga-clad invader and recognized the name and description given to him earlier by Cleatus. Without a word, the guard stepped to one side and opened the door of the apartment to the interloper.

Inside, Cato's stomach began to twist again. Onesimus was sitting on his cot, with his head in his hands. At first, the prisoner did not look up at his visitor. Finally, Cato broke the uneasy silence, "Onesimus, look at me. My name is Cato. I was in attendance at your trial. My purpose is to discuss what happens to you next."

With resignation, the slave slowly lifted his head. His eyes were bloodshot from many tears. He peered at the man dressed in the spotless toga. He did not stand up, nor did he speak. His lost facial expression resonated with Cato who forced himself to go on, "It is my duty to inform you of components associated to your case that Cleatus wants me to convey to you." The agent of Rome softened his tone and finished, "I also wish to advise you in ways I have learned through experience."

The accomplice to the deceivers looked about the room and sat down in the only chair, making sure it was sufficiently clean so as not to soil his toga. He maintained his air of official status. Onesimus' eyes followed Cato's movements, but he remained mum, dreading to hear the details of his sentence.

Cato changed his intended tactic, staring at the pathetic young human form in front of him. While he thought, he honed in on the slave's body language and withdrew a small cloth from inside his inner tunic. It was scented with spices to counter the rank smell of the room. He quietly covered his nose with the cloth and inhaled slowly. Onesimus watched the action of the Roman official with a blank stare.

Cato continued with his offer to Onesimus. "While you continue your apprenticeship with Paul, you shall continue to be paid by Antonius." Cato quickly expressed how unusual this was, "Normally slaves, especially runaway slaves, do not receive any compensation for their labors. However, in your particular case, there is some uncertainty, because Roman law allows the slave owner to dismiss all charges against a slave and give him his freedom. Cleatus awaits answer to this question from Philemon. Once Cleatus knows this answer, he shall judge accordingly."

What Cato did not tell Onesimus is the law he cited was very obscure and had not been invoked for decades. The real reason for allowing Onesimus payment for his labors was to determine what he did with the money. If any of the funds went to anyone other than Philemon, this would be construed as funding rebellion. It would be sufficient evidence to convict Onesimus and, possibly, Paul.

The runaway slave looked warily at his visitor and still did not react to his news in any way. He merely sat in resignation and waited for the next revelation. Without warning, Cato jolted the young slave with his next statement.

"Now I shall give you my personal advice. The decision you make after our discussion today will determine your fate. It really rests in your hands, despite your thinking otherwise at this low point in your life. You can either listen to what I offer you, or reject my attempt to assist you. It is your decision, and all I require is a simple yes or no. If your answer is yes, I will proceed with my recommendations to you. If it is no, I will simply get up, leave, inform Cleatus, and you are on your own. Which do you prefer?"

Onesimus sat upright on his bed cot and stared at the unknown man who was old enough to be his father. His eyes revealed a mixture of disbelief and sudden interest. Cato allowed time for the young slave to make his life-determining decision.

After several minutes, Onesimus uttered, "What are these recommendations you speak about?"

Relieved that the young slave had opted to listen to his advice, a pleased smile crept into the corner of Cato's mouth which he immediately hid by turning his head to cough. He sternly instructed, "First, you must control your emotions and not allow them to interfere with your thinking and reasoning! If you don't, you will sentence yourself to great pain and possibly even death." Cato stopped his discourse and pretended to adjust his toga while he gauged his target's reaction. Onesimus cocked his head to one side and stared intently with skeptical eyes at his messenger.

"Second, you must become cunning, shrewd, and calculating in how you deal with those who control your fate. You can devise a strategy to manipulate them into giving you what you want and need."

Before Cato could continue, Onesimus scowled and sarcastically spat, "What, exactly, is it you so knowingly perceive I want and need, Roman?"

Cato joined his hands together and placed his clasped fingers to his lips, all the while locking onto the slave's fiery eyes. He did not hurry his answer to the angry slave.

His answer was one word.

"Freedom."

Onesimus tilted his head backward and laughed scornfully, "Freedom! Surely you are mad! How is it possible for me to attain freedom in *my* circumstance?" He shook his head back and forth and glared at his visitor. "You are right, Roman, in that I do desire freedom. That is not difficult to determine. How do you propose I achieve my desire?" His words were laced with undisguised sarcasm.

The Roman agent did not allow the slave's tone and demeanor to deter him. Steadily, Cato fired the details at the prisoner. "You are foolish, and do not see the opportunity you have! Look around you, slave! Are you not in a cold, damp cell, shackled to the wall with iron that claws at your skin?" His words hit home and caused Onesimus to recoil at his harsh reality.

Cato continued his firing shots, "Do you not realize you have valuable time to be able to utilize your cobbler's talents and develop them into better skills? And in the process earn money for doing so? Are you oblivious to the fact you are a carrot being offered, to entice Paul into divulging secrets the Roman authorities want? Your actions in this game of inducement can propel you into becoming a freedman!"

Onesimus was now alert and attentive to the words of his potential benefactor. He remained wary. His eyes narrowed as he glared at Cato. "How do I know this is possible and not some ruse on your part to cause me more harm?"

"Because Cleatus is aware that Paul and Philemon know each other. What better way to learn if Paul has secret intentions to cause rebellion than to use you to get Paul to reveal his plans?"

The slave then began to lightly bump his head against the wall behind him as he thought this over. As he did so, he studied Cato's face. He leaned forward and said, "Are you trying to tell me that if I go along with this hoax, and provide Cleatus what he wants, he will declare me a freedman?"

"Exactly. With my assistance. When this conspiracy is completed, I will petition Cleatus to publicly pronounce your freedom." To give further proof of his intentions, Cato continued, "And it won't cost you the normal two thousand denarii to purchase your desired goal."

Onesimus' stared at Cato. "Why are you revealing this plot to me and not letting things take their planned course of action?"

Cato slowly got up from his chair and smoothed his toga. He took two slow steps forward until he was next to the slave's bed. His posture noticeably softened, along with his voice. With surprising emotion, he looked at Onesimus with eyes of compassion. Onesimus detected a hint of moistness in the corners of his eyes.

"Because many years ago, I, too, was a slave. I experienced the gut-wrenching nausea that goes with the realization you are considered property, no better than a dog." Cato stiffened, assuming the stance of a fighter. With his fists tightly clenched, and a hard edge to his voice, Cato pressed on, "I studied and learned how to manipulate those who owned me by using my talents to achieve what otherwise I could not do." With a touch of pride in his voice, he confessed, "I touched the slave master's heart in ways I learned were important to him, so that he yielded and even publicly announced my becoming a freedman. With my freedom I also became a citizen of Rome."

Onesimus was shocked as he listened and watched this stranger whom he never would have guessed would have such a story. He briefly hung his head, then looked up again with a humbled demeanor. He asked, "What did you do, and how long did it take before you were set free?"

With his regained regal bearing, Cato slowly paced the room as he spoke, "My father instructed me and provided for my formal education in my homeland of Cyprus. In addition, he sent me to Greece where I was tutored by several prestigious mentors. I returned to assist my father in his shipping business. On one of our journeys from Cyprus to Rome he died aboard ship and I was abducted by pirates. I was taken to an auction."

The revisited events caused Cato to stop. He pressed the cloth against his mouth to steady a trembling lip and pretended to cough. It had been years, but the memories were as if they had happened yesterday. He drew a deep breath, and went on, "There, the gods favored me. My speech and education were acknowledged by the auctioneer. A wealthy Roman purchased me to educate his offspring. He realized I could also assist him to make his business more profitable."

At that point, Cato became subdued. He lowered his head and softly uttered, "It took ten long years before I was freed. During that time, I never was beaten and did not have to wear the despicable collar around my neck or ankle shackles. I was treated fairly." Cato somberly looked down and shook his head slowly from side to side, before meeting the eyes of the runaway slave. "Nevertheless, I was a *slave*."

Cato's emotions caused him to involuntarily shudder as he remembered those dark days of his youth. He did not elaborate, and Onesimus did not inquire further about this man's background. Cato straightened up and adjusted his toga in preparation for his departure. He started towards the door of the apartment and stopped before opening it. Without looking backward at Onesimus, he made a final statement, "This shall be our only meeting. I cannot and will not offer you more advice. You have what you need. The choice now is yours for what you want to do." At that, Cato quickly opened the door and left.

The guard on duty entered the room and proceeded to inspect it for any hidden weapons that Cato might have left for the runaway slave. He did not realize that Cato had indeed delivered a powerful weapon to the slave prisoner—but not a physical one. Onesimus held the weapon not in his hand, but in his will.

When he was alone, Onesimus sat morosely on his cot. His mind whirled wildly as he thought about the counsel just presented to him. He struggled to remember all the profound words spoken by his unexpected benefactor. After a considerable time, he asked the guard about obtaining food. He suddenly felt famished, rejuvenated by his decision. He had decided to go along with the Roman conspiracy against Paul. This could be his vehicle to attain revenge against the man who had pretended to be his friend.

He swallowed hard and his stomach tightened at the prospect that Cato might not follow through on assisting him in becoming free and potentially a Roman citizen. The thought of being betrayed again was one he did not want to dwell on.

During the time Cato was offering his advice and assistance to the runaway slave, Aelia and Antonius were discussing a situation that had developed without any warning.

Antonius repeatedly fidgeted during their talk. At times, his nervousness caused his eyes to rapidly blink uncontrollably, and he would rub them with his hands. Aelia soon became annoyed at his twitches. "Antonius, calm yourself!" she cried. "Your anxiety causes you to overlook the reality of the situation and the opportunity we have."

Aelia forced the nervous man to sit and listen carefully. "Cleatus has allowed Onesimus to continue his apprenticeship with Paul. No doubt, Cleatus has some deceptive plan for doing this. It doesn't matter to us, because we will continue to have high quality goods to sell." The shrewd businesswoman ceased speaking so that her words could be absorbed by her emotionally weak business partner.

"I shall have my operatives attempt to learn what Cleatus' motive really is. This will allow us to make plans to capitalize on this state of affairs." Aelia became firm in her voice and her eyes blazed as she emphasized to Antonius, "Do not do anything, under any circumstances, that I do not first approve! Simply continue supplying both prisoners the supplies they need to produce our products. Do not go to Paul or to Onesimus. Have one of your employees deliver the raw supplies and pick up the finished boots."

Aelia suspended her commanding directives to determine if

Antonius was truly listening and understanding her firm order. Satisfied he was, she concluded, "Remember, Antonius, agents of Cleatus will be observing your activities. Anything that causes them concern will invite Cleatus to interfere with our business and potentially cause suffering to you." She then gave her partner the obvious analysis, "Do you not realize that when we first began our association with Paul that agents were monitoring our activities with this man accused of treason? By the gods, have you been blinded to this fact?"

Apparently, he was. Her business partner's eyes widened at this shocking news. He began to sweat at the knowledge he had overlooked Cleatus' strategy and the potential pain Cleatus could inflict on him. Timidly, he admitted to his partner, "I have been oblivious to all this and focused only on the business portion." Antonius straightened his shoulders and asserted in a stronger voice, "I will give Cleatus no cause for alarm; furthermore, I will do only as you direct."

Aelia's eyes softened and her body relaxed. "Good. I must continue with other business, but we shall meet again on my next regular visit. Do not attempt to contact me unless it's an absolute emergency." She turned decisively and left the cobbler's business to look after her other enterprises.

Meanwhile, Epaphras was visiting Paul concerning the events surrounding him and Onesimus. God's provision was that Lucilius, rather than Draba, was at this consultation. Because Lucilius was a convert to Christ, it allowed Epaphras to be more open and direct with Paul.

The trio held their conference in Paul's workshop, and the minister of Christ described to his fellow warrior in Christ all that took place during the trial. Lucilius was engrossed in the conversation about the happenings. He listened attentively and planned to relay his findings to Marcus. But Epaphras looked very concerned, and pleaded, "Paul, based on what you have said, I believe it is necessary for someone to return to Colosse and attempt an intervention with Philemon. We must inform him of Cleatus' ploy and, more importantly, urge him to go to Almighty God and seek the direction He wants for Onesimus."

Paul concurred with his spiritual brother's insight. "It is important to remind Philemon of his responsibility to God first, before the Romans. I know, Epaphras, you are deeply involved with the church here. You should continue your work here. We must spare Timothy to get word quickly to Philemon before the Romans do. Go get Timothy and bring him to me."

Epaphras clasped Paul's hands firmly in his. "We must also pray fervently to Almighty God that He will bless us with His discernment and wisdom in this matter."

After Epaphras left on his mission, Paul took the time to talk to both Lucilius and Marcus about the unfolding events. It was an opportunity for the mentees to learn some important spiritual principles for their own growing relationships with Christ.

They met in the courtyard where the dog handler was posted. Paul positioned himself to avoid blocking Marcus' official observation of activities in the grasslands behind the open wall of the townhouse.

"My brothers, I must address what is occurring with Philemon. It is also important for your walk in faith. You see, once you accept Christ as Lord and Savior, there comes a process of following Him. Your past allegiance to the ways of the world and its culture must be weaned like a grown lamb is weaned of its mother's milk."

Lucilius and Marcius once again were gripped by Paul's teaching. Neither interrupted with questions, but listened intently to their mentor. "Philemon is a Roman citizen and can deal with Onesimus in accordance with Roman law. This you already know. Philemon, the slave master, is also a follower of Christ and has the opportunity, as well as the obligation, to grow in his faith and to let all involved in this situation see Christ first and foremost."

As they moved through the courtyard, Paul briefly peered outside at the beckoning grasses that were waving in the early spring breeze. Then, he continued, "Philemon can obey the harsh laws of Rome and be perfectly within their law. Onesimus would be severely beaten and sold at auction. Rome would take their commission and Philemon would receive the balance to purchase a replacement slave. This is according to Roman law."

The spiritual mentor looked grieved at this possibility, before he proceeded, "But Christ has other ways for us. We are to have our eyes on heaven's ways, not on earthly ways. Philemon has the opportunity to give grace, kindness, and forgiveness to Onesimus, just as Christ has forgiven us, and as He did for Philemon, when Philemon put his trust in Christ. Philemon must be reminded Jesus told us to forgive as we have been forgiven by our heavenly Father. We live by grace, and are not bound to harsh dictates of laws that are for condemnation and punishment. Philemon can forgive Onesimus, and even free him." Paul's audience of two was all ears. It was a radical idea.

"The world would be astounded at this action, and not fully understand why Philemon would choose this path. They will inquire about his reasoning for such an unheard-of action. This is Philemon's opportunity to let others see Christ's love, forgiveness, and grace through his actions and words."

Again Paul held back a moment before continuing, "Philemon has professed to be God's new creation, transformed by Christ through the Holy Spirit. Should he put Roman law ahead of God's way, he displays hypocritical actions. If the world does not see Christ through your words and actions, there is no way for them to know that Christ indeed is the Way, the Truth, and the Life."

Both Marcus and Lucilius were overcome by Paul's teaching. They were mute, their minds wobbling back and forth attempting to absorb their mentor's words which conveyed an entirely different approach than what either had imagined.

Lucilius cleared his throat. In a hesitant voice, he asked, "But, Paul, doesn't Philemon have a duty to abide by Rome's laws since he is a Roman citizen?"

"Absolutely, he does. But, by obeying Christ first, Philemon can demonstrate that Almighty God's higher ways and higher thoughts are more beneficial to man than laws imposed by agents under the influence of the devil. Remember, Christ's ways are far better than man's and are the only true solution to the deception of the devil. Our Lord God defies the world and all its logic."

Marcus expressed his concern, "Many of Rome's laws are intended to protect both the empire as well as its citizens from those whose intent is to destroy the empire. Are they wrong in making and enforcing such laws?"

"Not in their own eyes, because they believe their laws to be correct. But when these laws do not show compassion to those under their domain, and when those laws do not honor and glorify Almighty God but rather contradict His commands, they are wrong and should not be honored."

Lucilius' expression gradually changed from confusion to understanding. "You are telling us, Paul, that we, as followers of Christ, ...we always put Him first and trust He will guide us in what action we should take?"

"Precisely, Lucilius. The unsaved world has only you as an example of who Christ is. Your words and actions can carry much weight in their answering 'yes' to the conviction of the Holy Spirit when they are prompted to accept Christ as Lord and Savior."

Marcus again offered his thoughts, "Paul, are you also saying,... " Marcus was almost afraid to verbalize his thought, "...that as we step forward into uncertainty, we are to live for Christ even to the point of ... death?"

Paul nodded decisively. "Yes, but perhaps not the death you are thinking of. The more we 'die' to our natural ungodly inclinations—our selfish ways—the stronger we become in Christ. To choose to die to that inner, sinful self, is to move forward in Christ. Your obedience to Christ first in all things allows Him to bless you and strengthen your spiritual life. And in the process, you build up your treasures in heaven that Christ will dispense to you on that glorious day you enter His heavenly kingdom and stand before His judgment seat."

Marcus asked with great interest, "What will these treasures be?"

Paul smiled and raised his hand to touch the much taller man's shoulder. "Only Christ Jesus knows, but be assured, they will be perfect in every way."

Marcus persisted, "But what is this judgment seat you speak of?"

Paul's tone was soothing as he answered, "It is when Christ evaluates what you did with your life here on earth through His power and your obedience. Your obedience to His promptings and guidance of the Holy Spirit that allowed Him to carry out his purposes will be rewarded."

Lucilius was thinking more of the immediate quandary. He shifted his weight from one foot to the other and changed the subject, "What decision do you think Philemon will make?"

Paul turned to face his mentee, and in a loving manner confessed, "I don't know. It is his choice. This I will say—the power of the world's influence on us is strong. At times, we need gentle reminders to keep our faith in Christ, totally surrender our will to His, and let Him lead us through the valley of the shadow of death."

Lucilius reacted as if he had an epiphany, "So, that is why I am sending Timothy to have an intervention with Philemon!"

Paul nodded. "We need to strengthen one another at times of temptation and difficult decisions. Making decisions according to God's will is an opportunity to serve Christ, exercise our faith, and further the kingdom of God. It is not always easy, but obedience brings surprising joy, even in the midst of difficulties."

Marcus reacted with a sincere and serious tone, "I shall pray that such will be the case."

Lucilius nodded and suggested they make their petition known to God. In perfect agreement, they joined their hands, looked upwards toward heaven, and prayed together.

Later that day, after their shift change, Marcus and Lucilius began their return to the palace barracks. Marcus purposely stopped before reaching their destination and turned toward his colleague. "Lucilius, Paul gave us weighty instruction to ponder. I must decide if I will truly surrender and follow Christ or not. In some ways, it is not easy. But I know Christ will hold me accountable for my actions, even if men do not. Under certain circumstances, this will not be an easy thing for me to do."

Lucilius agreed. "I foresee other occasions that will require great faith and firm resolve to choose God's way and possibly incur the wrath of men. We must rely on the Holy Spirit to guide us. After all, isn't that part of the reason our Lord God has given us His indwelling Spirit in our hearts?" The pair continued walking silently, each absorbed in their individual thoughts.

The two soldiers did not know it, but at that very moment, Seneca had just received notification that Nero would soon be back in Rome.

## Chapter 26

Timothy embodied a whirlwind of activity following his decisive meeting with his fellow spiritual warrior, Paul. He was able to secure passage on a merchant caravan heading to Ephesus the next day. He would be one of 26 passengers. The caravan would be traveling light and despite the 125 head of camels in the train, it would make good time on the journey.

Prior to his leaving, he went to a commercial pigeon vendor and sent a message ahead to notify one of the church elders that he would be returning to Colosse. Pigeon communication was a huge enterprise that spawned many vendors to engage in the business. For a small fee, anyone could send a message virtually anywhere in Rome's empire. This ability eliminated the costly expense of obtaining, training, and securing a base in the vast hubs of commerce spread throughout the empire.

During the winter months, cages of pigeons were a part of many caravans. Once a pigeon reached its destination, the bird handler would wait until a dozen or more could be sent back to their home base in a locked cage. When the birds arrived safely back at their home base, they were again available to make another trip to the same location. The birds were trained to go only to one location. As such, the vendor needed many pigeons in order to reach the many outlets throughout the empire.

It was not uncommon for Rome to employ pigeon vendors as spies. They could clandestinely read the messages before sending them aloft. Timothy was aware of this possibility, but he did not let it interfere with his message to the Colossian church.

Throughout the 18-day journey back to Colosse, Timothy had

ample opportunity to petition Almighty God for His direction concerning the situation with Philemon. As a willing servant of Christ, Timothy was confident that God would use him in a mighty way.

The camel caravan that Timothy had joined was three days out of Rome where it almost intersected a bigger caravan on its way to Rome. The two carriers of merchandise came within two miles of each other from different trails and with very different missions. The caravan heading east had Timothy, whose mission was to intervene for a godly purpose. The opposite caravan had Nero, Caesar of the Roman Empire whose mission was to use two current situations to stroke his pride and elevate himself— constructing the man-made port of Portus, and settling the issue with the citizen accused of treason, Paul.

Seneca was enjoying leisure time at his villa when a messenger announced Nero had returned to Rome and requested his presence immediately. Nero was not one to be kept waiting, and Seneca knew the purpose of the meeting. He bade Pompeia farewell and instructed his carriage driver to make haste back to Rome. Since the weather was mild, the journey was completed in just fifteen minutes.

The Roman consul was directed to Nero's palatial private living quarters where he was shown to Rome's esteemed emperor naked in his bath. "Seneca, you're in time to join me in a very relaxing warm bath. Come and enjoy the therapeutic water and answer my questions," said Nero in a coaxing voice. Nero had ordered engineers to construct a wood-fired boiler on the top floor of the palace. Its purpose was to heat water from one of the aqueducts that serviced the palace. The heated water made its way down to the second floor where Nero's living quarters were located. The simple piping transferred the heated water to one of the small baths used by the emperor. The addition of mint oil scented the water and Epsom salt provided healing qualities. After his tiresome journey from Athens, Nero reveled in this relief before he resumed his duties governing Rome.

As soon as Seneca had stripped and eased himself into the water, Nero came straight to the point. "Seneca, I will be addressing the Senate, day after tomorrow. I must know how things are progressing with the construction of Portus and also the status of our prisoner accused of treason. These are important items the Senate will demand to know."

Seneca could feel the combined effect of the mint-scented

water and the Epsom salt minerals. He let himself bask in relaxation briefly before giving Nero what he wanted. He took a deep breath and said, "Portus is making good progress. The central lighthouse is finished, as are several of the warehouses that will store grain from Egypt. There has been some issue with the entrance, but nothing major. I suggest, Nero, that tomorrow we tour the site for your personal inspection. During that time I can show you details that will give you better understanding."

Unexpectedly, the pot-bellied ruler reacted by raising his hands out of the warm water and clapping with glee. Droplets of water flew through the air. "Excellent suggestion you have, Consul. I shall also get comments directly from the chief engineer. This will assist me greatly in addressing the senators." Caesar giggled with delight at Seneca's suggestion.

Seneca pretended to be thinking while he simply enjoyed the scented warm water. He felt relieved and briefly closed his eyes, then tackled the topic of the prisoner of Rome. "We have some interesting developments with this accused Jewish citizen Paul that you can greatly benefit from and use to impress the Senate."

Nero raised himself slightly in the bath and cocked one eyebrow in response to the consul's announcement. He was always glad to have ways to impress men of influence and power, especially the Senate. He needed to strengthen others' perceptions of his abilities as supreme ruler over the empire. This was especially needed in light of the criticism he was receiving for his repeated stays in Athens. He rotated a wet hand energetically as a command for Seneca to not delay in giving him this intriguing news.

Seneca responded, "It has been determined—through detailed efforts on the part of myself and Cleatus—that this accused prisoner, Paul, has committed no crime of treason against Rome. His accusers were not Roman citizens, only Jews who based their false accusations on trivial religious grounds." Seneca studied Nero's reaction closely. He had hoped to add drama to this issue, but the impatience on Caesar's face was such that Seneca did not attempt to prolong the explanation. "What is developing with this man is his involvement with a runaway slave from Colosse, named Onesimus. The slave's owner is a man called Philemon who profits well from providing Rome necessary merchandise. He owns hundreds of slaves and is also a Roman citizen."

The combination of the warm water, the salt, and his vocalization was causing his throat to become dry. "Nero, would you grace me in providing some wine? My throat is parched."

Caesar snapped his fingers and a naked servant girl brought forth the beverage. As Seneca soothed his throat, he studied Nero's face again for any reaction. There was none, but the consul knew that was about to change with the addition of more information. "Our prisoner Paul knows this Philemon, and has converted him to this new sect called Christians. We are still determining if it presents any danger to Rome."

Nero suddenly demanded, "Come, Seneca! Get to your point! You are wearying me. Thus far, you have told me nothing of real interest."

Seneca's stress faded. He had Nero exactly where he had hoped the ruler would go. The consul knew he now had control over his superior. "The runaway slave has been working with Paul as a cobbler apprentice. Paul has sent one of his companions, a man named Timothy, back to Colosse to confer with Philemon as to what he wants to do with the slave. We have been monitoring the activities of all these people, plus others in Colosse, to determine if they are in the process of planning a slave revolt."

At that point, Seneca deliberately stopped to let Caesar absorb this new information. He casually took another sip of wine, knowing Nero would speak.

Nero sloshed the warm water around his neck and shoulders as he pondered Seneca's information. "This could be quite serious Seneca, quite serious. What are you doing to determine the status of these people?"

Seneca's plan of manipulating Nero was working well. "Cleatus and I are in complete agreement that the slave Onesimus shall continue to work as a cobbler alongside Paul. We will monitor their activities, as well as all who visit these two men. In addition, Cleatus has assigned one of his most seasoned operatives to interrogate the slave once a week. He is adept at applying pressure to this young rebel to get him to turn against Paul should the two be plotting a revolt together."

The consul paused for Nero's slower thinking to mentally track his scheme. Then he continued, "We are awaiting word from Philemon to learn if he wants the slave back, or will sell him at auction, or have him executed. As you know, Caesar, we cannot do anything until this Philemon sends us his signed document stating his preference. With sea travel interrupted due to winter's storms, our only available way of getting this document is via one of the camel merchant caravans. You know from your personal experience the time involved with the caravans."

Nero looked down and scratched his forehead. Water from his fingers mingled with the sweat on his forehead and dripped off his nose. He paused, deep in thought, then slowly lifted his head to look directly at Seneca. "It has been just over one hundred years since the last slave rebellion, led by the gladiator Spartacus. Despite destroying this revolt, Rome remains very wary of potential slave uprisings, especially with nearly 200,000 slaves in Rome at this time and one million slaves throughout the empire."

He straightened himself up as best he could in the warm water, and strongly warned Seneca, "We cannot allow another slave revolt to take place!" Nero relaxed and sank back down into the soothing water. In a calmer voice, he instructed his consul, "Do what is necessary to learn about these two prisoners. Neither man shall be allowed to go free until we are certain there will be no revolt. Be thorough."

Seneca nodded his head in understanding, and broached the matter of Paul, "Roman law requires you to hear the appeal of this citizen Paul within a timely manner. How do you propose avoiding this?"

A deep furrow formed in Nero's brow. He scowled and snapped, "The element of intent allows me to keep this citizen detained until we are certain he is not planning an uprising against Rome! The fact of his being a follower of this illegal sect called Christians gives me this authority without any time limit." He raised his voice for his definitive royal proclamation, "This I choose to do."

Nero narrowed his eyes and stroked his perspiring red face. "Seneca, you and Cleatus must remain vigilant, persistent, and use whatever means necessary to unravel the intent of this Jewish Roman citizen. Find out where his main loyalty lies. I require you to keep me notified on a timely basis as this case develops."

Seneca was barely able to resist revealing the satisfied smile he felt inside. He declared, "You have my pledge to do this, Caesar. I shall give your bath back to you now and meet you tomorrow for our inspection of Portus." The personal consul to Caesar eased out of the bath, dried himself off, and exited the palace, fighting back an impulse to laugh.

As his carriage made its way through the streets of Rome back to his villa, Seneca was jubilant over how his meeting had gone with Caesar. He was quite pleased with his ability to weave a scenario plausible enough to get Nero to delay his hearing of Paul's appeal. He was determined to use this opportunity to reestablish himself with Nero, who was distancing himself from him, his former mentor. As Caesar's main consul, Seneca did not want the embarrassment of being replaced, especially in the sight of his fellow senate colleagues.

Seneca relaxed in the carriage seat, enjoying the events of the day and planning the next step in his plot. He would now direct his attention to his fellow conspirators, Cleatus and Cato. They would provide the means for his strategy to unfold into reality.

The next day, Cato went to Seneca's villa for a meeting that Seneca had described as one of great importance. Cato tried not to speculate on its purpose, but was glad to confer with Seneca and notify him of a decision he had made concerning Onesimus.

The two met in Seneca's office, disappointed the rainy weather prevented them from enjoying the spring changes in the villa courtyard. Cato could tell that Seneca had been greatly impacted by something, and suggested he begin the conversation, which he did. "I've met with Cleatus about the situation with the runaway slave. It was my suggestion to have you periodically question the slave and obtain any information of merit to give to Nero pertaining to the prisoner Paul."

Seneca watched for Cato's reaction but, to his relief, his colleague was clearly just waiting for more information. Seneca continued, "Cleatus vetoed my suggestion, stating he wanted someone more forceful to handle this slave. He has chosen an operative he has utilized many times in the past. He is brutal and cruel in his efforts, but is known to be quite thorough and effective."

At the sound of this description, Cato cringed, imagining Onesimus being subjected to that style of interrogation. He remained silent and let Seneca complete his message. "As it stands now, you shall continue to question Paul and relay your findings only to me. Cleatus and I shall meet and compare his findings from Onesimus to what you give me concerning Paul. There should be no overlap between you and Cleatus' henchman. If there is, let me know immediately."

Cato quietly sighed with relief and realized he did not have to inform Seneca he could not interrogate Onesimus because of his unsteady emotions over his own slavery. Instead, Cato said, "I believe this separation is the best way to proceed. In this way, neither Onesimus nor Paul will suspect I'm playing one against the other, and I shall be free to gain more insight into Paul's intent."

Seneca tilted his head and his eyes showed surprise at Cato's words. "This is excellent, my friend. It could very well turn out that Cleatus' henchman will cause enough turmoil in Onesimus that he will confide in Paul and thereby allow you to gain valuable information for us. When do you propose to visit Paul?"

"Within the next day or so. I want to give sufficient time for Onesimus and Paul to continue their work together. I do not want to rush the process, for fear they will realize our motives and cease any involvement in their undercover activities."

Seneca immediately saw the ramifications. "I agree with you entirely, Cato," he said. "I do not wish to remain in my townhouse in Rome while all this unfolds. Since it is not that far between our residences, keep me informed by joining me here. We can have lunch or dinner together and make this unpleasantness more pleasant. Of course, if an emergency arises, send a messenger and I shall return to Rome without delay and meet with you."

The plan was in place.

The same day Timothy had embarked on his epic mission, Onesimus had begun implementing his plan to snatch his freedom out of his personal hell of slavery. His conversation with Cato had led him to devise a careful plan of action. Satisfied his strategy would not be exposed by Paul or any of his followers, Onesimus had appeared for his usual session with his target Paul, under an assumed pretense of light-heartedness. He did not believe his gambit would take long to achieve the desired result of satisfying Cleatus' and Seneca's concerns.

Onesimus was pleased with himself at the end of his first day of work with Paul. He believed his casual attitude around Paul had adequately hidden his true intentions. With his evening meal in one hand, he opened the door to his apartment and entered his residence.

He dropped his bagged supper when he noticed a seated figure in the only chair in the apartment. Regaining control of himself, he croaked, "Who are you, and why are you in my residence?"

The seated figure looked up at Onesimus, but took plenty of time in answering the runaway slave's question. The unknown intruder watched his quarry and knew he was unsettled. This reaction was just what the seated figure wanted. "I am Jarvis. Sent by Cleatus to instruct you on how to proceed in your duty to Rome to acquire needed information about this man Paul who you are working with."

Onesimus felt his knees trembling as he heard the details of his circumstances spoken by a stranger. The unknown figure seemed not to notice, or didn't care, because he continued speaking, "I shall be meeting here with you once a week for your verbal report concerning Paul's interaction with you." The seated figure stood up and motioned for Onesimus to sit down in the chair he vacated. "Please sit down. Go about eating your supper, if you like, before it gets cold."

At first Onesimus hesitated, but he felt helpless. He relented and did as the man instructed. He cautiously removed his supper from the leather bag and slowly began to feed his diminished appetite. Jarvis smiled faintly and continued his speech, "You are to tell no one of our weekly debriefing. Absolutely no one—including the guards and, obviously, Paul."

As the man relayed his instructions, Onesimus was frightened by his ominous tone. His fear elevated when the man ordered, "You should have information for me every week. If you do not or if what you give me is declared weak or insignificant, I shall have no recourse but to deal harshly with you. If this happens a third time, you will be taken to the mines as your punishment."

The thought of spending the rest of his life in the dreaded mines made Onesimus almost choke on the small morsel of food in his mouth. He stopped chewing and stared wide-eyed at his visitor. Jarvis recognized his words had instilled fear in the runaway slave and did not elaborate further. His point had been sufficiently made. Instead, he smiled an ugly smile at his prey and concluded, "I leave now, but expect me one week from today. This is the only place we shall meet." When he had finished, he casually exited the apartment and disappeared down the stairs.

Onesimus looked at what remained of his supper and knew he could not finish it. He opened the door to the apartment and offered the remaining food to the guard who declined, stating he was not allowed to eat or drink anything from the slave. The runaway slave dropped the food in the apartment's garbage container and lay down on his cot.

His thoughts were centered on Jarvis' threatening instructions and he wavered between the instruction and his own proposed strategy. After hours of assailing thoughts, exhaustion won the battle and Onesimus fell asleep.

## Chapter 27

Cato waited two days before informing his client there had been a delay in his appeal before Caesar. His emotional turmoil over the plight of the runaway slave Onesimus was one reason for his procrastination. The second reason was his desire to better prepare for Paul's reaction to the postponement.

As his carriage arrived at Paul's rented townhouse, Cato felt buoyed somewhat for his task by the beautiful spring weather. The trees were budding and new shoots were turning bright green. The birds had returned, bringing with them their cheerful songs. Cato strode briskly to the door and entered the townhouse with an air of renewed tenacity.

Paul noted his attorney's determination, but dared not guess the meaning behind Cato's deportment. The apostle did not have to wait long before it was revealed. True to his earlier demand for privacy, Cato sat alone with Paul in his office and put it to him directly, "Paul, Seneca has informed me that your appeal before Caesar has been postponed indefinitely. I do not know the reason for this and can only speculate." The attorney scratched behind his ear, and inquired, "Perhaps you may have knowledge of the reason for this suspension?"

At first, Paul was taken aback by Cato's announcement, but showed no signs of frustration or contempt towards Nero for the rearrangement. Christ's apostle only looked perplexed as he answered his attorney's question, "I cannot provide you any insight concerning this suspension. None of my visitors has indicated any such possibility to me. Had this been so, I would have immediately notified you so that you might intervene in the matter."

Cato proceeded with his next question, "Could there be some development by your followers in any of the cities where you have established your churches that would give cause for alarm to Nero?"

Again Paul answered honestly, shaking his head, "I know of nothing that would cause such a reaction by Caesar."

"I will consult with Seneca and others involved with this matter to determine why Nero has taken this action. In the meantime, continue receiving your visitors and working with the runaway slave." Cato fiddled uncharacteristically, brushing lint from his clothing, as he prepared his next question, "By the way, how is he progressing in his work with you?"

"Onesimus is a very talented cobbler. He learns quickly and makes adjustments that fit his ability. I can only give him a few techniques I have learned. Sometimes his anger manifests itself in his work."

Cato immediately seized this opportunity to get a glimpse into Paul's relationship with Onesimus. Perhaps it would reveal a tie-in to a secret motive of Paul for revolt against Rome, in spite of his doubts. "Has Onesimus mentioned to you why he has such anger? It's understandable for slaves to harbor anger against their masters. Could this be the source of our slave's attitude?"

Paul reflected a moment, then replied, "I'm sure Onesimus has some anger towards Philemon. As you say, this is common at times between slaves and their masters. However, I sense that Onesimus has other anger for reasons that he has not revealed to me."

To this, Cato gave a terse response, "I believe you should inquire with the slave about this. It could be associated with the delay of your hearing." Paul assured his attorney he would monitor the situation with Onesimus and inform Cato of any developments. Seneca's co-conspirator gave Paul a formal nod of his head and told him he would confer with him later, after he had time to probe elsewhere concerning the hearing delay.

While the principals assigned to Paul's case were secretly maneuvering in their quest to determine the apostle's ulterior motives for recruiting followers, Timothy safely arrived in Colosse and prepared to meet with Philemon. The onset of spring had reopened the sea routes and the ambassador for Paul had booked passage on one of the faster ships.

Timothy rested one day from his lengthy trip before he

scheduled an appointment with Philemon. He had only a brief amount of time to accomplish his mission. The ship he had secured passage on would be leaving immediately after it was loaded with goods bound for Rome.

While he waited for the rendezvous with Philemon, Timothy used his time to seek out church members, asking many questions and gathering valuable information that would factor into his summit with the slave master.

Philemon was suspicious of Timothy and at first did not want to converse with the much younger man. The Colossian slave master knew Timothy was highly regarded by Paul and surmised the younger mentee of Paul had been sent specifically to confront him about his runaway slave, Onesimus. Philemon felt the muscles in his neck and shoulders tighten as he thought about this confrontation. He had mixed feelings about the whole event.

Timothy was cordial with Philemon, but wasted no time in addressing the reason for the conference with the slave owner. "It is vitally important I talk with you about Onesimus. Have you sent back the document to Cleatus, indicating your decision concerning the fate of this young slave?"

Philemon stiffly answered, "I have not, but I am about to sign it with my instructions regarding the runaway." The Colossian businessman arched himself up in a defiant stance toward Timothy. "I know Paul sent you here, but I must inform you the slave is my property and I can do with him as I wish according to Roman law."

Philemon pointed his finger at Timothy and sternly declared, "Remember, I am a Roman citizen and this allows me to take whatever action I see fit to take. After all, I own several hundred other slaves and whatever my actions are will send them a clear message. If I'm lenient with Onesimus, assuredly the other slaves will view this as weakness and take advantage of me."

Timothy was puzzled by Philemon's anger. He had heard Paul speak of him in tender terms as a godly and beloved brother in Christ. The young disciple of Christ silently asked for God's blessing for discerning spirits to identify the unrighteous fears that sought control of the Gentile convert. In a calm voice, the servant of God addressed the spiritually conflicted older man. "You indeed are right on all accounts, Philemon. Paul is quite aware of your rights as a Roman citizen. After all, he, too, is a born Roman citizen with full rights and privileges, some of which you do not possess because you have a freedman citizenship." Timothy's mild reminder got Philemon's attention. He had overlooked Paul's Roman citizenship that he had by his birthright.

Timothy continued, "At this point, Paul wants you to consider the spiritual aspect of your situation. Are you sure this is how Christ Jesus wants you to represent Him in this matter?" The young disciple stopped respectfully and let Philemon grasp what was just said to him.

Philemon did not respond, so with a silent prayer for wisdom and guidance, Timothy carefully continued to speak truth, "A hasty decision that is not based on God's plan will not further the kingdom of God, nor give you peace in your mind or in your spirit."

The Colossian was very agitated by Timothy's words to the point he began to fidget, but he said nothing further. Timothy took advantage of the interlude. "In addition to Paul, other brothers—Epaphras, Ephroditus, Tychicus, and Aristarchus—all implore you to meditate on this from the spiritual standpoint, which supersedes any earthly viewpoint. This issue is about serving Christ and letting the world see Christ through your godly attitude and actions."

Philemon noticeably bristled at Timothy's exhortation. His already heightened emotions caused him to flush. He argued, "I recognize these men as disciples of Jesus and church leaders. They agreed to let me hold gatherings in my home; but I don't see how this concerns the church! Will the church and these men reimburse me for my loss? Will these church leaders come to my aid when my other slaves rebel? Who will intervene on my behalf when the Roman authorities castigate me and potentially fine me for allowing my slaves to rebel? You know how Rome feels about slaves and rebellion." When Philemon finished his argument, he believed he had adequately outwitted his young opponent. Now, with a calmer demeanor, he waited for Timothy's reaction.

The younger disciple looked sorrowful. "Philemon, you make a grave... very grave... mistake about this entire situation. It's not about Paul or the other church elders telling you what to do. It's not about your position with the Roman authorities, and it certainly isn't about your getting the best of me in a debate."

Timothy looked a long time at Philemon, deeply desiring to make him understand the importance of what he was about to say. "It's about your relationship with Christ Jesus and being His servant. It's about standing firm on the foundation Christ has given you, extending God's grace to a fellow believer, and striking a blow against the devil's deception."

The spiritual ambassador then lobbed the most preeminent truth to the slave master, "You have accepted Christ Jesus into your heart and all that He stands for. Your decision in this case will reveal your heart and it will reflect who Christ is to you. In essence, Philemon, this situation is as much about you as it is about Onesimus."

Philemon stepped backward as if he had just taken several hard body blows. His unblinking eyes seemed frozen until his gaze dropped to scan the floor. It was the conviction of the Holy Spirit, and the Colossian had no place to hide. After a deafening silence, the persuaded slave owner summoned enough strength to say, "You came from Paul. What does Paul recommend I do?"

Without hesitation, Timothy gave the instruction, "That you go to Christ in prayerful meditation and seek His face. Surrender your will to His, that He may guide you in this matter. Next, inform Cleatus, who is in charge of this matter, that you want more time to consider your options. You authorize Cleatus to continue detaining Onesimus until such time that you reach your final decision."

Philemon thoughtfully considered this option. If he indeed waited to make a decision, it might be possible for him to gain some advantage from Rome regarding his use of slavery. It was also possible that factors unknown to him were at play in Rome, and Paul could be his liaison and make a decision—thereby making it possible for Philemon to avoid going to Rome and disrupting his business in the process. Aside from his personal interests, though, he was really considering Timothy's admonishment about seeking God's face first. He didn't want his pride, arrogance, and control to prevent him from the right decision.

He rubbed his clean-shaven chin several times before he replied, "I will do as Paul says. But, mind you, the ultimate decision remains mine alone."

"That is all Paul and the church elders desire of you." The confrontation was over. Timothy left to think things over, and Philemon went back to taking care of his business concerns. Soon afterward, the Colossian slave master signed the document stating that he would wait on his final decision and authorizing Paul to be his liaison in the matter. Relieved the matter was settled, at least for the time being, Philemon put the issue out of his mind.

Timothy went to a private spot within the city of Colosse and spent time in prayer, thanking Almighty God for the opportunity presented to him, and for God's protection over him and His strength to confront Philemon.

The next day, the young ambassador boarded the ship that would take him back to Rome and to Paul. The winds would be favorable and despite the vessel's heavy load, Timothy calculated he would be able to relay the events of his intervention to Paul within five days.

Back in Rome, Paul continued to witness to the runaway slave, but was dubious of Onesimus' actions. When slaves decided to run away from their masters, often the reason was because of how they were treated. Christ's apostle previously had spent nearly three years living in Ephesus and was familiar with Colosse and the surrounding area, as they were geographically close to each other. He knew the issues involving slavery.

During those missionary journeys, a large number of Gentiles had come to accept Christ's salvation, including many businessmen who also were slave owners. Paul and the newly established church elders had worked diligently to get these slave masters to treat their slaves more humanely, and to even consider freeing their slaves after seven years, similar to the religious law of the Jews. This was, however, routinely rejected by many.

Paul had instructed the church elders to diligently teach how everyone should first and foremost be a bondservant to Christ Jesus rather than to man. The apostle of Christ did not like cultural worldly slavery, but he taught using Jesus's words concerning slavery, thereby letting the Holy Spirit guide and direct the slave owners' actions. It was a matter of choice that had to come from the heart and not a mere observance of law. In Philemon's case, the converted Gentile had continued in his earthly roots and retained his slaves.

This was troubling to Paul and the church elders because it became an opportunity for the Gnostics to espouse their legalism in an attempt to divide the church, and minimize Christ's word to them.

Each day that he worked with Onesimus, Paul attempted to make conversation with the young runaway to learn more about his situation with Philemon. While the slave had previously seemed congenial and candid after his trial before Cleatus, now Onesimus appeared to be distant and conniving.

The answer to Paul's concern about Onesimus came one day through Marcus and Lucilius. The pair was on the afternoon shift, and when Onesimus had finished his day and was gone, the two guards approached Paul.

Lucilius initiated the conversation, "Paul, Marcus and I have heavy hearts and must inform you about this runaway slave." The new mentee of Paul attempted to gauge his mentor's receptivity to the issue.

"Go ahead, Lucilius, tell me what is on your minds. You have nothing to fear."

The two guards looked at each other for reassurance and Lucilius spilled out, "Onesimus has reached an agreement with Cleatus to probe you to determine if you have operatives in the Roman colonies where you've established churches. They want to determine if you intend on igniting a rebellion that would include the many slaves that inhabit these colonies."

Marcus followed his fellow guard, revealing, "We have learned that should Onesimus obtain such information about your intent, he will be set free and be granted Roman freedman citizen status."

Lucilius jumped back in, "Onesimus answers to the orders of a man named Jarvis, who is one of Cleatus' close agents. It is Jarvis who applied pressure to Onesimus and instructed him not to tarry in his efforts, otherwise he will be scourged."

Marcus expanded with more details. "Should Onesimus not obtain the information Cleatus desires, the slave will be either sold at auction or returned to Philemon. Cleatus expects a document from Philemon to come by way of merchant caravan that reveals what Philemon desires to happen to his slave."

Paul could see his mentees' concerns written plainly on their anxious faces. When they had completed their explanation, he raised his hand gently, and expressed his appreciation, "Thank you, my brothers, for informing me of this deception. I have long suspected something between Onesimus and myself was not right. I shall take what you have told me to our Lord Jesus Christ in prayer and wait for His guidance through the Holy Spirit." Paul looked at both his mentees and wanted to know, "How did you come about this insightful information?"

"One of our fellow guards who is assigned to watch Onesimus overheard his conversation with Jarvis. He provided it to us. There are times when requests for information are made, especially when we guards are involved in a complex case such as yours, Paul."

Lucilius and Marcus had questions about handling the duplicity, so Paul engaged them in a spiritual teaching that lasted several hours. Topics of honesty, deception, fears, trust, faith, and prayer were discussed animatedly. When they had heard more than they could absorb, the guards joined Paul for a late dinner together. Afterwards, Paul retired to his bedroom to pray and meditate on what had been revealed to him.

The winds propelling the heavy-laden ships weren't quite as favorable as Timothy had hoped for. Instead of five days, it took seven for the vessel to travel to Ostia, the port of Rome. Finally back in the city, the tired spiritual envoy realized how fatigued he was. He elected to replenish his strength before giving Paul the news concerning his mission to Colosse. He fell gratefully into bed, still imagining the rocking of the ship as he fell asleep.

Early the next morning, feeling well-refreshed, Timothy took nourishment before he went to meet with Paul. The young evangelist had God's peace within him and did not let any nagging worry or anxiety press him to rush into the day's agenda.

Inside Paul's townhouse, Timothy was warmly received by his mentor who invited him into the office where they could talk. Timothy was accustomed to having guards attend these conferences with Paul, but he was feeling unsettled about the guard on this particular day. It was Draba, who listened very attentively to the discourse between Paul and his emissary. However, Paul seemed undisturbed by the guard's presence and talked openly.

When the session was over and Timothy was gone, Draba did not need to confront Paul for clarification of details. Paul took that initative. "Draba, I know you will be reporting my conversation with Timothy to Flavius. It is important for me to explain some things to you, so that your report will be accurate and not cause you any trouble or harm with your superiors." Draba was surprised at Paul's words, and grateful. Should he not have adequate answers for Flavius or Cleatus, he could get into serious trouble. The guard had a growing respect for this Roman citizen accused of treason.

Paul patiently and thoroughly explained the tie-in between himself and Philemon and why he sent Timothy to confer with the slave master. Draba was astounded at Paul's concern for a lowly slave. He was also impressed that Paul's suggestion to Philemon was actually in accordance with Roman law.

The Praetorian Guard member thanked Paul for his explanation, and as soon as his shift was over, he rushed to Flavius' office to give his report while it was fresh in his mind.

A big surprise took place the next morning when Onesimus arrived at the makeshift workshop for the day's cobbler projects. The runaway slave was cheerful and full of energy as he anticipated how he would engage Paul during their workday together. The cobbler mentor was already sitting at his workbench, finishing up a pair of boots for one of the Praetorian Guard members. It was a challenging project for a soldier who had foot damage from an earlier battle. Paul had the soldier come to his workshop to make a customized template for the boots.

Onesimus was glad Paul had taken the time to instruct him on the techniques required to make custom footwear. As the runaway slave peered down at the nearly finished boots, he was impressed with the quality of workmanship. He knew the soldier would be very appreciative of Paul's skills.

Paul put down his tools, then stood up and said to his cobbler mentee, "Onesimus, I would like to converse with you, but let's have some breakfast first, in the courtyard." The runaway was indeed hungry and agreed to Paul's proposal. Draba, too, felt famished and welcomed the opportunity to satisfy his own hunger.

After the meal was completed, they remained seated at the table and Paul initiated the prime conversation. Paul addressed Onesimus, "I have news that pertains to you and your situation here in Rome," he began. Both Onesimus and Draba were surprised there was news. They could see that Paul was relaxed as he spoke, so they also relaxed in anticipation of whatever the prisoner was about to reveal.

"I sent my emissary Timothy to Colosse to personally speak with Philemon on your behalf concerning the issue of your being his runaway slave." When Paul finished telling the entire scenario and its results, both Draba and Onesimus were stunned. They had not suspected anything quite like this from Paul's opening statement. Draba was able to compose himself and became very alert, knowing this could be vital information for Flavius. The guard sneaked a quick glance at the slave. He was sitting transfixed, almost in shock, at Paul's disclosure.

"I gave Timothy instructions that before Philemon signs any document affecting your life and future, he should first pray and meditate on his words and make sure he does not act out of selfishness, pride, or control. Obviously, his decision will decide your fate. I implored him to be fair concerning you, Onesimus. I realize there is much pressure on him but, still, he must resolve to do the right thing."

Draba turned from looking at Paul to ascertain Onesimus' reaction to this revelation. There was complete silence at the table. The only sounds were those of the small birds chirping their early morning praise songs in the courtyard bushes. Onesimus sat as if he were one of the marble statues furnishing the townhouse. He was completely shocked and speechless.

Paul took note of Onesimus' condition, but continued, "Timothy has returned by merchant ship and informed me he indeed spoke with Philemon who agreed to do as I requested. I believe his answer will arrive soon by courier from Colosse. I wanted you to know this, in preparation for what Cleatus will do once he receives Philemon's signed document of instruction."

Draba made a mental note of Paul's statement concerning the signed document and thought perhaps it, too, had arrived. Inwardly, the guard was excited at this development. He had valuable information to relay to his superior and, at the same time, insight into these two prisoners.

Finally, Onesimus recovered sufficiently to speak. Draba noticed color had returned to the slave's face since Paul's first announcement. The slave's eyes blinked and scanned the room as he searched for words to convey his thoughts and emotions. Draba prepared himself for any physical attack Onesimus might impulsively launch at Paul. The guard would be very quick in unleashing his short sword to nullify a lunge from the slave.

Onesimus swallowed hard and faced Paul. "Why have you done this for me? Are you doing this to also benefit your own appeal before Caesar?"

Paul was unruffled at Onesimus' question. He sat comfortably in his chair with his hands folded on his lap, looking as peaceful as if he were resting by a burbling stream. His eyes glistened and he smiled with understanding. "When you ran away, I believe you had cause for your actions that reflected your inner turmoil. It doesn't matter how impulsive you were in running away. What matters is to settle this dispute with fairness and in a way that pleases God."

Draba studied Paul very carefully to detect if the prisoner was merely attempting to placate the young slave. The guard decided Paul was being quite sincere and truthful in his statement, so he honed in on Paul's answer to the slave's second question. Evenly, Paul answered, "My intention is not to benefit myself. My appeal before Caesar will rest on other significant evidence that proves my innocence of the treason accusation. Helping you would not sway Caesar to declare me innocent."

Onesimus let himself relax somewhat, but he remained skeptical. "How do I know what you say is true and not merely a ploy of some sort to harm me?"

Paul was quick to answer him in a kind voice, "Come now, Onesimus, why should I want to harm you? You have done nothing against me. There would be nothing for me to gain by harming you in any way."

Silence once again shrouded the courtyard. It seemed that even the songbirds momentarily stopped their melodies in anticipation of Onesimus' next move. The runaway slave dropped his head. Draba correctly judged that Onesimus' questions had come from a fearful reaction, not through sound mental processing.

Both Draba and Paul watched the emotionally conflicted slave, patiently waiting for him to express the thoughts swirling in his head. Onesimus lifted his head, exposing a face that displayed only a numb expression. He softly stammered, "I ...I don't know what else to say. This is so confusing to me."

Paul stood up and went over to Onesimus. He placed his hand on the befuddled slave's shoulder and said, "I see you need time to consider what I've said to you. Remain here in the courtyard, collect your thoughts, and meditate on your next actions. Should you have more questions for me, I will be in the workshop. Take your time, Onesimus, in thinking this through, so you don't end up harming yourself further."

Draba agreed with Paul's advice to the slave and, knowing he would not be reprimanded for it, could not help but add his confirmation of its wisdom. "Slave, I agree with what this man has spoken. You would do well to heed his counsel."

Onesimus looked up at Draba, then at Paul, and lowered his head. He could not speak, only nodded his head in resignation. He could barely move. He slumped, deep in thought. He was vaguely aware that the birds had resumed their cheerful singing, but he had no song emanating from his confused, troubled heart.

## Chapter 28

Onesimus lingered in the courtyard quite some time until he was informed by Draba that the workday was over and he must return to his apartment with the assigned guard. Slowly and with great effort, the slave hoisted himself up and followed Draba to the townhouse atrium where both Paul and the assigned guard waited for him.

Paul gave the slave a warm smile and his eyes expressed compassion and love that comforted Onesimus in his confusion. The guard stood firm, ready to escort the slave the short distance to the apartment. Onesimus remained silent, but he was anxious to hear Paul's parting words.

"Do not be discouraged, Onesimus," Paul said to him. "Your thoughts will clear up concerning this matter. In my heart, I believe that Philemon will take the right course of action in his decision. Be not fearful—nor let fear lead you to react with anger. Instead of worrying, speak your needs to our heavenly Father, and let His peace take charge of your thoughts and feelings."

The crestfallen slave had no answer to the words just spoken to him. He merely began walking toward the front door with the assigned guard beside him.

Paul and Draba watched the slave depart the townhouse. Then Draba turned to Paul and said, "I must go make my daily report to Flavius. Of course, your conversation with Onesimus will be included; but rest assured, Citizen, my report will be accurate and not reflect any personal opinion I have concerning the slave or you."

Draba realized there was more he wanted to convey to the

prisoner, "I appreciate your enlightening me about your association with Philemon and the church elders in Colosse. This greatly helps my understanding and my report."

Christ's apostle flashed a genuine smile at the guard. "Draba, I have every confidence that you will report fairly and accurately what you have witnessed this day here. You are a man of honor and loyalty to Rome and I respect this."

The Praetorian Guard member and battle-hardened soldier felt slightly unnerved by Paul's unexpected commendation. He bowed to Paul, picked up his shield of wood and leather, and left to fulfill his duty.

Seneca was perplexed when a message arrived, compelling him to go to Cleatus' office in Caesar's palace. He knew it was time for their monthly meeting, but this normally took place in far more pleasant surroundings at Seneca's townhouse or villa. It was an oddity, and Seneca perceived something very unusual had taken place or was about to happen. He donned his cloak and instructed his driver to hurry to Caesar's palace.

Upon his swift arrival, the consul to Caesar stood apprehensively outside Cleatus' office. There were no signs of turmoil from any of the personnel designated as part of Cleatus' staff. Seneca construed whatever the emergency was it would be secretive, known only to Cleatus and himself. He gathered his composure, and entered the top Roman general's office.

Cleatus was seated behind his desk, poring over a document, when his secretary announced Seneca's presence in the doorway. The general laid his hands on the document and acknowledged the senator's presence, "Please be seated, Seneca. I have an interesting document that requires our immediate attention."

Seneca hastily sat down. His eyes were fixed on Cleatus who tapped his fingers on the document. "This is a daily report by one of the guards named Draba, who is assigned to our prisoner Paul. It states that Paul sent an envoy to Colosse to sway our runaway slave's owner, Philemon, in his decision about the fate of his slave."

The announcement caused Seneca to lean forward in his chair with astonishment. He was immediately curious, and impatiently urged Cleatus to tell him about this new development. Fortunately, Cleatus was just as eager to supply the details as Seneca was to hear them, and he quickly began to fill them in. "It appears this Timothy strongly suggested to Philemon that he should think through his decision concerning the fate of his runaway slave. Draba tells us that Philemon would be sending the signed document required of him to identify the fate of his runaway, like all slaveowners must do. Either Philemon will request his slave's return, or authorize the slave to be sold at auction." As Cleatus spoke, Seneca eased back into his chair and cupped his hands together, intently listening to the general.

At the conclusion of Cleatus' announcement, the Roman consul asked, "What are your thoughts or concerns that Paul may influence Philemon to do something that is contrary to Roman law with runaway slaves?"

Cleatus pursed his lips in thought before he spoke, "Paul and the sect he leads are unknown to us because it is new. At this point, it's quite possible Paul could be preparing for an uprising against Rome. If this is the case, there are numerous slaves throughout the empire that would join his cause. The fact Paul has established outlets in many of our prime commerce hubs makes this very suspicious and problematic."

Seneca then expressed his own thought, "This is most interesting. The vast number of slaves who potentially would join Paul could cause a rebellion far beyond that of Spartacus." Cleatus momentarily closed his eyes at this horrific thought. Spartacus had recruited over one hundred twenty thousand slaves to his cause and had come very close to overthrowing the Roman government.

The general began to nervously clasp and unclasp his hands as he spoke, "There are many slaves with military experience and training who could instruct such a following and this would be a major problem for us." Seneca intuitively sensed the magnitude of his co-conspirator's fear. The Roman consul knew that Cleatus would employ any means necessary to thwart such an uprising.

Seneca asked the general, "Do you believe Onesimus is capable of being a leader of any uprising?"

Cleatus quickly shook his head. "Not at all. His motivation is centered on his own life and wanting to escape Philemon. At best, he would be a follower to whoever is in charge of a rebellion. He has no leadership experience or skills to be a threat to us."

This answer made Seneca wonder, "Then, how do you see Onesimus fitting into this situation?"

Cleatus was quick to reply, "Not as a leader, but perhaps a purveyor of information. Obviously, Jarvis will be in close contact with the slave. He knows when and how much pressure to apply to this runaway slave to reveal any secret plans he may have knowledge of but is keeping to himself. It may include Paul or it may not. Time will tell."

Seneca offered another insight, "We don't want Jarvis to instill such fear into Onesimus that he panics. Should this occur, we would not learn of any complicity between the slave and Paul."

"I concur with your assessment, Seneca," said Cleatus. "At the present time, we must wait until Philemon notifies us of his decision regarding his slave. Once this is made known to us, we can adjust accordingly." Then the supreme military commander decisively lowered his fist on his desk to emphasize, "Rome must be protected against a slave rebellion, and I will not allow such a thing to happen!"

Seneca heard the stern resolve in Cleatus' voice. The Roman consul was alarmed the general might zealously invoke action that would supersede his own plans. Seneca desperately wanted to use Paul, and now Onesimus, to his advantage with Nero as well as with the Senate. He felt compelled by his growing fear over Nero's changing attitude toward him. Seneca did not want Cleatus or the military to usurp any glory due him from this new involvement between Paul and the runaway slave.

When Onesimus was escorted back to his apartment by the assigned guard, he was very somber. He informed the guard he would not be taking any supper. Once he was alone, he began thinking about his earlier encounter with Paul. After some time, the runaway slave fought to dismiss Paul's words, but he could not. They haunted him. The slave had never experienced anyone who took a genuine interest in him and his wellbeing. Paul's kindness, encouragement, and caring ways were completely foreign to him. Onesimus did not know it was possible to be valued and cared for by another human being.

The melancholy young slave also thought of how he had become angry towards Paul, not realizing that Paul was taking the necessary steps to help remedy his situation. Onesimus also remembered how his anger had led to him agree to solicit incriminating information that would damage Paul and possibly lead to his demise.

Onesimus' mind became a battlefield of conflicting thoughts and emotions. After several hours of inner chaos, the slave felt as though his mind was ready to explode. He felt flushed and hot, and he could hardly catch his breath. He could not stop pacing frantically around the small apartment.

Recurrent thoughts flooded his mind, despite attempts to cast them aside. Each thought renewed a severe emotional reaction with sickening physical effects. His stomach churned, his muscles cramped, and soon he had an intense headache from the relentless mental assault.

Finally in desperation, the besieged lost soul did what he had never envisioned doing—he audibly cried out to the one he least expected would help—such was the force of his total turmoil. Unsure whether he even would be heard, he implored Christ Jesus to give him relief, "Jesus, I've heard about you from Paul and others, but scoffed at the thought you were real. I went to the gods I learned about, but they have never answered my pleas, nor have they given me any solace in any of my troubles. I don't know if you are unlike these other gods, but if you are real, I cry out to you to help me!"

When he finished soliciting the Almighty God of the heavens, his exhausted body collapsed onto his bed. He did not move, except to curl up in a fetal position, his eyes tightly closed, listening to his own gasps and heavy, laborious breathing. Soon, he fell into a troubled sleep.

At some point during his deep slumber, he became mentally aroused, seeing things in a vivid dream which, oddly, at the same time seemed very real. He was above himself, looking down at the pathetic form he had become. He was watching everything that was happening to him. He saw he was on his hands and knees, straining to stand up, but he could not move. His back felt as if a huge boulder was pinning him down. The more he strained, the more the weight pushed him down, weakening his arms and back.

Attempts to take a deep breath were unsuccessful. His nostrils flared as he repeatedly drew desperate, short, labored breaths. He peered at his swollen hands which were lacerated and caked with dried blood. He realized the weight on his back was weakening him to the point he did not know how much longer his weakening arms could support his crouched position. He tried unsuccessfully to raise his head, but could not. Dried sweat on his face and neck was accumulating from his unsuccessful physical straining.

Just as he was about to succumb under the heavy weight, he heard a melodic voice softly speaking to him, saying, "Follow Me." Onesimus felt a warm sensation permeating his body. He still had great difficulty breathing, but the combination of the warmth and the compelling voice energized him.

He was barely able to lift his head, but as he fought, he saw an intense light in front of him. Despite the light's unusual brightness, it did not blind him or even cause him to squint. Its unearthly effect was mesmerizing.

Onesimus made one last attempt to stand up and was astonished that the enormous weight had somehow been removed, allowing him to get to his feet. He realized he could breathe much easier. He opened his eyes and was enveloped in the beautiful light. He thought of cocoons and equated his experience to being in a cocoon, ready to emerge into life. This event was unlike anything he had experienced before. Again, he heard the melodic voice beckon him, "Follow Me."

Onesimus lifted his outstretched arms and saw his hands—they were healed! There were no lacerations, the swelling was gone, and they were cleansed of the dry, caked blood. The dried sweat no longer coated his body.

Onesimus felt scrubbed clean and refreshed as if he were under a gushing waterfall removing all the dirt and grime from his body. He leaped forward, running towards the inviting voice and strange light.

As he hurried toward the center of the healing light, he was amazed at how effortless his movements were. The huge obstacles he encountered were formidable, yet he easily bounded over them. Every potential debilitating hurdle was rendered ineffective to impede him. After each surmounted obstacle, he turned his gaze to the riveting light source that was like a benevolent magnet drawing him closer.

The enthralled slave did not speak, but somehow he knew the magnetic personage could understand his thoughts without speaking. The more he focused on the voice and the light, the faster he could move. His quickened pace was full of joy, and his heart began to pound as he came closer to the presence which he realized was Jesus, the God-man Paul had spoken of.

Finally he stopped, and the radiance of the warm light went through every part of his body. For a third time, the lyrical voice said, "Follow Me." This time Onesimus shouted in an elated voice, "I will follow you, ... Jesus, I will follow you!"

Indescribable sensations of life came in waves and flowed throughout his body. He opened his arms wide and threw his head back, wanting the healing light to penetrate every inch of his being. Then the sensation ceased.

Astounded, Onesimus found himself awake on his bed in the same position as when he had fallen into his deep slumber. It had been a revelatory dream. He did not move, but opened his eyes and searched the apartment to ascertain where he was. He felt relief when his mind confirmed he was in his tiny apartment and he could feel the bed beneath his body.

The once-frantic, desperate slave now felt tranquility instead of torment. He felt peaceful, with a lightness he had not experienced ever before in his troubled young life.

Onesimus sighed deeply, not of despair or resignation, but of joy. He swung his legs over the edge of the cot and used his hands to sit upright on the bed. In one swift, easy effort, Onesimus stood up, then immediately dropped to the floor on his knees and placed his elbows on the bed.

In a joyful voice, he audibly proclaimed, "It was you, Jesus, that I just experienced, wasn't it!" Onesimus did not expect nor require an answer. His heart answered for him, verifying the truth of his exclamation. Onesimus lowered his head and he remained silent in his kneeling position, basking in the experience that he could hardly believe.

For the first time in his physically and mentally tortured life, he knew contentment, joy, and peace. It wasn't an emotion or a feeling, exactly. Rather, a new state of being that he was determined to enjoy and to safeguard at all cost.

As the sun rose to proclaim a new day, the morning shift's guard informed Onesimus it was time for him to leave for Paul's townhouse and begin his work. The guard noticed a difference in the prisoner's countenance. It wasn't dark and brooding, but full of confidence and purposefulness. The slave's features were softer; he was congenial, polite, and kinder. The guard wondered why he was so different, as he escorted the slave through the interplay of sun-streaked buildings and shadows.

Inside the townhouse, Paul had breakfast ready for his cobbler colleague in the residence's dining room. Lucilius was beside Paul as they waited for Onesimus' arrival. Both Paul and his personal guard noticed the difference in the young slave who had not yet revealed his extraordinary experience. Nevertheless, Paul smiled, believing he knew what was affecting the slave's noticeably changed demeanor.

Onesimus' face was almost glowing. It no longer had worry lines in every corner. His brow was free of his earlier signs of hidden anger and his eyes no longer flashed with hostility.

Lucilius secretly conjectured Onesimus had accepted Christ's salvation during the night. The slave's demeanor and appearance had a freedom and a brightness that resembled his own and Marcus's transformation when they allowed Christ into their respective lives. Lucilius wondered if Christ had revealed Himself to Onesimus the same way He did with them.

Paul studied Onesimus, as well, and believed that Christ had acquired another lost soul for all of eternity. Eagerly, the apostle of Christ wanted to shout for joy, but he waited for Onesimus to make it known to them. Paul had learned that after a lost soul becomes saved, part of God's sealing of this life-changing event is to manifest His glory through His new child's countenance and body language. It is part of the identification process that shows the lost world the power and supremacy of Almighty God; and to followers of Christ, it creates an unspoken recognition of one another in the faith.

After the satisfying morning meal, Onesimus could no longer contain himself. He blurted out, "Paul, is it possible for us to remain here a few minutes? I have something I want to speak about." Paul casually sat back down. Lucilius stared intently at the slave and predicted Onesimus was about to end the speculation that was captivating all their thoughts.

Onesimus tentatively voiced his acceptance of Christ's eternal salvation. Humbled and somewhat embarrassed, he related the entire dream scenario that took place between himself and his Savior. Lucilius was engrossed in Onesimus' story of his personal encounter with the Redeemer of the World. It was not like his experience at all, yet had the same result. At one point, he choked up and could not refrain from raising a hand high in the air, praising Almighty God for the miracle of another transformed life.

At the conclusion of Onesimus' life-changing testimony, Paul went around to where Onesimus was perched, to confirm what had happened to him. The evangelist took Onesimus by the arm, coaxed him to his feet, and proceeded to give him a hearty hug. "God hears the unspoken cries of our hearts, and answers in ways that sometimes surprise us! Your dream spoke to your needs, emotions, and honest submission to our savior, Christ Jesus! This is an answer to my prayer to our gracious God that you would receive the conviction of His Holy Spirit! Your name, Onesimus, is now permanently recorded in God's book of life. Praise Almighty God in the highest!"

Lucilius also came around and gave Onesimus a warm and powerful hug. "I'm so pleased to now call you my brother in Christ!" Onesimus was overcome with emotion, and tears began to slowly slide down his cheeks, but he smiled broadly. Lucilius turned and ran to the courtyard where he summoned Marcus to come to the dining room.

The startled warrior did as requested, and when he learned of Onesimus' conversion, he let out a loud holler and embraced the slave. The death ball that constantly hung at Marcus's side swung precariously in the commotion, and Lucilius moved swiftly to prevent it from scarring the new convert.

For the remainder of the shift, the foursome rejoiced in God's miracle. The celebration that took place in that earthly room was exceeded only by celebration joy in the heavens, while the devil and his demons gnashed their teeth over their loss.

## Chapter 29

Nearly a week after Onesimus accepted Christ's invitation to eternal life, Cleatus was handed a signed document from Philemon. Unceremoniously, the supreme military commander unrolled the short scroll and read it. He absorbed its contents, then nonchalantly dropped it on his desktop.

For a few moments, he merely sat there, contemplating his next step. He rose up, donned his black helmet, pausing only to inform his secretary he would be gone the rest of the afternoon. The secretary did not say anything, as Cleatus was moving too quickly for any reply to be made. It wasn't unusual for Rome's top military general to leave his office in the afternoon. The secretary supposed his superior was going for an afternoon ride in the countryside. He uttered a mournful sound to himself, wishing he, too, could leave his office duties that often felt stifling.

The secretary was correct in assuming that Cleatus was going for an afternoon ride on Nike. What the office clerk did not realize was Cleatus had a second motive for his actions. He was going to Seneca's villa for an impromptu summit. The news from Philemon needed to be addressed quickly.

Seneca was startled at the unannounced visit of his co-conspirator and knew it must be important. This was only the second time Cleatus had taken such action and the Roman consul/senator knew it had to do with either Paul or Onesimus, or both. He quickly led Cleatus into his private office.

Cleatus quickly gave the reason for his sudden appearance, "Seneca, I just received the signed document from Philemon stating his decision concerning his runaway slave. I felt Philemon's decree worthy of an immediate conference."

Before continuing, he waited while one of Seneca's house

slaves placed a tray of snacks and poured wine for their pleasure. When the slave left the private office, Cleatus resumed his report, "Philemon has declared he wants Onesimus detained until issues within his organization in Colosse are resolved. His said his decision could impact aspects of his business in a negative manner." Cleatus grabbed a piece of fruit and complained, "Philemon was not specific what the business concerns are, only that his decision on the slave could seriously impact his business. We can only wonder what Philemon's business issues are, and I don't believe we should engage in that mental futility."

Seneca was quick to respond, "I agree with you wholeheartedly, Cleatus. There could be many reasons behind Philemon's decision. Besides, we have time to wait. This allows us to further monitor the relationship between the slave and Paul, and gives us time to obtain more information concerning Paul's potential influence on a slave rebellion."

Cleatus asked his host, "Do you foresee any difficulty with this development when you inform Nero of Philemon's decision?"

The sharp-witted consul and senator answered, "None at all. Nero is as deeply concerned over a potential slave rebellion as the rest of Rome's ruling body. He will wait for all the facts to be presented to him before he takes any action that might go against him. At the present time, Nero is consumed with construction progress on the new Portus port. He is under considerable pressure to get it completed and fully functional. Rome's increasing demand for goods, especially grain, is great, and the new port is vital to Rome's sustainability. Nero's absence during his time in Athens sours the Senate, so the more progress on Portus, the better his relationship with the Senate."

Cleatus ate the fruit in his hand while he processed this information. He did not fully accept it. But he hoped that Seneca could convince Nero not to take any hasty action. In the back of his mind, Cleatus made a personal resolution that if this slave issue started to unravel, he would personally go to Nero with his alternative plan, one that Seneca did not know about.

The two schemers discussed what they each had learned from their spies about Paul, Onesimus, and now Philemon. The exchange was enlightening for both men. Each would take what the other shared and use it to fabricate his own strategy or make adjustments for his own personal benefit.

When the last item was deliberated, the summit was adjourned. Seneca lingered at his desk, munching and plotting, while

Cleatus enjoyed a relaxing ride back to his townhouse with renewed energy for the tasks that lay before him.

Spring was giving way to warmer summer months. During this period of time, Paul gave daily spiritual mentoring to his three mentees. Each session was rewarding, demonstrating how Marcus, Lucilius, and Onesimus thirsted for the word of God. The mentees asked probing questions of Paul who was never stymied or too fatigued by their insatiable spiritual hunger.

Paul organized his time effectively during his house arrest. During the day, he divided portions of the morning to mentor Marcus, Lucilius, and Onesimus. One day each week, Paul would verbally instruct his mentees in the word of God. During the remainder of the week, they individually meditated on the teaching and discussed it among themselves.

Paul was available for clarification of points and uncertainties associated with their earlier instruction, but, mainly, he allowed them to receive discernment of God's Word from the Holy Spirit. It was a special time for the mentees, who grew spiritually by leaps and bounds.

Paul focused on his cobbler projects and, usually four days each week, also ministered to the Roman church elders. The ambassador of Christ gave thanks to God each day for the miracle of life and opportunities given him to serve his Lord.

The same day Cleatus informed Seneca about Philemon's decision regarding Onesimus, Seneca sent a messenger to Aelia, whose villa was within two miles of his own. The Roman consul/senator invited the businesswoman to dinner the next day. Seneca's reasoning behind the invitation was he wanted Aelia to know directly from him what course of action would be taken concerning the runaway slave. Aelia's interest in the slave was based on his employment by Antonius and the management of the boot business that Aelia owned.

Seneca kept Aelia informed as a show of respect because her particular business interest in the cobbler trade could be negatively impacted if Onesimus would no longer be able to work. Whenever the Roman government made a decision that affected businesses, they made it a point to inform the various business owners as soon as possible after the decree was official. This allowed the business owner to make any necessary adjustments to adapt to the new decree.

Seneca realized that Aelia probably already knew of Philemon's decision from information obtained by her agents and secret spies that she and many other business people utilized. Intrigue was a normal part of the elite Roman class. Everyone clamored for inside knowledge to gain any kind of edge that would benefit them personally or monetarily.

The Roman consul wanted to inform Aelia personally, to correct any misinformation that might have been relayed to her. But it was not strictly business. Besides the political intrigue factor, both Seneca and his wife Pompeia enjoyed Aelia's company. They looked forward to their evening affair together.

The hosts stood in the atrium of the villa and were impressed, as always, by the appearance of their evening guest. Aelia wore a draped teal-colored gown that accentuated her slender curves and complemented her light olive-tone skin. Her intricate upswept hairstyle added a sense of regalness, as if crowning the statuesque woman. Aelia serenely glided toward her hosts with an appreciative smile. Her graceful strides across the marble floor in her flowing sea of blue-green seemed like gentle waves of the Mediterranean.

Seneca and Pompeia had also dressed elegantly for the occasion. They greeted their guest with kisses on the side of each cheek and invited her into their finely appointed dining room. Once they were seated, dinner began, and their conversation was light and cordial. Each was sizing up the other and making mental preparations for the after-dinner conversation that would be more weighty and detailed than the light-hearted banter they were currently enjoying.

With the multi-course dinner completed, Seneca broke off the casual talk by revealing Philemon's decision. Aelia deliberately appeared nonchalant in response to the news. She slightly lifted her head, and the movement of her curved neck added to her royal appearance. Pompeia was mildly jealous of Aelia's striking beauty; but the consul's wife sincerely admired her female friend.

Not many women were able to achieve the high level of success that Aelia enjoyed. Business was dominated by men who often resorted to harsh tactics to accomplish their desires. Such involvement was not for the faint at heart.

Aelia not only survived in such an environment, she excelled, and was able to consistently outwit her male counterparts. Her deceased husband had provided the business foundation, but it was Aelia's insight and attentive business knowledge that had brought her husband's businesses to power and influence.

Soon after she became involved in her husband's businesses, the male-dominated business community had taken note of her abilities, and began to give her respect women otherwise did not receive. In many circles, it was common knowledge that Aelia could be even more ruthless than some men.

Knowing this about Aelia, Pompeia sat primed for the ensuing conversation. She had spent the dinner hour imagining what was about to take place between the feminine business magnate and her husband. It would be engaging, and Pompeia was eager to witness Aelia's tactics in their game of wits.

"Seneca, I have heard rumors concerning this slave master in Colosse who owns Onesimus. What did you say his name is, again?" inquired Aelia.

The evening's host answered casually, "Philemon. He owns several businesses in the region that comprises Colosse, Laodicea, and Hierapolis. He owns nearly a thousand slaves, so the loss of one is miniscule. However, how he handles this runaway slave will impact the attitude of the other slaves, as well as other slave owners."

Aelia reflected, "I have no knowledge of this Philemon, but on occasion I do engage in trade with some vendors in that region. I am aware how the actions of one slave can have great impact on slavery there. I assume, Seneca, this Philemon is willing to wait on a final decision concerning Onesimus because he gains much from the present situation. After all, he receives half of the slave's earnings from his cobbler job without any expense incurred. This is quite profitable. I would do the same."

Pompeia discreetly smiled and lauded Aelia for her opening gambit in the evening's mind game. The hostess positioned herself to easily change her view from Aelia to Seneca without drawing undue notice or interrupting the proceedings. She waited expectantly for Aelia to continue.

As if on cue, Aelia said, "Rome provides the slave's housing and prevents him from escaping once again; and they give control to Philemon, the slave owner. Do you foresee Philemon making a final decision anytime soon?"

Seneca realized Aelia had just informed him she knew many details about Onesimus, and did not want Seneca to waste her time with the elementary basics. He was careful to give Aelia credit for her knowledge and business instincts, saying, "I anticipated you would have knowledge of Philemon's directive to

Cleatus regarding the status of the slave. I am aware that you would intervene and purchase Onesimus from Philemon. This would be of great benefit to your business interests, as Onesimus is becoming quite the accomplished cobbler, much due to his tutoring from Paul." Seneca continued, taking the opportunity to parry in this mind game with his guest. "However, I must implore you not to make any overtures to Philemon regarding such a purchase. Rome would not allow such a thing to take place at this particular time."

Pompeia keenly observed how her husband attempted to add tension in his warning to their guest. She knew Seneca well from their thirty years of marriage, and was confident he would not be cruel to their friend as he cautioned Aelia, "There are certain aspects to the issue involving Onesimus that, from a military point of view, could do harm to the empire. You are aware of the three slave rebellions that have occurred. Despite the most recent one, involving the slave Spartacus—even though it is over one hundred years old—Rome remains wary of any potential revolt involving slaves. Onesimus is deemed a potential rebel and, therefore, Rome demands top authority in resolving this matter."

Aelia serenely answered, "I fully understand what you are saying, Seneca. I have no intention of interfering with Rome's military involvement. Certainly not. And from a business standpoint, this is not a good time for me to make any offers to purchase the runaway slave. Philemon has too much control over this matter. Once things develop that causes his control to wane, I will step in and make an offer that obviously is advantageous for me."

Pompeia nearly let out a shout, but was able to contain her delight in how adeptly Aelia had handled Seneca's ploy. It was not often that the hostess had opportunity to witness Aelia in action against men. As such, Pompeia savored the moment. She particularly was impressed by how calmly and demurely Aelia presented herself, all the while holding her ground in this matter. Pompeia's respect and admiration for Aelia grew with the evening's activity.

Not to be deterred by Aelia's deflection, Seneca said, "I will confide in you that our investigation combines Onesimus with our concerns about Paul. As you are aware, your renter is the leader of an unknown sect that has outlets in many of Rome's main commerce cities. There are many slaves in these environs who could easily be swayed by Paul's teachings. He is very charismatic. His type of individual always warrants scrutiny by Rome. Do not let yourself come under the suspicion of Rome in this matter."

Pompeia was shocked at the blunt suggestion in her husband's words toward their guest and friend. Aelia and Seneca had several shared business interests. It was shocking to Pompeia to see how Seneca had drawn a definite line between their friendly association and his authoritative governmental position as the Consul to Caesar and Senator of Rome.

Aelia had received proof of her suspicions and detected Seneca's change of attitude. She knew it was time to appease her host. "I appreciate your disclosure with me about this investigation. I was not aware of such activity, but I'm not that surprised, either. Have no fear, dear Seneca, I will not become a wedge in Rome's involvement with these prisoners. Rest assured, my interests are purely business, and as you know, business is very fluid and adaptable to any given change."

Pompeia was relieved by how adroitly her friend offered an olive branch to her husband. Seneca had the power to mightily impact Aelia's business interests as well as her pursuit of intrigue. What took place at their villa was a microcosm of how Rome's culture among the elites regularly played out. Members of the elite ruling class always were activating schemes and spying on both friends and enemies. The various spying and clandestine undertakings were fear-based, and anything involving slaves often led to paranoia.

Pompeia regretted that she was in no position to align with her friend in respect to the events involving Paul and Onesimus. Nonetheless, she certainly would use her influence with Seneca to temper his actions involving Aelia.

The next day, Aelia made her usual trip to Rome. Because it was the first of the month, she had her normal pursuits to fulfill. Her first stop was to see Antonius. Her cobbler business manager was nervous by nature, and he needed consolation concerning the uncertainties over his top two cobblers, Paul and Onesimus.

Carefully, she informed Antonius that both Paul and Onesimus would continue their normal bootmaking projects. She also gave him hope and assurance that once the time was right, she would purchase Onesimus. Antonius was greatly relieved at this news. The prisoner and the slave accounted for forty-five percent of the profits from the military boot manufacturing.

Aelia's last stop in her business rounds was at her townhouse, rented to the current focal point of Rome's investigation, Paul. She again enjoyed the time spent with Rome's prisoner and delighted in how easily they always conversed. He made her feel warm, respected, and, in a manner, loved.

But she had to set aside her emotions and address the business side of the affair. She would make inquiries of both Paul and Onesimus that would give her insight for what to expect in the near future. Many times her agents and secret spies literally bumped into their counterparts employed by Seneca and Cleatus. There were sometimes comical surprises in these encounters, but physical conflicts occurred at other times.

The result of her covert maneuvers convinced her that Seneca and Cleatus were making a huge mistake in assuming that Paul and Onesimus were pillars of an impending slave rebellion. So firm was her belief about the two prisoners, she directed her agents and spies to focus on both Seneca's and Cleatus' activities. She believed what the two officials might do could cause her more setbacks in business than any threat the two cobblers might represent.

Despite all the secretly choreographed investigations into Paul and Onesimus, the two cobblers continued making quality boots for Aelia and Antonius. Paul often commented on the progress Onesimus was making to develop his considerable talent into high-level skills. The young runaway slave, now a pursuer of Christ, remained humbled at God's blessing to him and always gave Him glory and praise for his gifts.

The warm summer months were joyful days for Paul, Onesimus, and the converted guards, Marcus and Lucilius. The rented townhouse was alive with spiritual vitality. Even various visitors mentioned to Paul how they felt the Spirit of the Lord abound when they entered the townhouse. It was a time of blessing.

The lost souls, the other Roman guards assigned to Paul and Onesimus, could also feel the presence of the Lord but could not properly identify it. It was the sovereign God of the universe they experienced. Draba took note especially of the change in Onesimus' demeanor and mannerisms. The former hostile and volatile slave was now easygoing, polite, and cheerful. The intensely loyal guard reported to Flavius on this change. It didn't make sense to him. He was suspicious, and the consistently kind treatment he received from both Onesimus and Paul was unsettling to the guard.

In mid-August, Timothy had returned from his most recent trek to Colosse to monitor Philemon and determine his spiritual viewpoint concerning his runaway slave. The slave master was always cordial and enjoyed talking about things which he saw Christ doing in his life, until the topic of Onesimus emerged. Then he became brusque with Timothy, never confiding what, if anything, the Lord God was teaching him about the slave issue.

Paul's envoy sadly remarked, "Paul, I believe Philemon is in bondage to the devil concerning Onesimus. He is reluctant to do what you implored him to do. He is known for his faith, and continues using his home as one of the meeting places for Christ's followers, and shows great love for his fellow Christ followers, but he is incensed about Onesimus's escape."

The ambassador of Christ hung his head in dismay at Timothy's assessment. He rubbed his hand back and forth across his brow and finally said, "You have done well, Timothy. I agree with you that Philemon is under demonic pressure to cling to bitterness and anger. What have the other church elders to say about him?"

Timothy gently replied, "They have informed me that talks have taken place entreating Philemon to go to God in prayer and supplication, seeking His direction and guidance in the case involving Onesimus. Philemon now refuses to speak with them about the runaway slave." Timothy surveyed his mentor's distressed face and empathized. He, too, felt the frustration and disappointment.

Paul interlaced his fingers and folded his hands under his chin. He stared down at the floor, absorbed in his thoughts. Timothy silently watched his mentor ponder the situation in Colosse. After some time, Paul unclenched his hands, knowing what he must do. "This situation is very unfavorable and must be resolved to the Lord's satisfaction as soon as possible. I must go before His holy throne and seek His guidance and direction for resolving this spiritual conflict. Since your last communication with Philemon, something of great significance has happened. Onesimus has turned to Christ and is now our brother! Philemon does not know this yet, but it is something that he needs to hear, and I believe it will make a difference to him. It certainly should."

Timothy observed Paul's firm determination and knew that God's missionary and friend was preparing for battle. Timothy was thankful action would be taken to prevent Colossian followers of Christ from falling victim to the devil's controling deceptions.

Paul embraced Timothy, and in a firm, quiet tone said, "Wait for my summons of you. When the Lord God gives me His direction, I shall pass it on to you. Pray about this unsettling condition and prepare yourself for spiritual battle." Timothy assured him he would, and left the townhouse.

The consultation had turned into a mini-forum due to the ever-present Roman guards. Lucilius was on duty during the discussion between Paul and Timothy. He was highly interested in the session. Paul did not refrain from educating his mentee about the principles involved. When Paul finished, Lucilius immediately said, "I see no reason for me to report this event to Flavius. He will not understand what it's about, and such a report will only confuse him and possibly cause trouble in a matter that is under God's jurisdiction."

"You are correct in your understanding of the situation, Lucilius," said Paul. "This can be valuable for both you and Marcus in your spiritual growth. As this unfolds and God reveals His plan, I shall confer with both of you about the spiritual components and God's direction."

When the afternoon shift arrived, Paul sequestered himself in his bedroom to meditate on the issue Timothy had presented to him. God's direction and instructions to Paul did not occur right away. But after he had fervently prayed about Onesimus and Philemon, Paul was no longer fretful, and merely waited with faith that he would receive direction from God. In His perfect timing, Almighty God would work in Paul's mind and spirit to give him peace and the needed answer to his prayer.

The apostle of Christ went about his daily routines and enjoyed the time spent with his mentees, his various visitors, and cobbler projects for Antonius. Paul knew not to be worrisome or anxious about the matter that remained on his heart and mind.

Approximately five days after seeking God's face, guidance was given to him! God's timing was such that the directive was presented on the first day of a new shift rotation. Draba went from days to the evening stint, leaving Marcus and Lucilius to attend to Paul during the day.

Early that morning, during their breakfast time together, Paul made an announcement that greatly shook his mentees. The apostle addressed Onesimus directly, "Onesimus, I have been in prayer concerning you and the stalemate you are experiencing here in Rome. Last night our Heavenly Father gave me instructions concerning your predicament. I shall give His directive to you. It is your choice to accept or reject His plan."

The three mentees waited, startled, for Paul's explanation for his sudden announcement. They exchanged looks, each seeking insight on what to do. Onesimus surprised them all. He quickly turned away from his fellow spiritual learners and asked Paul, "Exactly what is God's plan concerning my situation with Philemon?" The question was offered in a tentative voice, and Onesimus could not help but feel tension in light of his limited options.

Definitively, Paul revealed, "You are to petition Cleatus to return to Colosse and face Philemon about your actions." Paul stopped to give his mentee sufficient time to grasp the shocking news. Marcus and Lucilius reacted to the unexpected proclamation by exchanging baffled looks, then turned their focus to Onesimus for his reaction.

The runaway slave was totally dismayed at this heavenly notice. He leaned back heavily in his seat and worry lines appeared on his forehead. He closed his eyes as he puzzled over the news. Onesimus desperately needed an explanation from Paul. With a slight tremor in his voice he asked his mentor, "Why does Almighty God want me to do this?"

Marcus and Lucilius sat riveted, barely containing their anxiety as they waited for Paul's response. In a gentle, consoling voice, Paul explained, "This is the best way to resolve the issue both legally and spiritually. Resolve it in such a manner that God gets all the glory and you become blessed."

Onesimus could not help but feel mildly irritated at Paul's answer. It was a natural emotional reaction to news that he neither expected nor liked. "How can I be blessed by returning myself to Philemon?" Marcus and Lucilius wondered the same thing. They shifted their inquisitive eyes from the runaway slave to Paul for his answer.

"You allow Rome and Philemon to see Christ through you. Your unexpected return will touch Philemon's heart and Rome will know you are not intent on creating a slave rebellion. Your act of surrendering to Christ will strengthen your faith and allow you to draw closer to Him."

Onesimus was extremely disconcerted over Paul's reasoning. He cocked his worried head at an angle, conveying his doubt.

Paul continued, "Remember what I have taught you about our Savior. He will never forsake you nor leave you! He will not allow the hounds of hell to destroy you. He has a plan and a purpose for your life, and this is but one step along that journey. This requires a great step of trust on your part. No matter how it seems, He works all things together for good to those who love and trust Him." The runaway slave just stared at Paul. His two fellow mentees were looking expectantly at him, knowing certainly this would be a huge test of faith.

Onesimus took his time in answering. Finally, he plaintively emitted, "I have prayed to Christ, believing He would release me from this bondage to Philemon and to Rome. I have envisioned He would put it on Philemon's heart to release me and declare me a freedman. As such I would be free to continue with you and carry out Christ's work. *This* I perceived would be what Christ wants of me. Your solution is not what I thought or believed."

Paul gently spoke, "Remember, Onesimus, that Almighty God has stated in his Word that His ways and thoughts are not our ways and thoughts, that He is higher and greater than mortal man in everything. To truly follow Christ, we are to totally surrender to Him and make our bodies a living sacrifice for His will to be done." Seeing startled reactions, Paul clarified, "It is a living sacrifice God asks. Living. While we live, we are given opportunities to be fully submitted to God's will as we live out our lives, even when it doesn't look reasonable to us. It is a form of worship to trust Him in all things and be willing to sacrifice our own plans."

A hush came over the dining room. Paul's statement of God's Holy Word caused Onesimus to look down in contemplation. He remained silent for some time. Finally, he raised his head and said, "Your words are quite the shock for me at this time. I must meditate on them and go to Christ in prayer and supplication to help me do the right thing."

Paul answered by agreeing with Onesimus' decision. "If you are unable to continue with your boot projects, do not fret. Take some time and go to the courtyard and commend your thoughts to the Lord."

Onesimus nodded his head soberly and left the table to make his way to the courtyard. Marcus accompanied him, while Lucilius remained behind per his assignment as personal guard to Paul. Lucilius had a whirlwind of thoughts, but he managed to ask his mentor, "Are you sure, Paul, this is what God wants Onesimus to do? The implications could be hazardous to our brother in Christ!"

Paul's jaw was set and his voice took on a commanding tone, "I am sure, Lucilius. God does not make light of these heavy situations, nor does He give foolish instructions. Many times, the recipient of His direction reacts in the flesh; the ways of the world overshadow God's guidance because of human emotions. These cloud his ability to rightly discern what is truly from God and what is not. Think about the issues involved in this case—what Roman law is and what God's law is. As you compare the two, pray for God's discernment to see how His law not only supersedes man's, but His solution is better than what man can devise."

"You have given both Marcus and me much to contemplate. Rest assured, Paul, neither of us will interfere with Onesimus as he seeks God's face in this matter. We will also do as you say and petition for His blessing of discernment."

As the day progressed, Paul worked fervently at his leather projects while Lucilius hung back, deep in spiritual contemplation. In the courtyard, Marcus leaned against the side of the rear opening wall, pondering what had taken place. Onesimus sat in one of the patio chairs, with his head bowed and his hands covering his face as he went to his Savior with a confused and troubled heart.

Two days after apprising Paul of the situation in Colosse regarding Philemon, Timothy informed Paul he would be returning to the region to continue monitoring the developments. Paul was in complete agreement and prayed with his young protégé that he would be a mighty servant to Christ. On the third day, Timothy sailed enroute to the smoldering issue that could explode like a volcano.

That same day during their daily breakfast time together, Onesimus informed Paul and his fellow converts, Marcus and Lucilius, that he had reached a decision pertaining to Paul's request. "I've prayed and meditated long on what you said to me, Paul, and now I have an announcement to make. I shall do as you say. I shall return to Philemon."

The tension in both Marcus and Lucilius escaped their bodies and minds at his proclamation, and was amply replaced by godly relief. The two soldiers felt Christ's love for Onesimus and wanted the best for him. At first, like Onesimus, they had been leery of Paul's petition. But after they prayed and discussed it together, they agreed Paul's wisdom and keenness to hear the Holy Spirit warranted their trust.

Onesimus went on to explain the reasoning behind his decision, "God's Holy Spirit has convinced me I must return and let myself be Christ's witness to Philemon, the other slaves, and those in the church in the region. Christ has moved in me not to be fearful of any repercussions on the part of Philemon." He looked at his audience—his spiritual brothers he had come to love, trust, and enjoy. He smiled at each of his brothers in Christ and humbly added, "I simply have to trust Christ Jesus, and follow Him, no matter how difficult it may be." In a hushed voice, the slave convert to Christ pleaded, "I seek your prayers for me in this situation. I fear my emotions will betray me and lead me astray before I can carry out His will and be Christ's servant."

Paul, Marcus and Lucilius surrounded the seated slave, laid their hands on him, and Marcus led the prayer, "Almighty God, our faith and trust is in You alone. We commend our brother Onesimus to You and beseech You to protect him and give him Your supreme power to carry out Your will, plan, and purpose in this matter with Philemon. May our brother be a mighty voice that will glorify You." Everyone said, "Amen!" and Onesimus felt a spiritual peace settle over him.

They returned to their seats at the table, and Paul said, "I will have one of the house messengers summon Flavius today. When he arrives, I shall assist you in making your request to return to Colosse and Philemon." Paul looked at his two guard mentees and informed them, "I want Flavius here while you are on duty. This will allow you both to witness how God works in these matters.

"I have gone to our Lord God about this matter. Onesimus, in addition to God's instruction for you to return to Philemon, the Holy Spirit has given me His thoughts that I've penned for Philemon, the Colossian church, and that of Ephesus, as well." Paul went to the office and retrieved three different-sized parchment scrolls made of fine goat leather.

The mentees stared at the writings and looked questioningly at their mentor. Paul gently but firmly directed his words to Onesimus, "This issue concerning you and Philemon, Onesimus, will have impact on the followers of Christ in Colosse and the entire region. In addition, it affects how the Romans will deal with Philemon, you, and the church in this region. It is important that everyone know the spiritual direction they must follow, otherwise the devil will rob and destroy what Christ has established in that area."

Onesimus gazed at the scroll Paul held in his powerful hands, then at his mentor's face. Softly, he said, "It is as you have taught me—that it is not my will, but Christ's to be done."

Paul called for the messenger boy.

## Chapter 30

Flavius was perplexed by the message sent to him from Paul, but surmised the reason for the urgency of the request. He mounted his horse and hastened to Paul's townhouse. When the centurion entered the residence, the front door guard escorted him to the back of the home where Paul and Onesimus were in the workshop. With each stride, Flavius' cloak fanned out and fluttered, as if it were propelling the soldier to his important destination.

Paul greeted Flavius warmly and suggested the small group go to the dining room for their conference. Once seated, Paul immediately got to the point, informing Flavius of Onesimus' desire to return to Philemon in Colosse. Flavius held his formal posture and looked first at Paul, then to Onesimus, then up at Lucilius who stood close to where Paul was seated.

The centurion pursed his lips at this news. He was aware that all eyes were focused on him. Coolly, he rubbed his cheek, then addressed the two detainees, "Your request is most unusual, Onesimus. Rarely do runaway slaves solicit to return to their masters. Tell me, why do you want to do this?"

Onesimus was prepared for the obvious question and easily replied, "It is the right thing for me to do. It is time to rectify my mistake and make amends with Philemon."

Flavius studied the slave, and in a matter-of-fact voice said, "You realize I have no authority to grant your request; this must come from Cleatus. I can only inform him of your entreaty. I will do so after we conclude our meeting here."

The centurion turned his attention to Paul and asked the prisoner, "Have you persuaded this slave to take this course of action?"

Paul also had anticipated such a question and quietly stated,

"I made the suggestion to Onesimus based on answer to prayer I made to Almighty God."

Flavius sat relaxed in his chair. It made no difference to him what was the reasoning for the application by the slave; his questions were posed mainly for his own curiosity. "You have made your appeal and it shall be given to Cleatus. If there are no other wishes, I shall proceed to Cleatus." Their silence gave indication no other issues were at hand and Flavius got up and left the townhouse.

When Cleatus was informed by Flavius of Onesimus' petition to return to Philemon, he was stunned. There was a brief discussion with his centurion commander who then left for his own office in Caesar's palace. Cleatus pondered the latest development in this strange case. Cleatus, the supreme military general, did not need to obtain approval for whatever decision he made concerning Onesimus' pleading. These situations had a definite protocol. Philemon's binding decree to wait on his final decision concerning the fate of his runaway slave had caused the delay.

Cleatus envisioned how the slave's petition would impact the investigation concerning his possible involvement in a slave revolt. The general took time to consider the various scenarios. When he finished his mental exercises, he dispatched a messenger. "Go quickly to this person! Time is of the essence and I must have an answer today!" he barked at the young lad. Cleatus got up and headed towards the end of the corridor to confer again with Flavius.

A winded messenger boy arrived at Paul's rented townhouse just before the daily shift change. Paul graciously accepted the message from the youngster, then went to his workshop to inform Onesimus of the update on his solicitation.

Lucilius stood next to Paul, and both peered down at the seated slave cobbler. Paul was quick to say, "Onesimus, Cleatus has made his decision concerning your request. You shall return to Colosse and to Philemon within the next two days."

Onesimus at first merely stared up at his mentor as the news was given to him. Lucilius waited anxiously for the slave's response to the fact he would return to uncertainty. Onesimus laid down his cobbler's tool and dully said, "It has begun. Let this be the time of the Lord."

After the shift change, Paul sent the house messenger boy to one of his trusted companions, asking for a consultation. Within a short period of time, Tychicus was sitting with Paul in the courtyard of the townhouse. The emissary of the Lord relayed the situation to his fellow evangelist, and made his pitch, "Tychicus, my brother, I would like for you to accompany Onesimus back to Colosse and deliver several letters for me. One is to Philemon, one to the church of the Colossians, and the final one to the Ephesians. The letters are in the hands of Flavius, the centurion assigned to my appeal. They are being copied and should be returned to me before Onesimus is escorted back."

Tychicus readily replied, "It is important for Onesimus to have someone he can rely on when he confronts Philemon. I am glad to do this. Your epistles will greatly affect the spiritual nature of this state of affairs, which needs to be addressed. I will remain there with Timothy until the situation is resolved."

Paul grabbed his fellow warrior's hands into his own and gripped them firmly, grateful for his eager willingness. "Let the Lord's sovereign power reign in all ways."

The morning of his departure, Onesimus was allowed to visit Paul prior to boarding the ship that would carry him to his destiny. Paul had secured Cleatus' permission for Tychicus to accompany the runaway slave. Before leaving, the trio prayed fervently together while Draba looked on with detachment. After the prayer, the small, armed escort took away Onesimus and Tychicus, plus Paul's priceless letters.

At the same time that General Cleatus had sent his messenger to the captain of the merchant ship to secure passage for his small delegation, the general also sent word to both Seneca and to Aelia. He fulfilled his obligation by petitioning them to meet at his villa since the two icons of Rome were in the vicinity of his country estate.

Both Seneca and Aelia appeared composed at the shocking news presented to them concerning Onesimus. However, each was mentally assessing the major change and calculating their respective next moves. The summit did not last long. When it was concluded, both Seneca and Aelia made haste to implement the initial phases of their individual plans.

Aelia promptly sent a message by carrier pigeon to one of her business assistants located in Ephesus. She instructed him to monitor Philemon. Should he elect to retain Onesimus, the business agent would present Philemon an offer to purchase the runaway slave. If Philemon chose to auction the slave, Aelia's agent was authorized to bid as high as 750 denarii—a high price, but one Aelia deemed worth the capital outlay. He had already proved his value to her. Onesimus would command a high price because he was young, strong, male, and healthy. Being skilled in a needed trade added to his value. Aelia speculated that at auction she could obtain the slave cheaper than through a private purchase agreement with Philemon. At auction, Aelia believed Onesimus could be had for around 500 denarii. It would be money well spent, considering the slave had already earned her double that amount by working for Antonius.

Seneca had a two-fold strategy to implement. First, he would send a message to a business friend in the region to determine what Philemon would do with his runaway slave. The Roman consul also saw value in Onesimus, and believed he could turn a profit by purchasing Onesimus, then reselling the slave first to Aelia or to Antonius or even another cobbler.

His second strategy focused on Nero. Seneca envisioned a way to use this development to help Nero gain favor with the Senate and for Seneca to be credited with his improved standing. He needed this fortification with Caesar. Caesar's respect for him had been slipping away in recent months.

Nero was ecstatic at Seneca's plan concerning Onesimus, and eagerly agreed to participate. This was a great relief to Seneca in his desperation for Caesar's favor. Although Cleatus was aware of Seneca's maneuverings, he did not object or interfere. The general was mostly amused by the political scheming and felt secure in believing he was the actual one who possessed real power in this matter.

The final element of Seneca's strategy was to inform Cato of the recent change in the status of the involvement with Onesimus and Paul.

Cato was beside himself with Seneca's report of the news. He was appalled at Onesimus' decision, and with his expectation that the young man's slave master would beat him to set an example to the other slaves. The thought of it made Cato ill.

Seneca presented Cato with copies of Paul's three epistles intended for the region of Colosse. "Flavius just delivered these to me. I haven't had time to peruse them. This I delegate to you." Seneca repeated the essentials so that the significance would be firmly set in their minds. "Obviously, as you analyze them, note any tie-in to potential rebellion. If there is such, I must know at once. Much is at stake."

The Roman consul then informed Cato about what Nero

would be doing within the next three days concerning the matter of the runaway slave. "If there is anything contained within those letters, I must know; otherwise Nero will make a fool of himself and we all will pay the price for that." Cato indicated he would not delay in dissecting the written materials and begged his leave that he could begin immediately.

On the ride back to his villa, Cato was deep in thought about young Onesimus and found himself tightly clutching the three scrolls he was to evaluate.

Soon after being informed of the imminent departure of the runaway slave, both Seneca and Aelia booked passage for their respective agents assigned to shadow the delegation headed for Colosse.

After receiving the news about Onesimus, Aelia spent the evening reviewing the various points involved with this snag in her affairs. She was confident her business operative in Colosse would be able to purchase Onesimus and thereby allow her to continue utilizing the slave's skills in bootmaking. To her, that would not be a formidable difficulty, only a time delay.

What the Roman businesswoman was more curious about was her renter's involvement in this scenario. Aelia resolved she would meet with Paul the next day and satisfy her curiosity. Besides, she would collect her monthly rent at the same time.

Aelia began her grilling of Paul in a very business-like manner, with probing questions concerning Paul and Onesimus. Paul remained cordial, but strongly emphasized how his decision was based on the prompting of God's Holy Spirit. His patron found herself becoming quite interested in this Christ Jesus whom Paul spoke about with great passion. Nobody, including herself, had that same passion for the numerous gods idolized by the Romans.

The business power broker made a mental note to herself to explore more about this Christ. She knew that many of her slave servants in Rome had converted to this sect Paul championed. On several occasions she witnessed a change in their attitudes and mannerisms that were opposite those of slaves who did not adhere to the teachings of the god Paul revered. She decided anyone or any deity who could effect such a change was worthy of learning more about.

Two days after receiving the three scrolls written by Paul, Cato delivered his assessment to Seneca at the consul/senator's country estate. His report was brief, per the custom of the Roman culture in government affairs. Cato, the assigned reviewer, reported, "The two epistles directed to the so-called church in Colosse and Ephesus are quite similar. Paul instructs the Colossians to be ever mindful of their completeness in their god, this Christ. It also has a very strong tone against false teachers and their teachings.

"To the Ephesians, Paul stresses unity in following this Christ's teachings and commandments. He maintains his Christ has full authority over the Ephesians. While Paul addresses the issue of the false teachers, he isn't as strong about it as he is with the Colossians." Cato paused in his report, allowing Seneca time to jot down some notes on papyrus paper he had imported from Egypt.

When Seneca finished, Cato continued, but his voice was much different, "The final scroll is a personal letter to Philemon concerning his slave, Onesimus. I found this scroll quite revealing in many respects. It also answers the majority of questions posed by you and Cleatus concerning a potential slave rebellion."

Seneca laid his sharp quill down and narrowed his eyes as he listened. He fiercely commanded, "Don't leave anything important out of your report! This is vital when next I speak with Nero before he addresses the Senate."

Cato bowed in compliance. "At different points, Paul reminds Philemon of the love Philemon had for this Christ and for a group Paul calls 'saints' and how Philemon's demonstration of this love refreshed the other saints, including Paul."

Cato adjusted his position in his cushioned chair and cleared his throat before he continued his summary of the letter to Philemon, "Paul next appeals to Philemon to act according to his belief in this Christ. Paul briefly lets Philemon know that Paul has some sort of authority to urge Philemon to accept Onesimus, but asks for Philemon to act out of love, not out of necessity or unwillingness. Because, he says, now that his slave Onesimus has converted to this sect, Onesimus is now much more profitable than what he was before he ran away."

Seneca leaned to one side, on the cushioned arm of his chair. "This is very, very interesting Cato. Please go on."

Cato raised his head with a quick nod, and continued, "Paul states it is he who is sending Onesimus back, despite his preference to keep Onesimus in Rome that the slave might minister to Paul." Cato lowered his written report and shook his head saying, "I have absolutely no idea what Paul refers to, having a lowly runaway slave 'minister' to him, or in what way. This part of the letter is confusing to me." Seneca nodded and gestured impatiently with a hand, urging him to go on.

"In line with this conversion, Paul instructs Philemon to receive Onesimus, not as a slave but as a brother member of this new sect." Cato moved to the edge of his chair and leaned toward Seneca. His voice became excited as he declared, "At the end of this personal letter, Paul implores Philemon that if Onesimus owes Philemon any money, Paul will gladly reimburse Philemon for the entire amount owed."

Seneca sat quietly, yet he was gripped by Cato's narrative. "I take it, Cato, there is still more in this letter..., please?"

"Indeed there is, Seneca. Paul exhorts Philemon to do more than what Paul commands in the way of accepting him back, but Paul isn't specific about what this entails. I don't have any notion what this could be."

Seneca put his fingers to his lips and remained silent. The Roman consul was puzzling over Paul's command to Philemon. Cato waited respectfully for Seneca to reveal his thoughts.

"Cato, as you know, I have operatives in Colosse who are closely observing Philemon and others who could be involved in this matter. None have sent back word about this, but then these letters haven't reached the recipients yet. I trust that should anything come about, they will inform me. Do you have more for me?"

Cato offered his own evaluation, "In comparing the three epistles, it is clear to me Paul perceives this issue with Onesimus is impacting a broad scope of the followers of this sect. Paul admonishes slaves in this region to respect, be obedient to, and remain humble in their service to their masters. He pleads for masters to do the same to their slaves. Finally, Paul states that both slaves and masters are free persons before this Christ they worship and revere."

Seneca shot up straight at Cato's final words of assessment. His eyes widened and he pointed his finger at Cato's notes, saying, "This... all of this... is contained in these scrolls?"

Cato replied confidently, "It is as I say."

Now Seneca raised an eyebrow and bent his head slightly to the side, all the while staring at Cato. "This is a tremendous breakthrough for us, Cato, ... truly tremendous! I trust you have written all this down in your report?" Cato nodded affirmatively. "Very good. I shall take your report, plus what we have discussed, and confer with both Nero and Cleatus immediately."

Seneca stood up and began his habit of slowly pacing about his office. Cato remained seated, watching his collaborator and entertaining himself with his own thoughts while he waited for Seneca to settle down. It was obvious the impact that Paul's epistles were having on the consul. There was excitement balanced with caution as Seneca moved about the room.

After some lengthy deliberation, Seneca finally turned and faced Cato. "We can only wait for these epistles to be read by the intended recipients. Notably, Philemon is at the center of this development. What he does will have great impact, not only on Onesimus and Philemon's status with Paul, but also on the action Rome takes as a result."

Cato sensed Seneca's anxiety and decided he ought to leave to prepare for a confrontation with Paul concerning the three scrolls. Seneca responded with a wave of his hand and blurted out, "Excellent, Cato, excellent! Be very thorough in your interrogation of our prisoner." Seneca's emotions were churning, and he leaned closer to his guest to emphasize the seriousness of the situation. He spoke quietly and seriously to Cato, "I want no aspects left unanswered in regard to these scrolls."

Two days later, Seneca sat down in his reserved Senate seat and nervously waited for Nero to address Rome's governing body. It was ironic that at the beginning of his reign, Nero had reinstated more power to the Senate than had been lost during the days of the previous Caesars. The Senate's power had grown to the point the Senate could command Nero and even hold his fate in their hands.

Seneca was anxious as he waited. If Nero did as he had briefed him to do, the pot-bellied monarch would increase his stature in the eyes of his new supervisors, the Senate. This would be good for Seneca, too, making him look like a hero to the Caesar.

Nero waddled into the Senate's chamber, and immediately the murmuring from the august ruling body ceased. All attention was directed toward Caesar. Seneca's neck muscles tightened in anticipation of Nero's discourse.

"My fellow Romans," snapped Nero, who studiously paused for effect, "I come to clarify an issue of great importance to Rome and one that you all have talked about these past few weeks."

As he spoke, Nero gestured with his pudgy hands, waving them about much like he did when performing his plays in Athens. He bobbed and weaved dramatically to emphasize his points. "It is a grave situation that confronts us in the region of Ephesus and Colosse involving slaves. I inform you that the runaway slave Onesimus, who is at the center of this issue, has been returned to his master in Colosse, at the slave's request." Nero didn't have to pause for effect; the Senate's sudden commotion took center stage.

Nero smiled at their reaction and let the group chatter, then thrust his hand at his audience and demanded, "Silence! Please! We all know how rare such a request from a runaway slave is. The remorse of this slave is deep and he willingly accepts whatever punishment his master may invoke." Nero paused in his monologue as he strutted back and forth in front of the Senate chamber's members.

"The slave has been aligned with a Roman citizen named Paul who is accused of treason and has appealed his case to me." Assuming an official pose, he announced, "I have purposely held off dealing with his appeal because of this alignment, while investigating a possible intent of sedition by the two prisoners." Again the voices began to mutter in response to Caesar's words. Seneca could see how much Nero was enjoying himself in his moment of self-glorification.

"Any threat of sedition must be taken seriously, especially one that could involve a slave rebellion! We all remember what happened not that long ago with the slave Spartacus!" Nero paused, allowing the gathering's emotional reaction to reach a crescendo to confirm his point.

"Our military and my personal consul Seneca have conducted a thorough investigation into this potential slave threat. We believe reuniting this slave with his master in Colosse will provide us necessary evidence of any such sedition. The decision of the master named Philemon regarding his slave will dictate how fast we intervene in this matter. His decision will impact the entire region and beyond."

Nero strode about dramatically. He finished by saying, "We shall not have to wait long for this slave master's decision. My agents in Colosse will send word to me as soon as his decision is made public." To heighten the effect, Nero whirled around and briskly left the Senate chamber. When the doors closed behind him, the Senate erupted in chaos and the voices echoed loudly as the senators forcefully debated among themselves.

Seneca was amused at the whole affair. Nero had successfully performed his one-act play, probably better than any of the plays given during his stay in Athens. Seneca, the planner and director of the performance, relaxed. Nero had done as he was instructed. Now they both had achieved their elevated status so badly needed from those who controlled their respective fates.

All that remained was the epilogue to this drama, and that would take place only after Onesimus presented himself to Philemon.

The producer of the one-act play enacted for the Senate met with Rome's Caesar shortly after Nero's performance. Nero profusely thanked Seneca for his clever conniving. There was great happiness in Caesar's voice and mannerisms as he told his consul, "The Senate is now fully convinced my tardiness in dealing with Paul was due to this slave sedition and not merely my extended stay in Athens. You have greatly enhanced my standing with the Senate, Seneca, and I'm exceedingly grateful."

Seneca did not speak. He bowed to his Caesar in recognition of the compliment. Nero adjusted his toga by wiggling his shoulders, and informed his consul with an air of dignity, "Octavia and I leave within the next few days for Athens. We have elected to travel by ship rather than wait and go via merchant caravan." In a pained voice, he added, "It was bad enough to travel that way on our return to Rome! We don't want to experience that dreary mode of travel more than we have to." He shuddered at the memory of the time, with its smells and discomforts.

Nero then added, "I trust you to notify the Senate when this Philemon sends us news of his decision regarding his runaway slave. I do not foresee the need for me to make another appearance before the Senate in this matter. They will accept your presence in my stead. You and Cleatus can take whatever action is needed, once the slave owner's news is known."

Seneca wasn't surprised at Nero's commission. In fact, he was pleased that Caesar would be leaving before Philemon's decision reached Rome. Appearing before the Senate with the verdict would allow him to reassert himself as a valuable consul to Nero and further enhance his standing with his peers. He was pleased his goals were being achieved magnificently.

With the slave matter in limbo, Seneca would apply pressure for Cato to do more research into the scrolls written by Paul. Cato would also have sufficient time to interrogate Paul more thoroughly. The bleakness of the forthcoming winter season began to glimmer with a bit of brightness for Seneca.

## Chapter 31

While Nero and his wife Octavia were boarding the merchant ship for Athens, the two servants of Christ, Tychicus and Onesimus, arrived in the port city of Ephesus. There was nothing to call attention to a seemingly ordinary arrival. Hardly anyone working the docks paid attention to the small party, despite the fact Onesimus was shackled both at the hands and his feet and four soldiers flanked him. It was common to see Roman soldiers escorting prisoners in this bustling hub of commerce.

Ephesus was the biggest port city in the Roman Empire; the city's size and importance was second only to Rome. The population base of 175,000 inhabitants came from throughout Asia Minor to engage in commerce. It boasted one of the finest libraries in the empire and was also known for its veneration of the Greek goddess Artemis. The open amphitheater seated over 20,000 people and was the site of many debates. Soon it would become an arena for gladiator contests.

There were three main roads that funneled into the city, and the small contingent took the one that led to Laodicea. From there it was a short journey to Colosse. Timothy met the small band of travelers there and proceeded with them to Philemon's estate.

The head of the four-man unit presented Onesimus to his master, Philemon. The tension in the air hung heavily. Despite praying and preparing for this event, Onesimus' angst was revealed by distended veins in his neck and at his temples. Philemon also was uncomfortable and shifted his weight awkwardly when the soldier handed him the keys to Onesimus' shackles.

Tychicus and Timothy keenly observed both men and hoped there would be no outburst on either man's part. The soldiers had their hands on their short swords to defend such an occurrence.

Onesimus remained subdued, and the transfer went without conflict. Philemon had one of his slaves take Onesimus to the cell he would occupy for the time being. Onesimus looked plaintively at his two supporters as he shuffled after his escort.

When Onesimus had disappeared from view, both Tychicus and Timothy turned their attention to Philemon who stared rigidly at the two men. He broke the silence and informed the two servants of Christ, "Onesimus will be taken care of and held in one of the cells I utilize for disobedient slaves. He will remain there until such time I decide what I want to do with him."

Tychicus stepped forward and withdrew one of the scrolls from his traveling bag. He handed it to Philemon and said, "Christ's apostle, Paul, wants you to read this letter before you make any decision regarding Onesimus. Timothy and I will remain here in Colosse to be proctors in this matter. Should you wish to discuss Paul's letter at length, we will be available to you."

Philemon took the short scroll into his hands and stated, "I will do as Paul requests." When he finished, Philemon turned his back on his inspectors and went inside his villa.

Tychicus looked at Timothy and said, "I have two other scrolls Paul has petitioned me to deliver. One is for the church here in Colosse and the other for the church in Ephesus. They both must be handed over to the church elders as soon as possible. Both are instructions based on principles that also pertain to this matter between Philemon and Onesimus."

Timothy looked at Tychicus' bag that contained the precious two scrolls, then at his brother in Christ. "If you allow me, Tychicus, I will distribute the scroll to the elders in Ephesus. I travel there tomorrow."

Tychicus agreed and handed the document to Paul's mentee. "Read the scroll before you release it to the church elders, Timothy. Paul has given you permission for this, knowing you will use it in your ministry to the elders."

Timothy gave Tychicus directions to where he could find the senior church elder, and left to prepare for his short trip to Ephesus. Tychicus followed Timothy's directions and made his way through the streets of Colosse until he reached the home of the Colossian church elder.

Paul's emissary spent the next two days discussing Paul's epistle to the Colossian church with its elders. It was a special time of blessing and the elders were thankful how Christ Jesus had supplied them His spiritual instruction in their time of need which was plagued with innuendo and confusion. The elders felt better prepared to be Christ's followers regarding Philemon and Onesimus and other pressing issues the church was facing.

For six days, Philemon struggled emotionally and spiritually. The Colossian slave master had read Paul's personal letter to him several times. With each reading, Philemon became more stressed. The contents of the letter caused him to wander about his villa during the day and get little sleep during the night. Later, he would realize it was the conviction of the Spirit of God working in him.

During this period of time, Onesimus was locked up in a small cell kept specifically for slaves who had run afoul of their master. Onesimus remembered this cell; it was the same one in which he had endured a month's punishment before making his escape to Rome. This time, he was determined to be sustained by his faith.

The shackles on both his hands and his feet remained intact, causing soreness and skin abrasions that drew blood. It was all too familiar. Despite his discomfort, the repentant slave remained upbeat. When other slaves brought his single daily meal to him, he was congenial and always thanked the slave with a smile. Word of his demeanor rapidly spread throughout Philemon's slave community.

But during the nights, Onesimus experienced turmoil. Often he would go to his Savior in prayer, confessing his doubts and anxiety, despite his earlier pledge to trust Him. There were nights Onesimus would literally pray himself asleep, seeking forgiveness, direction, and strength from his Savior. But each new day, he awoke refreshed and was again able to endure the waiting and uncertainty of Philemon's fateful decision.

Late in the afternoon of the sixth day, Philemon sent several messengers throughout Colosse and the nearby towns, heralding that the next day he would announce his plan for the runaway slave who had caused him such turmoil. Tychicus and Timothy received word of the momentous event and made plans to attend.

The day of his promised pronouncement, two main groups assembled at his villa. One group consisted of slave buyers interested in bidding for the runaway slave who was considered prime property. Among these buyers were representatives for Aelia, Seneca, and ten other slave owners.

The other group was of curious onlookers, wondering what would happen. The significance of this event caused many people to alter their schedules to attend what was assumed to be an auction of a discontented slave. Seldom had the actions of a single slave caused such a stir among the region's populace. Because fifty percent of the inhabitants were slaves, the free citizens were concerned about rumors spreading throughout the area about Onesimus being instrumental in a possible slave rebellion.

Both groups had a common interest in the action of Philemon, who was considered key in dealing with the supposed slave revolt. By mid-morning, the designated area for the auction had filled to capacity, much to the surprise of Philemon.

At the center of this designated area was a raised platform that consisted of five steps to the top floor. It was elevated enough for slave buyers to get an unobstructed view of the slaves, but not so high the view would be distorted to the buyers. The top floor could easily display up to ten slaves plus the auctioneer who happened to be Philemon. The Colossian slave master had conducted many such auctions of his specimens of humanity over the years.

Tychicus and Timothy arrived early enough to position themselves at the base of the auction platform and just to the right of center. The auctioneer would stand on the left side of the platform with the slaves on the right side. The two disciples of Christ chose their position to enable them to rush the platform should Onesimus erupt and attempt to hurt Philemon. Emotions were running high, and they weren't taking anything for granted.

While the crowd waited for the star participants in the drama, many murmurings could be overheard. The vast majority were speculations over how much Onesimus would fetch for the eventual buyer. Others complained that it was getting hot and why there should be such an event for the sale of a single slave. There had been no notification by Philemon that other slaves would be made available.

Finally, Philemon appeared and climbed the steps to the top of the platform. When he reached his position, the crowd stopped their chattering, and all eyes and ears concentrated on him. The host of the auction remained silent and looked over his left shoulder. Onesimus could be seen climbing the same steps on the back of the platform that Philemon had used.

Tychicus and Timothy stiffened in anticipation. The two disciples were jostled by buyers who attempted to position themselves for the best view of the slave. Representatives for both Aelia and Seneca were close to the two disciples. Tychicus slightly straightened, and leaned over to whisper into Timothy's ear, "My brother, notice that Onesimus is without the customary shackles. This is very odd."

Timothy nodded his agreement and whispered back to his older brother in Christ, "Yes, and also, Tychicus, there are only four soldiers stationed in front of the platform. Usually, there are double that number, plus cavalrymen, and yet there are none here today." They looked at each other with raised eyebrows.

The crowd quieted as the voice of Philemon could be heard. "Attention! Attention... I wish to speak!" shouted the slave master. The noisy mob hushed and several, including the two disciples, held their breath in anticipation. Philemon cleared his throat and continued his address loudly enough for even those in the back to hear clearly. "I have announced that this day I would declare the fate of my runaway slave named Onesimus." Philemon gestured with his left hand towards the slave who stood only three paces away. "And this I intend to do.

"After much deliberation and lengthy conversations with Onesimus over these past six days, I have resolved the only fair and compassionate solution is to declare this man to be *free*."

The audience was stunned. Some gasped. No one could utter a word. Philemon had done completely the opposite of what everyone expected. Tychicus and Timothy were also astonished at the announcement. Neither of the disciples had envisioned such a decision. In the background and unnoticed was the commander of the garrison who stood at attention, expressionless, as he listened to the shock announcement.

Before the human mass could react, Philemon quickly answered their unspoken question, "I confer this pardon in accordance with Roman law." Philemon reached out and grabbed a document handed to him by one of his slaves who had been at the bottom of the platform but now stepped up to his owner. Philemon held the document high in the air and said, "This is my written proclamation, making Onesimus a freedman. In addition, he is also a citizen of Rome by the authority given to me by Roman law!"

Philemon lowered the document and turned to face his now former slave who stood completely dumbfounded at the grace-filled pronouncement of his fate. The contrite slave master took two steps towards Onesimus and handed his freedom paper to him. With tears welling in his eyes, and an overwhelming sense of awe, Onesimus bowed in acceptance of the freedom passport. Suddenly it was over, and the two stars of the event disappeared down the back of the platform.

The flabbergasted mass suddenly overcame their shock and erupted, loudly exclaiming over the strange turn in this event. Aelia's and Seneca's representatives fought through the milling throng and made their way to two carrier pigeon vendors located nearby. Each agent had a brief message to send to their boss. One short sentence that would have profound efects back in Rome.

"Philemon freed the slave."

After each agent paid their separate vendors to send the remarkable news item, they retrieved their personal belongings and hurried to secure a place on a camel caravan scheduled to make its way to Rome with merchandise. Despite each agent traveling in a different merchant caravan, they would arrive in Rome within two days of each other and confer with their employers.

Tychicus and Timothy also fought their way through the crowd to the backside of the platform just in time to catch up with the two main attractions of the event. Philemon and Onesimus were headed into Philemon's villa, and Tychicus called out, "Philemon! Onesimus! We wish to speak with you!" Recognizing the voices, the two players stopped and Philemon waved for them to approach.

"I anticipated you would want to speak with us about my decision. Come and eat with us and we will be able to speak at will," said Philemon with a relaxed smile.

After being seated in the comfortable dining room of the villa, slave servants brought them goblets and new wine. The sun was hot and all four men were thirsty and hungry, as none had eaten much earlier in the day. Philemon requested his servants to bring them some good food. The forthcoming diversity of food items was reflective of Philemon's wealth and business ability to purchase uncommon delicacies that others could not.

Without delay, Philemon tackled the main question on the two disciples' minds. "For six days, I was under the conviction of the Holy Spirit, in great turmoil both night and day. Almighty God revealed to me my pride, arrogance, and control that was preventing me from being his humble servant and allowing Him to carry out His plan and purpose for both myself and Onesimus."

His rapt listeners carefully dipped their pieces of fresh bread into the lavender-flavored honey as they remained glued to Philemon's confession. "In some ways I have not followed our Savior, Christ Jesus. I've given Him lip service and enjoyed working with fellow believers, but I must confess I was not willing to submit to

God's faithful and consistent message to me about Onesimus. I realized that my treatment of him and other slaves was not honoring to Christ, and I have repented of my resistance to what I knew Christ Jesus wanted to change in me. I have asked forgiveness of God, and of Onesimus."

Philemon paused to satisfy his thirst, then continued, "Christ has shown me these past few days that I must either serve him or serve man; I cannot serve both. After much duress I finally have surrendered my spirit to Christ and elected to serve him in all things. Freeing Onesimus is the public statement I can make to show Christ's love and His transforming work in my heart."

The repentant Gentile lowered his head briefly to swallow the lump in his throat. When he had sufficiently composed himself, Philemon declared, "Paul's personal letter to me was Christ's way of convicting me of my sin against Him. His words touched my heart deeply. I read it four times before I realized how I had slipped spiritually. I've held church meetings here in my home but felt at a distance from Christ. No doubt, many members of the church weren't aware of it."

As Philemon looked at his guests, it was evident how disquieted he had been during the past week when he was allowed to experience a spiritual desert alone with his Savior. "I have much to repent of and this step was the first. I will institute more lenient measures with the other slaves and eventually free them all."

Tychicus and Timothy fleetingly glanced at each other, then at Philemon again. Timothy grinned and shook his head in amazement. "What a day and a time to glorify the Lord God Almighty and our Savior Christ Jesus! Your action, Philemon, indeed has shown Christ to not only those who attended this event. It will fan out like ripples on a pond throughout the entire region, reaching the minds and the hearts of many people."

Onesimus interrupted the proceeding by saying, "Philemon and I have agreed that I will work for him as a cobbler and go about evangelizing all who seek me out." With a new respect for his former slave master, the new freedman rejoiced, "Philemon has assured me I will have plenty of opportunity to speak of this momentous occasion to anyone interested in learning more about Christ."

Tychicus put down his wine goblet, turned towards Philemon, and asked, "What is the reaction from the Roman garrison commander here in Colosse?"

Philemon chuckled as he answered, "He was quite astonished

when I conferred with him about my plan. Once his shock abated, he was genuinely thankful and said this would be instrumental in quelling any thought of a slave rebellion in this region. He indicated he would be notifying Cleatus in Rome of this development."

Tychicus proclaimed with excitement, "This is how Almighty God so often works to achieve his plan and purpose! What a time to let our hearts sing praise and glory to Him."

Onesimus humbly added, "It is also a blessing to see God's ways and how he works in and through His children." The jubilant quartet raised their wine goblets in a toast to their Lord and Savior.

The pigeons received a favorable tailwind that allowed the winged messengers to make excellent time to Rome. Their breaking news elicited different reactions from the recipients Cleatus, Seneca, and Aelia. It fostered a series of meetings to discuss how to utilize Philemon's shocking decision.

Aelia met with Antonius who became despondent over losing the services of his skilled former employee. The businesswoman then sent a message to one of her business associates in Ephesus to contact Onesimus, hopefully to contract for his services. Finally, she visited her renter, most curious to hear his response to the decision that would soon be rippling throughout the empire.

Her meeting with Paul did not last long, but was very impactful. Paul's spiritually-based explanation of Philemon's decree moved Aelia, and she hastily left to control her emotions.

Seneca and Cleatus held an impromptu conference to share their thoughts and to prepare the plan they would activate once the unusual news spread throughout Rome. Cleatus opened the discussion saying, "Philemon's choice will spread throughout the entire region and I believe will influence the far eastern portion, as well. I've sent Quadratus a message to prepare for the ensuing impact. In addition, he will notify Festus to prepare for reactions in his province of Judea."

The supreme military general showed his wonderment as he pronounced, "Seneca, our prisoner Paul has squashed a potentially serious situation for Rome. His letter to Philemon, I believe, was the turning point in this precarious set of circumstances."

Seneca had a similar expression of awe as he concurred with Cleatus. "The other two epistles written by our prisoner will also enhance and explain Philemon's decree. Time will tell how Paul's followers of this Christian sect will implement his urgings. His advice could have great impact on us because these Jesus people enact what he instructs them to do."

Cleatus exhaled audibly, saying, "Of course, I will have my commanders scrutinize the resulting activity and censor anything that poses a threat to Rome." His voice became firmer as he quickly added, "But I am fully convinced our prisoner is innocent of any accusation of intent to incite rebellion."

Seneca nodded his head. "I completely agree. The evidence is sufficient to reach this conclusion, Cleatus. Now all that remains is to notify Nero of this development, so that he can release Citizen Paul from house arrest."

Cleatus stretched his neck, raised his chin, and waggled a finger. He stressed, "Nero must be fully convinced to take this action. He is becoming more unstable and unpredictable in his actions. Caesar could elect not to release this citizen should he believe there is personal gain for him not to do so."

Seneca clasped his hands together and placed his hands behind his head as he contemplated Cleatus' words. After a thoughtful moment, he declared, "I believe I have just the solution to this potential problem. It will resolve the appeal by Paul and, in the process, prevent Nero from taking irrational action."

Cleatus looked with great curiosity at his collaborator and uttered, "Whatever action you take, Seneca, must be done thoroughly, and you also must protect yourself in the process. Nero is vengeful and will not take lightly having his authority usurped."

Seneca smiled wryly at Cleatus. "My friend, have no fear. I shall refine my plan to make sure this matter is settled to the benefit of everyone."

On that note, the discussion ended.

After the meeting with Cleatus, Seneca had a similar conference with Cato. It was briefer than previous sessions between the two. Seneca saw how visibly relieved Cato was when he heard about Onesimus' newfound freedom. The Roman consul witnessed Cato's eyes misting over and his voice becoming somewhat subdued over the news. Seneca was not surprised by Cato's emotional reaction, understanding Cato's own experiences of being held in bondage.

The consul cleared his throat and said, "There is no need to further analyze Paul's writings. We have all that is needed to resolve Paul's involvement with Onesimus. His recent letters also serve to more than adequately refute the accusations of treason brought against him. Caesar will have no difficulty releasing him.

Your involvement as his attorney is completed." The two legal minds then shared some food and drink before Cato departed Seneca's villa.

That evening, Seneca had a lengthy conversation with Pompeia about the monumental news. He told her he had one more act to add to the drama in the Senate.

The following day, he proceeded to Rome. His mission was to address the Senate. He had earlier sent a messenger to the senior senators, requesting that he make a presentation to the full Senate. The senior senators had relayed they would hear him out.

The short carriage ride from his villa to the Senate chambers was sufficient time for Seneca to finalize his thoughts. Stepping from the carriage, he looked up at the government building where the Senate resided. Seneca hastened inside with determination and made his way to the Senate's chambers.

The chamber was a din of disjointed and varied conversations within the prestigious ruling body of Rome. Some of the senators took issue with being drawn away from their villas and into Rome's foul winter air. Others were curious why Seneca convened his colleagues at a time when government affairs were usually not decided. The speculation continued until Seneca made his appearance.

A slave attendant entered the chamber and announced his arrival. The senator's entrance was filled with pomp. Seneca purposefully strode into Rome's hallowed halls of government with his head held high, his chin thrust forward, and his facial expression firm. He looked straight ahead, taking each step slowly and decisively.

His toga was crisp, fresh, and had the distinctive colored band at its bottom hem that signified his position. His left hand firmly gripped the shoulder part of the toga. His undertunic shoulder revealed the same colored band that adorned the hem of the toga. Seneca's right arm swung loosely as he walked to the designated spot for speakers.

When the slave attendant made his announcement, the entire chamber became silent. All Senate members were in attendance. The majority of the rulers sat relaxed in their seats without any sign of formality. Some draped an arm over their seat, while others sat with one leg crossed over the other. All eyes remained fixed on Seneca's ceremonious entrance.

Only when Seneca reached the designated speaker's spot did he look at his contemporaries. He deliberately remained silent while his eyes surveyed the breadth of the room, starting on the left and progressing to the right. Taking a deep breath, he relaxed his posture somewhat and began his oratory.

"My fellow Senators, friends, and even a few enemies...," he paused and smiled, acknowledging the low chuckles of the assembly. "Thank you all for answering my request to address you at this time. I shall not delay or otherwise string out what I have to say. For some time now, two issues have plagued this chamber, ranging from mild interest to gravely professed concern for Rome's well-being. Today I have the privilege to give you solace on these two topics that have become intertwined. A resolution has been reached and it is one that will greatly benefit Rome."

Immediately, the senators sat up in their seats, wondering what their colleague was about to reveal to them. The commotion lasted a brief moment, giving Seneca time to prepare for his next salvo. He relaxed even more and let his facial features convey a softness to disguise his inner thoughts. Having the senators' complete attention, Seneca continued his drama.

"Two prisoners under house arrest have long been suspected of harboring secret plans for a slave rebellion in the eastern part of the empire. One, a citizen named Paul, is accused of treason and intent to incite sedition. The other is a slave named Onesimus, who ran away from his master in Colosse and made his way to Rome."

At that point, Seneca lowered his head and began to slowly walk about the room. He turned to face the Senate. In a powerful voice, he said, "General Cleatus and I have investigated these men and the rumored threat of their conspiracy to ignite a slave rebellion. It has been arduous, but several days ago our efforts were shown to have produced success."

Seneca took a deep breath and boomed out, "The slave master Philemon has acted upon the advice given him by the prisoner Paul concerning the runaway slave Onesimus. Philemon decreed the slave to be a *freedman* and a limited citizen of Rome!" Seneca abruptly stopped so that his words would resonate with his associates.

Pandemonium broke out. Many of the senators exclaimed and stood up in sudden reaction. Some called out loudly, either nodding in agreement or shaking their heads in vehement argument. Seneca allowed the chaos to continue for a few minutes, before ordering, "Gentlemen! Please let me continue!"

Order was restored to the room and the senators took their

331

seats, muttering the last of their unfinished sentences. All leaned toward Seneca, concentrating on his countenance and straining to hear his words. Seneca responded with a slight smile. He was enjoying what he had wrought.

With a passionate voice, he barked, "The citizen accused of treason, Paul, has done Rome a great service by intervening in this situation! I have personally read his correspondence to Philemon. It directed the slave master to think through his decision concerning the fate of his slave Onesimus."

Seneca began to walk the room with precision and purpose. He seemed relaxed, his right arm moving loosely at his side except for his well-chosen gestures. All eyes followed his every move. The senator faced his riveted throng and extended his right arm with an open palm towards the assembly. In a controlled, forceful voice, he declared, "Not only did Paul write to Philemon, he wrote two additional documents to his band of followers called Christians in Colosse and in Ephesus."

The orator let his words hang in the air, knowing each senator would internalize the significance of this act because of the status of the two commerce hubs.

With perfect dramatic timing, Seneca continued, "Paul's epistles to the Colossians and to the Ephesians are words of encouragement, instructions on how to deal with issues of authority and submission, and relationships between slaves and their masters. They directly include instructions against rebelliousness. The effect of these three epistles is that Rome is no longer under threat of a slave rebellion." Seneca emphasized his last sentence and waited.

The impact of his statement caused the assembly to decidedly react in their seats. Some put a closed fist to their mouth, some placed their hands on their heads, and some simply stared at the presenter with astonished eyes.

A barely noticeable smile returned to Seneca's face. All the senators were also slave owners, so the situation involving Onesimus was one close to their hearts and a topic of endless conversation. Now this earthshaking news was received with relief; it dissipated tension and worry over slave actions that were part of their daily lives.

Seneca demanded silence once again from the crowd. It was almost immediate as each senator thirsted for more information about what had occurred in an otherwise unheralded city. Their casual postures had changed to undivided attention, with many leaning forward in their seats, anxious to hear more.

Standing tall, Seneca thrust his right arm out towards the gathering, and in a booming voice he authoritatively declared, "Because of Paul's show of loyalty to Rome, what has taken place in Colosse is clear indication of his innocence of all accusations brought against him. When Caesar Nero returns to Rome later this spring, I will apprise him of what Paul has accomplished for Rome. I will also present Nero with undisputed evidence of Paul's innocence and Nero will release him from all charges."

Seneca lowered his arm to his side and gave a single, definitive nod of his head, accentuating that the evidence was quite conclusive. The Senate erupted with approval of their cohort's intelligent investigations and discoveries. Seneca closed his eyes and smiled unmistakably. He was completely satisfied with his oratorical performance. He enjoyed hearing the gratifying reaction of his colleagues.

Intellectually, Seneca was content. He had been able to defuse any possibility of Nero causing harm to Paul, a man whom Seneca had come to admire and greatly respect during the course of their involvement.

It also felt satisfying to have obtained a form of vengeance on Nero who had shunned his earlier advice, and had replaced him with two younger, less seasoned, advisors. Seneca could accept being replaced, but what had galled him was how Nero had belittled him before his Senate peers. This was totally unacceptable to the renowned politician-businessman-philosopher. But now he knew he had regained the respect he deserved from his fellow senators.

No other communication was necessary. Seneca ended the conclave. With his head high and chin forward, he made his way to the chamber door. When he reached the far end of the seating area, a junior senator caught his eye, smiled, and winked at him, then quickly bowed his head. It was Aelia's oldest son, who held the businesswoman's Senate seat among Rome's elite ruling body.

Women weren't allowed to hold political office, but because Aelia was a very powerful businesswoman, her proxy held the office for her. Virtually all senators were prominent businessmen. Seneca discreetly tilted his head and slightly smiled his acceptance of the accolade from the junior senator.

Without breaking stride, Seneca gloriously exited the chamber in what was to be his final appearance before his peers.

## Chapter 32

For seven days, Cato went into seclusion. The earthshaking news of Onesimus becoming a freedman and a Roman citizen affected Cato to such an extent he wanted to be alone to review and consider how the events had transpired. During his solitude, the prominent mentor and attorney repeatedly read Paul's three epistles.

His main focus was the personal letter Paul had written to Philemon. Cato dissected this letter with an approach similar to how he approached his business and legal duties. He took notes, and sought out any references that might assist him in obtaining a clearer understanding of Paul's thinking. Since there were no sources available concerning Paul, Cato felt frustrated with his inability to fully understand Paul's writing.

Parts of the epistle were simple enough and needed little explanation. Others stymied Cato, especially passages referring to a so-called salvation and to the shared relationship both Paul and Philemon had with their god, the Christ Jesus. Try as he might, these spiritual passages remained veiled to him.

On the seventh day, a very frustrated Cato cried out, "I don't know who you are, Jesus, but obviously you have great power over many people. The gods of Rome I understand, but no matter how hard I try to understand you, I cannot. My heart and mind are in turmoil over this letter to Philemon. I beseech you to reveal yourself to me that I may know you."

When he finished his pleading, Cato rested his head on his hands that covered the unrolled copy of Paul's letter to Philemon resting on the top of his desk. He felt completely devoid of energy.

Unable to fully comprehend what Paul wrote to his church followers, Cato decided to take a warm relaxing bath, with the hope that it would rejuvenate his mind.

Cato received more than he anticipated during that time—he received a personal encounter with Christ Jesus, to whom he had cried out earlier. The businessman/attorney and mentor to Rome's elite found himself being called out by the only One capable of answering his questions about salvation. Cato felt a quiet inner voice saying to him, "Trust Me." It wasn't audible, yet it was so prominent in his inner being that it was as if the voice was in the room.

The lost soul felt compelled to respond to the invisible voice, and he could only answer yes with a degree of boldness and eagerness that surprised even him. Cato felt a warmth in his soul that he knew was unrelated to the warm water that surrounded him. It penetrated him through and through. He felt his mind and body relaxing with a peace that he had never before experienced. He remembered Paul referring to a "peace that surpasses understanding." He knew now what Paul was referring to.

The strange feeling did not last very long, and when it subsided, Cato felt a desire to go back to his office and read Paul's admonition to Philemon again. He hurriedly left the bath, dried off, and hastily wrapped himself in a robe. This time, the inquisitive Roman began to understand Paul's instructions to the Gentile convert. When he finished the epistle to Philemon, Cato tackled the letter to the Colossians, again with the ability to comprehend what Paul was saying.

After finishing the letter to the Colossians, Cato immersed himself in the epistle directed to the Ephesians. As he read, it was as if a dark veil had been lifted from the words written on the scroll. He was amazed at the depth of Paul's writing. And more amazed at how he could now understand it with clarity. It seemed like an entirely different piece of writing. It thrilled and amazed him.

Once Cato completed his studies of the three epistles, the Roman sat for a few moments and began to sob. "Thank you, Jesus, not only for removing the veil that I can now understand your words, but I thank you for showing me you, indeed, are God."

The Roman seeker had never felt this closeness before. He had never encountered any one of the various Roman gods like this and, frankly, did not believe in any of them. This experience was totally different and unique. He longed to receive confirmation from someone that his unusual experience was real.

Cato's thoughts concerning his experience stirred up questions and doubts. He began pacing around his villa. All the while, he felt pressure building up in his thoughts, pressure that would not go away. He questioned the experience he had while reading the scrolls. It was so unlike the philosophy of Stoicism. Finally, he clumsily plopped down in one of his courtyard chairs, totally exhausted. He placed his head in his hands for a moment, before letting his arms fall limply to his sides. In exasperation, he called out, "Why am I so restless? Why am I unsure? I ask you to comfort me and give me peace. I need to know without question you indeed are real, ...then I will worship only you."

The next day, Cato left his villa early in the morning, and headed straight for Paul's rented townhouse. His heart was pounding as he knocked on the front door. He entreated the guard on duty to let him see Paul.

Christ's apostle could tell when he first set eyes on his attorney that something was new. Paul saw the light of Christ in Cato's eyes and knew his counselor had accepted Christ's love and invitation to eternal salvation. An excited joy welled up in his heart. Lucilius stood wide-eyed, for he also saw the change in Cato's persona and the presence of the Holy Spirit in the now saved soul.

Before Cato could describe his life-changing experience, both Lucilius and Paul wrapped their arms around him and exclaimed their joy for his salvation. This was the confirmation Cato needed, that indeed the change was real when he put his faith in Jesus Christ. The certainty, comfort, and peace that he had called out for was given to him through their immediate recognition of his transformation. Cato's eyes watered a little in awe and thankfulness. He felt light-hearted and free. Lucilius released Cato, and quickly ran to the courtyard, bringing back Marcus whose smile communicated he had just been told of Cato's salvation.

Cato was finally able to understand the events that led up to his recognizing and accepting Christ as his personal Lord and Savior. When he finished telling them, Marcus and Lucilius clapped their hands in joyful praise. Paul led them all in a prayer, praising God for leading Cato to seek Christ. Lucilius went to the kitchen and ordered a special meal as a feast, similar to what the prodigal son had received in Christ's parable.

During their shared meal, Cato revealed his delight in Paul's epistle to Philemon and the resulting decree of freedom for Onesimus. Paul responded by saying, "Solomon wrote that 'the discretion of a man makes him slow to anger and his glory is to overlook a transgression.' This is how the Holy Spirit moved deeply in Philemon. His public act showed Christ Jesus to many."

All smiled in agreement with Paul's statement. The newest convert said, "That's what I want—people to see Christ through me. Is that possible, Paul?"

Christ's evangelist affirmed, "Most certainly. You do not have to make it happen. Christ Jesus does it. He will show Himself through you!" Paul rejoiced. He was surrounded by God's children who were eager and thirsting for the word of God.

The mentees hardly noticed the harsh winter. They were so engrossed in learning more of God's Word and having Paul guide them in living out God's word in their daily lives. All three spent considerable time with the Roman church groups, putting their new faith into action. This was difficult for Marcus and Lucilius who had to be very discreet in their actions because of Rome's official suspicion of the sect known as Christians. But the two guards were members and eager participants. Nonetheless, all three converts worked diligently with the Roman church elders, and throughout the winter months, they all received God's blessing as they exercised their faith.

In March, the specter of winter began to lose its grip, despite its clawing and scratching to retain its hold. The emerging dominance of spring gradually ordered winter to beat a retreat into obscurity. The foul air from the wood burning stoves was gone, and spring breezes energized the inhabitants of the city.

Rome became alive again, along with the grasslands' new vibrant greens and flowers bursting forth with fragrant buds and blossoms. Newborn animals kicked with joy over the new life they explored. Men and women, beasts, and birds felt a strong feeling of hope and expectation.

For Nero, the advent of that particular spring was a bittersweet experience. Bitter because he had to leave his beloved adopted city of Athens and return to Rome. He hated to leave an environment that gave him life and freedom for musical and artistic expression. He hated to return to one that was mundane, full of drab duties, restricting his ability to immerse himself in the theater and playing his lyre.

Rome's Caesar, his wife Octavia, and their entourage sadly stepped aboard one of the first merchant ships bound for Rome. Their accommodations were comfortable, although they shared them with much-needed goods to satisfy the hungry and demanding inhabitants of Rome. Nero's assigned military guards slept in shifts on the deck of the ship.

At the end of one week of calm sea travel, Rome's ruling Caesar Nero arrived to resume his dreary duties as emperor over his vast and powerful empire.

Nero's servants met Caesar and his group at the port of Ostia and assisted getting the travelers and their belongings back to the palace quickly and safely. Inside the palace, Nero had his first reluctant encounter with his dreaded duties. His two younger advisors petitioned his presence on a matter of importance.

Caesar sat with a forlorn look on his face at the thought of having to conduct official business so soon after his return. But when his advisors described Seneca's performance before the Senate, regarding the case of the citizen accused of treason and sedition, his facial expression rapidly changed.

As his advisors gave twisted and faulty details to Nero about Seneca effectively usurping Caesar's power, Rome's Caesar became livid. He erupted from his large chair and marched around the room, shaking his head in fury. His red face began to twitch, causing the left corner of his mouth to elevate with each spasm. He was seething. As he crossed in front of his advisors, he periodically emitted unchecked sounds of gas.

Finally, the pot-bellied ruler stopped his venting, steadied himself by placing his hand on the corner of his grandiose desk, and looked at his two ashen-faced advisors. With glaring eyes of fire, he bellowed, "Bring Seneca to my office immediately! I don't care what hour it is! He is to report to me now!"

Seneca had received notification at his villa that Caesar would be arriving by merchant ship that day, so the Roman consul prepared himself to be summoned by Nero. He knew his replacement advisors would waste no time informing Caesar of his actions before the Senate. Seneca was not worried at the thought of Nero's reaction. In fact, he was quite calm and confident about what would come from this hasty meeting with Nero.

The consul to Caesar abruptly stopped in his path toward the carriage that would take him to meet with Caesar. Standing at the open door of the carriage was Pompeia. Seneca had confided in Pompeia earlier about what he would say to the unpredictable Caesar Nero. Now Pompeia told her husband, "I want to accompany you at this time of your need."

338

Seneca smiled at his lovely wife and replied, "I appreciate your love and your concern for me. Let's go and settle this matter without delay." Along the way to the palace, the two silently held hands, each consumed with their own thoughts. When the carriage stopped at the palace, Seneca leaned over and gave Pompeia a kiss, then quickly left her alone in the carriage, assuring her he would not be long.

Inside the palace, the Praetorian Guards were on the alert about Nero's anger, and one of the guards cautioned Seneca as he began his trek to Caesar's office, "Be careful, Consul, Caesar is very upset." It was an understatement. Seneca nodded his understanding and continued confidently down the hallway to face the roaring lion of Rome.

Nero was alone in his office when Caesar's secretary ushered Seneca in to meet his wrathful emperor, face to face. Nero stood facing the door, his face crimson, his eyes on fire, and his mouth compressed in a line so thin his lips were invisible. Nero was barely able to contain himself; his toga displayed sweat stains as further evidence of his violent agitation.

Seneca bowed slightly to acknowledge Rome's Caesar. His imperturbable appearance took Nero by surprise and momentarily caused the emperor to forget what he was about to demand. The two men looked each other directly in the eye, neither blinking. Seneca was calm, confident, and at ease. Nero's face once again resumed its twitching, but his face was returning to more of its original color.

Finally, Nero opened the inquisition, "Why did you dishonor me before the Senate and in essence take away my authority to decide the fate of this citizen named Paul?"

"I did not dishonor you, Nero. I simply laid the groundwork that you could release this innocent citizen immediately, and show the Senate you have been closely involved with this man's appeal."

Nero remained skeptical, cocking his head and squinting his fiery eyes at his once most trusted consul. "Your explanation does not sway me, Seneca. I know your action was to benefit you and dishonor me in the process." He looked and sounded almost petulant.

Seneca's voice became more firm and gruff, "Your young advisors have been filling your mind with false ideas, Nero. It is common knowledge that both the Senate and businessmen throughout the empire are quite concerned over your lengthy absences each winter, when you go to Athens to perform your plays and your music."

The consul straightened himself up to his full height and continued with oratory bluntness, "You are becoming the laughingstock of Rome. The Senate, in particular, wonders about your capability to truly govern Rome to retain its glory. You, O mighty Caesar, are on very unsteady ground with both the Senate and the military. You have much to prove to them; otherwise they will not hesitate in eliminating you."

Nero could only stare at his consul-turned-accuser with wide eyes similar to a deer coming face to face with its hunter. Seneca seized on Nero's show of weakness to add more, "I made you appear competent and gave you an easy opportunity to rule on the obvious. My report, as well as that of Cleatus, exonerates the citizen Paul from all accusations as well as intent to incite. Rome, and especially the region of Ephesus and Colosse, know this man saved the empire from a potentially serious slave uprising. To not release Paul will result in your own demise."

Seneca raised his eyebrows, lowered his chin, took in a deep breath, and stared at Caesar with steady eyes. He waited for the dumbfounded Nero to recover from the verbal onslaught he had just launched at him. Nero's eyes began to go back and forth as he contemplated the stinging words of his senator-consul. Several minutes went by without a word being said by either combatant.

Nero swallowed hard and began to speak, but his voice cracked. He coughed to cover it, and tried again, "I shall take your advice under consideration. Now go and leave me alone," he muttered grumpily.

Without hesitation, Seneca wheeled around and exited Caesar's office. He exchanged glances with Cleatus who was waiting to confer with Caesar. Hints of controlled smiles were on both men's faces, but went unnoticed by the office personnel.

As Seneca strode toward his carriage, Pompeia happily noted the relaxed state of her husband. His face no longer manifested the worry or concern so often displayed while dealing with Paul's appeal.

Seneca arrived at the carriage. He opened the door, looked lovingly at Pompeia, and said, "It is finished. Take me home."

The secretary led Cleatus into Nero's office and discreetly shut the door, just as he had done for Seneca's meeting. Nero remained standing with his back to the door even after his secretary announced Cleatus. The pot-bellied emperor did not want Rome's supreme military commander to see his loss of composure. Slowly, Caesar turned around and managed a weak smile to his visitor, "Cleatus, please sit down. What matter brings you here this day?"

The highest ranking military general, resplendent in his solid black uniform with the gold and brass adornments, remained standing. He held his helmet in the forearm of his left arm and he stuck out his barrel chest to enhance his power image. "What I have to say won't take long, so I shall remain standing."

Nero could see the intensity on Cleatus' face, and was surprised at the general's resistance to his instruction to sit. He nervously wondered what was about to be revealed to him. "Very well, proceed," said Nero rather weakly.

"I have come to inform you of my immediate retirement from Rome's military."

Nero was aghast at this revelation and stumbled to his chair where he flopped down. He looked up in disbelief at the imposing black-clad figure and queried, "Why do you want to retire now?"

Cleatus retained his stately composure and squared his shoulders. He looked down at the emperor of Rome and pronounced, "I am weary of the responsibility and duties I must execute. I have no fervor in dealing with the array of issues that arise on a regular basis. Perhaps I am too old for this position."

Nero sat, bewildered. He needed Cleatus to be on his side in many forthcoming issues. Rome's supreme general could be a very good buffer for the two main concerns still facing him, the citizen Paul's appeal, and the progress of the new port city Portus. Nero was counting on Cleatus to support him; and now he must find a substitute.

"Before you retire, will you assist me with the matters concerning the citizen's appeal and also the completion of Portus?"

Cleatus' jaw became firm, his lips tightened, and his steady eyes were steely. "There is no need for my assistance in these matters, Nero. It is obvious the citizen accused of treason is innocent and must be released; otherwise, you will incur the wrath of Rome and the empire. Concerning Portus, there is nothing you can't handle, once you learn what has been developing during your stay in Athens." Cleatus looked intently at Nero and repeated his decision, "I will not assist you any longer, Nero."

Caesar was shaken by the tone of Cleatus' voice and could only stare at the imposing figure towering over him. Finally, in a subdued voice, Nero said, "Very well, then, I accept your resignation. Is there anything else before you leave?"

This was the opportunity Cleatus sought. Boldly, he answered, "If you adhere to the advice of your new advisors and do not release the accused man Paul, I will personally return to duty and drive my short sword through your liver. I would do this, not because of any allegiance to this man Paul, but to protect Rome from your insanity."

Cleatus put on his helmet and stared down at the shaken emperor of the Roman Empire. After a few brief moments, Cleatus turned and exited the office with a defiant and settled bearing, similar to the one Seneca had displayed a few minutes earlier. Nero sat in a daze. He knew Cleatus did not merely threaten him, but gave him a promise he would surely keep.

Nero was shocked by the two encounters. The words of both Seneca and Cleatus repeatedly reverberated in his mind. He closed his eyes and thought long about the action he had to make concerning the appeal by the citizen Paul. His original idea to punish Paul to better himself in the eyes of the Senate was now changed because of Seneca's speech.

Paul's influential involvement in Philemon's decision about his slave Onesimus resulted in Paul being highly regarded by the military and the business community in Ephesus, Colosse, and even Rome.

Rome's Caesar realized how much he had missed during his stay in Athens, even though he did not regret the time he had spent pursuing his desires. After a considerable period of contemplation, Caesar weighed in his mind what he had to do regarding the citizen detained for treason. He summoned his secretary and gave orders for two messengers to be sent at once. After giving his instructions, Nero went to get a warm relaxing bath, massage, and then a good meal. This had been a very strenuous day—not the happy homecoming he had envisioned.

Three days later, Nero dressed in his finest purple toga that distinguished him as emperor. The expensive fabric was a combination of silk and cotton, both imported items from Egypt. He placed rings on every finger of each hand. He had Octavia rub some fragrant oil around the back of his neck and under his chin.

Caesar was about to make a ruling that was nearly two years in the making, one that many considered long overdue. Nero wanted to look his finest for this notable occasion, to reinforce his identity as the greatest ruler of the world.

Satisfied with his attire and his appearance, Caesar made his way to the room set aside for judgment. The Praetorian Guard members escorted him to his appointment. Just outside the back entrance door, Nero took a deep breath and assumed the official stance with the top left portion of his crisp, new toga clenched in his left hand. He draped part of the purple uniform over his right forearm and signaled the guard to open the door.

Inside the judgment room, Nero attempted to walk with elegance befitting a king. To the few inside the room who were waiting for his arrival, he came across as a fat-necked, pot-bellied duck, waddling towards his judgment nest.

At the back base of the platform where his judgment throne was placed, Nero carefully walked up the seven steps to the top of the platform. He momentarily stopped to admire his throne made of olive wood with padded stout arms to pillow his elbows. At the front of each arm was the carving of a lion's head looking menacingly at any who stood in front of the chair. The seat and back of the throne were upholstered in fine linen dyed a dark purple, with gold trim. Inlaid gold leaf embellished some of the carved wood that ran throughout the chair. Nero thought it fitting, and enjoyed the lavish ornamentation.

Lifting his head high, Nero lowered himself on the throne and looked imperiously down at his observers. He studied the faces of Seneca, Cato, and the detained prisoner Paul. They showed no emotion. Both Seneca and Cato wore the traditional white toga with a purple band highlighted by a gold stripe at both the hem of the toga and on the right shoulder of the undergarment tunic. The detainee was dressed in a natural-colored thin wool toga and matching tunic that reflected his status as a Roman citizen. Nero noted that Paul was also clean-shaven in the manner of all Roman males.

The three observers stood at the front base of the platform that led to the throne of Caesar. Nobody spoke. All looked on and waited for Nero to open the proceedings. He did not waste any time in starting the appeal. He was anxious to get on with it and be done with it.

Nero looked at Paul more closely than he previously had done. "You are the citizen named Paul who has appealed his case of treason before me?"

Paul answered briefly, "I am he." Both Seneca and Cato had dropped back two paces and stood in back and to one side of the defendant.

Caesar stated, "I have read two reports based on investigations into the charges against you. Each was thoroughly detailed and their conclusions are the same. I agree with these reports and do henceforth declare the charge of treason and the charge of intent to incite sedition invalid. You are no longer to be detained. You are allowed to enjoy all the privileges due a Roman citizen."

Nero spoke in a monotone. When he finished, he lifted his portly form from his throne and retreated down the back side of the platform. He did not look back, but headed toward the rear entrance of the room and waddled out the door. No one saw his clenched right fist and his compressed lips. The glory he had envisioned for this moment had not materialized. He was glad to get it over with.

Seneca and Cato stepped forward when Nero began to leave the judgment room. Each placed a hand on Paul's shoulder and offered their congratulations to the man they had been personally involved with for nearly two years. Paul acknowledged their gestures with a smile and simply turned to exit the judgment room. None of them spoke until they were outside the cavernous hall.

Seneca broke the silence. He was emotionally drained. He looked at Paul and said, "Now that you are no longer under house arrest, I assume you will be going elsewhere."

Paul detected weariness in Seneca's voice. He said, "It has been my prayer to Almighty God to go to Spain. Now it is possible to do so."

"When do you intend to leave Rome?"

Paul replied, "As soon as I can obtain passage on one of the merchant ships scheduled to leave for Spain."

Seneca added his personal assessment of Paul's detention, "You have proven yourself a noble citizen of Rome. I laud how masterfully you seized the opportunity to free both yourself as well as Onesimus. In the process, you garnered great respect from Rome for quelling a most serious potential slave uprising. You have shown me your ability to be shrewd, perceptive, and resourceful."

Cato watched both men during this exchange with great respect. He was mildly surprised by Seneca's next words, "I was present in Athens when you debated Greece's finest thinkers. At that time, I was impressed with your oratory ability. These long months have given me deeper insight into your character. You are a man who has my highest respect." Seneca bowed his head toward Paul to finalize his commendation, then quickly left the palace.

344

Cato stepped forward. "My carriage awaits us, and will take us back to your rented house. Let us now go."

When the two men walked into the rented townhouse, there were no guards. Flavius had ordered his troops to vacate the premises since Paul had been exonerated of all charges against him. Paul felt somewhat strange, not seeing the ever-present soldiers he had become accustomed to during the past two years. He asked Cato, "Do you know what has become of Marcus and Lucilius?"

Cato replied, "They are in the process of being reassigned." Paul's face fell at this update. Cato suggested they go into the dining room and partake of some lunch before the attorney would return to his villa. He opened the door to the dining room and motioned for Paul to enter first. The released defendant noticed Aelia standing there with a beautiful smile on her radiant face. Dressed elegantly in a stola, Aelia looked imperial in the gown.

She stepped towards her renter and offered her hand, which Paul took without hesitation. "Paul, I'm very pleased that Caesar did the right thing and invalidated the charges against you. I know you want to make your way to Spain as soon as possible. Come, let us sit down. I have important news for you."

The two sat at the highly polished table. At once, the kitchen door swung open and a house servant brought the first tray of food to the diners. As Aelia began to tell her news, Paul noticed how her eyes sparkled and her smile enhanced her elegant cheekbones. He wondered what news she would have, after all that had already transpired.

Aelia handed her renter a piece of papyrus and said, "This is to be given to the captain of one of my ships that will be leaving tomorrow morning for Barcelona. A portion of the ship has been set aside for you and up to six people total during your journey there. You will be quite comfortable."

Paul looked at the passage ticket, then at his patron. "You are most kind to me, Aelia. How much do I owe you for this passage?"

Aelia looked offended and gently scolded him, "Paul, there is no charge. This is my gift to you." Her smile returned and she continued, "The two years I've come to be associated with you have been wonderful. Your kindness, caring, and respect for me mean a great deal to me."

Aelia's eyes began to mist as she added, "Recently, I've asked Christ Jesus to come into my life. Your teachings that I've heard about from my servants, plus talks with Marcus and Lucilius, and your actions all combined, persuaded me that I need from Christ all that you have shown me. I am now a child of God." The female convert confessed, "I consider you a surrogate father, and I greatly appreciate your love. Thank you. This is the least I can do for you."

The flabbergasted emissary of Christ raised his goblet and motioned for Aelia to do the same. "I thank Almighty God for His grace to you and His salvation and in giving us this friendship— all praise and honor to Him."

Aelia raised her goblet in a salute. The two enjoyed a fine dinner and excellent conversation, focusing mainly on the joy of her new faith. Neither paid attention to the fact that Cato had departed after ushering Paul into the dining room.

When the evening came to an end, Paul took Aelia's hand and gently raised it to his lips. "I shall keep you in my prayers," he promised. Aelia withdrew her hand from Paul's and kissed him on the cheek, then quickly rushed out of her townhouse. She did not want Paul to see the tears she knew she couldn't contain.

Eight hours later, Paul awoke feeling refreshed, vitalized, and eager for his forthcoming journey to Barcelona. He had spent considerable time in prayer after Aelia exited her townhouse. The humble servant of Christ gave glory and praise for God's grace and blessing to him during the two years of his house arrest. Now it was time for the next phase of his mission—to evangelize throughout Spain! The Holy Spirit had made it clear to him it was his next assignment.

Aelia had arranged a carriage to take Paul to Ostia where he would board the merchant ship. It was still dark, but as the carriage drew closer to its destination, Paul could smell the salty sea air as it wafted inland. Retrieving his traveling bag of cobbler tools, a second pair of sandals, and his ample treasury that he had earned while working for Antonius, Paul began to walk the short distance to the gangplank of the merchant ship.

Suddenly, two predawn shadows appeared a short distance in front of him, blocking his path to the waiting vessel. One was larger than the other, and both looked stout. Paul could not make out any details. Although somewhat alarmed, he continued on his path, while observing the two shadows who did not speak to him.

Paul was dressed in the traditional Jewish garments of a long tunic covered by the mantle cloak for warmth. He adjusted his bag and stepped closer to the two shadows. As he slowly advanced, Paul squinted, attempting to make out details that would tell him who the shadows were.

Suddenly, one of the shadows stepped toward him and said, "Isn't this going to be a fine day to travel the sea?"

Paul immediately stopped and exclaimed, "Is that you, Lucilius?"

The shadow laughed, "Indeed, Paul, it is I, and with me is Marcus."

Paul laughingly took another step towards the friendly shadows saying, "Thank you for coming to see me off to Spain."

Before he could continue, Marcus interrupted, "We aren't here to bid you farewell. We are here to accompany you on your quest. Our hearts beat with the same desire you have to minister to the unsaved souls of Spain."

Paul was dumbfounded. "But Cato informed me you were to be reassigned by Flavius."

Lucilius clarified Cato's statement. "We had decided to retire from Rome's military since our service was completed. For Marcus, this is his second retirement. Flavius was kind, and expedited our retirement requests to make it possible for us to accompany you."

Marcus informed his mentor how Aelia had also lent her influence for the matter. It was she who had secured them passage on the same ship as Paul's. Lucilius added that Aelia would not accept any payment for the passage. When Lucilius finished his explanation, another voice was heard behind them.

"Not only did Aelia secure passage for the three of you, she did the same for me." Paul wheeled around and looked at the voice, proclaiming, "Cato! Why do you seek to join us?"

"You taught me about Christ's encounter with the rich young man who rejected our Savior's offer to follow Him. I do not want to be like that man. My heart's desire is to follow Christ. I can do this by accompanying you to Spain."

Cato then relayed how he had earlier sold everything. Part of his property was purchased by Aelia and the remainder by Seneca. "What I have is sufficient for me to assist you in evangelizing the lost in Spain."

The sound of orders being barked and sailors finishing up loading their limited merchandise for Spain grabbed the attention of the group. Lucilius exclaimed, "We must hurry, the ship is about to sail without us!" They laughed at what an irony that would be, and dashed up the gangplank.

Aboard the ship, the foursome made sure they were out of the way of the rushing sailors who were going about the final loading. The captain came up to them. "Are you are the ones Aelia has spoken to me about?" Paul answered they were. The captain said, "Good, because we are nearly ready to sail."

Just then, a panting, exhausted voice cried out, "Which one of you is Paul? I have something to give him!"

Christ's ambassador stepped forward and the out-of-breath youth held out a pouch and placed it in Paul's hand. Without further words, the young messenger turned and ran off the ship.

The early morning light was rising over the horizon and was barely sufficient for Paul to determine what was in the pouch. He took out a piece of papyrus, and read aloud, "This is rightfully yours. I underpaid you." It was signed Antonius. There were nearly 900 denarii contained in the pouch.

While Paul was marveling at God's provision, a voice rang out, calling his name. All four looked in the direction of the voice. A solitary man stepped forward for recognition. It was Onesimus.

The travelers were stunned to see the young man who had held the attention of an entire region of the Roman Empire. Four astonished voices shouted their amazement all at once, "Onesimus!" "What are you doing here?" "But you were in Colosse!" "How did you come here?" "Why are you here?" "What about Philemon?"

Grinning, the former runaway slave explained that the situation in Colosse was such that his new freedom had become a distracting issue while he sought to give the gospel. Many there wanted to hear from him about his slavery and freedom more than about the wonderful transformation of his life by Christ Jesus.

"Philemon and I were in agreement it would be best for me to return to Rome and accompany you on your quest to Spain where my story wouldn't be a distraction from doing Christ's work." Onesimus went on to explain how he had traveled back to Rome on a merchant ship three days before Nero returned.

While in Rome he had stayed with Teman until after Paul's trial. "Once word came to us that you were vindicated of the accusations, I inquired and learned you were to leave today. One of the church members put me in touch with Aelia and she secured my passage with you. She refused any payment, telling me to do God's work when we arrive in Spain."

A silence came over the five missionaries who were in awe

over how Christ the Lord had brought them together. Paul beckoned toward the bow of the ship and began walking towards the area where they would not interfere with the final preparations for departure. The apostle gathered his companions around him and suggested that they go before the Lord in prayer. Each man sang forth a hearty song of praise to God for His grace and timing that each of them would go forth as His servants.

When the last of them finished his prayer, they looked up at the tall masts of the ship, now visible against the rosy dawn. The mainsails were being released, and they began to unfurl and pop as the early morning breeze filled them, slowly propelling them out of the harbor.

Once on the open sea, the followers of Christ were still at the bow. They gazed at the tranquil water as the vessel slipped through the small whitecaps.

With the ship undulating in harmony with the waves, each man stood silently peering at the horizon, reflecting on how God had worked His wonders and His plan through all the events of the past two years. Their hearts seemed to cry out in unison, just as the prophet Isaiah once cried out to God,

"It is I, Lord God. Send me!"

## ABOUT THE AUTHOR

Tomas W. Schafer taught history and was a journalist for many years. After putting his faith in Jesus Christ, his increased interest in biblical history and the life of the apostle Paul inspired him to research and write this book.

His natural curiosity eggs him on to answer his imagination's innumerable questions. He is fascinated with the psychology that underlies power, politics, and people. As a journalist and interviewer, he enjoys talking to people and hearing their stories. His background of prison ministry, mentoring, business, and journalism brings a wide variety of experiences for authenticity in his writing.

Tomas has a passion for telling others about Jesus Christ, and mentoring others in their shared desire to follow Him. His first book was *MENTORING GOD'S WAY—Fulfilling the Great Commission*.


PrisonerOfRome@gmail.com

As a reader of *The Prisoner of Rome*, you are invited to contact the author with your questions or comments about the book through the above email address, which was set up for that one specific purpose.*

The author will enjoy communicating with you and will personally answer your inquiries.

*Unrelated correspondence will not be answered.*

Also available:

Mentoring is the high calling of Christ, who commanded His followers to "Go and make disciples."

It is not accomplished by a formula or pre-set rules. Mentoring is a heart-based ministry with twists and turns that can defy traditional thinking.

With this in mind, *MENTORING GOD'S WAY* gives us biblical references and real-life examples to illustrate the challenges and the wisdom needed to be an effective people-helper.

Along with guiding principles for mentoring, are twelve compelling case studies to consider individually or in a group study. They teach us to listen well, be prayerful, consider specific biblical principles, and follow the leading of the Holy Spirit as we respond to those who seek our counsel.

The thought-provoking examples are contemporary, and provide good preparation for individuals who desire to follow the Lord's command to go and make disciples, even in the most difficult situations.

ISBN: 978-1-940728-11-7
Library of Congress Control Number: 2017933391

www.ingramcontent.com/pod-product-compliance
Lightning Source LLC
Chambersburg PA
CBHW030812260626
47169CB00001B/289